Acclaim for *Our Kid*:
'Reading *Our Kid* was a very moving experience! I was born in Salford and so you can understand my deep emotion at reading your wonderfully written, deeply touching, extremely heart-warming memoirs. Congratulations!' John Sherlock, Hollywood producer

'I half-read my mother's copy of *Our Kid* when the team was playing in Italy. Enjoyed it so much I thought I'd better order my own copy' Brian Kidd, Deputy Team Manager, Manchester United

'Enjoyed *Our Kid* thoroughly. Read it in two days flat. Hardly paused for breath' William Mowbray, retired headmaster, France

'I read *Our Kid* on the train and I laughed so much I was getting funny looks off my fellow passengers' John Kennedy, *Catholic Pictorial*

'This rag to riches tale, set in my own lifetime, recalls wartime boyhood, is packed with nostalgia, filled with laughter and is often tinged with pain. As a tale it is compelling and difficult to put down' Robin Hull, Professor of General Practice

'*Our Kid* was so enjoyable that I did not want to come to the end of it' Jennie McWilliam, General Practitioner

'Altogether a very enjoyable read' *Bradford Telegraph and Argus*

Billy Hopkins, who is better known to his family and friends as Wilfred Hopkins, was born in Collyhurst in 1928 and attended schools in Manchester. Before going into higher education, he worked as a copy boy for the *Manchester Guardian*. He later studied at the Universities of London, Manchester and Leeds and has been involved in school-teaching and teacher-training in Liverpool, Manchester, Salford and Glasgow. He also worked in African universities in Kenya, Zimbabwe and Malawi.

Billy Hopkins is married with six grown-up children and now lives in retirement with his wife in Southport.

Our Kid was first published under the pseudonym Tim Lally.

First published in 1998
by HEADLINE BOOK PUBLISHING

First published in paperback in 1999
by HEADLINE BOOK PUBLISHING

First published in 1996
by The Limited Edition Press

41

ISBN 978-0-7553-3011-9

Typeset by Avon Dataset Ltd, Bidford-on-Avon, Warks

Printed and bound in Great Britain by
Clays Ltd, St Ives plc

HEADLINE BOOK PUBLISHING
A division of Hodder Headline
338 Euston Road
London NW1 3BH

Our Kid

Billy Hopkins

headline

For Clare

'Give me the child for the first seven years, and you may do what you like with him afterwards' Attributed as a Jesuit maxim, in *Lean's Collectanea* vol. 3 (1903) p. 472

'If only it were true!' Jesuit priest, 1998

Prologue

Another Bloody Mouth to Feed

'Come on now, Kate. Y're no' really tryin',' said the midwife. 'Pull on the towel and push! Push!'

'I am bloody well pushing,' Kate shouted back. 'I can't push any harder. Pull and push. It's like rowing a boat on Heaton Park lake. You'd think God would have thought of an easier way of having kids.'

'It won't be long now, luv,' said Lily Goodhart, her next-door neighbour, wiping Kate's glistening forehead.

'That dose o' castor oil should speed things up,' said Nurse McDonagh. 'Anyway, it's no' as if it's your first wean.'

'Aye, but it never gets any easier, no matter what they say,' said Kate.

A sudden contraction convulsed her.

'Glory be t'God, that was like a red-hot poker going through me!' she gasped.

'Bite on your hanky when it gets too bad, Kate,' said the nurse. 'We don't want the neighbours to hear. And your kids are in the other bedroom. Is your husband no' around?'

'No, I told him to take himself off to the pub outa the road. He'd only be in the way. Besides, he doesn't like trouble, y'know.'

'Lucky for him! Just the same, I think he should be here, just in case we have to fetch Dr McDowell. Lily, you'd best go across to the pub and bring Tommy over.'

'Eeh, I don't think he'll like that,' said Lily.

'Never you mind whether he likes it or no'. Tell him he's needed over here. Dinna come back without him.'

'Very well, if you say so,' said Lily doubtfully as she left the little cramped bedroom.

'I do hope we don't have to bring no doctor. I'd be so embarrassed, like . . .' said Kate after Lily had departed.

'But he's a *doctor*.'

'It doesn't matter. He's a man, isn't he? I don't want no man – not even me husband, for that matter – to see me like this. And anyroad, I think . . .'

But the nurse did not discover what it was she thought, for Kate was racked by another agonising spasm and was busy stifling a scream.

'Come on now, Kate,' urged the midwife. 'Nearly there! Now, pull and push! Pull and push!'

It was eight o'clock on that Sunday night in 1928. Tommy was already on his third pint and a feeling of bonhomie and goodwill had begun to flow over him. He felt completely at home and in his true element.

'This is the place for me,' he said to Jimmy Dixon, his bosom pal. 'This is where I really belong. The vault of Tubby Ainsworth's. Best bloody pub in Collyhurst.' Its real name was the Dalton Arms, but hardly anyone called it that.

The thick tobacco smoke and the excited babble of twenty male voices talking at once combined to produce in Tommy a deep sense of contentment and comradeship. In here, he felt safe and away from all those goings-on at home.

He took out a packet of Player's Weights, extracted the last remaining cigarette, tapped it slowly on his yellow, nicotined thumbnail, and struck a match. Puffing contentedly on his fag, he looked up from his cards and gazed round the vault, taking in the picture of the pasty-faced men in their flat caps and woollen mufflers which they wore like a uniform.

'Eeh, what a bloody fine bunch o' working men they all are,' Tommy said.

'Whadda you mean? Working men! Most of 'em are on the dole!' said Jimmy.

'Doesn't matter, they're the salt o' the earth. Except for that bastard Len Sharkey over there,' he added quickly as his eye lighted on his hated enemy, guffawing as usual with his mates over some joke or other.

They took a long pull at their pints.

In the main, then, Tommy was happy. A pint, a pal and a bit of peace – that was all he wanted. That wasn't asking too much, was it? But that Sunday night, he had more. It was his lucky night. He was on a winning streak, having just pegged twelve on the cribboard with a double pair royal. No doubt about it. He was well on the way to taking not only the game but the shilling bet that was riding on it. Mind you, Jimmy Dixon was a real Muggins and wasn't quick enough to add up even his own score, never mind Tommy's. But what the hell! Friend or no friend, a shilling was a shilling in this rotten old world. He downed the rest of his pint and stood up.

'My twist, Jimmy. Same again?'

Jimmy drained his own glass. 'Aye, ta. Don't mind if I do, Tommy. And see if you can't buy me a bit o' bleeding luck while you're at it.'

Tommy pushed his way through the men standing at the bar.

3

'When you're ready, Tubby. Pint o' usual for me and a pint o' bitter for Jimmy there. Oh aye . . . and ten Weights as well. Must have a smoke for the mornin'.'

'Right, Tommy. Pinta best mild, pint o' bitter, an' ten Weights. That'll be one and eleven altogether,' Tubby Ainsworth said, drawing the pints.

Tommy paid up, collected the beers and his cigarettes and returned to his seat at the card table.

'All the best!' said Jimmy.

'Bottoms up!' rejoined Tommy.

It was at that precise moment that his peace of mind was shattered. As he tilted his head back to drink, he saw through the bottom of his glass the shawled figure of Lily Goodhart hurrying towards him.

'Bugger it! Don't turn round now, Jimmy, but have you seen who's coming?'

'No. How the bloody hell could I?'

'It's Lily Goodhart, me next-door neighbour. And I know why she's here.'

As Lily threaded her way through the unyielding male bodies, she was greeted by various cat-calls.

'Women not allowed in the vault!'

'Men only in 'ere.'

'Go and fill your bloody jug at the snug.'

'S'all right,' she said. 'I just want a word with Tommy there.'

She went up to the card table. Tommy put his pint down.

'Yes, what is it, Lily?' he asked irritably – put out by her appearance in the vault and the fact that all eyes were on him. Especially those of Sharkey, who seemed to be enjoying yet another horse-laugh with his cronies.

'It's time, Tommy,' she said in an urgent whisper. 'It's Kate. I think you'd better come now. Her waters broke and the pains are coming faster. I don't think it'll be long now.'

'Bloody hell. No peace for the wicked – not even in the bloody pub. But what do they want me for? Kate told me to bugger off out of the way.'

'I think it's in case there's complications, like, and they have to call the doctor.'

'A doctor! I can't afford no two quid for a bloody doctor. Besides, I've heard they kill more than they cure with their bloody instruments.'

'I'm only telling you what they told me.'

'All right, Lily. I'll finish this game first. Mind you, I can't see what bloody use I'll be. She'd be better off if I just stop where I am. How long's the midwife been there?'

'Over half an hour. I think she's doing her best to hurry things along, like. Anyroad, Tommy, I'd better get out of the vault afore these men here chuck me out. But I promised to come and fetch you. Shall I wait for you?'

'Look, Lily, there's no bloody need for that. I've said I'll come when I've finished the game, and I will.'

'All right. If you say so.'

As if for protection, she pulled her shawl tightly around her shoulders and hurried out.

Tommy returned to his card game, but his heart was no longer in it. Lily's visit had put him off and he lost his concentration. He missed an obvious run of four and several other chances on the next deal. Jimmy Dixon wasn't as daft as Tommy thought and was quick to take advantage of the distraction. He soon caught up, and after a few more deals beat Tommy with a final flush of five, giving him a total of 121. Jimmy picked up his winnings and put them in his pocket.

'Hard luck, Tommy. I really thought you'd beat me there. Never mind, old son. Have another pint to wet the new baby's head. Pint o' best mild, isn't it?'

'Shouldn't really, Jimmy – the baby's not been born yet. But . . . er . . . go on then. Y've twisted me arm. Better make this the last one, though.'

Deep down he was feeling queasy at the thought of having to listen to Kate in the throes of childbirth.

Jimmy came back with their pints and they each took a long swig.

'Ah!' sighed Jimmy, smacking his lips. 'There's nowt to beat a drop o' good ale!' He leaned forward and adopted a confidential tone. 'How many kids have y'had now, Tommy?'

'I think I've bloody well lost count. Let's see.' He counted off on his fingers. 'There's our Flo, Polly, Jim, Sam and Les. How many's that?'

'Five.'

'That's right. Two girls and three boys and this new one'll make six if the little bugger makes it. But I'd best be off, Jimmy. Better go and see what's happening, I suppose. With any luck it'll all be over by the time I get there.'

He swallowed the rest of his pint and got to his feet.

'Thanks for the beer, Jimmy – though I won't say thanks for that bloody game o'crib. I'll win that bob back from you next time, you'll see.'

He headed towards the door to a chorus of ribald remarks from the Dalton Arms regulars.

'About time you was castrated, Tommy!'

'Y'ought to get yourself doctored!'

'Y'want to tie a bleeding knot in it, Tommy!'

Tommy turned to face the source of the last remark.

'And you want to keep that big mouth of yours shut, Sid Hardcastle, afore I fill it for you.'

The speaker went quiet, because he knew that,

6

although Tommy looked harmless enough, being only a small, bald man with knock knees, he had a vicious temper and was perfectly capable of carrying out his threat. He hadn't worked and survived in Smithfield Market for thirty-odd years without picking up something about the art of pub brawling.

As Tommy was going out of the door, Len Sharkey said in a loud, sarcastic voice:

'I don't know about *Tommy*. Tom-cat's more like it, eh, lads?'

His cronies rewarded him with a loud belly-laugh. Encouraged, Len added:

'Catholics are all the same round here . . . breed like bleeding rabbits.'

Tommy stopped, turned, and walked over to Sharkey. He looked up into the other man's face.

'Whadda you mean by all that? Tom-cat, Catholics and bleeding rabbits?'

'Piss off home, Tommy. I don't want no trouble. We was only joking.'

'Sharkey, you're full o' Malarkey. And I wanna tell you summat. We've got some big fellas in the market.'

'Oh, yeah. So what?'

'I've never come across a fella as big as you. You must be over six foot.'

'Six foot three,' answered Len proudly.

'I've never come across a fella as big as you, with so much muscle. I take me hat off to you,' Tommy continued, whipping off his cap.

Len preened himself.

'But you must be the only fella in Collyhurst with no balls.'

Then, without warning, in one swift, flowing motion, he nutted Sharkey with the skill of Dixie Dean heading

7

one home for Everton. Len went sprawling across the floor, and it was a good job there was sawdust down, for his nose began to pour blood as he lay there. There was a momentary pause, and then all hell broke loose. Len's mates began shouting abuse – 'You mad bastard!' 'You crazy sod!' – as they helped their leader to his feet. Jimmy Dixon was over at Tommy's side in a flash, restraining him from further action.

'Calm down, Tommy lad. Take it easy, mate,' Jimmy said.

'Right!' shouted Tubby Ainsworth, pointing to Tommy and Len Sharkey. 'You're both banned! I won't have no fighting in my pub. Now bugger off home, Tommy, for Christ's sake. They want you over there!'

'It's OK, Tubby,' said Jimmy, trying to cool the situation. 'He's going now. I'll see he gets on his way.'

He walked Tommy to the door.

'You'd best get home, Tommy lad, and get someone to see to that cut on top o'your head. But, by God, that Len Sharkey's been asking for a good hiding for some time now. He'll not be so free and easy with his mouth in future.'

'He'd no right saying all that, Jimmy. All that stuff about Catholics. I'd have murdered the get if y'hadn't stopped me. And now Tubby's banned me. Me – one of his best customers.'

Jimmy laughed. 'Banned you, be buggered! If Tubby banned everybody who'd had a fight in the vault, he'd have an empty pub. No, take it from me. He'll have forgotten it by tomorrow. I'll call over after, Tommy, and see how you've got on.'

Leaving the smoky atmosphere behind, Tommy emerged from the pub into the Collyhurst evening air. It was half past nine and not quite dark, but already the lamplighter was going his rounds down Collyhurst Road.

Tommy crossed over the road, cursing Len Sharkey for making him lose his rag like that. With his strange, shambling gait, he hurried along by the side of the River Irk – known simply in the district as the Cut.

As he approached the iron bridge which led to the Dwellings, he spotted Polly playing 'Queenie-o-Co-Co, who's got the ball?' with a lot of other kids. 'See I haven't got it!' 'See I haven't got it!' they chorused as they offered alternate hands for inspection.

'Come on, our Polly,' he ordered. 'Time you was in. And bring Jim with you. It's past his bedtime.'

'Aw, Dad. Can't we stay out a bit? S'only early.'

'No you can't. Up you go.'

'Yes, but Dad . . .'

'Will y'do as you're told, y'cheeky little sod. And less of your ole buck. Now get up them bloody stairs afore I land you one. It's time you packed up them bloody daft games. You're thirteen and you'll be starting work next year. You should be giving help at home, not playin' out here. Your mother's not well, y'know.'

'Yeah. I know. She's got that stomach ache again. It's through eating all them kippers on Friday. But we're out 'ere 'cos they chucked us out when the nurse came. Sam and Les are already in bed, though.'

'I should bloody well think so. But now it's time the two o' you was in. So up the Molly Dancers!'

Reluctantly, Polly collected her ball and her younger brother. Squeezing past a courting couple who were at it on the steps, she followed her dad up the stairwell until they reached the landing and the lobby which led to their tenement – number 6, Collyhurst Buildings.

* * *

The door was ajar. Inside, they found Lily stoking up a big fire at the black-leaded kitchen range. Flo, the eldest daughter, was filling a large iron kettle from the tap in the corner of the room.

'It's a boy, Dad,' announced Flo. 'Seven pounds. And he's lovely.'

'Oh aye,' sighed Tommy, resignedly. 'I thought it might be a boy the way your mother's been eating all that apple pie lately.'

'How d'you mean?' asked Lily.

'Well, fancying apple pie means a boy, and cherry pie, a girl. S'well known, that, in Lancashire. But by God, another boy, eh! Another bloody mouth to feed! That's six kids we've got.'

Nurse McDonagh, all bustling and businesslike, appeared from the bedroom carrying a brown paper parcel, which she thrust into the fire.

'What's that? It's not the baby, is it?' asked Jim, his little face aghast.

'Never you mind what it is, young man,' Nurse McDonagh said. 'And no, it's no' the baby. The very idea, indeed!'

She turned to Tommy.

'So the prodigal son has come back to the fold, eh? And you look as if you've been in the wars, as well.'

She fished in her medical bag, pulled out a small bottle of iodine, and applied a little to Tommy's wound. Tommy winced.

'It's only a scratch. Not worth botherin' about.'

'Dinna fash yoursel'. I'm no botherin' that much. If you daft men want to punch each other's heads at night, it's no skin off my nose. More like skin off your heid, I'm thinkin'!'

'You're a hard woman, Nurse.'

'Ye've got to be in my job. But you took your time gettin' here. Timed it just right, didn't you? Like the last time – arrivin' home when it's all over. Typical man! You think when you've put your wife in the puddin' club, that's you out. Your contribution to the birth process!'

'Now, you know very well I'd have been no use to you. I know nowt about bringing kids into the world, except that you need a lotta hot water.'

'Aye, and I suppose you think that's for mixing with your whisky to make yoursel' a hot toddy! All things considered, though, I think maybe you were better taking yoursel' off to the pub and keepin' outa ma way.'

'But how's Kate? How's me wife doing? Is she all right?'

'You've no need to worry on that score. I thought at one point we might need the doctor, but everything's turned out fine, and mother and son are both doing well. You've got a strong, healthy wife there. She had her baby without any fuss – hardly made a sound. The only noise was from your son, and judging by the strength of his lungs, there's not much wrong with him either.'

'I know I picked a good 'un when I picked Kate,' he said proudly.

'Well, anyway, I've cleaned things up as best I can. And now I suppose you'll be wanting to go in and see the bairn. I don't see any way I can stop you.'

'I should bloody well hope not,' he said indignantly.

'I don't suppose there's any harm as long as you don't go breathing your beer fumes and germs all over the baby. Not too much noise, either,' she said, looking pointedly at the younger end of the family. 'Now, I'm awa'. I've got another case over the road – a lot more urgent than yours. I'll call in again tomorrow morning to see how things are. See that Kate gets a good sleep tonight.'

She began packing up her mysterious black bag, and Polly asked:

'Is that what you brought the baby in?'

The nurse gave her an old-fashioned look, hesitated, looked as if she were going to say something, then changed her mind.

'In a way it is, I suppose.'

'We had a listen at your bag before, and we didn't hear no baby in there,' said Polly.

'Don't be daft,' said Jim. 'Everyone knows that babies are brought by an angel. Don't you know nowt, Polly?'

'How d'you make that out?' asked Polly.

'Well, when one person dies, another one gets born.'

'Straight away?'

'No, stupid. When a person dies, he has to go up to this room in the sky where he has to wait for, I dunno, maybe a hundred years until it's his turn to get born again.'

'I dinna ken what they're teachin' 'em at school these days,' said Nurse McDonagh, shaking her head.

Tommy gave the nurse a sealed envelope.

'Ta very much for all you've done, Nurse. Though I think we should be getting a discount for quantity.'

'That'll be the day – when a Scotswoman gives a discount!' And with those words, Nurse Flora McDonagh departed from the scene.

Less than a minute after she'd left, a little voice from the second bedroom piped up:

'Dad, can we come out? We want to see the new baby.'

'You little buggers should be asleep,' said Tommy. 'Not listening to all that's goin' on out here.'

'Go on, Tommy. Don't be so miserable,' said Lily Goodhart reprovingly. 'Let 'em see the baby. It's not every day that they get a little brother.'

'Aye, I suppose you're right, Lily. Go on then. We may as well all go in together – though it'll be a bit of a squash in that little bedroom. All right then, you little buggers. You can come out. But just for a minute.'

In a wink the two young 'uns, Sam and Les, were out of the bedroom, dressed in their everyday shirts which served also as their nightwear.

'Right!' said Tommy. 'In we all go.'

He knocked gently on the front bedroom door and called softly:

'Kate, is it all right if we come in?'

All held their breath to catch the answer.

'Yes. S'all right, Tommy. You can come in now,' said Kate.

He opened the door quietly, and all seven of them traipsed into the room and gathered round the bed. Kate was sitting up, smiling and looking radiantly happy, whilst the newborn baby – oblivious to all the fuss going on around it – slept soundly in the large wooden drawer which served as a cradle.

'How do, Kate,' said Tommy. 'How y'feeling?'

'Oh, I'm not so bad, Tommy. Not so bad. But what's that stuff on your head? You've not been fighting again, have you?'

'No. S'nowt to bother about. I bumped into Len Sharkey, that's all. You're the one to worry about – not me.'

'Did you pay the midwife, Tommy?'

'Aye, I did that. Ten bob as usual. Is that right?'

'Aye, that's right. Same price as last time. Well, what d'you think? Another boy, eh?'

'Aye, another boy,' he replied, with feigned brightness. 'That's four we've got now. And this one's just as welcome. Just as welcome. He's got to be fed. We'll look after him and see he's all right.'

He took a peek at his son but couldn't think of anything to say. To him, all babies looked alike. Wrinkly and red-faced – like miniature Chelsea pensioners without their uniforms. But he felt he had to say something.

'Well, he seems to have everything,' was the best he could manage. 'It's bloody marvellous. He's even got fingernails! Did y'put a penny on his belly button?'

'Aye, I did that.'

'What's that for?' asked Flo.

'That's to flatten it,' said Kate.

'A bit like when they put pennies on a dead person's eyes,' said Polly.

'Well, not quite . . .' replied Kate.

Meanwhile, the three boys stood silent, taking in the scene: the big brass bedstead, the heavy dressing table with the swivel mirror, the large jug and basin, and the huge mahogany wardrobe with Dad's pot hat on the top – the one he took down for funerals.

'Do you want to see your new baby brother?' Kate asked.

They nodded, and Kate folded back the blanket a little to give them a better view.

'He looks like a big red tomato,' observed Jim. 'Though on second thoughts, p'raps he's more like a beetroot.'

Jim had recently started a Saturday-morning job helping Joe Ogden, the greengrocer.

Sam and Les looked on. They weren't too keen on a new baby sharing their things and their space, but as compensation they wondered if they could make use of this tiny doll-like creature as a prop in one of their games.

'Are we goin' to keep him? And will he be able to play out with us?' asked young Sam.

He had in mind the idea of using the baby on Guy Fawkes night, not only to augment their collection of money but as a possible real-life effigy to put on the fire.

'Course we can keep him. He's ours now,' said Kate. 'And he'll play out with you when he's a bit bigger.'

'I think he's got your hair, Tommy,' Lily announced.

'Well, some bugger has,' said Tommy. 'But it doesn't matter about his hair as long as he's not skenny-eyed or hare-lipped or anything like that.'

'I think he's the loveliest baby I've ever seen,' said Polly. 'What are you going to call 'im, Mam? What about Rupert? That's a lovely name; it's the name of a prince, you know.'

'We don't want no princes in this house,' said Kate. 'Though I really haven't had no time to think about names much. I usually leave that to your father. What do you think, Tommy?'

'I've named them all up to now,' replied Tommy. 'But I think we've just about run through the Litany o' Saints. So I don't mind what you call him as long as it's not summat like Marmaduke or Archibald . . . or Winston like that bastard Winston Churchill.' Tommy had never forgiven Churchill for the Dardanelles.

'What do you think, our Flo?' asked Kate.

'Well, the boss at work has ever such a lovely name,' said Flo. 'His name's William Armstrong . . . And then there's that poet they learned us about in school – William Wordsworth, I think he was called. It was a poem all about daffodils. "I wandered lonely as a cloud" – summat like that. Why don't we call him William? It's ever such a nice name.'

'Aye. I like the sound o' that,' said Kate. 'It's got a nice ring to it.' She pronounced the full title in her best imitation of a posh-voiced flunkey announcing an important dignitary at a royal banquet: 'William Hopkins! Yes, I like it,' she declared. 'As long as he

15

doesn't get called "Willy" or "Billy".'

'I don't like the name William,' Polly proclaimed petulantly. 'I think it sounds dead sissy. And anyroad, if you're going t'give the names of poets and all that, what about Rupert Brooke? He's a poet too, isn't he? They're learning us a poem by him at school. Something about "If I should die . . ." '

'Oh, bloody hell,' said Tommy, putting both hands on top of his head. 'She's got death on the brain! The kid's only just been born and already she's talking about dying.'

'Now, I've told you before,' said Kate. 'We don't want no Ruperts and no princes in this house.'

Flo said: 'Besides, he'd get called Rupie.'

'Yeah, loopy Rupie!' added Jim.

Polly pouted. 'Everybody's always laughing at me in this rotten house! I'm fed up, I am. If Flo says anything, oh yes, that's all right. But not if I say it. Everybody just picks on me.'

'Will you stop causing trouble, our Polly. You're an awkward little bugger. You should learn to keep *that* shut,' said Tommy, indicating his mouth.

'Then why can't we give him two names?' Polly insisted, not to be talked down. 'What's wrong with Rupert William?'

'Listen, you little madam,' retorted Kate. 'Two names is for toffs. All our kids have just the one name and that's enough. Anyroad, there'll be no more arguments. It's settled. His name's William and that's the end of it.'

The others gave murmurs and nods of agreement. Not that their opinion mattered once Kate had made up her mind.

'There's something none of you have noticed,' Lily declared. 'Today is Sunday, and you know what they say about a Sunday child: *The child who is born on the Sabbath day/Is lucky and happy and good and gay.*'

'P'raps he's going to win Littlewoods or the Irish Sweepstake,' said Tommy.

'I think you may be right,' said Kate. 'I spilt some sugar the other day, and that's a sure sign that we're going to have some good luck.'

'Let's hope so,' Tommy said. 'Now then, the nurse said we wasn't to tire you, Kate. So I think that'll do for tonight. All told, it's been a very busy day – you might even say a productive day, especially for you. But not a bad night's work, eh – even if I say so myself!'

'Cheeky bugger,' retorted Kate.

He looked at the big alarm clock on the dressing table, and, thinking about the market, continued: 'Anyroad, I've got to be up at four o'clock tomorrow morning. Someone's got to carn the money now we've another mouth to feed. So come on, you lot. Say good night and off to bed with you.'

After their good nights, they all left. The three boys got into their big bed, top and tail fashion, in the other bedroom, and the two girls climbed into theirs in the same room.

'I'll be on my way now, Tommy,' Lily said. 'Me family will be thinking I've fell in the Cut. I haven't seen 'em all day. I'll call in again tomorrow to see how she is and if there's anything she wants.'

'Ta very much, Lily, for all you've done,' Tommy said. 'We couldn't ask for a better neighbour. You're a brick . . . the best.'

'Oh, don't mention it, Tommy,' she said. 'That's what neighbours are for.'

When everyone had left, Tommy decided to go on to the front landing of the Buildings for a last smoke. It was a

bright night and the Cut was bathed in moonlight, giving
it a beautiful romantic aspect. Lighting his fag, he looked
out towards Collyhurst Road. It was closing time at Tubby
Ainsworth's and he could hear the last customers shouting
their slurred good nights. From below, he heard a familiar
voice calling him. It was Jimmy Dixon, about to go into
his ground-floor tenement.

'Aye, aye, Tommy. How did you get on?'

'Oh, not so bad. I've had another boy.'

'Another boy, eh? It must be all that bloody Boddies
you've been supping. We'll have a pint o' two to celebrate
in Tubby's tomorrow night. G'night, mate.'

'G'night, Jimmy.'

Another son, Tommy said to himself. God, look at
these here hovels – stone-flagged floors and walls dripping
with damp. Three rooms and a lavatory between two
adults and six kids. Not much of a place to bring 'em up.
The landlords have a bloody cheek charging us five bob a
week rent for these holes. They slung these tenements up
in the 1880s and called 'em artisans' dwellings. Well, I
don't know what the bloody artisans thought about 'em
but I know what this here bloody market porter thinks
about 'em. Slums for the working class, that's what they
are. Only fit for the bloody cockroaches that share the
dump with us.

Then there's the Cut over there. Looks a bit of all right
in the moonlight. Like a picture postcard. But it's nothing
but a bloody sewer, and everyone round here dumps
their shit in it – especially that dye works up the road. 'Is
it any wonder the kids round 'ere get scarlet fever with all
them bloody colours,' he added aloud, seeing the irony of
it.

But this is no bloody place to rear a family, he thought.
As for this latest little bugger . . . What chance does he

stand here in Collyhurst? I think we'll have to flit. There's got to be something better than this, though I don't know where.

He ground out his fag and went in to get some sleep.

Chapter One

A Mixed Infant

Billy was six and he knew how to whistle. He had many other accomplishments, of course: he could read, tell the time, throw stones, catch a ball, and climb the railway fence. But his whistle was the thing he was most proud of; he simply puckered up his lips, blew, and out came the one and only tune he knew: 'The Stars and Stripes Forever', which he'd heard on his Dad's HMV wind-up gramophone. 'Whistling Rufus', Mam called him. Only that morning when he'd been on their veranda lavatory, she'd called through the door:

'Come on out, Whistling Rufus – come an' wet your whistle.'

She had a funny way of saying things like that. Why, at breakfast, when he was eating his Quaker Oats, she'd said:

'That's right. Get that down you; it'll stick to your ribs.'

The idea of all that gooey porridge clinging to the inside of his ribs didn't appeal to him at all. But then her list of wise sayings was endless:

'Crusts make your hair curly.'

'Fish makes you brainy.'

'Stew puts a lining on your stomach.'

All true, of course, because Mam was forty-seven and knew everything.

Whistling Sousa's march, he set out for school and soon crossed the bridge over the Cut, which that morning was flowing a sickly yellow. He waited on the edging of Collyhurst Road and, like he'd been told, looked both ways, finding the speed of the horses and carts easy to judge but not so the post office vans which came tearing out of the recently built depot. He made it safely to the other side, however, and stopped just outside the Rechabite Hall and looked up at the big sign-board emblazoned with the words:

ORDER OF RECHABITES: FOUNDED 1835
TEMPERANCE MISSIONARY HALL

Billy thought about the truly wonderful Christmas party they'd had in there the previous night. But at the same time he felt a twinge of guilt on account of the sin he'd committed by attending it.

Now, it was common knowledge amongst the Catholics of Collyhurst that the Rechabites – despite the fame of their kazoo and comb-and-paper band – were misguided heretics who were bound to go straight to hell for not believing in the right religion. At Holy Mass only yesterday, hadn't Father O'Brien, the parish priest, warned everyone about the dangers of false religions and the worship of false gods. From his pulpit, he had thundered:

'Remember, my dear brethren, that God has said, "Thou shalt not have strange gods before me!" Any Catholic who takes part in the worship or prayers of a false religion is guilty of a grievous sin and will be doomed to hell for all eternity.'

On the other hand, it was common knowledge amongst the people of Collyhurst that the Rechabites organised an annual children's Christmas party of breathtaking magnificence. For those children who were lucky enough to get a ticket, the party was undoubtedly a never-to-be-forgotten affair. And Billy had a ticket! Given to him by Dad! It was the equivalent of a Cup Final ticket for an adult, and how his dad had come by it was anybody's guess – certainly not for any feat of sobriety. Perhaps he'd won it in a game of crib, or found it outside Tubby Ainsworth's pub. But Billy wasn't interested in the whys and wherefores – he had a ticket, and that was good enough for him!

The party was due to start at six o'clock. Before Billy was allowed to put a foot outside the tenement, Mam washed him and scrubbed him until he shone like a polished red apple. Then on with his best jersey, navy-blue trousers with striped elastic belt, long stockings with the colourful tops, and finally his black leather boots which Dad had buffed and buffed until they were gleaming. Mam issued dire warnings about not losing the cup and saucer he had to take, and about being on his best behaviour. At last a spotless, luminous Billy set out with a final piece of advice ringing in his ears:

'Eat their cakes an' jelly, son,' Mam had said. 'But try not to join in their prayers and hymns if you can help it. That's a good boy.'

Over at the Rechabite Hall, ten tables had been laid with colourful paper covers, serviettes, crackers and party hats – the latter being the well-made, expensive variety – not the cheap, flimsy kind. The eyes of all the children, however, were focused not on the tables but on the open kitchen doors through which they could see the waiting banquet. Around the sides of the hall stood the Rechabite Sunday-school staff smiling in welcome but dressed in sombre clothes as if going to a funeral.

So that's what heretics look like, thought Billy. But what's making them smile like that?

Seated at the tables, sixty boisterous kids – nearly wetting themselves with excitement – all looking unnaturally clean and laundered, and holding a motley collection of crockery of different shapes, sizes and colours, waited impatiently for the festivities to begin. At six fifteen, a tall, bearded gentleman in a black suit – not unlike the pictures of Abraham Lincoln that Billy had seen at school – appeared on the stage, clapped his hands for attention and intoned in his best church voice:

'It does my heart good to see so many bright and shining little faces here before me. The Lord Jesus has said: "Suffer the little children to come unto me." And this is what we are doing tonight, for the dear little children of Collyhurst have indeed come unto us to celebrate the birth of our Lord and Saviour, Jesus Christ. But before we begin our feast, my dear children, let us stand, bow our heads and thank the great Lord above for his munificence.'

For the young listeners, this speech was not only incomprehensible but unbearably long, for they were eager to get on with the serious business in hand, namely the dispatch of all that seductive food sitting out there in the kitchen. The kids of Collyhurst, however, had learned a pragmatism that John Dewey would have been proud of. They knew which side their bread was buttered on, and if to get at all those lovely comestibles they had to take part in a few curious rituals, so be it.

Billy was worried, though, about that word 'suffer' the Lincoln character had used. He'd met the word before, in 'Suffered under Pontius Pilate', and he wasn't too happy about what these Rechabites had in mind.

All present bowed their heads. Surreptitiously, Billy made a cross with his two index fingers, like he'd seen in a Dracula picture, to ward off evil spirits.

The Rechabite intoned solemnly:

'O let Israel bless the Lord: let him praise and exalt him above all for ever. We give thanks to Thee, O Lord most holy, Father almighty, God everlasting, for this bounteous food which Thou hast placed before us in celebration of the birth of Thy son, Jesus Christ. Impart unto us, we beseech Thee, O Lord, the grace to quench within ourselves the fire of evil desires; grant that no flame of guilt lay waste the souls of Thy servants here present tonight. Amen.'

This strange incantation was enough for Billy. Lucifer had been summoned up as the unseen guest.

But now the food was brought on, and any thoughts of Lucifer were temporarily suspended. For some time, the only sound in the hall was kids chomping their way through mountains of food. And what food! They had never seen such a spread! Potted meat sandwiches, quickly gobbled up, followed by mince pies, chocolate cake and a choice of three kinds of jelly – the whole lot being washed down with copious quantities of sweet, milky tea served by the funereal Rechabites from large metal tea-pots.

When the repast had been devoured, it became time to pay the piper, and the price was the singing of hymns – Rechabite hymns and only just short of devil-worship. The kazoo band assembled on stage and began to tune up like the Hallé Orchestra. A large grubby chart containing the words of the heretical hymns was rolled out on display. The band struck up with its tinny zuzzing sound and they were off. With great gusto, the Rechabites and their followers sang out, their voices ringing to the rafters.

The first one, 'Stand up! Stand up for Jesus', sounded

particularly depraved, but there followed others equally wicked, like 'Fight the Good Fight' and 'Tell me the old, old story'. As not a single one of these had ever been heard in St Patrick's Church, Billy became more and more convinced that his soul was turning blacker and blacker with every note he sang.

There was a temporary respite from all this, however, when silent films were shown on an 8 mm projector, featuring celebrities like Charlie Chaplin, Harold Lloyd and Buster Keaton. The memory of the hymn-singing episode was soon lost in laughter at the antics of Charlie and the deadpan face of Buster.

Like any good production, the party had a finale. An authentically dressed Father Christmas ho-hoed his way into the hall and proceeded to give out presents of all kinds of games and toys. The fact that they were distributed by a sinful Rechabite Santa – or was that Satan? – was irrelevant since they were lavish beyond the Collyhurst kids' wildest dreams. The red-robed figure must have been mad. With wild abandon he handed out boxed games of ludo, lotto, draughts, tiddlywinks, and snakes and ladders.

But like all the other delights that evening, they had to be paid for. This time with the prayers of this misguided religion.

What would Father O'Brien say if he could see me now? thought Billy. He could hear the priest's voice echoing in his head: 'Prayers of a false religion . . . grievous sin . . . doomed to hell for ever.' Meanwhile, the staff had lined up on the stage – like the cast at a pantomime taking its final bows – for the concluding ceremony.

Now the sinfulness of the hymn-singing was compounded by the recitation of Rechabite versions of well-known prayers, like their unauthorised phrasing of the Lord's Prayer which contained various words different from those Billy was used to: 'Our Father *Which* art in heaven' instead of the orthodox and correct 'Our Father *Who* art in heaven'. And sin of sins – surely the work of Old Nick himself – there was a postscript at the end, which instead of finishing at 'deliver us from evil. Amen' actually went on with 'For Thine is the kingdom, the power and the glory, For ever and ever. Amen.' As Billy uttered this final sinful supplement, he felt sure that he'd sold his soul to the devil for a set of snakes and ladders.

Maybe he had. But then it really was a very good set.

Now Billy awoke from his reverie and continued his journey. At Dalton Street, he was joined by his two best friends, Teddy Smith and Joey Murray.

'Hiya, Billy,' said Teddy. 'Goin' to school?'

'Course I am!' replied Billy. 'D'you think I'm wagging it or somethin'?'

Teddy's pants had more patches than pant, his shoes were scuffed dusty grey, there were great spuds in his stockings, and he had a snotty nose. Just the same, he was well-liked – after all, he was a very good fighter and a very good stone-thrower.

Joey Murray was better dressed because his dad had a job with a pension at the new post office depot and consequently had a position to keep up.

'What a stink!' said Teddy as they passed the Phillips rubber works. 'It's nearly as bad as the Cut.'

'Aye, but not as bad as the boneworks over there,' remarked Joey.

'I wonder what do they do at the boneworks,' said Teddy suspiciously.

'Dunno,' said Billy. 'But me mam says they make glue out of bones.'

'Whose bones? They don't use dead people, do they?' Teddy asked in horror.

'No, I think they use mainly horses. But I suppose they must use people sometimes – if there's a shortage,' said Billy, always a mine of information.

They passed under the big railway arches at Aspin Lane.

'I played in the Cut yesterday,' said Teddy. 'It was dead smashin'. We was all throwing stones at the rats. I hit one a beauty.'

'I'll bet y'had it for your Sunday dinner,' said Joey.

'Oh no we didn't,' replied Teddy defiantly. 'Me mam got a sheep's head from the butcher's, so there!'

'Oh yeah,' replied Billy. 'Well, me and our Les climbed over the railway fence an' went picking coke an' cinders on the tip. An' after, we followed a cart out o' the gas works; it was piled up with coke – warm an' steaming, like. We picked up some really big pieces what fell off. We got nearly half a bag for me mam. But me dad wouldn't half belt us if he knew we'd been on the tip.'

At Sharp Street Ragged School, Teddy asked:

'Why do they call it the Ragged School, I wonder?'

'P'raps it's because all the kids who go there are ragged,' said Billy.

'Like you, eh, Teddy?' said Joey.

'Don't be such a cheeky sod, Joey, or I'll belt you one,' said Teddy, giving him a friendly cuff.

'Hey, I saw a dead body yesterday,' said Billy. 'In a coffin.'

'Did yer heck,' said Teddy. 'Where?'

'In the Fannings' toffee shop. It was their lad; I think he'd swallowed a huge tube o' summat. They said he'd died of a tube o' colossal. That's what it sounded like, anyroad. He looked dead beltin' in his coffin'; he was smiling, like, as if he'd just heard a good joke, an' he was dressed up in altar boy's clothes. Funny, that, 'cos they're not Catholics.'

'I wonder what it's like bein' dead,' said Teddy. 'I'll bet it's smashin'. Like being in the pictures all the time an' watchin' Mickey Mouse an' with as many toffees as you can eat.'

'You might have to go to purgatory first,' said Joey, 'if you've done a lotta sins.'

'How long for?' asked Teddy.

'About ten billion billion years,' replied Billy pessimistically. 'That's what Miss Gibson says, anyroad.'

At Dantzig Street, there was a newspaper boy yelling in a street-seller's sing-song voice: 'News! Latest News! Hitler next German Chancellor! Gordon Richards now champion jockey! Loch Ness Monster seen again!'

Teddy couldn't help having a go at the paper boy's strident call:

'News! Latest new-ew-ews! Donald Duck dead!' he bawled in an uncannily accurate imitation.

They arrived at the Salvation Army hostel, where they crouched down with knees bent to peer into the basement dining hall at the down-and-outs slurping their soup at the long wooden tables. There was a powerful pong of stew and steaming underpants and singlets coming through the open windows.

The three boys poked their heads in and shouted: 'Get your hair cut!'

Immediately one of the derelicts left his place at the table and came running towards the window, bawling:

'Get away with you. Cheeky little buggers.'

They ran off quickly up Angel Meadow, chanting as

they did so a rhyme that was compulsory for Collyhurst children passing that way:

'*Jack, Jack, turn around/Turn your face to the Burial Ground.*'

'Jack' was the revolving air-vent on the top of the CWS Tobacco factory, whilst the Burial Ground was St Michael's Flags – an ancient parish cemetery now being used as a recreation ground.

'Are there any people buried under there?' asked Teddy, pointing to the stone flags now worn smooth by the feet of two centuries.

'Miss Gibson said there are thousands and thousands,' said Billy. 'They all died of some collar disease.'

'How do you die of a collar disease?' asked Teddy, anxiously fingering his neck.

'I dunno. I suppose it's when your collar's too tight. But don't ask me!' said Billy, getting a little impatient. He could see himself being cast in the role of medical consultant just because he'd seen a dead body. 'I don't know everything!'

'Is it haunted, do you think?' asked Teddy nervously.

'Don't be daft, Teddy,' answered Billy. 'Course it is. Must be. I wouldn't come down here on a dark night. Not for anything. You'd see all the ghosts come out moaning an' clutching their collars.'

At the bacon warehouse, they followed their usual routine with the man at the bacon hoist:

'Got any rickers, mister?' Billy called out.

'Got any knickers, mister?' Joey shouted cheekily.

'Here!' said the man, throwing out a whole lot of small, flat pieces of wood which the boys then put between two fingers and clicked like castanets. Rattling their rickers, they turned the corner into Sinclair Street. Straight into trouble!

There, lying in wait for them, was their hated and feared enemy, the skenny-eyed kid. His squint seemed to have given him the distinct advantage of being able to look in two directions at once, like the swivel eyes of a chameleon. He was about thirteen years old, and his close-cropped, basin-barbered head and the area around his mouth were painted with a hideous purple ointment – the standard treatment for ringworm and impetigo at the school clinic. In his hand he held a large catapult, which he pointed at the three youngsters.

'Right, what've you gorr on yer? Empty your pockets or you get this,' he snarled, indicating the fully loaded catapult.

The three boys took out all their prized possessions and placed them at the feet of the highway robber. The booty consisted of one yo-yo, one piece of chalk, one tin soldier, three pairs of rickers, two marbles, a piece of string, and one Uncle Joe's mint ball.

'Whorrabout money? Where's yer money?' the robber demanded.

The three lads shook their heads in reply.

'Right,' the young thug said. 'Next time I see you lot, you berra 'ave money!'

The three victims were then allowed to go on their way. Trembling with fear, they reached the sanctuary of the yard of St Wilfred's Mixed Infants.

The school was accommodated in a large hall which served as a church on Sundays and a place of learning on weekdays – curtains being the only means of separating the classes. As the boys arrived, Sister Helen of the Santa Maria Order was ringing her large handbell to start the school day.

Sister Helen! Beautiful Sister Helen! What mixed

thoughts her name conjured up in Billy's mind. When he had first started school two years previously, he had looked up to her as a saint. Even in appearance she resembled his statue of St Thérèse of Lisieux, the Little Flower of Jesus, which he had won for answering catechism questions.

After his mam, Sister had been his favourite person. When all was said and done, she had been the one who had taught him to read when he was only four; the one who'd called him in from the playground to tell him that he had made such progress in his reading that he was to be promoted. She had said:

'William' – only teachers, priests and others in authority ever gave him his full title – 'you are the first in the class at reading and so you are to come off cards and start on a real book!'

The book in question was all about a family where the dad wore a suit and a tie, the mother a lovely silk dress, and they had a pretty little daughter named Kitty who spent all her time playing with their pedigree Collie dog called Rover. They all lived together in a big house with a large garden in which the dog would run about freely whenever a member of the family gave it the command: '*Run, Rover, run.*' At which they exclaimed to each other with obvious pride: '*Rover is running. See Rover run.*'

Again, Sister had been the one to award him countless religious prizes for his ever-widening religious knowledge, until his drawer at home had become a veritable Aladdin's cave of crucifixes, rosary beads, holy pictures, statues of major saints, holy water fonts, and enough medals to make an African general jealous.

Yes, Billy had placed Sister on a pedestal, and from his lowly position, he had sat at her feet and worshipped her and hung on to her every word.

But the relationship was too fervent and did not – indeed, could not – last. One dark day, he found that his heroine had feet of clay. She used bad language! He found her out in lesson time. She was teaching nursery rhymes, and the children had had all the usual stuff about amorous Georgie Porgie and the neurotic Miss Muffet when Sister turned to a new one which went:

> *Curly locks, Curly locks,*
> *Wilt thou be mine?*
> *Thou shalt not wash dishes*
> *Nor yet feed the swine;*
> *But sit on a cushion*
> *And sew a fine seam,*
> *And feed upon strawberries,*
> *Sugar and cream.*

Billy could not believe his ears. The term 'swine' was a very bad swearword in Collyhurst, as in the expression: 'Bugger off, you little swine.' And here was the holy nun using the 'S' word in a nursery rhyme! Billy had reported the obscenity to Mam, but she had merely laughed and told him not to worry.

Nevertheless, in his mind, the reputation of his heroine had become tarnished. And there was worse to come. His suspicion about her tendency to use profane words was confirmed when towards Christmas he heard her employing yet another 'S' word. She was teaching a carol all about some king called Wenceslas who was having problems with snow and ice. Everything had been going fine until she reached the fifth verse, when he heard her sing:

> *In his master's steps he trod,*
> *Where the snow lay dinted.*

Heat was in the very sod
Which the saint had printed.

Everyone knew that the word 'sod' was a major term of abuse, as in the phrase: 'You cheeky little sod' or the command: 'Sod off!' Once again, Billy reported the matter at home. And once again, Mam laughed and advised him not to worry. He found this very difficult to understand, for on the odd occasion when he had tried using these words himself, he had been given a swift clip round the ear and told not to be such a cheeky little bugger.

In his turn, he let Sister down. In the playground one day he made a disgrace of himself by failing to make it to the lavatory in time. His brother Les had to be called out of class to take a weeping, wet William home for a change of pants. So ended a beautiful relationship.

At the age of six, Billy was promoted to Miss Gibson's class. Sarah Gibson was a dark-haired, frosty-faced spinster about forty years old, her powerful pebble glasses giving her the look of a bullfrog. On her upper lip there was a hint of a moustache, whilst on her cheek she had a large hairy mole. In her class, he devoted nearly all of his time to the hard grind of the three Rs and the acquisition of basic literacy and numeracy. Day by day, he fought his way through book after book and table after table until he had reached the dizzy heights of his five times. In religion, he had completed the initial training for his First Confession and First Communion whilst at the same time battling through the Penny Catechism until his store of religious emblems had grown to the point where he was considering opening a shop specialising in the sale of sacred objects.

There was no doubt, though, that his favourite lessons

were fairy tales and poetry – especially the nonsense verses of Lewis Carroll:

> *'Will you walk a little faster?' said a whiting to a snail,*
> *'There's a porpoise close behind us, and he's treading on my tail.'*

and:

> *'The time has come,' the Walrus said,*
> *'To talk of many things;*
> *Of shoes – and ships – and sealing wax –*
> *Of cabbages – and kings –*
> *And why the sea is boiling hot –*
> *And whether pigs have wings.'*

They also recited poetry all about 'The house that Jack built' and the maiden all forlorn who had a cow with a crumpled horn.

Came the day when Miss Gibson thought she would round off the afternoon lessons with a half-hour of class entertainment.

'Who would like to make a start?' she asked. 'Will anyone here sing or dance for us?'

Her request was met with complete silence. Most of the children of Collyhurst had learned at an early age the first rule of survival: never volunteer for anything – unless you're going to get paid for it!

'Come along, children,' she said impatiently. 'Surely someone can do something.'

Unable to stand the tension any longer, Billy raised his hand.

'I can dance like Fred Astaire, miss,' he said.

'Come along then, William. Let's see this dance of yours.'

He went to the front of the class and executed a kind of tap dance à la Fred Astaire but more economical, as Billy used only one foot – his right. When he felt that his audience had had enough, he stopped to assess their reactions. He need not have worried. Miss Gibson said:

'That was very good, William. I think it deserves a round of applause. Come along, children.'

The clapping and the admiration which followed were meat and drink to Billy – especially that of June Gladwin, his sweetheart, who sat in the front row watching him admiringly. He sat down triumphantly.

'Now, I'm sure there must be somebody else who wants to do their little party piece,' Miss Gibson said.

Silence, while most of the kids tried to puzzle out what she meant by 'little party piece'.

'Come along now, children. Surely there must be someone else,' she coaxed, sounding a little desperate.

For Billy, this lack of response became unbearable, and he wondered if he should volunteer his services again to solve Miss Gibson's embarrassment. He remembered a little act of his which always caused great laughter and amusement at home with Mam and his two sisters when they were fooling around with the latest craze from America, the Shimmy – danced to a pop song of the day, 'I wish I could shimmy like my sister Kate'.

He raised his hand again.

'I know another dance if you want, miss.'

'Very well, William. You seem to be the only one who's willing to do anything today. Let us see this other dance.'

Billy went out to the front and began his rendering of the Shimmy. This involved raising both arms above his head and wiggling his hips voluptuously in the style of Miss Dorothy Lamour doing a hula-hula dance in the

South Sea Islands. Miss Gibson took one look and frowned.

'Sit down,' she commanded. 'That is disgusting.'

Billy sat down deflated – bewildered that his perform-ance could cause happy laughter in one place and disgust in another. There was no understanding the adult world!

Perhaps the Shimmy was associated with sin in Miss Gibson's mind, because before they finished school that day, she said:

'Remember, children, that tomorrow morning our young curate, Father Conroy, is coming over to hear practice confessions. Remember to have a sin ready to tell him, and don't forget all that I have taught you.'

After the usual prayers, Miss Gibson dismissed the class.

On the way home, Billy and his friends – boys and girls – gathered together in a little secluded corner near the Burial Ground to play their favourite game – Truth or Dare. The boys consisted of Teddy Smith, Joey Murray and Billy, whilst the girls – also a trio – were Patsy McGivern, Wendy Killick and June Gladwin. Patsy McGivern was a brown-eyed belle with dark hair arranged in a neat fringe across her forehead; Wendy a rosy-cheeked girl with fair hair plaited in two long tails; but the greatest beauty of all was June Gladwin, with her gentle blue eyes, her long light-brown tresses which cascaded down her back, and a lovely little smile that could melt a heart of stone. Billy was hopelessly in love with her.

The game started with Joey Murray asking the questions.

'Truth or Dare?' he enquired of Teddy Smith.

'Dare!' said Teddy, always ready for action.

'I dare you to climb up that lamppost, swing round it, spit twice, and then come back to your place.'

Teddy executed the deed with the skill of a Hollywood stuntman and was back in his place in a flash.

'Truth or Dare?' to June Gladwin.

'Truth,' said Billy's heroine.

'Is it true you love Billy?'

'Yes, it's true,' she said, blushing. Billy's heart leapt for joy.

'Truth or Dare?' to Wendy Killick.

'Dare,' she answered.

'I dare you to hug me,' Joey said.

Typically selfish, thought Billy.

Then came his turn:

'Truth or Dare?'

'Dare,' answered Billy boldly.

'I dare you to kiss June Gladwin,' said Joey obligingly.

Billy carried out the command readily by giving June a smacker on the cheek.

'Awwww!' exclaimed the other two girls admiringly. 'He went and did it!'

Joey now turned to Patsy McGivern: 'Truth or Dare?'

'Dare,' she said, not to be outdone by her friend Wendy.

'I dare you to show us your knickers!' said Joey.

A long-drawn-out 'Awwwww!' came from the three girls. Then, 'We're telling on you . . .' And on that shocked note, the game broke up.

Disconsolately, Billy and the other two boys began the journey back together until they reached the forge, where they parted company. Billy wanted to watch the horses being shod, but the other two had to get back to help with babies at home.

Through the open top half of the smithy door, he watched fascinated as the blacksmith and his mate hammered and shaped the white-hot metal into a horseshoe, which they then nailed on to the horse's hoof.

Why, he asked himself, doesn't the poor horse feel the hot shoes being nailed on to its feet?

Still puzzling about this, he set off for home. But as he turned into Collyhurst Road, there was the skenny-eyed kid! For the second time that day! Waylaid by the wretch who seemed to have a grudge against the rest of the world.

'Stop! You're not going past! Worravyer gorrin yer pockets, kid?' he demanded.

'Nothin'. Honest to God. You took everythin' this morning.'

'I told you to get some money for the next time I saw yer, din't I?' he said. 'An' you 'aven't got it, 'ave you? So just for that, you get this.'

He wrestled with Billy and pulled him to the ground. Then, kneeling on him, he took from his pocket a box of ointment – the very same evil-smelling purple ointment which was smeared on his own head and mouth.

'Try some of this, you little bastard,' he snarled, rubbing the foul stuff on Billy's face and head. 'Now let that be a bloody lesson to you, you little sod. Next time, 'ave some money or else you'll get some more!' the juvenile footpad growled.

Released from the bully's grip, Billy wept and wailed his way down the length of Collyhurst Road, causing passers-by to tut-tut in sympathy.

'What've they done to you, son?'

'What's that horrible purple stuff on your face, son?'

'They should set the coppers on to 'em.'

These sympathetic noises only served to make Billy howl the louder. He reached his own door at last and for good effect turned up the volume of his bawling by several decibels as he crossed the threshold. Mam was black-leading the grate with Zebo when she clapped eyes on him. He made such a sorry sight, she almost went berserk.

'Who in God's name has done that to you? And what *is* that awful stuff? Whoever done this should be locked up! If I get my hands on the swine . . .'

Billy never did find out what she'd have done to the skenny-eyed kid because she was too busy putting pans of water on the gas rings. In double-quick time, she began washing his hair so vigorously that she got soap in his eyes and his ears, thus causing a fresh outburst of blubbing. Then it was all over and his natural colour was restored. As a special treat for being so brave, she cut him a very thin slice of Mother's Pride, covering it generously with 'best' butter.

That night the family gathered round the table for their evening tea of 'tater-ash' – Lancashire hot-pot covered over with a golden pastry crust. The conversation turned to the bullying and brigandry of the skenny-eyed kid and the effect it was having on 'our kid', who had now become frightened to walk home from school on his own.

Billy's hero was his brother Jim, who was now thirteen years of age and in his last year at St Chad's Elementary School in Cheetham. Every night after school, he could be seen running home down Collyhurst Road to do his paper round at the Fannings' corner shop. In the evenings however, he had been receiving boxing instruction for some considerable time at the Welcome Boys' Recreation Club just near the Dwellings. Now, when he heard this conversation at the dinner table, his ears pricked up.

'What time does this cock-eyed kid start his bullyin'?' he asked Billy.

'After school lets out – at half past three.'

'Right. We let out at four o'clock. So if I run fast . . .' said Jim, working out some calculation. 'OK. Leave it to me,' he said finally. 'An' I think it's time I started givin' you boxing lessons so you can look after yourself.'

After tea, there occurred a rare event. Dad climbed on to a chair and, reaching up to the very top shelf of the built-in wall cupboard, took down his most prized possession – the one which had a picture of a dog listening to a loudspeaker horn on its lid. His portable gramophone! Nobody, but nobody – except himself – was ever allowed to operate this piece of amazing technology. In fact, the machine was only brought down on very special occasions, for example when Dad was in an unusually happy frame of mind, or alternatively when there had been perhaps a minor family crisis and someone needed to be cheered up. This particular evening seemed to slot into the latter category. The trouble was that there was only a limited selection of records to choose from. But that evening, Dad played the complete repertoire. There was, of course, 'The Stars and Stripes Forever', and in addition Waldteufl's 'Skater's Waltz', Arthur Tracy's street-singer's 'Marta', Harry Richman's 'King for a Day', Sandy Powell's monologues ('Can y'hear me, Mother?') and the top songs of 1934 – recently purchased by Billy's two sisters – 'Sing as We Go' and 'Isle of Capri', both sung by Lancashire's own Gracie Fields.

Billy's favourite was still 'Underneath the Arches' sung by Flanagan and Allen, because it reminded him of that Christmas two years ago and his wonderful first visit to town with Flo and Polly when they had bought the record at Woolworth's. He would never forget that trip – not as long as he lived. He had been just four years of age, and his two sisters had met him after school at the top of Angel Meadow. Together they had walked down Thompson Street and Oldham Street, and the sheer splendour of the scene – the bright lights, the gleaming store windows, the honking of the traffic, and the visit to meet Father Christmas in Lewis's store – had so filled him with awe and wonder that he could only gaze open-mouthed at the fairyland world to which he had been transported. On the way back, they had bought black puddings as a special treat for Mam and Dad, plus, of course, the record. As these thoughts went through his head, Sam and Jim began their Flanagan and Allen act, singing and strolling about the tenement.

Mam brought him back to the land of the living.

'Come on, tough guy. Time for bed.'

The day of drama ended on a happy note. As Mam was tucking him into bed, she asked him the question she always liked to ask:

'What are you?'

And he gave the James Cagney answer she wanted to hear:

'A smart guy and a tough kid!'

'Now,' she said, 'time for sleep. Before you close your eyes, say the prayer our Flo learned you.'

He began, 'Now I lay me down to sleep, I pray the Lord my soul to keep; And if I die before I wake, I pray the Lord my soul to take.' And as a postscript, he added: 'And by the way, God, if I meet the skenny-eyed kid tomorrow, will You please fix it so that I can run faster than him!'

The next day began like any other. The journey to school had become a routine. Billy whistled as he strode across the bridge. His two friends joined him at Dalton Street, and they shouted their usual 'Get yer hair cut' through the Sally Army's window, and collected more rickers from the bacon man at the hoist.

The skenny-eyed kid, however, was nowhere to be seen that morning.

School started off as usual, but on this particular morning, religious instruction was devoted to role-playing confessions with Father Conroy. As Billy watched his adorable June Gladwin go in first, he wondered what sins this lovely blue-eyed creature could possibly have committed. How could an angel sin? The class of children waited their turn to be called to the confessional box – each one anxious not to make a mistake, each one ready with a sin. As the queue went down, their nervousness went up. Like waiting to be shot, thought Billy. Too soon, Miss Gibson called:

'Next – William Hopkins.'

His heart fluttering, Billy entered the confessional box and began:

'Bless me, Father, for I have sinned. This is my first confession.'

'Good boy, William,' said Father Conroy. 'Now the sin part. Tell me a sin.'

'Please, Father, Joey Murray asked Patsy McGivern to show him her knickers.'

There was a long pause before Father Conroy continued. He appeared to be weeping, because he had a handkerchief up to his eyes and he was making little snorting noises. Billy didn't think that Joey's sin was that serious.

'Now, William, tell me *your* sin,' Father Conroy said when he had recovered his composure.

Billy didn't really have another sin ready, as they'd been told to prepare just one for practice. He thought very quickly and came up with:

'Please, Father, I did the Shimmy dance.'

He didn't know what it was, but Father Conroy had started crying again.

Billy began the walk home after school feeling very nervous and apprehensive. This journey back – fraught with danger and possible violence – was beginning to resemble a walk through a dark African forest with wild animals lurking behind every bush. He passed the corner where he had been attacked – now forever associated with assault and evil-smelling ointment. He strode bravely alongside the Cut, whistling his tune to cover up his nervousness – when suddenly, he was there! The skenny-eyed kid! Legs astride, catapult in hand.

'Right, kid,' he rasped. 'Empty yer pockets. Where's yer money?'

Billy was about to answer but didn't get a chance. For without warning, the bully was sent reeling by a blow of the ox-felling kind. Jim stood over him and said:

'If I ever see you near our kid again, I'll give you the hiding of your life. Now scram!'

Jim then continued his run to Fanning's so as not to be late for his paper round.

Now it was the turn of the squint-eyed mugger to howl. But before the young thug could obey the order to scram, Billy got in the final word:

'Listen, kid! That was me brother and he's a boxer, see. You pick on me and you pick on me family.'

And he stepped over the prostrate body and swaggered home, whistling 'The Stars and Stripes Forever'.

The following Monday, Billy set off for school as usual. At Dalton Street he was met – as usual – by Joey Murray. But there was no sign of Teddy Smith.

Later that morning, Sister Helen called a meeting of the whole school and announced that Teddy Smith had drowned in the River Irk whilst throwing stones at the water rats. He had fallen in at a deep part of the Cut, where the swift current had swept him away into the sewers.

On the way home, Joey and Billy stopped at the railings of the Cut. They looked down at the river, which was a dirty grey cesspool of filth and garbage containing rusty bedsteads, decayed mattresses, twisted bicycles and decomposing dogs. But over near the bank, there was a tiny section of the river where the water swirled and eddied in a whirlpool of technicolour dyes, and as it pirouetted over stones and rocks, it seemed to be enjoying a fit of bubbling laughter.

'Poor Teddy,' said Billy. 'I wonder if he's down there watching Mickey Mouse, and with all the toffees he can eat.'

Chapter Two

Honeypot Street

Moira McGurk was giving her favourite lesson on the British Empire.

'You see, boys,' she began. 'When David Livingstone went to Africa, he found that many tribes had not even discovered the wheel – they didn't even have calendars . . .'

'Then how did they know which year it was, miss?' asked Billy.

'Well, William,' she answered. 'They remembered each year by calling it after some big event that had happened in that particular year. For example, if they had had millions of locusts, they might call that "The Year of the Locusts". Now, what do you think they would call it if they had no food?'

This was something the Red Bank kids could relate to.

' "The Hungry Year",' suggested Carrots Campbell.

' "The Year of Famine",' said Billy.

'Good, good,' said Miss McGurk. 'What about a year with no rain?'

' "The Thirsty Year",' said Joey Flewitt.

'Excellent,' said Miss McGurk. 'Or "The Year of the Drought". Now then. What about this year – 1935? What could we call this year?'

The class was stuck for a moment.

'Something that happened in May. You were all given special mugs. Think of King George and Queen Mary,' she prompted.

'Ah, I've got it,' said Henry Sykes triumphantly. ' "Silver Jubilee Year"!'

'Good lad, Henry,' said Miss McGurk. Then, warming to her subject, she asked: 'But what would you call this year for you and your family – personally? I mean, it might be "The Year Your Grandad Came to Stay" or something like that.'

'Please, miss,' said Stan White. 'For our family, it's the year me Dad ran off with our lodger.'

'Yes. Yes,' she said, doubtfully. 'But we don't want to hear about that. You mustn't tell us about that here!'

'Please, miss,' said Billy. 'It's the year we did a flit from the Dwellings to Honeypot Street.'

'You mean a "moonlight flit",' said Stan White.

'No I don't,' replied Billy defiantly. 'We moved in the daylight when everyone could see us.'

'Now stop it, you two!' said Miss McGurk ominously. 'But anyway, nice people don't say "flit", William – when they mean "remove" or "move house". What does "flit" really mean, does anyone know?'

'Please, miss,' said Carrots. 'It's that stuff me mam squirts to kill the bugs in the wallpaper.'

'No, no,' said Miss McGurk. ' "Flit" is what little birds do when they fly lightly from one branch to another.'

Exactly, thought Billy.

The overcrowding in the Collyhurst tenement had become too much. Mam and Dad had talked and talked about it for months. It was time to move. Through her half-sister, Hetty, Mam got wind of an empty house – rent eight and six a week – at number 17, Honeypot Street, Red Bank, on the other side of the railway. She didn't waste any time but went straight over to see the landlord and put down the key-money. It was as simple as that and the house was theirs.

On Wednesday 2 October 1935, Rolls-Royce announced their new 50hp, twelve-cylinder Phantom III saloon costing £1,850. It was also Dad's birthday and the day they upped sticks and began their move. For the whole weekend before, the family – aided by a sorrowful Lily Goodhart – had been employed on the job of wrapping up their most fragile possessions in newspapers: the holy statues, the glass-domed shades, the picture-frames, and the oddments of crockery not immediately required.

'Eeh, I'll miss you all when you've gone,' sighed Lily. 'I don't know what I shall do, I really don't. I think we might flit ourselves; we've heard about some nice houses on that new estate in Benchill.'

'You can always come up and see us, Lily. We're only on the other side of the railway, you know,' said Mam.

Now, in Smithfield Market, Tommy had a mate, Sid Lawson, who had a horse and cart. After he'd bought him about ten pints of beer, he agreed to 'flit' them. It would have been cheaper to have paid a removal firm to do it, but that was by the by. With the help of Jim and Sam, the two men loaded up the furniture and the other few bits and pieces, securing the whole lot with a few stout ropes. They set off to make the three-mile journey by road whilst the rest of the family walked by a shorter and quicker route – each one carrying a different household item. Mam had two heavy shopping bags of groceries; Flo the bucket and mop; Polly a sweeping brush and dustpan; Les the gramophone – God help him if he'd dropped it – and Billy the large iron kettle. They made a strange sight as they processed down Collyhurst Road past all the familiar landmarks.

'Goodbye, Rechabite Hall!' said Billy.

'Goodbye, Fanning's shop!' said Les.

'Goodbye, Welcome Boys' Club!' said Polly.

'And goodbye, River Irk, and also you, Teddy Smith,' said Billy. 'Are you still down there in the pictures with your toffees?'

They climbed the seventy-seven steps and crossed over the huge railway bridge.

'It's like climbing the stairway to heaven,' said Flo breathlessly.

'S'more like climbing up Mount Everest, if y'ask me,' Mam gasped.

They trudged along by the railway fence on Barney's waste ground, then turned the corner and there it was: Honeypot Street and the start of a new life!

'Why do they call it Honeypot Street?' asked Billy. 'I don't see any bees around here.'

'Well, what about Angel Meadow then?' said Les. 'You didn't see any angels there, did you?'

'And we didn't see no meadows neither,' added Polly.

Billy had to admit they had a point.

At the beginning of the street, they were welcomed by a pack of mangy-looking mongrels which, disturbed by the unusual sight, barked and growled at their heels whilst a small gang of ragged, snotty-nosed urchins called after them:

'Eh, look at this lot. It's a Whit Friday procession.'

'No it's not,' said a bigger one. 'It's a strike by the railway cleaners.'

The family ignored them and walked on past a bakehouse which boasted the sign: 'NATHAN COHEN:

BAKER & CONFECTIONER' and from which there wafted the delicious aroma of hot crusty loaves and freshly baked bagels.

'That'll be useful,' said Mam, indicating the bakery.

'But we don't eat Jewish food,' said Polly.

'You'll eat what you're given and like it,' said Mam.

As they progressed along the street, they chanted together the countdown of the odd numbers: 25 . . . 23 . . . 21 . . . 19 . . . 17! Number 17! Their house at last! The five of them gazed up at it in awe. After Collyhurst Buildings, it was a palace! It was one of three houses raised above street level and was approached by six steps.

'Eh, we're going up in the world,' said Billy.

'First thing we do,' said Mam, 'is donkey-stone them steps. We can't have the neighbours talking about us. That's your job, Polly, d'y'hear?'

'Why does it always have to be me? I always get the rotten jobs,' complained Polly, though deep down she was secretly proud to be given such an important task so early in the 'flitting' process.

Half an hour later, Dad, Sid and the lads arrived with the furniture. Watched by prying neighbours from behind their curtains, the Hopkins family began unloading their possessions.

'Right, our Flo,' said Mam. 'Start by getting our old curtains up to the front bedroom window.'

'But suppose they don't fit?' said Flo.

'Don't make problems,' said Mam. 'Get your father to nail them up for the time being. We don't want them nosy neighbours over there watching us undress for bed, do we?'

'What about us?' said Polly. 'What if they're watching me and our Flo?'

'Who'd want to watch you?' answered Mam. 'Anyroad, you're at the back of the house.'

'Yes, but there might be somebody in the back entry looking up at us,' said Polly.

'Listen, Miss Yes-But, get on with the unpacking and stop arguifying,' said Mam. 'And you, our Sam, see if the Gas Board have turned the gas on, and if they have, get the kettle on. We could all do with a cuppa tea. I'll start mopping out the scullery. If there's one thing I can't abide, it's dirt.'

The house was in chaos, with half-opened tea-chests everywhere, wrappings strewn about the floor, ornaments and chairs and bedding all mixed up higgledy-piggledy. As a first priority, Dad and Jim had gone upstairs to assemble all the beds with a spanner. When disorder was at its peak, there came a knock at the door.

'I wonder who that can be,' Mam snapped. 'It can't be anyone we know; we've only been here five minutes. Go and see who it is, Polly.'

Polly came back: 'It's one o' them nosy neighbours you was talking about. Mrs Sykes from next door,' she said.

'Hush. They might hear you,' said Mam. 'Ask her to come in.'

Polly returned with Mrs Sykes and a young boy about Billy's age. She was a big, heavy woman with asthmatic breathing problems.

'Hello, Mrs 'Opkins. I heard you was coming,' she panted. 'I'm Mrs Sykes from next door. And this is me son, Henery. I just thought I'd pop in and ask if there's anything I can do for you. A bit a shopping or summat.'

As she spoke, she flicked glances about the room, noting the disarray and taking an inventory of their possessions like an eagle-eyed bailiff from the Assistance Board.

'That's very nice of you, Mrs Sykes,' said Mam. 'But we're all right, ta. I brought a lotta food with me for emergencies, like. We're just brewing up. Would you care for a cup?'

'Oh no, Mrs 'Opkins,' she wheezed. 'I don't want to put you to no trouble. I thought I'd better let you know about the shops in the street and that, though.'

'That's right thoughtful of you.'

'We always shop at Ormeroyd's,' Mrs Sykes went on. 'It's a nice clean shop and Elsie Ormeroyd is ever so obliging if you're a bit short o' the ready, like, and you want to put it in the book. There's Sidebotham's at the other end, but we don't trust that shop.'

'You mean Sidebottoms?'

'Yes, that's right. Only they like to be called Siddy-both-ams, not Sidebottoms. Anyroad, we don't like 'em.'

'Oh, and why is that?'

'There's always a funny musty smell in there, like – sort of mouldy, if y'know what I mean. I think she keeps the firelighters next to the bread. Besides that, she has one o' them there notices which says: "Please do not ask for credit as refusal often offends." Y've probably seen 'em.'

'Oh, I don't think we want no tick.'

'We've also got a chippy at the end of the street if you're stuck for summat t'eat,' she continued, ignoring Mam's protestation. 'There's a nice pub as well – the Queen's Arms, which we all call Capper's on account of that's the name of the lan'lord. We gen'rly go in there at weekend for a gill or two; they're all very nice, friendly people as goes in there. I dare say you'll get to know it all when you've been here a bit. Anyroad, I can see you're busy so I won't take up no more o' your time.'

'That's very good of you, Mrs Sykes. It's as well to

know we've got neighbours like you,' said Mam.

'Don't mention it, Mrs 'Opkins,' she said. 'And my Harry, me husband, is a rag-and-bone merchant. So he can get you one or two things that you might need. For a start, I've brought you this donkey stone. I'm sure you'll want to do your steps.'

'Ta very much,' said Mam. 'I was just saying to our Polly that the steps needed doing, wasn't I, Polly?'

'Yes, Mam, you was,' said Polly obligingly.

Throughout this conversation, Billy and Henry Sykes had been eyeing and weighing each other up, like two boxers in the ring assessing the other's strengths and weaknesses. Billy quite liked the look of Henry, who seemed friendly enough and not a bit like the runny-nosed brats they'd seen at the bottom end of Honeypot Street.

Mrs Sykes and her son made their way to the front door and Mrs Sykes took one last look over her shoulder to make sure she hadn't missed anything.

'Remember now,' she said. 'If there's anything . . . anything at all.'

The door had no sooner closed behind her than Mam said:

'I do hope 'er next door isn't one of those who's always coming in and out, 'cos I believe in keeping y'self to y'self. And who the hell does she think she is, anyroad? Does she think we're one o' them there rough families who have more dinner-times than dinners? We're a respectable family in this house, we are. For a start, there'll be no tick as long as I'm in charge. I believe in paying my way, I do. None of this here putting it on the slate. As for fish and chips! There'll be none o' that muck in here – not as long as I've got a pair of hands to cook with.'

'You're right there, Mam,' said Polly.

'And what was all that there stuff about a pub? She must think we're drunkards or summat. Then the cheeky bugger starts telling us to donkey-stone our steps when we've only just bloody well got here.'

She turned to Polly:

'Get out there and get them steps cleaned – now! Be sharp about it! And no buts.'

'Look at this, Mam,' shouted Polly some time later, when she had completed the step-cleaning chore. 'We've got a lovely parlour. It's got wallpaper with lovely blue flowers. We can have parties and all that.' Polly's interest in parties was not unconnected with the fact that she had recently acquired a boyfriend, a certain Steve Keenan, and it was beginning to look serious.

'We can't afford no parties – what with a rent of eight and six a week,' said Mam. 'Don't mention parties to your father, for God's sake – you know what he is.'

'Yes, but . . .' began Polly.

'There you go again.'

'Sorry, Mam. I'll try to stop arguing and I'll try to help out a bit more. This house means a new life for all of us. And p'raps me and our Flo could start our own little sideline, like. But honest, I'm dead happy we've come here. Me and our Flo have even got a whole bedroom to ourselves at last.'

'I know. It's been a good move. We should've done it years ago. There's no bathroom, mind you, and the lav's outside in the yard. But considering the smells, specially when your father's been on the beer, it's probably best out there. And then you can't expect to have everything, can you?'

'We'll freeze to death out there in winter,' complained Polly.

'Good. It'll stop you from sitting out there reading the lavatory papers. And that reminds me – get one o' the lads to cut up some newspapers and tie 'em on the nail out there. Enough about the lavatory. We've got a good living room with a posh gas mantle – you've only to pull that there chain and it plops on. Isn't it marvellous what they can do nowadays? And just look at that range! I'll be able to bake me own bread in that oven. That's another job for you, by the way, our Polly.'

'What, me baking bread?'

'No, y'daft ha'porth – black-leading the oven and the grate.'

'Aw, Mam. That's not . . .' Then she remembered. 'Sorry, Mam.'

'And it's not a bad scullery either,' Mam went on. 'It's got a big slopstone and a good gas stove. Eeh, I'm proper glad to be out o' them Dwellings – though I'll miss Lily Goodhart. We'll probably spend the rest of our lives in this house. In fact, I'm sure we will.'

'I do hope so,' said Polly. 'I do hope so.'

Whilst all this talk was going on, Billy and Les were charging through the house, inspecting and commenting on every room and facility.

'Eh, our Les,' shouted Billy happily. 'Take a look at this yard. Have you seen how big it is? We can play football in it. I could even make a cart or a guider here.'

'Yeah,' said Les. 'And what about the cellars? We can hide in the dark down there.'

'I don't fancy that much,' answered Billy. 'It's dead dark, and besides, it's cold and damp.'

As the two boys scampered about the house, little did they know how much time they were to spend down there in the years ahead.

Chapter Three

We're in the Money

The family settled into a new routine, and a year later Collyhurst Buildings and the Cut seemed like another world, a million years and a million miles away.

It was a Saturday morning in July. Billy had recently had his eighth birthday – not that anyone had noticed. Today he awoke at his usual time, around seven o'clock, and lay in bed thinking. Saturday! His favourite day of the week. No school, of course. Instead he would be going to the matinée at the local flea-pit. But more important, it was money-making day!

All the family seemed to be at it! What Dad did for a living, Billy wasn't too sure. He only knew that Dad got up very early in the morning and went off to Smithfield Market, where he carried things about on a cart. But beyond that, Billy was pretty vague. There were two things, though, he was sure about. Dad was always bringing home lots of fresh fruit and vegetables. And fish! Loads and loads of it! To the point where he felt that he had eaten so much of the stuff his true home was not Red Bank but Dogger Bank! The other thing Billy knew for sure was that after work, Dad drank enough beer to float a battleship, and if he went over his limit – as he usually did on a Saturday – it was best to keep well out of his road or else!

The rest of the family were also on the money-earning trail. Jim had started work in a warehouse on Salford Docks, whilst Sam and Les had their paper rounds at Blount's, the newsagent's on Cheetham Hill Road.

But it was Flo and Polly who had hit the jackpot with their sideline. They worked as seamstresses for Northcotes, the fur-coat manufacturer, on Oldham Road, and one of the perks of the job was being allowed to take home any useless fur remnants left lying around the factory. With typical Collyhurst acumen they had spotted a golden opportunity and had built up a lucrative business making fur mittens at fourpence a pair from the unwanted scraps. Already they seemed to have kitted out most of the residents of Honeypot Street, and several streets beyond. A few months previously, they had boldly intro-duced a new line in Cossack hats, using larger fragments of fur – which the family had to assume were true waste scraps and not deliberate errors made by fellow workers hoping for a share of the profits. The hats had been an immediate winner, as people had soon realised that they could double as tea-cosies when not being used as headgear. So popular were the hats in winter, the neigh-bours had begun to look like extras in a Chekhov play. Billy's part in this Russianisation of the Red Bank residents had been to hire out his hands – at the reason-able charge of a farthing a pair – as templates for children's gloves. He had to make a living too.

Apart from this, Billy had his own ways of coining it – in the heating and lighting business. It had taken him some considerable time to build up his clientele and win their goodwill. The thing was, he had his eye on a beautiful model yacht which he had seen displayed in the big plate-glass window of Baxendale's store on Miller Street. For several weeks now he had drooled over this magnificent boat, and had even spent one or two hours sketching it in his drawing book. To raise the seventy-five shillings required to secure this glittering prize, he had worked out that he would need to put aside one shilling and sixpence a week for one whole year, and already he was halfway to reaching his goal. In his mind's eye, he could see himself at the end of the year proudly carrying the boat under his arm up to Queen's Park lake, to launch the vessel on her maiden voyage to the applause and envy of all his friends and brothers.

'I now christen this ship the SS *Jolly Jim*. May God bless her and all who sail in her!' said King Edward. He could dream, couldn't he? He emerged from his fantasy world and went down to breakfast.

Mam also had her dreams. That same morning, she looked at her bank book. With compressed lips, she carried out a complex mental calculation, counting with her fingers on her chin and throwing away imaginary numbers into the air – as she had been taught at the Board School many years ago. It had taken almost twenty-five years of scrimping and saving to put aside the amount she had. She checked the total – £42.17.3d. She prided herself on being a good manager; that is, being able to make a little go a long way. In her world, the worst insult for a housewife was to be called a bad manager – one who spent more than the family earned and who relied on tick to buy the groceries. Hire purchase was something those funny Americans did, and certainly nobody in the working class – nobody who wanted to be thought respectable, at any rate – would even dream of buying on the never-never. Anyway, today Kate was going to spend a good part of her nest egg. She didn't know how Tommy would take it. Sometimes he didn't take kindly to the idea of her buying something as important as furniture without first asking him.

But, she thought to herself, I know how to pacify him all right. An hour in bed with him this afternoon will soften him up. I'll tell him about it after we've done it; that's when he's in a good mood – the daft ha'porth – and he'll agree to anything.

Kate's attitude to sex was simple – it was a duty women had to put up with in order to satisfy a man's bestial nature and keep the peace. She took no pleasure, and indeed expected none, for herself. On the other hand, she saw no harm in occasionally exploiting the situation and making use of Tommy's Achilles' heel – though in fact, she thought naughtily, his weakness was situated at the other end of his leg.

After a breakfast of toast and tea, she called Flo and Polly together.

'I want you to come to town with me this morning,' she said.

'What for?' asked Polly, her usual agreeable self.

'I'm going in for a new three-piece suite, and I want you to help me pick one out.'

'Oh, that's smashing, Mam,' said Polly. 'I've seen some lovely ones in Dobbins, that new store on Oldham Street.'

'We're not going to no Dobbins. We're going to the Co-op in Downing Street where we'll get a sensible suite and the divvy as well. Should be a lot of divvy on furniture.'

'Oh, that'll be really good,' said Flo. 'We can make that room look lovely. And me and our Polly have got a few pounds saved from selling our mittens. You can have some of that to buy a few bits and bobs to finish off the room.

Y'know – pictures, mirrors and oilcloth, and all that.'

'And p'raps we can have a few friends round as well, if we've got a nice parlour,' said Polly – though she wasn't too keen on Flo mentioning their 'mitten money', as she had earmarked her own share for her bottom-drawer. Her two-year courtship with Steve Keenan had developed into a full-blown romance, and they were now officially engaged. Hence her desire for parties, and the chance to bring him home to introduce him to all her family and friends.

Billy had already met this boyfriend for a few minutes, and those moments were indelibly imprinted on his mind.

It had been one early Sunday morning – was it only two weeks ago? – that he had been coming down the stairs still rubbing the dreams from his eyes. Suddenly there had been a rat-a-tat-tat on the front door. After drawing back the two bolts, he had opened the door and there, silhouetted against the newly risen sun, had towered the apparition of Douglas Fairbanks, the aviator star of *Dawn Patrol*. The colossus had been rigged out in full battle regalia of leather suit, helmet and goggles. Billy had simply gaped open-mouthed. And the giant, god-like creature had spoken in a deep, sonorous voice:

'Hello, young man. You must be Billy. I've heard a lot about you from your sister Pauline.'

Mam had appeared and had said in her poshest, up-market voice:

'Oh, good morning, Mr Keenan. Won't you step h'inside for a moment. Polly won't be too long.'

'Many thanks, Mrs Hopkins. That's fine. Please call me Steve, by the way.'

The hero had actually stood waiting in their living room whilst Polly had been putting the finishing touches to her outfit. Why, even Dad had cringed and deferred before this well-spoken visitor. But then he always did when he felt he was in the presence of anyone 'higher-up'. If he'd had a forelock he'd have tugged it.

'So, young Billy,' said Steve. 'Pauline tells me you're very clever at school.'

Billy's chest swelled with pride and he took an immediate liking to this tall, handsome stranger.

'What's your teacher's name?' he asked.

'Miss McGurk.'

'Is she kind or is she nasty?'

'A bit of both, I think.'

'What's your favourite subject?'

'I've got two really – composition and sums.'

'You'll not go far wrong with those. You can write a book and then count all the money you'll make from it, eh?'

Polly, looking like Amy Johnson, had come downstairs then, and the couple had greeted each other fondly. But none of that kissing or anything. Not in front of Mam and Dad.

'We'll be off now, folks,' Steve said. 'We're going for a run over to Scarborough.'

'Where's Scarborough?' asked Billy. It might have been on the other side of the world for all he knew.

'On the east coast of Yorkshire. It's about two hundred miles there and back,' he'd replied nonchalantly.

Two hundred miles! said Billy to himself. I was right. It *is* on the other side of the world!

Douglas Fairbanks and Amy Johnson had then mounted Steve's 250cc BSA motorbike and roared off into the unknown.

Now Billy was brought back to the present by Mam's reaction to Polly's suggestion of a party.

'Now I've told you before. You'd better not let your

father hear you talking about having friends round,' she said. 'He'll throw a fit.'

Tommy was a very strict father and ruled the household with an iron hand. All the kids were afraid of him because they knew how easily he could flare up, especially after the pub. Sometimes, like dogs with hypersensitive hearing, they sensed his approach long before he arrived, and when he walked through the front door, a hush fell over the living room.

'I'll be careful, Mam,' said Polly. 'Don't worry.'

'What'll we do with our Billy?' asked Flo. 'All the lads are out and he's there in the back yard by himself.'

'Well, we can't take him with us,' said Polly. 'It'd take too long to get him cleaned up.'

Billy came in from the lavatory.

'Listen,' said Mam. 'We're going into town. Why don't you go and play with Les and Sam?'

'They won't let me go with 'em. They've gone off with their gang to Queen's Park. They told me to scram.'

'Why've they done that?' asked Mam.

'They said I'm a telltale just 'cos I told you when they went swimming in their bare skins in Cauley's Millpond. When I try to go with 'em now, Alfie Rigsby – 'e's the boss of the Honeypot Street gang – says: "Eh, Sam and Les. Tell your kid to scram. He'll tell on us".'

'P'raps it's because you are a telltale! You're telling on 'em now! You should learn to keep *that* shut,' said Polly, pointing to her mouth – a mannerism learned from her father.

'Well, Billy,' said Mam. 'What are you going to do with yourself while we're in town?'

'I've got a very busy morning ahead of me,' replied Billy. 'First my religious work with the Jewish people. Then Henry Sykes is coming round and his dad's brought him an old kitchen door that we're gonna chop up for firewood. When we've sold the bundles of wood, we should have enough money for the pictures and some toffees.'

'All right,' said Mam. 'See that you do your chopping in the back entry, though – not in the yard. Your father'll go mad if he sees a mess. Now, we'll be back about twelve o'clock to make the dinner for your father coming in. See that you behave yourself.'

The three females of the Hopkins family put on their best coats and departed to catch the 62 bus to town.

Billy went into the house and checked the time. Half past nine and time to start the Saturday-morning routine – fires and lights. The quickest money he'd ever made.

He went first to the easiest job of the day, at the Beth Shalom Synagogue on Cheetham Hill Road. Rabbi Greenberg was in charge, an oddball who'd claimed last week that, according to his Jewish calendar, the date was 5696. But his money was good. The rabbi was already waiting, and as soon as Billy arrived, he indicated the electricity control cupboard. Billy stood on a chair to reach the panel of light switches, and, on a signal from the rabbi, flicked them all on, flooding the synagogue in bright illumination. That was it! He was told to return just before one o'clock to switch them all off again.

It's a mad world we live in, he said to himself, quoting one of his mam's favourite sayings.

Next in line was the firelighting end of the business – equally puzzling but equally rewarding. First port of call was in Stock Street to Mrs Gluckman, a superstitious old soul if ever there was one.

'So, come in then, William,' she said. 'The fire's already

set. Try to jump over the step though, or we'll have bad luck.'

Billy was ushered into the front room, where an ancient Jewess at least two hundred years old lay propped up on pillows on the bed. There was an overpowering smell of camphor oil and embrocation. Casting a professional eye over the arrangement of newspapers, firewood, clinkers and coal, he selected a lump of coal, which he placed on the pyramid in the grate with the delicate touch of a master-craftsman.

When he was sure that all was in order, he applied the match and the fire ignited. That was not the end of it, however, for he now had to apply a blower to encourage a good, healthy blaze. There were on the market metal blowers, but none of his customers had ever taken the trouble to afford one and it was necessary to get by with a makeshift device consisting of a shovel balanced on the bars of the grate with a large sheet of newspaper placed across it. Suction from the chimney then activated the blaze, but great care had to be taken to avoid setting the paper blower itself alight – a disaster which had happened to him on one or two occasions. For this simple service he was paid the princely sum of threepence.

As he left the room, he took a surreptitious look at the decrepit old woman, who reminded him of a hideous old witch in a Grimm Brothers' fairy tale. At that moment, the old crone sneezed loudly. Mrs Gluckman shot over to her like a rocket and tugged both her ears in an upward direction.

'To long, lucky years,' she recited piously.

The old woman's ears might be long, but they weren't so lucky, thought Billy as he prepared to leave. Still, it was none of his business. He shrugged his shoulders, pocketed his wage and walked happily along the lobby whistling 'We're in the Money'.

'Stop!' cried Mrs Gluckman, holding up her hands in horror. 'Shaydem! Shaydem! Demons. Whistling attracts them, didn't you know that? Aren't there enough things to go wrong in this house without inviting them in?'

She ran back into the house and emerged with a large packet of Sankey's salt, which she sprinkled liberally about the lobby and the threshold.

'That should fix 'em!' she said.

'Sorry about that, Mrs Gluckman,' said Billy. 'See you next Saturday.'

I'll never understand adults, he thought as he strode off. What's that other thing me Mam says: 'There's nowt so quare as fowk.'

On from there to Mrs Levy. Another fire. Another threepence.

'I'm well on my way to buying a yacht,' he remarked to Mrs Levy as he was leaving.

'With your head for business, I'm not surprised,' answered the woman.

His final domestic job involved quite a long walk to Elizabeth Street, to the house of old Mr Benjamin Hymans, who always wore his skull cap and prayer-shawl on Saturdays and who always haggled over the price. This week was no different.

'Come in, Villiam,' he mumbled as he shuffled back into his kitchen. 'So, this veek I need two fires. Von in the kitchen for me and von in the bedroom for Becky, my vife, who is not very vell. So it should be cheaper for two. Vat d'y say? Fo'pence for two.'

'Sorry, Mr Hymans,' Billy said. 'The best I can do is fivepence – a cut price – specially for you as an old customer.'

'Then we split the difference,' said Benjamin. 'Fourpence ha'penny.'

'It's a deal. Just for you,' said Billy. 'But please don't tell the others or they'll all want a cut price.'

This last job finished, Billy ran like the wind to get back and join his pal, Henry, in the firewood-production end of the enterprise.

Billy and Henry were experienced woodchoppers. They had never counted how many bundles of firewood they had chopped but it must have run into many hundreds – even thousands, who knows? Their method of breaking up a kitchen door was simplicity itself. Though they lacked a knowledge of basic mechanics, they knew that the weakest part of an object was its centre point. So, resting the door against a wall, they were able to break it apart by heaving a very heavy stone on to its middle. Once the door had cracked into two parts, it was child's play to break it down further by leaning the pieces against a big stone and jumping on to the wood with both feet, preferably wearing heavy boots.

The final stages required tools, and Billy went inside the house to fetch his dad's hammer and pincers. An axe – or better still a hatchet like those Indians had in *Last of the Mohicans* – would have made the job easier, but beggars couldn't be choosers. He and Henry worked hard with skill and dedication, splitting the kindling with the claw end of the hammer. Inside an hour, they had twelve bundles all neatly tied up and ready for sale. They placed the firewood in the wooden cart they had made earlier in the year from a soap box and a set of pram wheels. Mr Sykes's profession really had proved most fruitful in the matter of supplying raw materials for that particular joint enterprise.

With a full load on board, they set about the business of selling the morning's production.

Their first call was on the Hardman family at the bottom end of Honeypot Street. It was not a success. There were ten kids in the Hardman family, five dogs and Billy didn't know how many cats. The Hardmans were also noted for their strong on-going relationship with the police: almost every other day, a representative of the law seemed to call at their home to pay his respects. Billy knocked at their door nervously, afraid they might drag him in and eat him for dinner. His knocking triggered off hysterical weeping from several babies and ferocious barking from a pack of hounds somewhere in the bowels of the house. Eventually, after much rattling of chains and the sound of bolts being drawn back, Wally Hardman – looking like one of the meths drinkers Billy had seen on Barney's brickyard – appeared, restraining a big, snarling Alsatian that obviously fancied Billy as a tasty tit-bit.

'Yeah. Whaddya want?' demanded Wally.

'D'you want to buy any firewood, Mr Hardman?' Billy asked anxiously. 'Only a penny a bundle.'

'Me! Buy firewood!' bawled Wally Hardman. 'Bloody 'ell! That'll be the day! If we want firewood, son – which we don't – we just tear out one o'them bloody railway posts growing at the end o' the yard. Now go on! Bugger off! Try somebody else!'

They walked on and reached old Mrs Finkelstein's house. Here they had better luck – but they had to bargain a little with her.

'Very well, lads,' she said. 'So I'll take three bundles already. Threepence, you said. But what about a bit o' discount for an old lady? Say tuppence for three.'

'Sorry, Mrs Finkelstein. No discount,' said Billy. He'd

learned the ways of Cheetham Hill at a very early stage in his career as a salesman. 'Business is business. But I'll tell you what I'll do. Today's Saturday and you're not supposed to light fires yourself, right? So I'll light yours for you for an extra penny. I usually charge thr'pence for lighting a fire. Today I'm feeling generous, so give us fourpence for the lot and we'll call it square.'

The old lady thought for a minute. Billy was right – the going rate was threepence to get a youngster to come and light the fire on a Saturday. She made a rapid mental calculation and came to a prompt decision:

'All right. If you light the gas stove as well, it's a deal. You should be in business, Billy,' she said. 'Oh, and by the way, would you untie the bundles for me? We're not allowed to do that ourselves on a Saturday either.'

Billy thought she was asking a lot for the extra penny but puzzled by all these do's and don'ts, he went into her house, lit a burner on the stove, applied a match to the fire and collected fourpence. On the way out he asked:

'Tell me, Mrs Finkelstein. Why do Jewish people have so many rules about this and that?'

'So, we're not allowed to work on the Sabbath; it's in the Old Testament. There are thirty-nine things we're not allowed to do; lighting a fire and untying things are just two of 'em.'

Billy joined Henry, who was waiting in the street.

'Thank God,' he said, 'I belong to a nice, simple, straightforward religion like the Catholic Church. No daft rules for us!'

Further along the street, they called on the Priestleys – a very religious Catholic family made up of mother, father and three children – two daughters and one son. The daughters were fairly grown-up: Jean, aged sixteen, was very pretty, always bright and cheerful, and had been seen once or twice lately in the company of Billy's brother Jim; Teresa, aged fourteen, never smiled because she was going to be a nun. David, the only son, was eleven years old.

The family was obviously a cut above the rest of the street, as the father smoked a pipe and possessed a clarinet which he kept on top of a cupboard. No one had heard him play it, but that wasn't the point. To top it all, he wore a trilby instead of a flat cap like the other men. When it came to the social ladder of the street, Billy had often tried to puzzle out just where his own family stood. It wasn't easy to work out. He knew they were higher than the Hardmans. But the Priestleys? Billy's dad smoked lowly Player's Weights, and the only musical instrument they had in the house was Les's mouth organ, which probably didn't count. Then again, their house did have six steps and three feet of a sort-of garden at the front. So he supposed they cancelled out the pipe, the clarinet and the trilby. On balance, he thought, that made them about equal. But if that was the case, it meant that the Sykes family was top of the street, because they had not only six steps and three feet of garden, but also a piano – out of tune, admittedly – which Henry's dad had saved from the rubbish tip. Billy gave up trying to solve the sociological problem; it was too complicated.

Mrs Priestley was a very solemn but friendly lady, who gave the impression of being very efficient and someone who would stand for no nonsense.

'Come in, William,' she said. 'You too, Henry. What is it you're selling? Firewood? And at a penny a bundle! That's a lot cheaper than the shop. I'll take them all. Take your cart out to our back yard and put the wood in the shed.'

Billy and Henry could hardly believe their ears and

their luck as she handed ninepence to them.

As they were going out, Mrs Priestley looked at Billy and asked:

'Why are you wearing that big scarf on a hot day like today, William? It's summer and I'm sure you don't need it.'

'That's to hide me dirty neck,' said Billy truthfully.

And for some reason that he never understood, the whole family – except for Teresa, of course, who succeeded in holding herself back – broke out into paroxysms of laughter as if they had heard the funniest joke in the world. Even Mrs Priestley smiled. Forever after that, Billy was regarded as a natural comedian by the Priestley family, and whenever he appeared they broke out into amused smiles and waited for him to say something funny.

'P'raps they're not used to telling each other the truth,' Billy said to Henry.

They left pushing their empty cart before them and with one shilling and a penny in their pockets from the firewood end of the enterprise.

'We're in the money! We're in the money!' they sang laughingly as they strutted up back Honeypot Street to their back doors.

'That's sixpence ha'penny each,' said Billy. 'We can go to the matinée at the Shakespeare; it's Buck Jones in *McKenna of the Mounted*. Should be smashing.'

'I'd rather 'ave Ken Maynard,' sighed Henry. 'But I suppose Buck Jones will 'ave to do. Have we got enough for a toffee apple?'

'Of course we have,' replied Billy, the accountant. 'We can afford not only a toffee apple but some pear drops and all. See you after dinner, Henery.'

Billy ran back to the synagogue to complete his duties there. He was a trifle early when he arrived but he always liked to get there a little ahead of time to watch and listen to the closing ceremony. He went in through the main door and up to the gallery from where all the ladies observed the proceedings. Standing behind them, he had a first-class view.

There were one or two men wearing wide-rimmed fur hats – might be some additional business here for Flo and Polly, thought Billy – embroidered silk caftans, white half-length stockings and, strangest thing of all, slippers! But the great majority of the men were dressed like black-bearded undertakers, with long, untidy tufts of hair straggling out from under their black homburgs – which, horror of horrors, they were wearing in church! – whilst on their feet they wore white plimsolls. Over their 'mourning' suits, they had draped black-and-blue-striped bedsheets, and four of the worshippers began processing down the main aisle carrying a large canopy above Rabbi Greenberg. As all this was going on, the whole congregation, sounding as if they were in great pain, wailed sorrowfully and pitifully in Yiddish. Young skull-capped boys then went out in turn to a central altar where, under a shawl held by one of their friends, they chanted in sing-song fashion from a large parchment scroll. After each reading, the congregation rocked back and forth and chorused what sounded like: 'Whadda shame!'

These curious rituals were rounded off by the rabbi taking a collection, placing the proceeds in a large red handkerchief and whirling it around his head three times, at the same time intoning Jewish prayers to which the people responded once again with their exclamation: 'Whadda shame!' perhaps referring to the shameful way in which the rabbi was treating their good money. The day's ceremonies concluded with the blowing of a very long and very old horn whose strong, piercing sound almost blasted Billy out of his perch in the gallery.

The tantivy signalled the end of the strange and weird service, and the congregation filed out of the synagogue. When the last one had departed, Billy went downstairs to meet the rabbi, who showed him to the control panel once again. A quick flick of the switches, off went the lights and the job was done! For this he collected eightpence – a small fortune for a small job of work.

'It's a mad, mad, mad world,' said Billy aloud to himself. 'And I'm buggered if I can make any sense out of it!'

He strode triumphantly down Derby Street with a jingle of coins in his pocket, a dream of a yacht in his heart and a song of joy on his lips.

About the time that Billy was doing his fire and light round, Tommy, his dad, was finishing a seven-hour stint of portering in Smithfield Market. He had worked hard and fast until gone eleven o'clock, when the pace had finally slowed down and the market had become relatively quiet.

That'll do for today, he said to himself. Not a bad day. Nearly fifteen shillings and a good lot o' stuff to take home. I think I've earned meself a drink o' two. He made his way to the Hare and Hounds on Shudehill, and as he went in he was met by that lovely, familiar, inviting smell of beer and tobacco smoke and the buzz of the market porters' heated arguments about football players and racehorses.

'Pint o' the usual?' said Geoff Docherty, the landlord, as Tommy walked through the door.

'Aye, ta,' said Tommy. 'Who d'you fancy for the Steward's Cup today, Geoff?'

'I like the look of that Solerina,' said Geoff. 'Might be worth having a little flutter on it.'

Two hours and six pints later, Tommy thought it was time to be making tracks. As he wobbled his way back, he thought about the nice dinner Kate would have ready on the table for him.

I like Sat'day, he said to himself. Life's not so bad now we're in Honeypot Street. I'll go home now and have a kip after me dinner. P'raps Kate might get into bed with me if the kids go out. Now she's forty-eight there's no danger of kids no more, thank God.

Thinking of kids suddenly reminded him that he'd promised her he would try and mend Les's boots on his shoe-last – though he usually made a pig's ear of it and had to take them to the cobbler in the end.

'Aye, I'll do them right after me dinner,' he said aloud. 'It'll save a few bob.' A sensual thought struck him. 'That should please her. It might just get her in the right mood.'

Speeding up his erratic walk a little, he planned the details of his campaign for a Saturday-afternoon seduction.

Tommy and Kate had certain signals to indicate to each other a willingness or otherwise to have sex. He was still somewhat shy on the subject. Despite all their kids, for example, he'd never seen Kate naked. When he came to think of it, she'd never seen him naked either. And when it came to asking for his oats, he hadn't the cheek to come straight out with a direct request like he imagined the toffs might do. He had to be more subtle and throw out hints in suggestive remarks. At night, he might say:

'I don't think I'll be long out o' bed tonight, Kate. I want to be up early.'

Kate knew what he meant by 'up', and if she felt in the mood she would answer:

'Go on up then, Tommy, and I'll join you.'

For an afternoon session, he would say:

'I'm feeling tired, Kate. I've had a hard day. I wouldn't mind going to bed for a bit.'

If Kate was willing, she would answer:

'Aye, I wouldn't mind getting off me pins for a while and lying down for a bit meself.'

Thinking these salacious thoughts, Tommy felt a stirring in his loins and, swaying a little, hurried back to Honeypot Street.

Billy reached home well after one o'clock and found Dad reading the *Daily Dispatch* while Mam and his two sisters prepared his favourite dinner – chips and egg. They had bought some tripe and onions from the UCP shop in town for Dad. They sat down to their meal, and whilst Billy made chip and egg butties, Dad slurped his tripe noisily.

'I've had a little bet on a horse called Solerina, Kate,' announced Dad. 'Only a bob each way. A tip from Geoff Docherty.'

'That'll be the day, when you win summat,' she said.

They continued eating. After a while, Dad said:

'I see here in the paper that some writer-fella called McMahon has tried to shoot King Edward.'

Dad often read out choice items of news from the paper to Mam. It was his way of educating her and keeping her up to date on current affairs.

'I hope they caught him,' she said.

'Aye. They caught him red-handed, all right. With a bloody loaded revolver in his hand.' Changing the subject, Tommy asked: 'Where are the lads, then?'

'Well, our Jim's upstairs, getting himself all spruced up to take that Jean Priestley from across the road out rowing on Heaton Park lake this afternoon.'

Jim was now sixteen and had discovered girls. Which

explained why he had become very fastidious about his personal appearance, spending a lot of time shining his shoes, brilliantining his hair and examining his face in the mirror for spots. It had to be said, though, that the green suit he had bought from Weaver to Wearer left something to be desired in the matter of taste. He was earning quite a decent wage – about 17s.6d. a week – as a labourer in a bonded warehouse on Salford Docks. In the evenings, however, he continued his boxing lessons at the Welcome Club, and had now achieved a creditable standard, and had won several cups and medals. He had also been giving Billy lessons in the art of self-defence for a couple of years – since the skenny-eyed kid incident – and he too had reached quite a good level for his age. Fortunately, though, there had been no footpads on Red Bank and so Billy's boxing skills had never been put to the test.

'Aye,' said Dad. 'What about the other lads?'

'They've all gone out to Queen's Park for the day, sailing their boats,' said Mam. 'Oh, and Tommy, me and the girls've been out this morning doing a bit o' shopping to beautify the front room, like. I'll tell you about it later. I think you'll be pleased.'

'Aye, we're definitely going lah-de-dah, Kate,' he said. 'A posh parlour. What next? The neighbours'll soon be calling us stuck-up if we're not careful.'

He began to lead up gradually towards the subject uppermost in his mind – the one that had been gnawing at him since he'd left the pub.

'Well, it's Sat'day. What's everybody doing today?' he asked brightly, looking round the table.

'Me and Polly are going out to tea at Patty Bristow's. Then we're going to the pictures at the Temple,' said Flo.

'And I'm going to the Shaky with Henry Sykes to see Buck Jones,' said Billy.

Tommy's hopes began to rise.

'I thought I might mend Les's best boots after me dinner and then go and lie down for a bit,' said Tommy, throwing out the hint.

Still thinking about her three-piece with its brown rexine cover and brass studs, Kate took the bait and said warmly:

'Aye, that'll be good if you mend Les's boots. You've been promising to do that for weeks. And, er . . . I wouldn't mind a rest meself for a bit, after all that walking about I did this morning. And I thought, if you fancy it, we might go for a drink tonight in Capper's.'

It's on. I'm on a winner here, thought Tommy. He could hardly wait to get the boot-mending bit over with. He went into the scullery to his tool-box. It was then that he made the discovery!

'Have you seen me hammer and pinchers?' he asked Kate.

'No,' said Mam. 'Why, aren't they there?'

She turned to Billy, who had gone white to the lips.

'Have you had 'em, Billy?' she asked anxiously.

'Yeah, I had 'em,' mumbled Billy. 'But, er, I thought I put 'em back. They must still be in the back entry.'

He ran out to check, followed closely by his dad.

In the entry, there was no sign of any tools.

'You stupid little bastard!' yelled Dad. 'I'll give you losing me 'ammer.' And he hit Billy a smack across the face that knocked him off his feet. 'You stupid, stupid little get,' he bawled, now beside himself with rage, and continued to smack Billy across the legs mercilessly, propelling him back across the yard. 'I'll bleedin' show you who's boss in this bleedin' house,' he bellowed, removing the belt from around his waist. He was about to strike when Kate got between them.

'Don't you bloody well dare hit my son with that bloody belt or you'll get a taste o' this,' she screamed, brandishing the poker. 'Now I'm warning you, Tommy. I'll swing for you, God help me, I will.'

Then Dad took the whimpering Billy by the scruff of the neck and thrust him into the cellar, slamming the door behind him. Sobbing uncontrollably, Billy sat in the dark on the cellar steps whilst the screaming and the shouting continued unabated in the scullery.

'I never wanted the bloody kid in the first place,' Tommy roared. 'Now he's messing up me life losing all me tools. He deserves a bloody good hiding to teach him a lesson. You're too bloody soft with 'im.'

'Oh, shurrup, you bloody big bully,' Mam screeched. 'I'll buy you a bloody hammer and pinchers if that's all you're worried about.'

Jim's voice could be heard shouting angrily above the fracas:

'Listen, you. If you ever hit our Billy like that again, you'll have me to reckon with. I don't care if y'are me father. I'll thump you, mark my words.'

Billy listened to the rowing and the wrangling through the cellar door. Gradually, very gradually, the commotion died down. After half an hour or so, Mam called softly through the door:

'Are y'all right, our Billy? Y'can come out now. The big bully's gone to bed to sleep it off.'

Filled with self-pity and still racked by involuntary sobs, Billy emerged from the gloom of the cellar.

'I'm not staying in this house. I'll run away and join the circus,' he said tearfully. 'I'm going to see me pal next door.' And he ran out of the house.

Henry came out of the back door as soon as Billy called his name.

'Are we going to the Shaky then?' he asked.

'No, I'm not going now,' replied Billy. 'I'm running away from home.'

'I'll come wi' you,' said Henry without hesitation. 'Where'll we go?'

'Dunno,' said Billy, still choking back the occasional catch in his voice. 'What about them gypsies you see at the fair on the croft sometimes? P'raps they would have us.'

'We could run away to Africa. Stow away on a boat,' said Henry.

'Yeah, and they'd never see us again. Then they'd be sorry. We might even get killed by the Fuzzy Wuzzies and then when we were dead they'd be crying when they saw us in our coffins in altar boy's clothes and then it'd be too late. And I'd be dead glad,' said Billy. But the thought of his own death and funeral nearly started him off whimpering again.

'Wait there,' said Henry, 'and I'll get some of that cold toast left over from our breakfast this morning, and we've got a big bottle of dandelion and burdock.'

'We'll run away to Barney's,' said Billy, 'and join the army with Mad Jack. They'll never find us there.'

The two friends set off together across Barney's wasteground until they reached Mad Jack's cabin. Here was a man they admired and looked up to. He was dressed in a ragged army greatcoat secured around the waist by a piece of string, whilst on his head he wore a faded military cap at a lop-sided angle matching his disfigured, lop-sided face. On his arm he wore three faded stripes. Sergeant Mad Jack was a shell-shock victim from the Great War, and he lived with his flea-bitten, one-eyed dog in a ramshackle hut which he had built with his own hands out of oil drums and corrugated-iron sheets in an attempt to create a replica of his dugout. He cooked his own food – usually bacon and sausage plus a potato baked on the end of a fork at a coke fire at the entrance to his shack. Here was true happiness!

'I'll bet his dad doesn't belt him for losing his hammer,' Billy said to Henry. 'He can come and go as he pleases, like that poem they're learning us at school:

> *'Give to me the life I love,*
> *Let the lave go by me.*
> *Bed in the bush, with stars to see,*
> *Bread I dip in the river.*
> *There's the life for a man like me.*
> *There's the life forever.'*

'Yak,' exclaimed Henry. 'Don't think I fancy bread dipped in a river. It'd be all soggy, like – a bit like them pobs me dad had to have when they took all his teeth out.'

Bubbles of spittle appeared round Mad Jack's mouth and he broke out into one of his babbling fits, having an imaginary conversation with unseen companions:

'Yes, Lieutenant Marsh. Yes, sir. Very good, sir. Jerries at three o'clock in no man's land. Take aim. Fire. Got that one, sir. Get your 'eads down, lads. Here comes a whizzbang!'

'Private Billy and Private Henry reporting for duty, Sarge,' said Billy, saluting.

'Have you two lads taken the shilling?' Mad Jack asked.

'Yes, Sarge,' they answered in unison.

'*On Saturday I'm willing,*' Jack sang. '*If you'll only take the shilling, To make a man of any one of you.*'

'Have you been over the top today, Sarge, into no man's land?' asked Henry.

'Any chep not going over the top when I blow my

whistle will get a bullet in the back of the head,' recited Mad Jack in a public-school accent.

Billy and Henry ate their toast, offering some to Mad Jack and his derelict dog, both of whom gladly accepted their visitors' hospitality. When it came to the dandelion and burdock, though, Billy didn't fancy drinking any of it after Mad Jack and his dog had had their swig. As they sat there sharing their fare and their conversation with the Old Contemptible and his mongrel, they really felt that they had run away and left their homes forever. They were never, never going back as long as they both lived. Though exactly why Henry had run away was not entirely clear.

'How's the weather been, Sarge?' asked Billy.

'*Raining, raining, raining,*' sang Jack. '*Always bloody well raining./Raining all the morning/And raining all the day.*'

' 'Ow many Jerries have you shot today, Sarge?' asked Henry.

'*If you vant to see your Vater und der Vaterland,*' sang Jack. '*Keep your 'ead down Fritzy boy.*'

After about an hour of this, Henry said: 'It'll be getting dark soon, Billy.'

'D'you fancy staying the night in Jack's dugout?' asked Billy.

'I would, Billy,' said Henry, 'but we allus have beans on toast for tea at home on Sat'days. What d'you think, eh? Is it time to go back yet?'

'Yeah, OK then. I think we've taught 'em all a lesson. I think that's enough. They won't try hitting me again. 'Cos if they do, I'll run away again. Next time to Africa. Come on, Henry, we'll go back.'

After saying goodbye to Mad Jack, who gave them a smart military salute, they wandered home and parted at Henry's back yard gate.

* * *

Billy went in by the rear door and found Mam, his two sisters and Jim, along with Jean Priestley, sitting round the table waiting for him.

'Where've you been, our Billy?' Mam asked. 'We thought you'd run away to the circus and left us forever. While you've been out, Mrs Priestley, Jean's mam, has been over to see us. And guess what? You left the hammer and the pinchers at their house in their shed. So all that ranting and raving was for nowt. And that big bully upstairs can go to hell. I won't be talking to him for a while. You can be sure about that.'

When he heard all this, Billy's lip began to tremble and he almost started blubbering again at the thought of the terrible injustice he had suffered. However, he managed to control his tearfulness and Flo said:

'We've talked it over while you were gone and we've got a nice little surprise for you. We've all changed our plans and we're going to take you to the Rivoli.'

'You've never been to the Rivoli, have you?' said Polly. 'It's the poshest picture house in the whole o' Manchester.'

At this news, Billy's eyes filled up once again, at the idea of such kindness after all the brutality.

'What's on?' he asked tearfully.

'Freddie Bartholomew in *David Copperfield*,' answered Mam.

They went – six of them – to the first house, in the best seats at the front of the balcony. Sixpence each for the grown-ups and threepence for him. The cinema was more like a royal palace than a picture house. Such magnificence! The only cinema he'd ever visited had been the Saturday-afternoon matinée in Collyhurst where the seats were hard wooden benches. Now, here in the Rivoli – fragrant with exotic perfumes – there was subtle, subdued lighting and silk illuminated pendant drapes on a giant stage which gave the whole place an air of mystery and elegance. Before the big picture started, a theatre organ played the popular number of the day: 'The Way You Look Tonight' after which the organist announced:

'And now for the song made famous by Lancashire's own star comedian, Mr George Formby.'

There followed the most popular song of all, 'When I'm Cleaning Windows'. This was high living indeed! The theatre lights began to dim and the organ, still playing as if protesting at the interruption, descended miraculously into the orchestra stalls. The huge velvet curtain opened slowly and noisily on its track rods, revealing yet more layers of silk curtain which rolled back one after another until at last there was the silver screen.

As for the film! Billy sat in a trance as he was transported into the fantasy world of Dickens' favourite child.

They were about ten minutes into the film when Billy turned to Mam and whispered:

'Who was Betsy Trotwood, Mam?'

'That was David's father's aunt, d'y'see?' she replied – a bit too loudly for Billy's liking.

A lady behind spoke up:

'Excuse me,' she said.

Here it comes, Billy said to himself. She's going to tell us to hush up.

But he was quite wrong, for the lady continued:

'Does that mean she's David's great-aunt, then?'

'Correct,' Mam answered authoritatively.

'Wasn't Betsy married?' asked the lady's husband.

'Yes, she was. But her husband died in India,' Billy's all-wise mam answered.

'Then why is she called *Miss* Betsy Trotwood?' another gent asked triumphantly.

'Because she didn't like her husband so she decided to go back to her maiden name. Now d'you understand?' said Mam.

It looked very much as if a full-scale debate and discussion might soon develop, but an usherette came and, flashing her torch, ordered silence.

As Dickens' story unfolded, four of Billy's companions wept unashamedly with tears overflowing and even Jim gave an occasional sniff as they watched Basil Rathbone being heartless and cruel to Freddie Bartholomew. What a coincidence that Billy should witness such hard-heartedness on this day of days. Mind you, Mrs Murdstone was weak and did little to stand up to Basil Rathbone and defend little David. Not like his own mam, who was brave and defied bullies by threatening them with pokers. And then David didn't have a brother like Jim either.

Ninety minutes later, they left the cinema cleansed and purged, having identified closely with the characters and the story. Aristotle would have been pleased to see that his cathartic principle had been so roundly vindicated.

'What did you think of it all, then?' asked Mam.

'I thought it was the best picture I've ever seen in all me life,' replied Billy.

'And what about the picture house itself?' asked Polly. 'I told you it was the poshest place in all Manchester.'

'It was all right, I suppose,' answered Billy. 'But I didn't think much o' their seats. They was dead hard and narrow.'

'How d'you mean?' asked Flo, puzzled. Then it dawned on her. 'You forgot to turn the seat down, y'daft devil!' she exclaimed. 'You've sat on that upturned seat for over two hours!'

And they laughed and laughed as they walked home. Then for a minute or two they all went quiet, until suddenly one of them remembered and set the others off. So they laughed all the way back.

Chapter Four

Oh No! Not Another Sermon!

'No man can serve two masters,' Canon Calder had said. 'Ye cannot serve God and Mammon.'

Billy didn't see why not. Yesterday he had served Mammon, and today, Sunday, he'd serve God. Simple.

The day after the flare-up, Dad was abashed and abased. Earlier that morning Billy had heard him – an habitual early riser – come upstairs to Mam with a cup of tea as an olive branch.

'I've brought you a nice cuppa tea, Kate,' he said humbly.

'Don't bother. I don't want no tea from you, thenk y'very much,' she had retorted. 'Drink it yourself, Mussolini. You're nowt but a big bully like . . . er . . .'

She was temporarily stuck for a word, but then it came to her.

'Like . . . er . . . Basil Rathbone!' she shouted triumphantly.

Uh-oh! thought Billy. War's been declared!

Immediately he felt sorry for Dad, as he was about to get the fish-eye treatment – God help him! The whole family knew what it was like when Mam decided to freeze somebody out. It was all a question of how long she would keep it up; she had been known to go for a whole week, like the occasion when Dad had been particularly loathsome after a marathon drinking session. Billy hoped it wouldn't last that long this time. Still, there was nothing he could do about it.

He put on his best pants, thumbed his braces over his shirt and went downstairs to have a cold-water 'swill' at the scullery slopstone. He had to go to the nine o'clock children's Mass at St Chad's on Cheetham Hill Road.

In the living room, he found that Dad had already made and raked the fire, put the big kettle on the hob, and was busy blacking and buffing all the family's shoes. He wore a contrite and hangdog expression.

'How are you, our Billy?' he asked anxiously. 'I've blacked your boots and you can see your face in 'em now.'

'Ta, Dad,' answered Billy, ready to let bygones be bygones.

'What d'you want for your breakfast, son?' Dad asked gently.

It was hard to believe that this man, who only yesterday had been a roaring, raging bull, had now become this quiet, subdued character cleaning shoes and enquiring about his breakfast.

'It's Sunday, Dad,' Billy answered. 'An' I'm going to Communion. I always have my breakfast when I come back.'

'Righto, son. Then just have a cuppa tea. It's freshly made.'

'Can't, Dad. The rule says "fasting from midnight", and if I swallowed even one tiny drop o' water, I couldn't go.'

'No one'll know. Just us two. And I'll not tell.'

'No good, Dad. God'd know and then I'd go to hell for

ever and ever. Miss McGurk said.'

'That seems a bit unfair. Just for a drop o' water.'

Mam came downstairs looking as if she'd sucked half a pound of lemons.

'I've done all the shoes, Kate,' said Tommy ingratiatingly.

'So I see,' she said icily, looking straight through him. Addressing Billy, she said:

'When you've had your swill, our Billy, your Sunday jersey and your stockings are laid out on y'bed. And tell the others to get a move on or we're gonna be late.'

Mam was in the Catholic Mothers' Union whilst Flo and Polly were both members of the Children of Mary. Every Sunday the three ladies of the family and the three younger boys went to the same Mass, though the lads preferred to make their own way there. As for Jim, he supposedly went to a later service but Billy knew that secretly he went to a nearby croft and played pitch-and-toss.

There had even been a time when Dad had started going to Mass. How much praying he did was very much in question, for he always returned with detailed accounts not only of who was there, but of what they had been wearing, together with scathing comments on their moral and financial standing.

'I saw that Mrs O'Brien there – all done up to the nines,' he would say. 'Mutton dressed as lamb. I wouldn't mind but they've not got two bloody ha'pennies to rub together, that lot. As for him, he wants to try doing a day's work for a change.'

When they told him that he went to church to pray, perhaps he thought they meant 'prey'.

As Billy was about to go through the back door, Dad called out:

'Whilst you're on Cheetham Hill, Billy, you can take the accumulator to Forman's radio shop for an exchange. Here's a bob and y'can keep the change, son. I backed a winner yesterday, y'see,' he added by way of explanation.

Here was real generosity, as the refill for their big Cossor wireless cost only a tanner. At this price, Billy thought it was almost worth getting belted.

'Mind y'don't spill acid down your new stockings,' said Mam. 'And don't wiggle the accumulator about or you'll get the programmes mixed up and we'll be getting Hilversum when we want the BBC.'

After dropping off the used accumulator at Forman's, Billy went into St Chad's Church, where Mass was about to begin. The front rows were reserved for the pupils and teachers of the school, the remaining rows being occupied by the various church organisations – the Children of Mary, the Men's Confraternity, and the Mothers' Union. The high altar was bedecked with a profusion of beautiful summer flowers – roses, carnations and lilies – and the various brass ornaments gleamed in the candlelight.

The sanctuary bell signalled the beginning of Mass. Mr Thomas, the headmaster, led the school prayers, the rest of the congregation joining in:

'O my God, I offer this Mass; first to give Thee supreme honour and glory; secondly to thank Thee for all the blessings I have received from Thee.'

Billy followed the Mass with the others.

The whole congregation rose to its feet when, in clear, ringing tones, Canon Calder announced:

'A reading from the Holy Gospel according to Matthew: "Jesus said to his disciples: 'You have learnt how it was said: An eye for an eye and a tooth for a tooth. But I say this to you: offer the wicked man no resistance. On the contrary, if anyone hits you on the right cheek, offer him the other as well . . .' " '

Then the Canon sermonised movingly and passionately on the theme of loving your enemy.

'In the Lord's Prayer, we all say: "Forgive us our trespasses as we forgive those who trespass against us." But do we mean it? Do we understand it? Do we apply it in our daily lives? Turn the other cheek! It means you must not bear hatred for your brother in your heart! It means you must openly tell him, your neighbour, of his offence; this way you will not take a sin upon yourself. You must not exact vengeance nor must you bear a grudge. It means you must love your neighbour as yourself no matter what he has done.'

Billy wondered if Mam was taking any of this in, and he could not resist taking a quick peek to see if she was listening, but her deadpan expression gave nothing away. Oddly enough, though, his brother Sam had a strange look in his eye, and appeared to be paying unusually close attention.

Wonder what's got into our Sam? Billy asked himself. Let him try turning the other cheek in St Chad's school yard and he'll find out what'll happen!

At the Consecration – the gravest part of the Mass – the warning bell sounded. Billy had never seen what happened at this juncture because Mr Thomas always made everyone bow down their heads as he intoned: 'My Lord and My God!'

Finally, '*Domine non sum dignus*'. Billy struck his breast three times and joined the line of kids queueing up at the altar rail. Canon Calder, in his magnificent silk vestments, bearing the chalice, progressed along the kneeling figures, repeating, '*Corpus Domini nostri Jesu Christi custodiat animam tuam in vitam aeternam. Amen,*' over and over again as he placed the consecrated host in the mouth of each communicant. The wafer felt large and tasteless on Billy's tongue, and in his dry mouth it stuck to his palate, but although he was tempted to release it with his finger, he knew that to do so would mean eternal damnation and suffering in the fires of hell. Miss McGurk had said so. So he buried his face in his hands and, freeing the host with his tongue, managed to work up enough saliva to swallow it. Then he joined the congregation in the prayers after Communion.

After Mass, Billy picked up the spare accumulator from Forman's and, having rolled his stockings down, carried it gingerly in his right hand, away from his legs. He crossed Cheetham Hill Road to make his way home and had walked only a few yards down St Chad Street when he was joined by David Priestley, who'd been one of the altar boys who'd served the Mass.

'Hello, Billy,' he said. 'I'll walk back with you, if that's OK.'

'Sure. But it'll be best if you walk on the side away from the accumulator.'

They walked on a little while in silence until Billy asked:

'How d'you like serving on the altar?'

'Oh, it's really great. The Canon even gives us a little cash at the end of the week, if we've served our full quota.'

At the mention of cash, Billy's ears pricked up. He was still thinking about that yacht.

'What d'you have to do to be an altar boy?'

'Well, if you fancy it, you'd have to learn the Latin, but I can teach that to you if you're really interested. I know there is a shortage of servers at the moment. The Canon was saying we need a few more.'

'I'm not sure I have the brains to learn all the Latin that's said in the Mass.'

'Sure you have. Say this: "Dominus, have the biscuits come?" '

'OK. "Dominus, have the biscuits come?" So, what is it – a daft game?'

'No, no. Now say: "Yes, and the spirits too." '

'Seems barmy to me, but OK. "Yes, and the spirits too." '

'You've just had your first Latin lesson. Try it. I say: "Dominus, have the biscuits come?" and you say. . .'

'Yes, and the spirits too.'

'Got it first time. Now I'll tell you a daft joke. There were once three men. Now, two of them were Irishmen – one called Carey and the other Christy; the third man was a Jew called Abie. They all wanted to open a shop and so they applied to the town hall for a licence. After a week, the two Irishmen got their licences but Abie got nothing. "How did you two manage it so quickly?" he asked the Irish fellas. "We went to Mass and prayed," they said. "Why don't you do the same?" So Abie went to Mass, and when it came to the Kyrie, the priest turned to the people and said: "*Kyrie Eleison. Christe Eleison.*" Straightaway, Abie stood up in the church and shouted: "Never mind 'Carey a licence' and 'Christy a licence'! They've already got licences! It's Abie who needs the licence!" '

Billy laughed heartily. 'That's a good'un,' he said.

'That's your second lesson,' said David. 'I'll tell you what. Come with me on the altar tomorrow at half past seven Mass. You won't have to do anything and we'll see if you remember the Latin you've just learned.'

'OK, I'll give it a go. But which people speak Latin anyway?'

'It's a dead language.'

'You mean it's spoken by the dead, by ghosts?'

'No, no,' laughed David. 'I mean that it's no longer used by normal living people.'

'I see. Just us in the Catholic Church.'

Billy was trying to live up to his reputation in the Priestley family of being the street comedian.

'I'll soon be learning the language properly,' said David. 'I've just heard that I've passed the scholarship.'

'The scholarship? What's that?'

'It's a test you can take when you're about eleven, and if you pass you go to a grammar school. I'm going to Damian College.'

'What's wrong with St Chad's? It's good enough for me.'

'Nothing wrong with St Chad's, but I'd like to be a priest one day, like my uncle in Aberystwyth.'

'With a name like yours, what choice do you have? But can't you be a priest from St Chad's?'

'You could – but it wouldn't be easy. Better to go to grammar school first and then to a seminary. If you stay at St Chad's you'd leave at fourteen and go out to work.'

'I think that's what me dad wants me and me brothers to do. He says that the best jobs are at the Wallworks factory on Red Bank.'

They had reached home.

'I'll call for you tomorrow about seven o'clock. Make sure you're ready,' said David as he crossed the street.

Inside, Billy's mam said:

'I hope you didn't spill no acid on your stockings.'

'No. I rolled me stockings down but I spilt a tiny bit on me leg.'

'That's all right then. As long as you didn't spill none on your new stockings.'

He handed over the accumulator to Dad – who was

apparently still in the dog-box – and he made a great show connecting it up to the wireless as if it was a complicated operation like brain surgery.

Billy sat down at the table with the others for the special Sunday breakfast which Mam and his sisters had already prepared. For a while there was temporary silence as they all concentrated on the serious business of tucking into their bacon and egg.

' "Hunger's the best sauce",' announced Mam after a while, quoting one of her many sayings. 'Oh, and by the way, our Polly,' she continued. 'I noticed you weren't at Communion this morning. Why was that, may I ask?'

'Oh, Mam!' exclaimed Polly, turning red. 'I think that's my business!'

'I know why she didn't go,' said Billy darkly.

'Oh, and why was that, clever clogs?' asked Mam, now very interested.

' 'Cos she's on a diet!'

Everyone laughed except Polly, who got to her feet angrily.

'You've been going through my things,' she snapped.

'I saw him go into your room,' said Sam maliciously. 'And he was in there a very long time.'

'That's not very nice,' said Flo. 'Our room's supposed to be private. Have you really been going through our things, our Billy?'

Now it was Billy's turn to go red.

'No, I haven't,' he protested. 'I haven't been going through your rotten things.'

But Billy was telling fibs! He had indeed been in their room and had pried through their things. On Friday, his mam had asked him to take up their clean clothes, and whilst in there, he had become fascinated by all their belongings. On their dressing table he'd noticed the couple of books Polly had been reading. One, called *Release the Real You!*, asked:

> *Do you know what to say but don't know how to say it?*
> *Cat got your TONGUE?*
> *Do you wish to be SILVER-TONGUED?*
> *Then amaze your friends with this miraculous new method!*
> *WHO you are and WHAT you are depend on your*
> *COMMAND OF LANGUAGE!*
> *SPEAK THE KING'S ENGLISH CORRECTLY!*

The other book was entitled *A Slimmer, Slender You! A Diet For The Modern Miss.*

Billy had skipped through the books quickly, for his interest had been drawn to his sisters' clothes – especially their underwear, which they had left lying about the room in their hurry to get out to work. There was something about the room that was essentially feminine: perhaps it was the smell of face powder and cream, or perhaps that strange, mysterious perfume. Whatever it was, he found that he was enjoying a new and inexplicable pleasure in examining the various items of female apparel – silk slips, suspender belts and girdles, bras and lace panties. He had experienced the same peculiar thrill a couple of weeks back when he'd looked at women in their undies in the Empire mail-order catalogue. Was it sinful? It must have been because he'd enjoyed it, and therefore he'd had to tell it in Confession.

'Bless me, Father, for I have sinned against the sixth commandment,' he'd said.

'Oh? In what way?' Father Maguire, the curate, had asked.

'I looked at women in their corsets.'

'I see, my son. And exactly where did you see these women?'

'On page 216 in the Empire catalogue,' said Billy, always ready to supply detailed information to anyone interested.

The priest had given him a penance of five Our Fathers and ten Hail Marys. Billy had never unravelled the mystery of how the priests managed to arrive at these numbers, and how they assessed the value of each sin in terms of prayers. Maybe they had a ready reckoner drawn up by the Pope. As he recited his act of contrition, the priest had said: '*Ego te absolvo in nomine Patris, et Filii, et Spiritus Sancti. Amen.*'

Then he'd added:

'And pray for me, my son.'

Perhaps he has the same problem, said Billy to himself. Perhaps he's even been lookin' at the same catalogue.

Now his mind came back to the breakfast table, however, and he said:

'Mam told me to take up your clean clothes and I just happened to see your book on the table.'

'It's true,' Mam said. 'I did ask him.'

Billy was saved any further recriminations by the appearance of Jim, who came downstairs for his breakfast. As he was sixteen, working and a man, there was no pressure on him to go to Holy Communion. He was his own boss.

Billy seized the opportunity to go upstairs to change out of his best things and make his escape. In Back Honeypot Street, he met Henry, who had acquired a huge lorry tyre – courtesy of his scrap-dealer dad. Henry didn't appreciate how lucky he was to have a father with access to such rich booty. For the next half-hour, they took turns at crouching inside the rim and pushing each other down the slope of the street until the tyre crashed into a wall at the bottom.

After a while, Jim, dressed in his hideous green suit, appeared on the street.

'I'm just going on Barney's tip for a game of pitch-and-toss,' he said. 'You can earn a tanner between you if you dog-out for us.'

'I thought you were supposed to be going to eleven o'clock Mass,' said Billy mischievously.

'Nah. I went last month. That's enough for me. Come on, the two o' you. Watch out for the rozzers and if you see one coming, whistle as loud as you can.'

'OK, our Jim,' said Billy. 'We was getting tired of that game anyroad.'

'Huh! Funny!' said Jim.

On the tip Jim joined a number of his mates in the illegal game of pitch-and-toss, which involved gambling on the outcome of tossing five ha'pennies into the air. Why it should be illegal was anybody's guess but, if anything, its illicit nature was one of its chief attractions. Billy and Henry left off their tyre game and climbed into good spots in two withered trees on top of the hill. From these vantage points, they kept a sharp lookout, like two eagles surveying their territory from high up in their eyries. Each time the coins were tossed into the air, there was an excited shout from all the young men, engaged in their own particular form of Sunday worship. An hour later, Jim came down the hill, whistling. A sure sign that he'd won. He threw a thr'penny bit to each of his sentries.

'That'll do for today,' he said. 'Right, Billy. Time for your boxing lesson in the back yard. Let's go!'

Pushing the two of them inside the tyre along the back street, Jim started to sing:

> *'Red stains on the carpet*
> *Red stains on the stairs . . .'*

'That's supposed to be "Red sails in the sunset",' called Billy from inside the tyre. 'We've got the record by Gracie Fields. What're you singin' them words for?'

'It's because of that murder by Dr Buck Ruxton,' Jim shouted back. 'Didn't you hear about it? He cut up his missus and her maid. He was hanged at Strangeways a few weeks ago. There's another one we sing about him as well:

> *'When you grow too cold to steam*
> *I'll have you to dismember . . .'*

'That should be "When I grow too old to dream",' called out Henry.

They reached their back doors. The young 'uns disembarked, and Henry managed, with Jim's help, to push the giant tyre into his own back yard.

Jim went inside the house while Billy waited in the yard. Five minutes later Jim appeared in full boxing regalia – shorts, shirt and canvas shoes – and carrying two pairs of boxing gloves. He tied one pair on to Billy's fists, leaving his own on loosely.

'Right,' he said. 'What are the four things ever to be remembered?'

'Death, Judgement, Hell and Heaven,' replied Billy promptly.

'No, daftie. In boxing!'

'Oh, right! The rules, the stance, correct punching and active defence.'

'Good lad! You're not behind the door. Now, why do we box?'

'To score points. To hit the opponent more than he hits you.'

'OK. Take up your position like I showed you.'

Billy took up his boxing stance, with his left foot a little forward, the toes of both feet pointing to the right.

'Good,' said Jim. 'Feel the floor with the balls of your feet. That's it. Now take up the peek-a-boo style that I learnt you. Carry your hands high, close to your cheeks, and punch from that defensive position. That's it! You've got it!'

Billy went into his shadow-boxing routine with all the skill of two years' practice.

'Elbows in! Chin into your left shoulder! Great! Light on your feet like you was dancing. Good! Good!'

Jim started to dance around, from time to time holding out an open glove for Billy to punch into. Billy's reflexes had been well trained, and every time Jim proffered a glove, he gave it a sharp, swift jab, varying the routine with the occasional uppercut.

'You've done well, our Billy. I can see you now in the ring against Jock McAvoy.'

'Don't act daft, Jim.'

'OK! OK! Remember – a boxer is a kind o' liar. A feint is a lie. You pretend you're gonna hit your opponent in one place, he covers the spot, and what d'you do?'

'You punch him on the other side instead!'

'Right! A punch that starts out as a left jab then turns into a left hook – that's a lie! Like starting with a straight "I" then making it into an "L". Making openings – that's what it's all about, see! You start a conversation with your left fist – say three or four quick jabs – so that your other fist can come out of its shell and hit your opponent like a rocket. Got it!'

'Got it!'

'Right! Let's get Bennie out.'

Bennie, short for 'Benito', was Jim's own invention. It was a special apparatus consisting of a mattress wrapped around a post which had been sunk in a bucket of concrete. An obese human figure had been painted on it in white, and superimposed on this Jim had put numbers on all the vulnerable spots (jaw, ribs, solar plexus, stomach).

'OK, Billy, get down in the Benny Lynch crouch. That's it! And duck, bob and weave! Duck, bob and weave! You've got it! Ready! When I call out the numbers, let's see you hit 'em! Right, 7–2–1!'

Billy dodged from side to side and let fly with a left jab, a straight right and a left hook – all on target on the wretched inanimate Bennie.

'Good! Good!' Jim called excitely. 'Now 4–2–1!'

Like quicksilver, Billy hit a right uppercut, a right cross and a left hook. Poor Bennie! He was taking a hammering!

'That's enough with Bennie,' said Jim. 'He can't hit back. So you can now have a go at me!'

Jim fastened two small pads to his knees and knelt to bring himself down to his brother's height.

'Okey-doke,' he said. 'Let's see you hit me!'

The two of them moved around the yard – Billy dancing lightly and Jim shuffling around clumsily. Billy tried to land a punch but in vain, as his brother was too quick for him in his ducking and his dodging. Billy's punches simply bounced off his gloves. Jim then moved forward and, with the speed of a cobra, gave Billy three rapid light jabs in quick succession – one-two-three.

'Just stop for a minute,' he said. 'If you were standing on railway lines and the train came, what would you do?'

'Jump to the side, of course.'

'Right. Well, do that when your opponent comes

forward at you. Weave to the side and watch for an opening. If you're ever in a fight, it's not just a matter of who's strongest or biggest, it's more a question of who's got the most skill and the most determination. Spirit is what counts! Remember that. One day you'll thank me for these boxing lessons, because you'll know how to take care of yourself. You'll see!'

'Ta for the sermon, our Jim. That's the second I've had today.'

Mam appeared at the back door.

'Come on, you two. Time for dinner.'

Lowering his gloves, Jim turned in her direction.

'OK, Mam. We've just finished.'

Like lightning, Billy landed three quick light jabs to his head – rat-a-tat-tat.

'Always keep your guard up, Jim! And you did say look for an opening, didn't you!'

'Y'cheeky little bugger,' said Jim, laughing.

Together, they went inside.

Whilst Billy was having a wash at the slopstone, he heard Dad giving Mam the nearest thing to an apology.

Thank God! Billy said to himself. At least they've started talking again. He hated the strained atmosphere in the house when Mam went into one of her 'freezing-off' moods.

'I'd had a skinful, y'see, Kate. Too much o' the bevy,' Billy heard his dad say.

'There's nowt wrong with having a drink, Tommy, but you always go too far. I know a man needs his pint and his smoke, but within reason is what I always say. Otherwise, you'll drink us out of house and home.'

'Aye, you're right there, Kate. Never no more. I'll not touch another drop.'

'I'll believe that when I see it,' she said.

She called up the stairs.

'Right, you lot. Dinner is served.'

The rest of the family – with the exception of Polly – appeared and sat down to Sunday dinner, the main meal of the week. Mam believed firmly in having a good table, and this meant a fully stocked one rather than a balanced diet. Her family wanted something solid down 'em – none of that rabbit food for dinner. The Sunday midday meal was a family ritual which never, never varied. Roast beef, Yorkshire pudding, cabbage – or sprouts or cauliflower, whichever happened to be in season – green peas, boiled potatoes, and one – and only one – roast potato each, the whole lot being covered by a generous helping of 'Ah, Bisto!' gravy. This first course was consumed and savoured in reverent silence and with near-religious dedication, so beautifully cooked and tastily flavoured was the fare. Pudding time, however, was the time for talking, and as Flo and Mam brought in the rice pudding, the three youngest boys chorused:

'No skin on ours!'

'I'll have their share,' announced Jim promptly – a bit too promptly.

Mam was almost sure that at some point in the past, Jim had put the young ones off the skin by telling them it was human skin and only fit for cannibals, but she couldn't prove it.

'Where's our Polly?' asked Dad. 'She was actin' a bit funny this mornin', wasn't she?'

'Oh, she's all right. Just a funny mood. It's her time of the month,' Kate whispered. 'Anyroad,' she continued, 'she's gone off to Southport with Steve on his motorbike. They said they'd be back for a bit o' tea about six o'clock.'

'Oh, aye,' answered Dad. 'Then we'd best get the good cups out.'

'You mean the ones with the handles,' said Billy.

There was a few moments' silence as they turned their attention to the rice pudding. Jim had already reached the stage of scraping the skin from the large dish.

'I see in the *Empire News*, Kate, that the GPO have started a speaking clock on the telephones,' announced Dad.

'Isn't it marvellous what they can do nowadays. How does it work?'

Dad made funny shapes with his hands, as if trying to explain the intricacies of the telephone system.

'Oh, it's too complicated, Kate. Y'wouldn't understand it.'

'I see,' she said, looking straight at him.

'I've heard one of them clocks on the telephone at work,' said Jim. 'There's a woman keeps giving the time over and over again. She says: "At the third stroke, it will be three twenty-five precisely." She goes on and on all day long.'

'What a boring job!' remarked Les.

'What if she wants to go to the lavatory?' asked Sam.

'She has to take the phone in with her!' said Billy, not to be left out of the speculations.

'That means she has to sit there with the phone in her hand, telling people the time,' added Les. 'I definitely wouldn't fancy that for a job.'

'Anyroad,' said Dad. 'Over a quarter of a million rung up to ask the time during the first week.'

'Eeh,' observed Flo. 'She must have been hoarse!'

'And wouldn't you think the toffs with telephones could afford clocks of their own like ours?' remarked Mam.

Dinner over, Flo and Mam sided the table and washed

up, after which the family dispersed to their various Sunday-afternoon recreations. Sam and Les went out to join in the never-ending activity of their gang; Jim announced that he was taking Jean Priestley rowing on Heaton Park lake – postponed from the previous day; Flo said she would be going out to tea again with her friend Patty Bristow; and Billy that he would be spending the afternoon reading his comics – *Chips*, *Film Fun* and the *Rover*.

As for Kate and Tommy, they too had a postponed appointment.

'Right, our Billy. No noise, d'y hear me? Me and your father's going for a lay-down for an hour. Then you and me'll go and see your Auntie Cissie and your Uncle Eddy over in Greengate. So think on.'

For the next hour and a half, peace and tranquillity reigned over the Hopkins household.

Chapter Five

No Green in Greengate

To reach the Greengate district in Salford, Billy and his mam had to cross Cheetham Hill Road and pass by the terrifying towers of Strangeways Prison with its massive twenty-foot walls.

'Our Jim said this is where they hung that fella for cutting up his missus and her maid,' said Billy.

'He's not the only one that's been hanged here. Not by a long chalk.'

'I hope his ghost isn't still hanging about,' Billy said with an involuntary shudder. 'I don't think we should hang about neither. Come on, Mam, let's hurry up!'

Over Great Ducie Street and past the assize courts they walked, passing street after street and row after row of shoddy back-to-back houses – every one the same – criss-crossed by a pattern of foul-smelling back entries and mean, squalid little courts. There were no green fields in Greengate, not even blue skies – a permanent half-fog drifted over the place. The smoking, huddled houses were dominated on all sides by dark, gloomy factories – notably the Greengate Rubber Works – and the services which attended them: the goods depots and the gasometers. The viaducts interweaved with the railway lines and with

103

the canals below, and here and there they passed a church or a Methodist chapel, whilst at every street corner there was the inevitable dingy little pub.

At last they reached Cable Street, where Auntie Cissie and her brood resided. At number 11, they found the front door already wide open, so Mam called down the lobby.

'Cissie! Are y'in? It's Kate! I've come to see you!'

The voice which responded was so strident, so piercing, it could have shattered glass or bent steel.

'Chuck thy cap in, Kate, and come inside!' Auntie Cissie screeched. 'Well, I'll be buggered!'

Reassured by this warm welcome, Billy and Mam went down the lobby and into the living room. Cissie was an extraordinarily thin, scrawny woman. It was difficult to understand how such a loud, shrieking sound could have emanated from such a bony frame. She was about forty-five years of age and obviously overjoycd to see her sister, for she clasped her in a long, affectionate embrace. Then she turned her attention to Billy and said:

'Hasn't he got big? I'm sure he's grown another foot since I last seen 'im.'

Billy looked down at his shoes.

'No,' he said. 'Still got only two.'

'I can see we've got a bloody comic in the family and all,' she said. 'Anyroad, I won't kiss him, 'cos I know little lads don't like to be kissed.'

Billy was truly grateful for this omission, especially as Cissie's three young daughters – Rose, Violet and Iris – were busy sniggering at something. He saw that they were pointing in the direction of his genitals from the corner of the room where they had been engaged in dishing out tea to their numerous dolls. Their dog, Scamp, appeared to be part of the conspiracy as it began nuzzling his crotch.

Seated by the fireside was Uncle Ernie, Cissie's husband – a morose, grumpy-looking individual who was engrossed in raking, poking and rearranging the coal on the fire. Billy could have given him a few pointers. Ernie acknowledged their presence and existence with a typical Lancashire greeting which was brief, economical and to the point.

' 'Ow do,' he said, and spat a great wet gozzler into the fire.

'You'll put t'bloody fire out doing that!' Auntie Cissie squawked.

Mam and Auntie Cissie retired to the kitchen for a private, sisterly chinwag, and Billy, not wishing to be left alone with the taciturn, expectorating Ernie, the giggling girls and the perverted dog, followed them.

He didn't understand much of their whispered conversation and confidences but he caught intermittent snatches:

'We've had some right times, you and me, Kate, since we was in service together.'

'We have and all, Cissie. A few heartaches and a few laughs.'

'That's all life is, isn't it? But how's Tommy treating you, Kate?'

'Mustn't grumble, Cissie. He doesn't ask for it much, if y'know what I mean. He's earning good money in the market, gives me thirty-five bob a week – so it's not so bad. We manage. We keep our heads above water. I even bought a new three-piece t'other day at the Co-op. What about Ernie in there?'

'He's all right. A bit of a miserable bugger but, like Tommy, he's not allus wanting to have it off like some men do. He gets good money at the rubber works but he doesn't half stink when he comes in at night! But never mind him. How's your Flo and Polly getting on nowadays?'

'Not so bad, Cissie. Our Polly's walking out with a very nice young man – well-off and a very posh talker. But I hope she settles down soon, 'cos she's a bit of an awkward bugger. Our Flo's lovely, but no prospects as yet. There's plenty of time, though; she's only twenty-four. She might as well enjoy herself while she's still young – that's what I say.'

'You're right there, Kate.'

Cissie adopted a conspiratorial tone and whispered:

'Eh, whatever happened to that there Bridget Sharples who lives in your street – the one who . . .'

She glanced over in Billy's direction, but he was absorbed in a copy of the *News of the World* which had been left lying on the kitchen table. He was reading the various headlines: *Sex-crazed choirmaster tells his story; 'They tempted me,' claims vicar; Climbed into nudist colony – lost his trousers.*

'. . . the one who, you know, had that illegible baby?' said Auntie Cissie, trying in vain to keep her voice down.

'That wasn't her first, you know,' Mam whispered. 'She'd had another one by another fella, about three year ago.'

'Tut-tut-tut. Get away. Just goes to show, a slice off a cut cake is never missed, eh?'

'You're right there, Cissie. They say you don't open t'oven door for just one loaf.'

'You'd think a girl like her would have used one of them contraspective things.'

'Aye. But I've heard that they put a hole in 'em every so often to keep the population up.'

'Tut-tut-tut. It's this here bloody Baldwin gover'ment. You can't trust the higher-ups, can you?'

'It's allus been the same, Cissie. They're all in a click and they're all twisters.'

'And what about your Billy, there? They say he's the brains of the family, eh?'

'Eeh, I tell you, our Cissie – he comes out with some things for his age. I get that worried, I do. I'm sure his brain's gonna burst one day!'

'You want to be careful there, Kate. You want to make sure that all the goodness of his body doesn't go into his head, 'cos then it can come out in his hair, specially if it's too long like it is now. You should allus make sure he gets a good haircut or y'might find his body goes weak and then he'd get poorly very easy. That'd be my advice t'you.'

'I think you're right there, Cissie. I'll have him at the barber's tomorrow. Anyway, I think we'd better be off now. We've got two more visits to make – to me mother's and to our Eddy's.'

'Eddy's!' said Cissie. 'You'll find they've got problems there all right. Mona'll tell ya. I won't keep you, but it's been right nice seeing you – just like old times.'

As they made their way down the lobby, Mam called out, 'Ta-rah, girls! Ta-rah, Ernie!'

When they reached the front door, Auntie Cissie shoved a shilling into Billy's hand, and in his mind's eye, his yacht hove into view.

Grandma McGuinness lived in a little two-up, two-down in Viaduct Street, opposite the railway goods yard. Mam knocked on her door and a voice in the house croaked:

'Who is it?'

'It's Kate, Mam. I've come to see how you're getting on,' Mam shouted through the letter box.

'Hang on! I'm coming,' Grandma said.

The door was eventually opened by an old lady who

was swathed completely from head to foot in black, with a simple cameo brooch at her neck; she was the image of the old Queen Victoria in mourning for her beloved Albert. They returned to the sitting room where Grandma sat down heavily in her rocking chair and returned her attention to the glass of stout she had been nursing.

'Take your coats off, and if y'want a cuppa tea, Kate, y'know where the stuff is. And bring this lad here that there bit o' roast beef left over from me dinner. He looks to me as if he needs feeding up. Why, he's just a bag o' bones.'

'S'all right, Mam,' Kate bawled in Gran's earhole. 'We've only just finished our dinner and we'll not take our coats off 'cos we can't stop. We're going over to our Eddy's.'

'I don't know why y'bother coming if y'can't stop. But bring that bloody bit o' beef for this here lad anyroad and stop arguifying.'

Billy was presented with a large piece of beef covered in fat and gristle. His stomach heaved.

'Get that down you and shurrup,' his gran said. 'And as for you, our Kate, you spoil yer kids, y'do. They won't eat this and they won't eat that. Not like our Hetty's kids – they'll eat anything.'

Billy looked round frantically for some way out of the impasse, searching for, as Jim would have put it, an opening. Mam pointed to a boat-shaped teapot on the mantelpiece.

'I notice you've still got your Coalport teapot, Mam.'

Grandma's gaze was momentarily diverted towards her most valuable possession, which had pride of place amongst all the ornaments. Billy seized his chance and, with the speed of a Joe Louis, thrust the fatty beef into her aspidistra plant-pot. Jim would have been proud of him.

'That's proper porcelain is that, Kate, and it's stopping where it is. As you well know, it belonged to me grandmother, Mary Molly McGinty, and it was given to her by her father, Sean McGinty, as a wedding present in Dublin in 1815.'

'Have you ever had tea in it, Gran?' asked Billy.

'I have not, young man,' she answered haughtily. 'It's a family heirloom is that and not for drinking tea out of. When I'm kicking up daisies, Kate, it'll come to you as me eldest daughter.'

'I'm sure I'll take care of it as you've done. But don't talk like that, Mam. That day's a long way off, I'm sure,' Kate said. 'Anyroad, we just come over to see if you're all right and if there's anything you want.'

'That's right; you just leave me 'ere. I dare say I won't be troubling you all that much longer. And there's nothing I want. I can look after meself. I like to be independent, I do. But tell our Eddy when y'see him that I'm very upset with him. I don't like the way he's knocking and bashing Mona about. If he can't behave himself and start looking after her, 'e needn't bother coming to me funeral. I don't want him there weeping over me coffin. Just tell him from me to think on. Oh, aye, and tell him I'm running out o' stout and to get me a drop in when he goes to the boozer tonight.'

Mam washed up a few dishes for Gran, including the one which had borne the vanished beef. Billy's brothers, when faced with dollops of Gran's inedible blubbery beef, had opted for the same solution. One day, somebody would clean out that plant-pot and discover a new species of meat-bearing aspidistra which shed steak instead of leaves.

Eddy, who lived appropriately – by either accident or design – in Brewery Street, facing Boddington's, was a rough diamond and a bully of the first order. All his life he had worked at tough jobs – as railway carter, market porter, slaughterman and meat packer. For Billy, however, his most remarkable feature was his right hand, which was missing a couple of fingers severed at the top joint some time previously in mysterious industrial accidents. He constantly bullied and badgered his wife, Mona, for her inability to provide him with offspring, with the result that she had developed not only a nervous tic but a high-pitched, plaintive whine.

Mam knocked on Eddy's door.

'Anybody in? It's Kate come to see you!'

The door was opened by Mona, a short, dark-haired woman on whose face was etched a permanent expression of anguish and apprehension, as if she was expecting to be struck a blow at any moment. Grimacing a painful smile, she said sorrowfully:

'Come in, Kate. It's so good t'see a friendly face again. Eddy's out at the moment – at the boozer as usual. I think he must have hollow legs; I don't know where he puts it all, I don't.'

'How do, Mona,' replied Mam. 'How are things with you?'

'Not so good, Kate. Not so good. It's your Eddy. He's all right when 'e's sober – he can be charming – but he's terrible when he's had a drop.'

'Why, has 'e been knocking you about again?'

'He has that, Kate. Something terrible,' she whimpered. 'Only yesterday he come in and . . . Hey up! He's here!' Mona cringed visibly. 'I better get his dinner out of the oven,' she wailed.

Eddy appeared obviously the worse for drink. He was

swaying and his eyes were bloodshot.

'How do, our Kate,' he said drunkenly. 'What's this bleeding woman been saying about me? Where's me bleeding dinner, you? Yer bleeding useless get!'

'Here's your dinner, Eddy. It's a bit dried up now from being in t'oven so long,' Mona stammered, placing his meal on the table.

'I'll show you what I think of yer bleeding dried-up dinner,' he bawled. Taking the plate, he flung it against the wall. The plate shattered into a thousand pieces and the amorphous mess slithered slowly down the wall.

'Oh, Kate,' Mona sobbed. 'What am I going to do? What am I going to do?'

'Go on, cry, you stupid bitch, cry! You'll piss less,' Eddy snarled.

It was time for Mam to act.

'Look you, you drunken pig!' she bawled at him. 'I won't have you using that dirty language in front of our Billy here. I'm ashamed of you as a brother. Now get to bed!'

Through his alcoholic haze, Eddy noticed for the first time that Billy was indeed in the room, witnessing his drunken, barbaric behaviour. Eddy nodded stupidly at his older sister and mumbled:

'Sorry, our Kate. I didn't see him there. I'll get meself off to bed. But *she's* no bloody use to nobody. Neither use nor ornament.'

Eddy stumbled off to bed, almost falling on his face as he went through the bedroom door. The three of them were left alone. Mona and Mam began cleaning the dinner from the wall.

'It's not my fault that I can't have kids, Kate,' wailed Mona. 'He's no right to treat me like this.'

'He'll be back to his charming self when he's slept it

111

off,' said Mam. 'But I wouldn't stand for it no more. You can either set the cruelty man on to him or you can leave home. If it were me, I'd leave.'

'I think you're right,' said Mona.

'Well, Mona, I've got to be getting back to make the master's tea. But think on what I've told you.'

On the way back, Mam said to Billy:

'You know, your father's not so bad really. You see, it's his work; they're a rough lot in the market and they all drink. He could be a lot worse!'

Mam turned the key in her own door.

'Eeh, I'm right glad to get back to civilisation!'

Billy fully agreed with her, for after that to-do at Uncle Eddy's, his own home and his own family really did seem like civilisation.

In the scullery, they found that Dad had already half-prepared the high tea which they had on Sunday nights: a magnificent salad – as befitted a Smithfield Market worker – consisting of lettuce, spring onions, tomatoes, radish, cucumber and beetroot, with a wide choice of condiments like pickles, piccalilli and chutney, plus, of course, the obligatory mayonnaise. In addition there was usually boiled ham or corned beef, but this Sunday, seeing there was a guest, there was a delicious middle-cut of West's red salmon – though it was for the adults only. To mark Sunday as something extra special, the bread was sliced diagonally into thin triangles instead of the customary weekday rectangles.

It wasn't long before young Sam and Les – prompted, no doubt, by healthy appetites – came in looking for food.

'The only time we see you two,' Mam said, 'is when you're hungry. I'm not kidding. You use this house like a Blackpool boarding house. What do you get up to in that Honeypot Street gang of yours?'

'We're collecting wood for Bonfire Night,' replied Les.

'Glory be t'God! Not already! It's three months off!'

'Aye. But we're gonna have a bigger blaze than Derby Street this year,' said Sam.

Shortly after that, Jim returned from his romantic boating expedition, and a little later Steve and Polly arrived looking as if they'd just flown in from Australia.

'Hello, Steve,' said Billy. 'When are you going to give me a ride on that motorbike of yours?'

'We'll see,' replied Steve. 'One of these days. I don't know when. But we'll see.'

That seemed pretty vague to Billy and so he didn't pursue it. He'd only been trying it on, anyway.

'Good evening, Mr Keenan . . . Steve,' said Mam, in her posh voice. 'Would you care for a little swill?'

'A swill, Mrs Hopkins? Sorry, I don't . . .' Steve said, glancing anxiously towards the table, which had been set out for tea, then quizzically towards Polly for a translation.

'You know, a wash, like. To freshen up,' explained Polly.

'Oh, that would be lovely, Mrs Hopkins,' said Steve, looking distinctly relieved. 'Is it upstairs?'

'No,' replied Polly apologetically. 'You have to use the slopstone in the scullery. Sorry.'

'No problems,' said Steve. 'That's fine.'

The great man went into the scullery for a swill and then joined the family at the table.

'Why can't we have salmon?' complained Sam.

'Because! That's why!' replied Mam. 'Eat what you're given and shurrup!'

'What d'you do for a living, Steve?' asked Dad as he made a large butty of salad and salmon – much to the embarrassment of Polly, who had raised her eyes to heaven in supplication.

'I'm an engineer at Avro Ansons, Mr Hopkins. We make aeroplanes,' answered Steve modestly.

Billy had always suspected that Steve had something to do with the aviation business.

'That's very useful,' said Mam.

'It will be if there's a war,' said Jim.

'I don't think there's going to be no war,' said Polly. 'Not according to that Hitler in Germany.'

'There'll be a war all right,' said Dad as he poured his tea into his saucer, blew on it and slurped it noisily. 'Mark my words! I wouldn't trust that bloody goose-stepping Hitler fella as far as I could throw him.'

'I'll get the dessert,' said Polly, now looking pale and drawn.

The Sunday dessert was usually pineapple chunks, but today, in honour of the important guest, there was tinned peaches and cream as well, but once again, for adults only.

'Why can't we have peaches too?' asked Sam, always the disgruntled one and a bit of a socialist to boot.

'You be happy with them chunks,' said Mam. 'A family in Africa'd be glad o' them.'

'But that's where they come from!' said Sam.

'Will you stop being so obstroculous,' Mam said. 'And while we're about it, let's change the subject as well,' she continued. 'All that miserable talk about war! Have you visited a picture house lately, Steve?'

'No, Mrs Hopkins. Not lately. I'm waiting for the picture house to visit me. It will one day.'

'How d'you mean?' asked Jim.

'The BBC have started transmitting the first talking pictures,' said Steve, 'on something called television.'

'Get away,' said Jim. 'Never. S'not possible.'

'Oh, it is,' replied Steve. 'The first broadcast covered

114

only a distance of ten miles from Alexandra Palace to Olympia, but it worked, though we're told in the paper that the announcer, Leslie Mitchell, looked as if he had two black eyes.'

'Isn't it marvellous what they can do nowadays? What will they think of next?' said Mam. 'Pictures in your own home. But I don't think I want one of them big screens and one of them projectiles in our front room.'

'You won't have to,' said Steve. 'Your set will be no bigger than that wireless there.'

Up to this point, Dad hadn't said a word, because he didn't understand the concept of television. He was also busy removing a piece of tomato skin from his upper denture, which he had taken out of his mouth to facilitate the operation. Polly had turned a funny colour. But now, when he had cleared the irritation, Dad felt it was time to deliver his opinion.

'It'll never work,' he said. 'Not in a month o' Sundays!'

Billy was sure he was right. Dad always was.

After tea, the family formed the usual big half-circle round the hearth, with Dad in the big chair near the wireless where he could operate the controls. In deathly silence, they listened to the news, which was all about Adolf Hitler recognising Mussolini's occupation of Abyssinia, King Edward opening a memorial on Vimy Ridge and England winning the Davis Cup.

'There's nowt else on,' Dad said. 'Not on a Sunday night. Nowt but religion! And that Mr Middleton and his bloody garden!'

If Dad said there was nowt on, there was nowt on. For when it came to judging wireless programmes, there was none better. Performers were either 'in' or 'out'. If somebody was awarded the accolade of a thumbs-up, he'd say: 'He's a good 'un!' or, alternatively, 'He's a good turn!' But if the thumb was turned south, he'd mutter, 'Bloody rubbish!' or 'Should be shot!' Henry Hall, Gracie Fields, George Formby, Arthur Tracy and Robb Wilton were all 'in', but Vic Oliver, Jack Warner, Harry Roy and, most especially, the languid, public-school Western Brothers with their 'Keep it up, chaps! Keep it up!' were definitely 'out'.

Dad switched the wireless off and the family was allowed to make conversation. Billy was the first to seize the opportunity.

'I met David Priestley today and he wants me to go on the altar with him.'

'Oh, aye,' Mam said. 'That'll be nice, but it means you'll have to get up early every morning.'

'That's all right. He also said he'd passed his scholar-ship and was leaving St Chad's to go to another school called Damian College.'

'That's a very good school,' said Steve. 'He must be a clever lad.'

'Oh, he is and all,' said Mam. 'I was talking to his mam after church this morning and she says he wants to be a priest.'

'D'y'ever fancy going to a higher school, our Billy?' asked Polly.

Dad responded for him.

'No, that's not for the likes of us. I believe in doing right by the lads and getting a good trade in their hands.'

'You mean like yours,' asked Kate contemptuously.

'No, not like mine. I never had a chance. But I'll tell you this, Kate – I've worked hard all me life and can look anyone in the face.'

'And look what you've got to show for it,' Mam snapped back. 'Nowt! If our Billy's got brains, he should get the chance to make something of himself.'

'Book-learning never did nobody no good,' replied Dad. 'Are they any happier, these bloody clever dicks, with their heads full of nowt but theories?'

'Education can lead to a better-paid job,' said Steve. 'Besides that, you know what they say: "Don't hide your talent under a bushel." '

'I don't want none o' my kids getting above themselves, being lah-de-dah and giving themselves airs and all that. A good apprenticeship at the Wallworks is worth more than all that book rubbish they learn 'em at them stuck-up schools.'

'That's what I want to do,' said Sam, chipping in. 'Billy's not the only one in this house with brains, y'know. But I want to start earning good money, not waste me time at one of them daft schools.'

'Me and all,' added Les.

'Y'see, Steve,' went on Dad, 'I want me kids to be nice, friendly people who can get on with others and not to be thinking about money all the time.'

'I agree with you, Dad,' said Polly, looking pointedly at Steve. 'I don't think it's right to try and alter people. You've got to take people as you find 'em.'

'Money isn't everything, I know,' conceded Steve. 'But just the same, the very top jobs, the interesting jobs, the well-paid jobs go to those who are well educated.'

'I think the big pay,' said Jim, 'the *really* big pay, goes to those at the very top of the tree, like our champion boxers – Jock McAvoy, Benny Lynch, Eddie Phillips. But I don't know what we're arguing about here, 'cos Billy's only eight and it's at least another three years before he can even think about scholarships and all that. A lot can happen in three years.'

How right he was!

* * *

The family discussion broke up when Dad said:

'I think I'll just slip out to Capper's for an hour and a game o' crib.'

'I thought you'd stopped drinking,' said Mam.

'Just a quick one,' said Dad. 'I won't be late as I've got to be up early again tomorrow.'

He went into his getting-ready-for-Capper's routine – a performance which the family always watched with fascination.

He went to the slopstone and soused thoroughly, snorting and snuffling and splashing water in all directions like an elephant. Next came the ritual dressing. He rolled up a brown silk scarf into a long sausage, put it round his neck, crossed it in front and secured the ends in his braces. He did not wear a tie. That was for Saturdays. Instead, he closed the top of his striped woollen shirt with a collar stud. On with his jacket, and then the final touch. He warmed his cap at the fire and placed it carefully on his head. Grooming completed, he went out. There was always a sense of relief when he left.

Jim also went out – in his case to some unknown destination, probably more games of pitch-and-toss, since it did not get dark at this time of year until after ten o'clock.

With Jim gone, things went dead for Billy.

'I want to go to the pictures, Mam,' he announced.

' "I want" doesn't get,' replied Mam automatically. 'Besides, it's Sunday and there are no pictures, except maybe Jewish ones.'

'Then I wanna go to the Jewish pictures,' he whined.

'They're in Yiddish, so you won't understand 'em.'

'It don't matter. I WANNA GO!'

Steve picked Billy up and hung him by his braces on

the coat hook on the living-room door.

'I suppose you think you look like Christ on the cross,' said Sam.

'Why have y'put me up here, Steve? Come on, don't keep me in suspense!'

'Right,' said Steve. 'You're up there for being cheeky to your mother. What's the fourth commandment?'

'Honour thy father and thy mother.'

'OK, remember that, and also that the most important people in the world for you are your mother and father and your family. Always show respect to them and you won't come to any harm. With your brains and your talent, you could get to the top one day, but you won't get anywhere if you give cheek. Got it?'

'Oh, no! Not another sermon! That's the third I've had today. From up here, I feel as if it's me as should be giving the sermon,' said Billy, laughing. 'Come on, Steve, let me down!'

'Only if you promise to behave yourself.'

'OK, OK,' replied Billy. 'I promise to behave if you promise to take me for a ride on your motorbike!'

'This brother of yours is a real wheeler-dealer,' said Steve to Polly. 'OK, Little Lord Fauntleroy. It's a deal! But we leave the date open.'

Steve took him down.

'He's learned all this bargaining and making deals,' said Mam, 'working amongst the Jewish people on Sat'day morning. Maybe he should go into business.'

There was an hour before bedtime, and the three younger lads settled down to scanning their comics avidly, as if they might find the answer to the riddle of the universe in one of them. The *Rover*, the *Hotspur*, the *Skipper* and the *Adventure* were passed around from hand to hand whilst Mam turned her attention to the 'Bullets'

competition in *John Bull* – not that she'd ever won anything. Steve and Polly retired to the front room for a bit
of courting.

Around ten o'clock, the three young lads were given their
marching orders, and together they trooped out. Before
going up the stairs, they paused outside the front room to
eavesdrop on the courting couple, making mock kissing
and hugging gestures as they did so. Through the door,
though, they could hear Steve and Polly talking earnestly,
and, judging from the sound of it, there was an almighty
row brewing.

'You've got to live and let live, Steve. You can't change
human nature,' Polly was saying angrily. 'You've got to
remember that it takes all sorts to make a world.'

'I'm not trying to change you. I'm just saying that
everybody can improve themselves – me included.'

'Yes, you may have opinions about that, but you're
always pushing 'em down people's throats – like y'did
with me dad tonight.'

'I did nothing of the sort. We were having a friendly
discussion, that's all.'

'I think you look down on us, y'know. The way me dad
eats, the way I speak and the way we live. You're always
correcting me! I think you just turn your nose up at other
people. And another thing. I didn't like the way you hung
our Billy up on that door tonight.'

'It was just a bit of fun, that's all. I think you're just
talking rubbish.'

'Oh, rubbish, is it . . .'

The three lads fled up the stairs as it suddenly sounded
as if the lovers were coming out of the room. From the
top of the stairs they heard Polly storm at Steve:

'Go and find someone who speaks proper. And you

can take your lousy ring back. I don't want to see you again!'

'There goes me motorbike ride!' said Billy.

They heard Polly run up to her room, and the sobbing which followed. Poor Steve left quietly by the front door, and a few moments later they heard his motorbike roar off down Honeypot Street.

As Billy lay in bed, he couldn't help reciting quietly to himself: '*This is the man all tattered and torn,/That kissed the maiden all forlorn . . .*'

But his thoughts soon turned to happier things – to a beautiful, graceful yacht gliding across Queen's Park lake. And tonight there was added a second dream: he saw himself going up on to the school stage at St Chad's to the applause of all his teachers, friends and family to be told by Mr Thomas that he had passed the scholarship to – what was the name of that school again? – Damian College. Then he was asleep.

Chapter Six

Monday-morning Blues

Monday came, and the morning sky was grey, grey as Greengate on a sunny afternoon.

Billy rose early and was ready when David Priestley called to take him to St Chad's Church for 7.30 Mass. As they were setting off, Mam called from the scullery:

'On your way back from church, I want you to call at the Jewish bakery and buy threepenn'orth of reject bagels or buns or whatever they've got.'

In the vestry of St Chad's, David showed Billy how to put on a cassock and a cotta, making a few fussy adjustments as if dressing a dummy in Lewis's window.

'There,' he said finally. 'St William of Cheetham.'

The two boys lit the altar candles, and processed with Canon Calder, the parish priest, into the silent old church. At that time in the morning it had an eerie atmosphere, their footsteps on the terrazzo-tiled floor echoing round the empty building. Empty, that is, except for two devoted worshippers: old 'Brother' Kelly, whose private 'silent' devotions sibilated round the near-deserted nave; and silver-haired Sally Sweeney, who was noted for her dedicated attendance at all church services, including weddings and funerals. Especially funerals, which were her favourite.

The Canon's voice reverberated round the hollow church as he intoned the beginning of the Mass:

'*In nomine Patris, et Filii et Spiritus Sancti. Amen.*'

David responded with a fluency born of long practice. Five minutes into the Mass, he caught Billy's eye and gave him a broad grin and a meaningful nod. The priest turned to face the congregation of two.

'*Dominus vobiscum.*'

'Dominus, have the biscuits come?' Billy said quietly.

Giving a big wink in Billy's direction, David responded, '*Et cum spiritu tuo.*'

'Yes, and the spirits too,' Billy mouthed.

A minute later, the priest whirled round and raised his arms.

'*Kyrie eleison.*'

Sotto voce, Billy replied, 'Carey a licence,' whilst David, grinning even more broadly, answered correctly: '*Kyrie eleison.*'

'*Christe eleison,*' said the priest.

'Christy a licence,' said Billy, adding under his breath, 'But it's Abie who needs the licence.'

The rest of the ceremony passed without incident, and Billy watched and imitated everything that David did, enjoying the experience immensely.

'At the end of the week,' David said, on the way home, 'the Canon gives us sixpence if we've served our quota. Then there's tips from weddings and funerals. Funerals are the best, 'cos not only do you get good tips but also a ride home in a big black limousine.'

'It seems quite easy, David.'

'I told you it was easy. And it will get easier still as you go along. Just follow in my footsteps and you'll be OK.'

'I'll try to do that,' Billy said.

They parted and Billy went to the Jewish bakery. He waited around for twenty minutes or so, then bought a big bag of bagels and seeded buns for threepence.

At home, he found the usual breakfast chaos. His brothers argued and bickered amongst themselves whilst Mam made toast, one piece at a time, by holding a round of bread, speared on an ordinary dinner fork, up to the bars of the living-room fire. Every weekday morning it was the same. She burned the thumb of her right hand, while the boys fought and squabbled noisily over who was first in line for the piece of toast due to come off the assembly line.

'The next one's mine!' wailed Sam as Mam threw a finished piece on to the table.

Jim was too fast for him and snaffled the toast with practised ease.

'Workers first,' he said.

Sam's whining reached fever pitch:

'Aw, that's not fair, Mam. I've been waiting I don't know how long for that piece. It was my turn and now he's rotten well swiped it.'

'Shurrup, the lot of you,' yelled Mam, her thumb resembling a well-done steak. 'Shurrup. I've only got one pair of hands.'

'I'm fed up of this rotten house and this rotten lot. That was my piece of toast.'

'Shurrup, I said,' Mam shouted, and she winged Sam a beauty across his left cheek.

Sam's whingeing took on a new urgency.

'Go on,' he howled, turning the other cheek. 'Hit the other side now!'

Mam duly obliged by landing a second slap right on target.

It was at that juncture that Billy, bearing buns and bagels, arrived like the relieving US cavalry.

'I saw you in church yesterday listening to that sermon,' Billy said as he deposited the provender on the table. 'You shouldn't do everything that the Bible tells you, 'cos sometimes it tells you some funny things like if your eye looks at something bad, you're supposed to pluck it out. Next thing we know, you'll be walking around like Lord Nelson!'

There was a loud knocking at the front door.

'Glory be t'God!' said Mam. 'Who can that be at this time o' the morning? I hope it's not her-next-door on the cadge for sugar or summat. Go and see who it is, our Les.'

Les was back in a minute.

'It's the postman. He sez he has an unstamped letter for us. There's a double surcharge or summat on it.'

'Now who can that be from?' Mam said, puzzled.

She went to the door to find out. The boys heard the postman say:

'Sorry, Mrs Hopkins. There's no stamp on it, though someone's tried to draw one in pencil there in the corner. Anyroad, the charge is double, I'm sorry to say. That's twice three-halfpence, making threepence due altogether.'

Mam took three pennies from her purse and paid up. She came back into the living room still perplexed, carrying the surcharged letter.

'It's addressed to "Master Samuel Hopkins". Here, it's yours,' she said, handing over the letter.

Billy and Jim had gone strangely quiet and were grimacing at each other as Sam, wearing a confused expression, opened up his mysterious letter.

'Well, what does it say?' Mam asked.

'It says: "Dear Sam, You are daft and potty. From your brothers Billy and Jim."'

'You daft devil, Billy,' said Jim. 'I told you to put it in the letter box of the door, not the pillar box at the corner of the street.'

'Right, you pair of daft buggers,' said Mam. 'You can both pay me threepence each for worrying me like that.'

This incident was only one of many against Sam, who had been cast in the role of family scapegoat. The other boys enjoyed baiting him, because he never failed to oblige them by reacting in exactly the way they had hoped. One of Dad's gramophone records began, 'And it's Pom! And it's Pom! Pom! Pom! Pom!' Whenever they were short of entertainment, they had only to chant, 'And it's Sam! And it's Sam! Sam! Sam! Sam!' for him to reward them by throwing a fit of purple rage. He was also the most faddy kid in the family. And that was saying something, for they were all a fussy lot as Grandma McGuinness had rightly asserted. Jim was chief tormentor, especially in the matter of food, for it usually meant an extra helping for him. Whenever there was meat pie for dinner Jim always sang – *sotto voce*, of course:

> *'Our John Willie's got scabby eyes,*
> *A dirty snotty nose,*
> *And he makes meat-pies.'*

On cue, Sam would begin yowling:

'I can't eat this pie now, Mam. Our Jim's put me off.'

This morning's breakfast scene was no different from usual.

'Right,' said Mam. 'No more toast. I'm fed up burning me hand. Get stuck into the buns!'

Jim was leaving for work, but as he hurried through the door, he found time to say:

'See all those little bits of things on the buns?' indicating the poppy seeds. 'Rats' droppings from the bakery!' Then he was gone.

'Can't eat 'em now!' Sam wailed. 'I'm fed up in this rotten house. If it's not our Jim putting me off everything, it's everybody going on about Billy and how brainy he is. Right, I've tried all that stuff about turning the other cheek. From now on, it's gonna be "An eye for an eye, and a tooth for a tooth"!'

After breakfast, Billy looked at the clock. It was already quarter to nine. He hadn't realised how much time he'd spent at church and queueing up for bagels. Being late at St Chad's was serious and meant the strap. Mr Thomas's rules were inflexible; no exceptions – no excuses.

Henry Sykes had told Billy that if you put a single horse-hair on the palm of the hand, there was no pain. This morning, in anticipation of the strap which was sure to follow, he took precautions, extracting a strand from their horse-hair sofa before running as fast as his legs would carry him to try to beat the nine o'clock deadline. He arrived at the school gate at 9.02 and found the headmaster waiting with a queue of latecomers already lined up.

'Right, all of you. In to morning assembly,' he ordered.

Billy was lined up with six others on the stage in front of the whole school.

'Now,' announced Mr Thomas, 'Charles Dickens has a character called Mr Micawber who says "Annual income twenty pounds, annual expenditure nineteen pounds nineteen and six, result happiness. Annual income twenty pounds, annual expenditure twenty pounds and sixpence, result misery." In this school, arrival eight fifty-nine, result happiness; arrival nine oh one, result misery.

'Now, in this world, being on time, being punctual, is one of the most important things in life. A great French

127

king once said: "Punctuality is the politeness of princes." But there is a lot more to it than just politeness. Oh, yes. Everything depends on being on time: the rising and setting of the sun, the moon, the stars, the tides. Our great British industry and our commerce all depend on it. The factories and the mills must start on time; the trains, the trams and the buses all must run on time. If you go to catch the nine o'clock train and you arrive at five past, it's too late, lads. The train has gone! Remember this, boys: "Punctuality is the soul of business." I read the other day that a man called Lucas said: "People who are late are often so much jollier than the people who have to wait for them." That might be true where he comes from, but not here, not in St Chad's school!'

He turned to the first latecomer:

'White, you were late every day last week. What's your excuse this time?'

'Please, sir, me mam forgot to wind the alarm clock up.'

'Remind your mother then. Hand out!'

Thwack. White shrugged his shoulders impassively.

'Next. Hardman, what's your excuse?'

'Please, sir. Please, sir, I had to go to the lavatory and I had to wait me turn.'

'Be first in the queue next time!'

'But please, sir, I have five brothers and I'm the youngest.'

'No excuse. Hand out!'

Thwack. A cry of 'Ow! Ow!'

'Tarpey! What have you to say for yourself?'

'Please, sir, I had to wait for me mam to finish patching me keks.'

'We don't say "keks" in polite society, we say "trousers". Anyway, it won't do. Hand out!'

Thwack. A yelp.

At last it came to Billy's turn to have his excuse assessed.

'Hopkins, you're not usually late. What excuse?'

'Please, sir, I served half-past-seven Mass and then I had to get the family breakfast from the Jewish bakery.'

'Not good enough. You should set off earlier. Hand out!'

Surreptitiously, Billy managed to stick the horse-hair on to the palm of his right hand. Mr Thomas brought the tawse smartly down and then, spotting the hair, looked Billy straight in the eye.

'It doesn't work, lad,' he said. 'Now hold out your other hand for trying to deceive your headmaster!'

Smarting from the burning pain, and blowing and shaking each hand in turn, Billy joined the main body of the school for prayers.

'Oh Lord, send me here my purgatory,' he recited with the others.

After prayers, Mr Thomas gave his little talk, as he did every morning.

'There was once a father with six sons. One day he made them all bend down and he covered them over with a big sheet. Then, even though they hadn't done anything wrong, he started belting them with a big strap. He didn't know which one he was belting as they were all hidden under the sheet. Very unfair, you all think. But when he'd finished, he took the sheet off them and said: "Let that be a lesson to all of you for the rest of your days. Life is very unfair and it's no good moaning about it. You have to learn to take the knocks and the blows even when you haven't done anything and you don't deserve them. Remember – that's life!"

'Now, we've come to the end of another school year.

129

Today the school will break up at dinnertime instead of the usual four o'clock.'

The school could not restrain a loud cheer in spite of the glares and cuffs of the supervising teachers. For most of them, school was a prison with no court of appeal and no time off for good behaviour. The lucky kids, they thought, were those who were off sick or in hospital with TB.

'We shall return to school after the holidays on Monday the thirty-first of August. During the holidays, keep out of mischief and try not to get yourselves killed.'

Then, in military fashion and in time to Miss McGurk's rendering of 'Christ the Lord is risen today!' on the old battered piano, the various classes filed out to their classrooms.

Seated two to a desk and in absolute silence, Billy's class waited for Miss McGurk to make the trip from hall to classroom. In this five-minute period, the ink monitors seized the opportunity to make their rounds, filling the ink-wells with their watery, freshly made-up ink. Then their mistress arrived.

Miss McGurk was the most feared and hated teacher at St Chad's. She was an Irish teacher of the old school – stern, unbending and often cruel as a disciplinarian. She was about forty years of age and she wore flat, sensible shoes and carried with her everywhere a massive leather handbag. On her lip – unlike Miss Gibson – there was no hint of a moustache. No hint. It was a definite moustache. All the kids in the class, except the very tough ones – like Stan White – lived in mortal fear of her, and some of them were nervous wrecks, their fingernails bitten down to the quick. On her desk she had a brown strap always hot from use, and she hit out on the flimsiest pretext and sometimes when there was no pretext. It was rumoured that in the locked drawer of her desk she had a green strap which she had had specially made up for her in Ireland. When it came to straps, this, it was said, was the jewel in the crown, the mother of all straps. Punishment with this piece of Irish leather was reserved for specially evil crimes, like swearing, farting, playing with oneself or making too many blots or mistakes. Some of the kids were mental defectives or of very low intelligence. It didn't matter. She made no allowance for handicaps.

She began by calling the register to make sure no one had escaped. At the same time, she checked on Mass attendances, which were recorded on a chart on the classroom wall. She lifted the lid of her desk and took out a box of Sharp's toffees and a tin of chocolate biscuits. The kids in her class watched her every move like dogs waiting for their meal. The first name always to be called was one of her special favourites.

'Flewitt!'

'Nine o'clock Mass and Holy Communion, miss.'

'Excellent, Joey. Here you are – one toffee and one biscuit. And another gold star for you!'

Flewitt went out to the front, collected his reward and stuck a small star on the long row of gold stars he had already accumulated against his name.

'Hopkins!'

'Nine o'clock Mass and Holy Communion, miss.'

'Very good, William. A toffee, a biscuit and a gold star.'

Billy accepted his prizes and placed his star on his row of mixed gold and silver honours.

'Sykes!'

'Nine o'clock Mass, miss.'

'Why weren't you at Communion?'

' 'Cos I swallowed a little bit o' water, miss.'

'You were quite right not to go, Henry. Listen, class. There was once a little boy who swallowed a drop of water when he was brushing his teeth and he thought it didn't matter so he went to Communion anyway. On the way home from Mass, he was knocked down and killed by a bus. Where do you think he is now?'

'Burning in hell,' the class chorused – all impressed and moved not only by the story of the little boy's tragic death but also by that bit about the boy brushing his teeth, since none of them possessed a toothbrush – as the school dentist would have confirmed.

'Right, Henry. One toffee and a silver star. White!'

'Never went, miss.'

'Not "never went", White, but "didn't go"! Why didn't you go?'

'Miss, since me dad left us, me mam sleeps with me uncles and they never wake up in time.'

'You mustn't tell us about your uncles here. And you must learn to get up yourself. Get out here and hold out your hand!'

The brown strap whacked White's hand.

'Now go and put a black star against your name.'

Stan White did so. When it came to his personal record of stars, White was all black.

In St Chad's school, there were many tough kids. None came tougher than Stan White, who had raised swearing and blaspheming to an art form. His dad had run off with a younger woman the year before, and his mam had had to go on the game in order to support her young family. Stan was nearly nine and already streetwise and the senior male in his family. Not only was he cock-of-the-class, he could fight many of the older boys in the two classes above. He was scared of no one and was incorrigible. At playtime he would, for a ha'penny, let anyone have as many whacks at his hands as they wished with a strap that he had stolen.

Only one punishment scared him – Miss McGurk's ladder! It was the equivalent of walking a pirate's plank. The classroom had a high ceiling with a trap-door to the loft. Leading to this there was a ladder permanently in position.

'Up there in the roof,' Miss McGurk had told them, 'it is very dark and there are hundreds and hundreds of rats ready to gnaw the very eyes out of any boy who's sent up there. If I find anyone in this class being sinful and wicked, up there he goes, I promise you!'

It was the one threat that worked, for even the hardest kids in the class quaked at the thought of being made to climb that ladder.

'You never go to Mass,' barked Miss McGurk at Stan White. 'Call yourself a Catholic? A Whit Friday Catholic is all you'll ever be. Who knows what a Whit Friday Catholic is? Hands up!'

The very term 'Whit Friday' was enough to trigger off powerful memories in Billy's mind.

Whit Week walks! These were an annual affair and a most important event in the school's calendar. Every year, about three or four weeks before Whit, all the Hopkins boys were taken to Mays', the pawnbroker's and outfitter's on Rochdale Road, to be kitted out: new shoes and stockings, grey breeches, a brightly coloured elastic belt with a hooked clasp, a new white shirt and a silk tie, a beautiful navy-blue blazer with an embroidered emblem on the pocket, and to crown it all, a new cap with the letters 'SC' emblazoned on the front. Billy didn't know how it was all paid for – perhaps by weekly payments, but then his mam didn't believe in the never-never.

Whit Monday was for Protestant processions. If it was sunny, the Protestants said: 'God knows his own!' and if it rained, 'God waters his little flowers!' Catholics used the same expressions – it was one of the few things they had in common.

Whit Friday was reserved for the Catholics, and for them it was a public demonstration of faith. Churches from all over the Salford diocese blew the dust off their banners, statues, crucifixes and display floats, and brought them out of storage. These were decked and covered in a profusion of beautiful flowers, ribbons and gaily coloured silks.

When the St Chad's processors gathered outside the school in preparation, Billy stood open-mouthed with awe and wonderment at the utter splendour and beauty of the people and the pageantry of the occasion.

Here were the scrubbed-faced young boys – Stan White among them – newly suited, hair gleaming and plastered flat with barber's hair oil, and each with a bright-red sash tied around his torso like an ambassador; the small girls in their brightly coloured silks; the young ladies in their bridesmaid's dresses and long white gloves; the teachers with their unaccustomed well-groomed, shining look; and the parish priest in black suit and gaiters, silk topper and silver-headed cane.

And when the proud banners bearing the St Chad's legend, and the silken streamers held by the beautiful maidens were raised, when the statue of Our Lady of Lourdes was lifted on to the decorated carriage and the Children of Mary took up their positions, when the schoolchildren were arranged in military order by the teachers, then Billy's heart swelled and overflowed with pride that he belonged and was part of such an august body of people!

The band struck up with 'Colonel Bogey' and they were on their way!

Down Cheetham Hill they flowed like tributaries as other churches joined them, and other bands struck up with rival tunes. Forward marched the glorious procession, swelling to even greater lengths as church after church merged. St Chad's, Corpus Christi, St Anne's, St Boniface's, St Malachy's, St Patrick's. Was there no end to these churches from such far-flung places as Blackley, Miles Platting and Ancoats? On down Corporation Street, along Market Street, the thronging crowds cheering and shouting tumultuously – 'Keep your 'ead up, son!' and 'Swing yer arms, our Billy!' – as they made their way majestically to Albert Square. From time to time a proud mother would break away from the cheering bystanders and rush out to her son or daughter to give advice and thrust money or sweets into their hands.

Finally they reached Albert Square, where a vast multitude – beyond anything Billy had ever seen or imagined – had assembled. Then the strains of 'Faith of Our Fathers' broke out and that massive crowd stopped its excited gabble, men and boys removed their hats and, standing to attention, everyone joined in the hymn – many moved to tears and sobbing at the sheer emotion of the scene.

> *Faith of our Fathers, living still*
> *In spite of dungeon, fire, and sword;*
> *Oh, how our hearts*
> *beat high with joy*
> *when e'er we hear that glorious word!*
> *Faith of our fathers! Holy Faith!*
> *We will be true to thee till death,*
> *We will be true to thee till death.*

* * *

Then there was the anti-climax of the slow and somewhat wistful march back to school, and the final dismissal. Back home to Honeypot Street to be told to get 'them new clothes off sharpish' and to see them stored in the wardrobe, where they had now become the new Sunday best. So, rather deflated and dejected, they went back to their normal routine and play, though without much enthusiasm.

In the pubs in town, however, heavy drinking and sentimental speeches were the order of the day. There were declarations of undying faith and loyalty to the Holy Mother Church from men, and sometimes women, who had not been near a church in years. A wrong word, though, in the wrong ear and a powder keg would be ignited and drunken brawls would explode: 'No man is going to insult my church or my religion! Take that, y'idiot!' Thus was born the expression 'Whit Friday Catholic'.

'Please, miss,' said Billy now, in answer to Miss McGurk's question. 'It means someone who never goes to church but says 'e's a Catholic on Whit Friday.'

'That's right, William. Someone who claims once a year to be a Catholic – usually in a pub in order to start a fight.'

Miss McGurk set the class to learning about baptism from the catechism whilst she sat at her high desk and tackled the daily calculation of register totals. It was a task she did not find easy, and she squirmed and shifted position several times, inadvertently revealing a little of her thighs as she did so.

White, who was sitting in the front row and

immediately in front of her, had a first-class view. Suddenly he turned to the class, leered and said in a loud whisper:

'Blue today, lads!'

'Who said that?' she snapped angrily. 'Was it you, Sykes?'

'No, miss. Honest to God, miss.'

'Don't take the name of the Lord thy God in vain. Then it must have been you, White!'

'Me, miss?' he exclaimed in feigned innocence. 'Not me, miss. I wouldn't look up your clothes, miss. Honest!'

'Well, it was either you or Sykes. Was it White who said it, Sykes?'

'I think it might have been, miss. But I'm not sure,' said Henry, not wishing to take the blame for something he hadn't done.

'Right, White. I've had enough of you and your impudence. Up the ladder you go. See what colour the rats are, since you're so interested in colour.'

White had indeed turned white.

'Please, miss, I won't do it again. Honest. Please, miss.'

Miss McGurk was adamant and unforgiving.

'Up you go, White. You filthy beast!'

Stan began the slow ascent up the ladder whilst the class, spellbound with horror, had become still and silent.

'Keep going, White!' she bawled. 'Right to the top!'

White was now terror-stricken at the thought of the rats waiting in the loft above.

'Please, miss. I promise never to look up your clothes again. I promise I won't tell anyone the colour of your knickers. Honest to God, miss. Please, miss.'

'Very well. You may come down this time. But if I ever catch you doing anything like that again . . . I promise you . . .'

Stan returned to his place, but when an opportunity arose, he turned to Henry, showed him a clenched fist and whispered:

'You wait till playtime, Sykes. You're gonna get thumped for tellin' on me.'

Miss McGurk turned to the class, who were still mesmerised by the Stan White drama.

'Right,' she said. 'You're supposed to have been learning your catechism. What is Baptism? You, Flewitt!'

'Baptism,' answered Flewitt, 'is a Sacrament which cleanses us from original sin, makes us Christians, children of God, and members of the Church.'

'Good. Does it have to be a priest that baptises you or can anyone do it?'

'Anyone can do it in an emergency,' answered Billy. 'You could even use tea or beer if there was no water handy.'

'Right. But let's hope that it doesn't come to that. Now. What do we promise in Baptism? You, White!'

'We promise in Baptism, miss,' he said, 'to renounce the devil and all his work and pimps.'

After religious instruction, Miss McGurk turned to her favourite subject and her favourite method of torturing her charges – mental arithmetic. She began:

'I went to the greengrocer's and I bought: three cabbages at a penny three farthings; two pounds of potatoes at twopence halfpenny; a pound of apples at twopence three farthings; a pound of carrots at a penny halfpenny; a pound of onions at a penny farthing. Right. How much change did I get out of half a crown? You, Campbell!'

The hapless Campbell was one of those pupils with no fingernails, and as far as he was concerned, mental arithmetic may as well have been advanced calculus.

'Please, miss, I don't know. Would it be fourpence ha'penny?' he said, making a wild stab at the answer.

'It would not. Get out here!'

Carrots Campbell went out to take his punishment like a man – as did many others in that lesson. The one thing they seemed to be learning was fear and the arbitrary nature of pain and punishment. Maybe Mr Thomas had been right.

Cuffing and clouting also accompanied the handwriting lesson – and handwriting meant copperplate script with lots of whirls, curls, loops and flourishes. Great store was set by having a good hand. The trouble was that writing was done with standard issue pens and the watery ink which the monitors had put into the inkwell of each desk. Nibs had a dual purpose, since they could be used either for writing or for dart-throwing, and, even though they inevitably wore out, it was almost impossible to obtain a replacement, with the result that attempts at calligraphy often resulted in scratches and ink blots.

'Handwriting time!' Miss McGurk announced. 'Copy the first two verses of "Daffodils" from your poetry books into your English exercise books!'

In fairy tales, King Midas had the misfortune to turn everything he touched into gold. For many of the St Chad's kids, everything they touched turned into an ink smudge. They already had grubby hands to start with, and they seemed to drip ink from the ends of their fingers like monsters in a science-fiction story. Add to this the fact that many of them trembled with nervousness and it was easy to understand why their exercise books were a mass of blots and blotches. Miss McGurk did her best to help by walking up and down the rows administering blows with shouts of 'You donkeys! You dafties! You dolts!' causing the ink-drippers to be even more nervous and prolific. 'Campbell,' she yelled. 'Your writing looks as if a swarm of ants has escaped from your inkwell and walked all over your exercise book without wiping their feet!'

Creative writing followed.

'See that funny mark on the blackboard?' she asked. 'Tell me what it reminds you of! You first, Shacklady!'

Shacklady was a mental defective with a hare-lip and a ferret-like face, and in all fairness he should have been in a special school.

'It reminds me of a funny mark on the blackboard,' he answered.

'Out here!' she bawled. 'I'll teach you to be funny in my class!'

The brown strap swished and found its mark – twice.

By this time Billy was panicking and put his hand up in desperation.

'Please, miss, it reminds me of a man looking out to sea watching the white, screaming seagulls skimming the tops of the waves.'

Tears sprang to Miss McGurk's eyes. She went to her capacious handbag and pulled out a Sharp's caramel.

'Here you are, William,' she said. 'For you. You should go a long way one day.'

'Yeah,' said Stan White. 'To Timbuktu.'

'Out here, White!' said Miss McGurk.

At playtime, the kids were turfed out and the teachers retired to their staffroom to recover their strength and their spirits. St Chad's playground resembled Strangeways prison yard with its high wall topped with broken glass embedded in cement. There was normally a teacher acting as a warder on duty, but as this was the last day of term, they had all gone to celebrate the event with a glass of sherry in the staffroom.

Billy was playing a game of 'Which-hand-is-it-in?' with Henry when Stan White strode up to them, held out his fist and said:

'Right, Sykes, you're in for a good thumping for telling on me.'

'Oh no you don't,' said Billy. 'Leave him alone. McGurk made him tell.'

'Keep outa this, Hockey. It's nowt to do with you. S'none of your business.'

'Henry's me pal. So I'm making it me business.'

As soon as he said this, an excited and expectant shout went up from the other kids in the vicinity: 'A fight! White and Hockey! A fight! A fight!'

White pushed his shoulder against Billy's and snarled: 'Wanna start something, Hockey? I can lick you easy.'

Billy pushed back and said:

'Oh, yeah. Y'couldn't lick a toffee apple.'

'I'm warning you – you gonna get a knuckle butty. I'll mollycrush you.'

'Oh, yeah. You and whose army?'

'Scram, Hockey, afore I spit in your eye.'

'You're just a big mouth, Whitey. If your mouth was any bigger, you wouldn't have no face left to wash. That's all y'are – just one big mouth!'

'Say that again, Hockey, and I'll paste you.'

'Big mouth! Big mouth!'

In an instant the two boys were grappling with each other and rolling over and over on the stone flags, clinging to each other like wild cats. Panting like two steam engines, they tugged and tore at each other's hair and jerseys, and Billy forgot all his boxing lessons as he tried to gain the upper hand on his savage, flailing opponent. By some miracle, he managed to roll away, get to his feet and adopt his Len Harvey stance. Now his blood was up.

'Get up, Whitey, and fight fair.'

White struggled to his feet, and as he did so, Billy rapped him on the forehead with three rapid straight jabs – rat-a-tat-tat.

White's face registered complete amazement, as well as a purplish swelling above his right eye. With a roar, and with arms opened wide as if to embrace him, he charged at Billy. As they wrestled about, White kicked Billy in both shins and followed this with a head-butt. Billy's nose began to bleed, but he managed to land a right hook on White's jaw. Then he felt himself being held back by a strong hand on the scruff of his neck.

'Right, you two. Enough,' shouted Mr Woodley, the deputy head. 'Go and wait outside the staff room for Mr Thomas.'

Holding his head back, Billy stemmed the blood from his nose with his hanky and, accompanied by White, whose face was looking none too good, went to await Mr Thomas's dispensation of justice.

As the two boys waited, they could hear through the half-open door of the staff room the voice of Mr Kinsella, who was in charge of Standard 5 and the most popular teacher in the school:

'For the past ten years, I've been a jailer in a children's prison. It's been my job to clamp down their bubbling energy and to chain them to their desks for six hours a day. You can see in their eyes that they hate school, for it's only when the bell rings at four o'clock that their eyes light up with delight at the thought of getting away from our clutches for a few hours. Did you notice how they cheered when they were reminded that today is the start of the long holidays? We pump rubbish into one ear and watch it come out the other. What's that old rhyme again?

> *Ram it in! Cram it in!*
> *Children's heads are hollow.*
> *Jam it in! Slam it in!*
> *Still there's more to follow!'*

'Most of the kids from this school are going to be "hewers of wood and drawers of water",' argued Miss McGurk. 'I treat them all with loving kindness but I think it doesn't do to go putting ideas into their heads.'

'But that's what we get paid for,' replied Mr Kinsella.

'I think Miss McGurk's right,' said Mr Thomas. 'I see our job as bringing a little order and discipline into their disorganised lives and . . .'

He noticed Billy and Stan White standing at the door.

'What have you two been up to?' he asked. 'As if I can't tell. Who won? Never mind, I don't want to know. As it's the last day of term, you can go. I think you've punished each other enough. The school nurse is coming round the classes just now so you'd better let her have a look at your injuries. Now, be off with you.'

Heaving great sighs of relief at the unusual leniency, the two boys went back to Miss McGurk and the last lesson of the day. It was the one they hated most – music!

Before the dreaded lesson began, the school nurse came into the class and did a quick check on all the kids' heads, looking for any lice or nits that might be lurking there, or ringworm that might have developed since her last visit. Billy always wondered why the nurse never examined Miss McGurk's hair for nits, as she was just as likely to have acquired a few from her wards.

When it came to his turn, his nose-bleed had stopped and so special attention was not required. But the visit of the nurse had at least delayed the start of the music.

On the blackboard, Miss McGurk had painstakingly

drawn music staves on which she had written various notes of music – quavers, semiquavers, crotchets, dotted crotchets, minims, dotted minims – all Double Dutch to the kids in her class.

'We shall start by clapping out the rhythms you see I've written up on the board. Ready! Now!'

The class began clapping but they could tell it wasn't right by the way she screeched at them:

'No, no, no! You set of donkeys! You imbeciles! Try saying it with me! Ta. Ta. Ta. Tay. Ta-a-a-tay. Ta-ta-ta-ta tay.'

But to no avail. The kids just did not understand what they were required to do. Miss McGurk flipped her lid.

'Right. We'll try again,' she screamed in an apoplectic frenzy. 'Anyone fooling about gets the green strap!'

'Ta-tay. Ta-tay. Ta-tay,' chorused the class nervously.

'Ti-tee. Ti-tee. Ti-tee,' chanted White, unable to resist the challenge and curiosity of a new experience offered by the much-vaunted green strap.

'You've asked for it, White. Get out here!'

She went to her desk drawer and withdrew the dreaded green strap. There was a gasp of excitement and horror at the sight of the Irish tawse which, up to this point, had existed only in myth and legend.

'Hold your hand out, White, and see how you like this!'

White held his hand out to the side and, with professional proficiency, waggled it about in a jerky, see-sawing motion, making it very difficult for Miss McGurk to hit the target accurately. The first whack was slightly off course and clipped the tips of his fingers, causing even that hardened character to cry out in pain. The second stroke, however, missed his wobbly hand altogether and struck Miss McGurk on the thigh, sending her into a paroxysm of rage.

'Out! Out! Get out! Go home! You vile wretch! And don't bother coming back!' she shrieked.

Whitey slunk to the classroom door, but before he disappeared he gave the whole class a cheeky grin and a broad wink.

'See you next term, miss,' he said as he departed.

After he had gone, the class was joined by boys from Standard 6 and 7, and the real music began as they worked their way through their repertoire of sea shanties. They sang them all with great gusto and enthusiasm: 'Hearts of Oak', 'Shenandoah', 'A-roving', 'Drunken Sailor' and the great favourite with them all, 'Bobby Shaftoe'.

'One day,' said Miss McGurk, 'some of you will join the Royal Navy and maybe have the privilege to fight for the British Empire and all that she stands for. Remember these shanties then, boys, and cherish them.'

Thus ended the term and the academic year at St Chad's Elementary School.

Chapter Seven

Say it with Flowers

When the school bell finally rang, there was a mad rush to escape. Woe betide any member of the public who got in the way of that tide of young humanity which erupted from the school gates like lava from a volcano.

Billy ran all the way home, as his energetic morning had given him a tremendous appetite. Monday meant nourishing lentil soup made up of the stock from the remainder of the Sunday joint plus a mixture of sundry vegetables. Mam had had an energetic morning too, for Monday meant wash-day in the front cellar. Somehow she always managed the miracle of preparing a lunch for five people at the same time as washing, mangling, wringing, drying and ironing the clothes for eight.

'What have you been doing to your nose?' she asked as they sat at the table. 'Have you been fighting?'

'Yeah,' Billy answered. 'I was nutted by Stan White.'

'You should be taking lessons from your father then – not from Jim. Your dad can show you what to do in a dirty fight.'

'P'raps you're right.'

'Anyroad,' Mam continued, 'your hair needs cutting badly.'

'I'd rather get it cut properly.'

'Stop acting daft,' she said. 'I want you to go and get your hair cut this afternoon. Your Aunt Cissie says it'll help you keep your strength up. Your father allus likes Larry's on Cheetham Hill – specially as it only costs fourpence.'

After dinner, Billy set off for the barber's but not to Larry's. Billy knew another barber – Lenny's, on Rochdale Road, who charged only threepence provided you didn't cry out during the comb-and-scissors bit. He walked along by the railway fence, over the big bridge until he reached the top of the steps, from where he spotted a big lorry way below pulling out of the dyeworks yard. The big truck was heading slowly towards Collyhurst Road, where it would have to stop. Billy leapt pell-mell down the steps and reached the bottom in time to catch up to the lorry as it was crawling the last thirty yards to the major road. Just in time to steal a ride on the back for that short distance. The vehicle manufacturers had thoughtfully provided a rail for the purpose at exactly the right height. Gleefully, feeling like a trapeze artist at the circus, Billy hung on to the back.

This is smashing fun, he thought, as the lorry crawled out of the compound.

Suddenly there was a rapid change of gears and the lorry accelerated at breakneck speed down Collyhurst Road, with Billy clinging for dear life on to the back. Instinctively, he sensed that to release his grip meant certain death. His head would have smashed like an egg on the cobbled road rushing giddily behind and away from him.

Screaming desperately for help, he grasped the metal bar in a grip of iron as the vehicle tore at full speed down the road. Streets, shops, pubs, factories became one dizzy blur in a crazy, nightmare whirl through Collyhurst. Completely unaware of his hysterical stowaway passenger swinging wildly on the rail at the back, the driver, in carefree mood, whistled 'Pennies from Heaven' as he took his load, the last of the day, on its routine journey back to the depot.

Billy's screams rang across the district, alerting pedestrians and bystanders on the pavements. But always too late to signal to the driver.

The huge truck changed gear to negotiate an incline, and as it did so, it began belching suffocating exhaust fumes into Billy's face. The acrid smoke got into his throat and his lungs. He felt himself losing consciousness. He could not hang on much longer. His grip was weakening.

'Move over Teddy Smith and make room for one more at the picture show,' he said aloud to himself. 'And save me a few toffees as well!'

But Billy's time had not come. By some miracle never fully explained or understood – perhaps his Guardian Angel had applied the brakes – the lorry stopped its ride of death. Simply stopped at the corner of Roger Street. Billy dropped off the back like a wet dishcloth, got to his feet and fled down a side street howling like a wounded animal.

He managed to totter into Lenny's shop, where he got himself a good haircut. Throughout the whole shearing operation, he was strangely silent, not even uttering a sound when it came to the scissors-and-comb bit, and earned himself a penny discount.

Home for the ritual hair-wash which always followed the school nurse's inspection and a visit to the barber's. Mam went at the task with passionate fervour.

'Just look at the dirt rolling out!' she exclaimed. 'Have you ever seen such muck? I'm not kidding, you could grow taters in your hair, you could!'

Billy enjoyed the sensual experience of having his scalp massaged, but then followed the part he hated most.

'Close your eyes and get your head down!' ordered Mam.

He set up a howl of protest when she poured a large jug of hot water over his head. She always managed to get a considerable quantity down his earhole, an occurrence which was to have long-term repercussions.

After the hair-drying stage came the hunt for any lice or nits that had miraculously survived this intensive decontamination. This had all the excitement and drama of a big-time African safari. Operation Dragnet began! The search for the parasites called for specialist equipment, and a fine-tooth comb was brought out and tugged through the tangled locks to trap any hardy and unwary survivors hiding with their offspring in the undergrowth. Short work was made of them as Mam, now the female White Hunter, cracked them on the comb under her thumb nail with dramatic commentary and cries of: 'Here's a big 'un! Gotcher!'

Feeling thoroughly purged and purified, Billy escaped into the street for an afternoon of freedom and frivolity. No school! No teachers! No Miss McGurk! A shiver of sheer pleasure and ecstasy ran through his body at the thought of the five weeks of liberty which lay ahead.

There was no such thing as being bored in Honeypot Street, as there was always something going on – a wedding or a funeral, an attempted suicide, an ambulance, a street-singer or a knife-sharpener, a chimney on fire, or a family fight that could be heard several streets away.

But most enthralling of all for Billy were the street games, with the flagstones, the red pillar box and the lamppost serving as props.

Billy and his pals played only with boys. After all, who wanted to join in with the girls, who were always playing sissy games like 'Hospitals' or 'House' – especially if they could borrow somebody's baby. If not that, they were always skipping to daft poems like:

> *Who's that coming down the street?*
> *Mrs Simpson's sweaty feet!*
> *She's been married twice before,*
> *Now she's knocking on Eddie's door.*

Boys' games were more intelligent, even though they changed with the seasons. Last month, yo-yos had been the thing, and the month before that whips-and-tops, but the current game was alleys – what the posh people called 'marbles' – which were ranked in status according to colour and killing-power – blood-reds being the most scarce and the most valuable. Billy was the proud possessor of six murderous 'bloodies'.

But the real favourite amongst his pals was bowling their hoops, or 'garfs', along the street – propelling them with a stick round impossible obstacles. Billy and Henry were the envy of all the other lads, as their garfs were bicycle wheels with pumped-up tyres.

'Watch this, Henery!' Billy called to his pal as he executed a particularly difficult bit of garf-guiding in and out of a set of bricks specially laid out for the purpose. He had completed the obstacle course when he was thrown off his stride by the roar of a motorbike coming down the street. It was Steve Keenan on his BSA.

'Righto, Billy,' called Steve above the noise of his engine. 'I promised you a ride on my motorbike. How about now? You still want a ride, don't you?'

'Do I!' exclaimed Billy. 'Let's go and tell me mam!

Quick, afore you change your mind!'

Mam wasn't too keen on the idea at first. She eventually came round but insisted on a big clean-up and a change into Sunday best.

'But I'm going on a motorbike – not to church.'

'Doesn't matter. Someone might see you!'

Steve made him put on a helmet and goggles and they went out into the street, where a gang of admiring kids were inspecting the motorbike. Their eyes nearly popped out of their heads when they saw young Billy 'Biggles' appear.

'By Jove, you young chaps, kindly stand aside, will you,' ordered Billy. 'My chum and I here are just going for a jolly old spin before tea, don'cha know!'

He sat astride the pillion and Steve started the engine.

'We'll go for a ride to Heaton Park. Hang on tight!'

With a roar, the two of them rode down Honeypot Street, leaving behind a gang of goggle-eyed kids.

'This is the greatest day of my life!' Billy called out as they sped along Cheetham Hill Road.

Street after street, shop after shop seemed to whizz by as the bike zipped through Cheetham Village and past the halfway house – a journey which took ages by bus and eternity on foot. In no time they had reached Heaton Park gates, but instead of turning in to the park, Steve steered the bike into a very affluent housing estate. They stopped outside a detached red-bricked house.

'Come in and meet the rest of the Keenan family,' he said.

Billy had seen one of these houses before – in his first reading book at St Wilfred's. He'd never thought he would ever go into one. Steve opened up the garden gate and wheeled his bike along the path.

They found Steve's parents and his sister, Constance,

sitting on deckchairs on the patio at the back of the house.

Mr Keenan Senior, in his early sixties and well over six feet in height, was a distinguished-looking gentleman with a silver George V beard. He was smartly dressed in flannels, white shirt and blue tie, and looked as if he had just stepped off a film set. Steve's mother was wearing a blue flowery summer dress, whilst Constance had on a smart tweed two-piece costume.

Straight out of the Beacon readers, Billy said to himself. The only thing missing is that pedigree dog.

As if it had read his thoughts, a beautiful sheepdog bounded into the garden and began licking his hand.

'This is Pauline's youngest brother, Billy,' announced Steve.

'How do you do?' said Constance. 'So nice to meet you.'

'Don't listen to her,' said Steve playfully. 'She's a teacher and doesn't know anything.'

'Glad to know you, young man,' said Steve's George V father.

'Now, Billy,' said Mrs Keenan. 'What about a nice glass of cold home-made lemonade on this hot afternoon?'

'Ta very much,' he answered. 'That ud be smashing.'

'With ice?' she asked.

'No, ta,' he replied, not used to being treated in this royal fashion. And anyway, ice-cream didn't go with lemonade.

He sat quietly in the deckchair that was offered to him, not daring to speak in case he said the wrong thing or put his foot in it. His mam had always told him: 'Speak only when you're spoke to and then your mouth won't get you into trouble.'

Mrs Keenan returned with his lemonade in a tall glass with a striped straw sticking out of it. Here was a new world, a new style of living.

This I could get used to, said Billy to himself, imitating one of his Jewish friends' expressions.

As the conversation flowed Billy swivelled his head from person to person. He listened to their adult talk about the weather, about the news, about the cost of the living, about Mussolini, about Constance's planned holiday in Italy, about the dog, and about the garden.

'I must say, Mother,' Constance observed, 'your petunias are looking very colourful this year.'

'Yes, aren't they? And they go on flowering for such a long time throughout the summer. That's why I like them.'

'Petunias are very nice,' said Mr Keenan, not to be left out. 'But my favourites are geraniums – they're always so bright and cheerful.'

'Do you have a garden, Billy?' asked Mrs Keenan.

'We do have a little patch at the front of our house where me dad's growing thistles, dock-leaves and dandelion and burdock. And me mam has a window-box in the back scullery – but I think she's growing water-cress. Either that or shamrocks.'

To Billy's bewilderment, this contribution to the horticultural discussion caused great amusement – especially to Mrs Keenan, who laughed till the tears ran down her cheeks.

'Steve told us you were a comedian,' she said, dabbing her eyes.

'I've even got the red nose for it,' Billy said.

'It looks quite sore, Billy. How did it happen?' asked Constance.

'Yeah,' replied Billy. 'I had a scrap at school today with the class bully. A lad called Stan White. He give me a Wigan kiss.'

'A Wigan kiss?' asked Mrs Keenan.

'Yeah, he tupped me with his head. Butted me, y'know.'

'I do hope you managed to hit him back,' said Mr Keenan.

'Oh, yeah. I socked him a beauty with a right uppercut.'

'Oh, I am glad to hear that,' said Constance. 'We mustn't let bullies get away with it, must we? Not in school. Not on the political scene. Not anywhere!'

I like her, thought Billy. It's not her fault she can't talk properly. And I like this family, their garden and their dog. I hope our Polly stops acting daft and marries this fella and gets to live in a house like this.

'Well, I'll have to take this young chap home, as I promised not to keep him out too long,' said Steve. 'If there's time, though, I thought we might take a little excursion before I drive him back. Come on, Billy 'Laugh-a-Minute' Hopkins, let's go!'

As they got up to leave, Mrs Keenan thrust a shilling into Billy's hand.

'You're worth a guinea a box. Here you are. Buy yourself something.'

'Ta very much. I've been very pleased to meetcha,' he said, and he meant it. 'By the way, what kind of dog is this?'

'It's a Collie type,' said Constance.

'So am I!' said Billy. 'And what's 'is name?'

'Why, it's Rover!' replied Constance.

'Thought so!' said Billy, as he waved goodbye.

They went back in the direction of Heaton Park.

'I've got a surprise for you,' Steve called over his shoulder, and they drove into the park until they reached an open space. Steve parked and locked his bike.

'Come on, Billy. Let's hire a motorboat!'

First a motorbike! Then a motorboat! Billy's heart turned somersaults at the thought of riding around the lake in one of those mechanised boats-for-two which he had seen but had never hoped to ride in. More than that, Steve actually trusted him enough to let him drive!

With both hands holding the steering wheel in a tight grip, Billy guided the chugging craft around the island and into the wide expanse that was Heaton Park lake.

After a while, Steve asked casually:

'How's Pauline today?'

'She was all upset last night, but she was OK when she went off to work this morning.'

'Yes, but how did she seem? I mean, did she look happy or what?'

'Oh no, she didn't seem happy. But she can be moody sometimes,' said Billy, more interested in the small family of ducks he had narrowly avoided decapitating.

'I wonder if she'll see me again.'

'I'm sure she will.'

'Perhaps if I wrote her a letter she might come round to seeing me once more . . .'

'I know how to get round our Polly – sorry, I mean Pauline.'

'Tell me, O great wise one!'

'Easy! Flowers! Especially roses. She loves them. That's your answer! Send her roses.'

'You think they might work?'

'I know they will.'

They finished their tour of the lake confining their attention and their conversation to more mundane, nautical matters. At the quayside, the lake attendant held their bobbing boat steady with his hook whilst they clambered out.

'Come on, young 'un,' said Steve. 'Time to get you home or I'll be in deeper trouble with your sister!'

On the way back, Steve stopped off at a florist's on

Queens Road, and a few minutes later he emerged with a beautiful bunch of red roses wrapped in cellophane.

'Billy,' he said, 'I want you to give these to Pauline for me. Tell her I need to have a reply by tomorrow night. I'll come by Honeypot Street at about half past four to get her answer from you. You can be our go-between.'

'Go-between!' said Billy. 'That's a new word on me, or is it two words?'

Steve dropped him off outside number 17, remounted his mechanical steed and sped off.

Billy rushed into the house bearing Steve's peace offering. He found Polly sitting at the kitchen table in earnest conversation with Mam.

'Polly! Polly!' he blurted, not stopping to catch his breath. 'I've been for a ride on Steve's motorbike and we went on a motorboat as well on Heaton Park lake. And I met all his family. And he's sent you these. And he says I'm to be your go-between.'

'Really?' she answered haughtily. 'Calm down! Come upstairs and tell me all about it.'

In her room, she put the bouquet on the dressing table.

'Just look at these flowers he's sent, Polly,' Billy said. 'Aren't they smashing?'

'Sending me flowers doesn't change nothing,' she said, not too convincingly.

With her young brother looking over her shoulder, Polly read the card attached to the cellophane:

> *O my Luve's like a red, red rose*
> *That's newly sprung in June:*
> *O my Luve's like the melodie*
> *That's sweetly play'd in tune.*

'That poem's a belter,' said Billy. 'But that Robbie Burns fella didn't know how to spell, did he?'

'Never mind all that. I don't want nowt to do with them. They'll all have to go back anyway. I can't be bribed with a few flowers. Steve's just trying to get round me, that's all. What did you think of his family, anyroad? Didn't you think they were a bit stuck-up?'

'Oh, no. Not a bit! I like 'em. They all talk very posh; his mam and dad sound as if they've each got a plum in their mouth, and their Constance as if she's got two. But they can't help it if they talk funny. And I still like 'em. They're nice and friendly.'

'What about Steve? D'you like Steve? How did he look? Was he happy? Was he depressed? Did he talk about me?'

'I think he's great. I like him no matter what you say about him. He's very kind and he thinks the world of you, our Polly. He was talkin' about you nearly all the time. And he did look a bit depressed, like, 'cos he's missing you already. Not only that, he's nice-looking and all. Reminds me of Douglas Fairbanks without his moustache.'

Polly looked pleased.

'And what about me?' she asked. 'Who do I remind you of?'

Billy thought for a minute or so. He had to be careful here.

'Ginger Rogers. Definitely. Only her hair is sort of gold and – er... yours is light brown. But, yeah. Ginger Rogers!'

'Ginger Rogers! D'you really think so?' Obviously enjoying the game of 'Look-alike', she asked, 'What about our Flo? Who's she like?'

'Gracie Fields!' answered Billy promptly.

'What about our Jim?'

157

'Easy. He's the spitting image of James Cagney. Sometimes he thinks he *is* James Cagney. Combs his hair like him, and dresses like him. But what about me then? Who am I like? I suppose you're going to say Freddie Bartholomew.'

'No, no,' she said. 'He's much too sissy. No, you're more like that lad in *Treasure Island*. Jackie Cooper, I think his name was.'

Billy felt ten feet tall, as it so happened that Jackie Cooper was one of his favourites.

'Oh, there's one thing I've been wanting to ask you,' he said. 'Why have you changed your name to Pauline? I like it 'cos it sounds real posh. But what was wrong with Polly?'

'I think the name Polly's horrible. Whoever heard of a heroine called Polly? It rhymes with Dolly, and Golly. And besides, it's the name of a parrot.'

'You're wrong, Polly. Look at the heroine in that song "Sweet Polly Oliver". And what about my name? Sometimes kids call me Silly Billy. Then there's our Flo. I won't say what her name rhymes with.'

Polly laughed, and she really did look like Ginger Rogers.

'Honestly, do you like the name Pauline or are you just saying that to please me?'

'No, honestly, I do like it. You're named after one of the saints – St Paul. And at school they've learnt us not only that song "Polly Oliver" but another one called "Pretty Pollie Pillicote". So what more do you want?'

'Oh, I do like talking to you, our Billy.'

'Remember, I'm your go-between,' Billy replied. 'What do you want me to tell Steve tomorrow?'

'Well, William Go-Between,' she said. 'Just tell Steve the flowers were lovely. He'll know what I mean.'

* * *

Three months later, Steve and Pauline were married at St Chad's Church. Billy and his friend David Priestley served the Nuptial Mass, and their tips were wildly generous.

A week after the wedding, Billy – accompanied by his brothers, Jim, Sam and Les, plus, of course, his pal Henry Sykes – launched a beautiful yacht called *Jolly Jim* on Queen's Park lake.

Chapter Eight

A Momentous Year

When 1939 began with a death, Billy knew that it was going to be a memorable year. After talking for so long about it, old Grandma McGuinness finally carried out her threat and went to join her stout-drinking cronies in the great snug in the sky.

From the top of the wardrobe, Dad took down his pot hat and brushed the dust from it. Uncle Eddy wept nonstop from the moment he heard the news.

She was laid out in her coffin in front of her livingroom window. Just before the funeral, Auntie Cissie and Mam took Billy in to view the corpse.

'Ooh, she does look well!' said Auntie Cissie. 'And what a lovely dress she's got on.'

'Aye, we showed her one of them shroud things just before she died,' said Mam.

'And what did she say?'

'She said, "I'm not wearing that bloody thing. I wouldn't be seen dead in it." '

'But what a lovely smile on 'er face,' observed Auntie Cissie.

'I never seen her smile once when she were alive,' said Billy.

'It don't matter, Billy,' said Mam. 'She's happy now, wherever she's gone.'

'Pr'aps she doesn't realise she's dead,' said Billy.

'Then she's in for a bit of a surprise when she wakes up tomorrow,' said Auntie Cissie.

'Not half,' said Mam. 'It'll be enough to give her a heart attack.'

'I just hope she never found all that meat in the aspidistra plant-pot,' said Billy.

'Did you have any money on her, Cissie?' asked Mam.

It sounded like a bet, and Billy half-expected to hear something like 'Aye, a bob each way', but instead Cissie said:

'I had a tanner a week with the Royal London club man. What about you, Kate?'

'I've had a bob a week on her for the last thirty years – ever since I was in service.'

'You must have a tidy sum coming to you then.'

'Aye, not so bad. Enough to rig out the whole family for the funeral.'

'Who did you get to do the funeral then, Kate?' asked Cissie.

'I got the Co-op. No sense in missing the divvy,' said Mam. 'Besides, they do a lovely send-off. You've probably seen their advertisement: "A funeral you will really enjoy." '

A week after the funeral, Ikey Goldstein, the second-hand furniture dealer, came round to value Grandma's bits and pieces. As Mam was the eldest child, it fell to her to administer the estate and arrange for the sale of the goods and chattels.

'There's no call for all this Victorian and Edwardian furniture any more,' he said. 'It's too old-fashioned.'

'Aye, I suppose it is,' sighed Mam.

'I mean, look at that mahogany dresser and that marble washstand, not to mention the old grandfather clock. All too big and too heavy for the modern home.'

'How much would you say then altogether?'

'I like you, Mrs Hopkins. I can see you're a straightforward woman. So, all right. For you I'll do a very big favour. I'll risk ruining myself. Say ten pounds for the lot.'

'Ten pounds! That's ridiculous!'

'So, I should need another dresser – another washstand! My shop's full of 'em. Well, I'll tell you what I'll do. I'll make it twelve pounds ten and that's my very last offer. I must be going mad – giving money away.'

Then he saw the teapot on the mantelpiece.

'Wait a minute, though,' he said. 'Let me have a look at that.'

He turned the boat-shaped pot over with an expert hand and read out loud:

'ANSTIC, HORTON AND ROSE, 1805. Never heard of them. It's just an old teapot worth a couple of bob, that's all.'

'I'm not selling that,' Mam said. 'It's a family heirloom.'

'It's my crazy day. Fifteen pounds for the lot with the teapot thrown in.'

'I'm very sorry. Just give me the twelve pounds ten. I'm not selling the teapot. It's been in the family too long.'

Ike had been in business long enough to know when it was pointless arguing. This was one of those times. He paid over the money and arranged for his van to collect the stuff the next day.

Mam worked it out that each one of Grandma's children would receive two pounds ten. But as it happened, Auntie Cissie had no need of the money. Two weeks after the funeral, her fate, her future and her fortune

162

were tragically transformed when Ernie, her husband, was knocked down and killed by a lorry reversing into him at work. The company admitted liability. The record compensation of £4,000 was, by any standard, immense. Billy's dad, who was earning £3 a week, worked it out at thirty years' wages.

Cissie bought a 'little gold-mine' of a shop which had the monopoly of supplying groceries to three blocks of nearby flats. She also bought a complete range of new furniture, including a Bluthner upright piano which no one knew how to play, and the whole family appeared dressed in the latest Kendal Milne outfits.

Unfortunately, just around the corner was the Golden Lion, and Cissie, along with her new-found friends, spent more time drinking in the pub than tending the shop. It wasn't long before the drinking sessions extended late into the night, with the result that the shop failed to open until around midday. The residents of the flats were not slow to weigh up the situation and began to help themselves to the free milk and bread which had been delivered to the doorstep of the shop.

'You see,' explained Mam to Billy one day as they were returning from a visit to Cissie's 'gold-mine'. 'Money doesn't always mean happiness.'

Back in Honeypot Street, it was all happening.

One night in February there was the usual silence as Dad listened to the news.

'Pope Pius XI is dead,' said the announcer. 'He died early this morning at his residence in the Vatican. The Pope was noted for his outspoken attack on the evils of Nazism.

'The Home Office,' continued the broadcaster, 'has announced plans today to provide free shelters to thousands of homes in the London districts most likely to be bombed. The steel-built shelters are made in sections and can be erected by two people without skill or experience.'

'Does that mean there's going to be a war, Tommy?' asked Mam.

'Most definitely. Never mind what that Chamberpot fella with the umberella says.'

'Glory be t'God! I hope you're wrong, Tommy. And all that stuff about shelters. Does that mean we're gonna get bombed?'

'Them poor buggers in London will. But not us. The bombers won't be able to get this far.'

To the Hopkins family, it certainly looked as if war was coming. Flo had given up sewing in the fur-coat factory to begin war work tending a conveyor belt at the Dunlop Rubber Company. Les, who had just left school, was working as a raincoat maker at Louis Epstein's on Cheetham Hill. Mainly military raincoats, he'd said.

'With you two working in rubber,' said Mam, 'it's no wonder this house is beginning to smell like a blooming factory. Why can't you get a decent, clean job like our Sam's?'

Sam was now sixteen and had been working as a lift attendant for over a year at Dobbin's, the new super store on Oldham Street. He was required to wear a page-boy's uniform complete with pill-box hat, and he certainly looked very smart.

The previous Saturday afternoon, the whole family – Mam, Dad, Les, Flo, Jim and Billy – had gone into town to listen to Sam at his work. They had crowded into his lift and had heard him call in a loud, confident voice:

'Mind the gates, please! Watch the gap!'

'Any chance of a lift, brother?' asked Jim.

They had more or less occupied the whole lift as it rode up and down the floors.

'Ground floor,' said Sam in his very poshest voice. ' 'Orticulture! 'Ardware! H'ironmongery!'

'Eeh, don't 'e sound posh?' said Mam. 'Like a real toff.'

'First floor,' Sam continued. ' 'Aberdashery! Perfumery! Lingerie.'

'You mean "corsets and suspender-belts",' said Billy.

'Here, where did you get to learn about such things?' asked Dad. 'You shouldn't know about things like that at your age.'

'Second floor. Men's wear. Shirts. Underwear.'

'You could do with a new pair o' long johns, Tommy,' said Mam.

'Oh, Mam, you're embarrassing us,' said Flo, red-faced.

'Don't you be so stuck-up,' Mam said. 'There's nowt wrong with sayin' long johns in a lift.'

'Top floor,' announced Sam. 'Beds, bunks and bassinets.'

'I allus knew he'd get to the top one day,' said Jim.

'Go on,' said Dad. 'Take us down to the bottom and we'll hear it all again.'

'It does my heart good to hear him,' said Mam. 'In charge of so many people. And he talks so nicely. No one would ever guess he comes from Collyhurst.'

The family rode up and down five times, encouraging Sam with their comments and their praise. On the sixth ride up, Dad turned to the gentleman who had managed to squeeze into the lift.

'This is my lad, y'know, what's doing all this announcing.'

'Oh, really,' said the gentleman. 'And I'm the manager of this store and I've been wondering when you are going to finish riding the lift and let some of our other customers use it!'

Shamefaced, the family left the store. It was already lighting-up time and so they wandered across Oldham Street towards Tib Street Market, which was a hive of activity on a Saturday night.

As they crossed the street, Dad said to Billy:

'Now that job that Sam has. That's a really good job, that is. Steady, secure and you don't have to dirty your hands. Sam gets twenty-five bob a week and he likes the job. Just riding up and down all day and announcing things.'

'It probably gets a bit boring, though,' said Jim. 'Just saying the same things over and over again. I know I wouldn't fancy it.'

'Just the same,' said Dad. 'He's bringing money in. And not wasting his time in one o' them colleges. Take a leaf out of his book.'

'That's right,' said Les, who didn't usually join in these intellectual discussions. 'Look at me. Only fourteen and already earning seventeen and a tanner just putting glue on raincoats with me finger.'

'If you like it,' said Jim, 'you just stick it out. But don't expect our Billy to give up his chance of education for seventeen and six a week. You'll probably end up with your finger sticking up in the air for good.'

They had reached Tib Street Market, a maze of narrow streets choked by stalls and hawkers' barrows, crowded with a happy-go-lucky throng of Saturday-night shoppers all pushing, jostling and shouting, intent on having a good time.

A simple-minded-looking youth in a grubby raincoat emerged from the crowd. 'Wanna buy a pup?' he asked, holding out a tiny, emaciated, shivering puppy. 'Only one and a tanner!'

There was no chance whatsoever of Dad ever buying a dog, especially one so disease-ridden as the one being offered. He had allowed a black cat, named Snowy, as a big concession, but beyond that he was not prepared to go.

They came to the first stall, lit by a bright, hissing naphtha flare, where a red-faced man with long flowing hair was extolling the virtues of his sulphurous ointment and his foul-looking medicine.

'This ointment and this medicine are the result of a secret recipe stolen by Buffalo Bill from the Apaches. The ointment will cure anything. Boils, pimples, ulcers, blisters, abscesses and carbuncles. It's so pure you can eat it! Just watch this!'

He took a great dollop of the glutinous yellow ointment in his hand and swallowed it, washing it down with a swig of the medicine.

'You said it will cure anything, but will it cure piles?' a lady asked.

'This will cure piles on your bum and piles on your carpet.'

'You mean haemorrhoids?' said a male by-stander, anxious to show off his knowledge of medical terms.

'This ointment will cure fibroids, haemorrhoids, rheumotoids, adenoids and asteroids. If you've got an "oid" this will fix you up!'

They moved on to the linoleum stall. How fascinated Billy was by the histrionic performance of the salesman as he emphasised each point by striking the lino with the flat of his hand.

'This lino has been laid in the kitchen of the Duke o' Devonshire. (SLAP) We've got these offcuts (SLAP) at a special price. I'm not asking a pound (SLAP), not even ten bob. (SLAP) Give me seven and six!'

On to the crockery stall, where the salesman performed impossible juggling acts with his Chinese porcelain.

'These eighteen-piece sets are five pounds in Kendals! I'm not greedy. I'm not asking even a pound. Not fifteen bob. Not ten bob! Who'll give me five bob? What, nobody? You bloody mean lot. Go on then, I'll give 'em away. Give me 'arf a crown! One for the lady over there, Bert!'

So, on to the home-made toffee.

'Only the best stuff goes into this treacle toffee. Try one. Go on, it's free.'

'A perfect night's entertainment,' said Jim. 'Who needs the wireless or the pictures when you've got this lot for free?'

At the corner of Swan Street, against all Mam's principles, Dad bought fish and chips for everyone, and they walked down Miller Street eating them straight from the paper.

'I wonder why fish and chips always taste better from newspaper,' said Flo.

'Not every newspaper,' said Dad. 'Only out o' working-class papers like the *Daily Mirror*. I wouldn't fancy eating them out o' the *Manchester Guardian*.'

They walked on for a little while, munching away happily. Then Jim dropped his bombshell.

'By the way,' he said nonchalantly, 'I've joined the Royal Navy. I report to HMS *Exmouth* training ship next week.'

'You've done what?' exclaimed Mam incredulously. 'What made you go and do a thing like that?'

'You daft bugger,' said Dad. 'If there's a war, you'll be right in the thick of it.'

'War or no war, I would have joined anyroad,' said Jim. 'I want to see something of the world.'

'It'll be the bloody next world, if there's a war,' said Dad.

'I want to go and visit all those places I've seen in the school atlas,' said Jim. 'Singapore, Hong Kong, Sydney, Cape Town.'

'What makes you want to go mixing with a lot of bloody foreigners? What's wrong with here?' said Dad.

'There's more to life than just working in a warehouse on Salford Docks and living in Cheetham Hill. There's a great big world out there and I want to see it.'

'How does that song go?' asked Mam. ' *"I joined the Navy to see the world./And what did I see? I saw the sea."* '

'It'll be the bloody bottom of the sea if Adolf Hitler has anything to do with it,' said Dad.

'I'm gonna miss you, our Jim,' said Billy. 'Who'll show me how to box now?'

'Don't worry, old son,' said Jim. 'I'll be back afore you know where you are. I'll get plenty of leave. And if I do get to see those far-away places, I'll bring you back some smashing presents, you'll see. And as for boxing, you don't need any more lessons now. You can stick up for yourself if you watch out for the head-butters and the dirty fighters.'

'I suppose so,' said Billy, not convinced and beginning to feel thoroughly miserable. After all, his brother, his friend, his mentor, and his hero was leaving. Somehow, his fish and chips had lost their flavour, and at the next litter bin, he dumped them.

The following day was the start of the Easter holiday. Billy went to spend a few days with Steve and Pauline, who lived in Prestwich in a small, comfortable semi-detached house – a wedding present from the Keenan family. Steve and Pauline now had two small sons, Oliver and Danny, who even at the tender ages of two and one, regarded Billy as the family comedian – the one who was always good for a laugh. The house, which was on an estate of new, red-bricked residences set in wide, clean avenues, had all the latest amenities, including lawns at front and back, a through lounge, a modern kitchen and, wonder of wonders, a bathroom with an inside lavatory!

On Saturday afternoon Billy found Steve digging a great hole in the back lawn.

'What's happening, Steve?' he asked. 'Why are you ruining your lovely lawn with that big hole?'

'This is to build an Anderson air-raid shelter,' replied Steve. 'In case there's a war.'

'But me dad says that even if there is a war, the German bombers will never reach us here.'

'Since when is your dad an expert in modern aerial warfare? Take it from me, Billy, if the war starts, the Germans have got the bombers all right.'

'Which ones could reach here?'

'There's the Dornier 217 for a start, and then there's the Heinkel 111. All part of Goering's Luftwaffe when it starts a Blitzkrieg.'

'What's that, Steve – a blitz-what-you-said?'

'It means a lightning war – a massive air attack to bring a quick victory.'

'Do you think there will be a war like that here, Steve?'

'I'm almost sure there'll be a war, but we'll be ready for them. Hitler won't just walk in here as he did in Czechoslovakia. At Avro's, we're working flat out every hour that God sends. Winston Churchill seems to think there's going to be a war. Neville Chamberlain is doing his level best to avoid one, but I don't think he'll succeed in the end.'

'I notice that everywhere I go men are building shelters and filling sand-bags,' said Billy.

'Better to be safe than sorry. There's no doubt the

whole country is getting geared up for a big fight. But never mind about war for a minute. What about you and your scholarship? I hope you're going to try for it – war or no war.'

'I'd like to, but I don't think me Dad wants me to go. He says it's a waste of time and I should get a job at fourteen like the others.'

'Take my tip. You have a go. It could change your whole life, believe me. Imagine yourself as a teacher, say. Taking the boys for cricket and football. Teaching them to understand things. Taking them out on school trips. Treating them like human beings – unlike some of the teachers we have in schools today. Apart from that, look at the long school holidays. Don't be daft, Billy. Go for the scholarship if you can.'

'You've convinced me, Steve! I like the idea of being a teacher. Especially after all that talk about holidays. But I've got to pass the scholarship first. I'm not even sure me dad's gonna let me sit for it.'

Pauline was trying to join the middle classes. She was most anxious to be accepted by her neighbours, and spent much of her time cleaning and polishing the steps, the brasswork, the windows, the paintwork, and even the brickwork, as well as trimming the hedges and mowing the front lawn. She had even taken to organising middle-class birthday parties for her children. At these shindigs, Billy was appointed as unpaid entertainer and funny-man.

On Oliver's second birthday, Billy prepared for his act in Pauline's bathroom. He put on the Nazi armband Mam had sewn up for him, then made up his Adolf face by combing his hair across his forehead and applying burnt cork to produce the effect of a small, square moustache; finally, using Pauline's lipstick, he painted small swastikas all over his face. He checked the final effect in the mirror, and, after satisfying himself that all was in order, strode downstairs to await his cue to begin his performance.

When the moment came, Billy marched into the lounge doing a goose-step, and with his right arm raised in the Nazi salute. Most of the kids at the party were too young to understand the full significance of the political satire and innuendo which was put before them, but that didn't matter. There was a howl of approval and much applause as Billy entered the room to begin his Adolf routine.

'*Achtung! Achtung! Mein namen ist Adolf Hitler! Vat ist mein namen?*' called Billy.

'Adolf Hitler!' all the kids yelled back.

'Gut. I am ze king of all ze vorld. Vat am I?'

'King of all ze vorld,' they shouted.

'I vant peace! Vat do I vant?'

'Peace! You vant peace!' they chorused.

'*Ja!* I vant peace. A piece of Poland! A piece of Czechoslovakia! A piece of Belgium! And a piece of . . .'

Grabbing Oliver and holding him up in the sky, he finished:

'And a piece of zis little boy!'

There were squeals of delight from all the kids.

'What are those funny things on your face?' called out Angus Greenhalgh, the precocious little four-year-old who lived next door.

'*Ja.* I am glad you ask about zese funny things on my face. Who knows vat is wrong mit me?'

All the kids shook their heads.

'*Kommen.* Someone must know vat these svastikas mean.'

No one knew.

Finally Billy delivered the punch line:

'Zese svastikas mean I am haffing ze German measles!'

The kids squealed their pleasure even though they didn't get it. It wasn't what he said; it was the way he said it. But the middle-class mothers who were there with their children seemed to like that one.

Finally the party was over and the guests all departed, leaving a chaotic aftermath. Pauline and Billy sat down, exhausted from all the effort expended in feeding and entertaining ten toddlers. There had been only one complaint, from Angus Greenhalgh, who had gone home weeping and wailing:

'I wanna Unca Billy like theirs! I wanna Unca Billy!'

Billy was still a pupil at St Chad's Elementary School, where little had changed – Mr Thomas saw to that. It was the same class of kids, the same ink-drippers, and the same impudent rascals like Stan White. But now, by simply getting older, they had been elevated to Standard 4 under the tutelage of Miss Susan Eager, a buxom young Irish teacher who went in and out in all the right places. The work – at least for some of the brighter ones – had moved on to a more difficult and challenging level.

Miss Eager was something of a slave-driver. One day she announced to the class:

'Some of you could go on to do great things if you worked hard. Think about taking the scholarship this May, because if you pass you could become doctors, dentists, solicitors, priests, and the very clever ones amongst you could even become teachers. But that requires very special ability. Those of you who wish to enter for the scholarship should take a form home today and bring it back completed and signed by your parent or guardian.'

In sums, her charges hacked their way through a jungle of long multiplication and division, of fractions both vulgar and improper, of decimals – 'I can't see any point in 'em,' said Henry Sykes – and finally of endless arithmetical problems about baths – something which not one boy in the class possessed – whose careless, stupid owners had left both taps running with the plug pulled out.

In English, they waded through the swamp of punctuation where crocodiles and alligators in the form of commas, apostrophes and semi-colons lurked in the undergrowth, ready to snap up the unwary. In spelling, they learned to tackle the imbecilic, illogical patterns of English words. Miss Eager made everyone learn her favourite rhyming verse:

> *I take it you already know*
> *Of tough and bough and cough and dough?*
> *Others may stumble, but not you*
> *On hiccough, thorough, laugh and through?*
>
> *Well done! And now you wish perhaps,*
> *To learn of less familiar traps?*
> *Beware of heard, a dreadful word*
> *That looks like beard and sounds like bird.*
>
> *And dead: it's said like bed, not bead –*
> *For goodness sake don't call it 'deed'!*
> *Watch out for meat and great and threat,*
> *They rhyme with suite and straight and debt.*
>
> *And cork and work and card and ward,*
> *And font and front and word and sword,*
> *And do and go and thwart and cart –*
> *Come, come, I've hardly made a start!*
>
> *A dreadful language? Man alive,*
> *I'd mastered it when I was five.*

Billy learned the finer points of writing compositions on any given subject, from 'What I did in my holidays' to 'My ambitions in life'.

'When you write compositions,' said Miss Eager, 'remember the interrogative pronouns that I told you about last month. Do you remember what they were?'

'Yes, miss,' answered Joey Flewitt. 'Please, miss, they are what, why, who, how, where and when.'

'Well done, Joey,' she said. 'They are what Rudyard Kipling called his six honest serving men. Now you must always use as many of these as you can in the very first sentence of your composition.'

'Please, miss,' said Joey. 'Can you give us an example?'

'No,' said Miss Eager. 'You can all make one up for me. Now!'

The class got their heads down, and for the next ten minutes there was no sound but the scratching of nibs on school exercise paper, and the sucking of pens. Finally, Miss Eager said:

'Right, that's enough. Let's hear what you've written. We'll begin with you, Henry Sykes.'

' "On Saturday afternoon, in our scullery, me dad kindly give me a tanner for cleaning his shoes." That tells you when, where, who, what, how and why, miss.'

'That's not bad, Henry. Next Campbell.'

' "At home last week, me dad hit me with his belt very hard because I said bugger off to my brother." Where, when, who, what, how and why, miss,' said Carrots Campbell proudly.

'I suppose you couldn't help bringing in a bit of swearing. But apart from that, it was correct. Next you, White,' said Miss Eager.

' "Last night at two o'clock in the morning, me mam crept into bed very quietly with uncle number three because she needed the money." '

'How many times have I told you not to bring tales about your mother into my classroom?' said Miss Eager. 'The English is correct but I want no more of those stories, do you understand?'

'Yes, miss. But they're all true, miss, and so I can't help it.'

'Very well. We'll let it go. Now let's hear yours, William.'

' "Many years ago, there lived in the village of Redbank two hunchbacked brothers, Kevin and Desmond, who were both woodcutters, but sadly, they were always down in the dumps because of their humps." That would be the beginning of a fairy tale, miss.'

'Excellent, William. I'm not altogether sure about the rhyming couplet, but full marks. Now I shall collect all the others in and mark them at home tonight. Since you have all worked so hard this morning, I shall read you a story.'

How Billy loved those stories she read to them – from books published by some coloured family called Blackie and Sons. Stories from Hans Andersen and the Grimm Brothers with opening sentences like: 'There was once a man who had five sons. One day, he called them together and said . . .'

But today, Miss Eager's story was from Greek legend.

' "Many many years ago, there was a great king called Dionysius who lived in great magnificence at Syracuse. One of his courtiers named Damocles tried to win his favour by flattery, telling him constantly how marvellous it must be to be king.

' "If that's what you think," said the monarch. "Come to my banquet and try sitting on the throne. See how you like it."

' "In the midst of the feast, the king told him to look

up at the ceiling. There Damocles saw, hanging above him by a single hair, a naked sword. Damocles was so terrified that he went on his knees and begged Dionysius to let him move to another place which did not involve such danger.

' "Now you see," said the king, "that I am under constant threat and my power hangs by a single thread." '

'That also warned Damocles not to be such a flatterer,' said Miss Eager. 'We use the expression "a sword of Damocles" whenever there's an ever-threatening danger.'

'Is it a bit like Britain today, miss,' asked Joey Flewitt, 'with war and all that hanging over us?'

'Exactly right,' said Susan Eager. 'The sword of Damocles is hanging over all of us at the present time.'

Religious instruction still loomed large in the school curriculum, mainly because teachers' efficiency and thus their security of tenure depended heavily on the successful outcome of an annual religious inspection. The rote-learning and memorisation of the Penny Catechism continued unabated, and Miss Eager employed every method she knew, from persuasion, bribery and pleading to unbridled use of the strap, in order to cram Catholic doctrine into her pupils' unwilling heads. What was more, the answers had become harder, deeper and perhaps more philosophical.

'Which are the four sins crying to heaven for vengeance?' she asked one day.

'Wilful murder,' said Stan White, thinking about his dad.

'Sin of Sodom,' said Joey Flewitt. 'Please, miss, what is the Sin of Sodom?'

'Never you mind,' said Miss Eager, blushing. 'What's the third, Campbell?'

'Oppression of the poor,' replied Campbell, whose family was on the means test.

'Defrauding labourers of their wages is the fourth,' said Henry Sykes, thinking about his Mam, who had refused to give him his spends last Saturday when he'd given her old buck.

'Next week,' announced Miss Eager, 'we shall be having our religious inspection, and a priest specially sent by the Bishop of Salford will be coming to test you. We shall have to go over the catechism many times. We will begin by revising the eight Beatitudes. Right, you, Henry Sykes, what's the third Beatitude?'

'Blessed are they that mourn; for they shall be comforted,' said Henry in a confident voice.

White farted. The whole class roared with laughter and approval. Miss Eager blew her top.

'White! Get out here, you filthy creature,' she screamed.

Thereupon six of the strap followed – all of which, as everyone knew, were totally ineffective on Stan's elephant-hide hands.

'Now, get back to your place, you disgusting animal, and keep quiet.'

'What is the fifth Beatitude?' she asked softly of the class.

'Blessed are the merciful,' answered Billy; 'for they shall obtain mercy.'

'Very good, William,' she said. 'And the Eighth – anybody?'

'Blessed are they that suffer persecution,' said Stan White; 'for theirs is the kingdom of heaven.'

On the day of the religious inspection, Miss Eager was on edge. As she said the early-morning prayers, she appeared unnaturally cheerful and she smiled too much.

'I shall want Flewitt, Hopkins and Sykes at the front and White, Campbell and Shacklady at the back,' she said. 'And woe betide anyone who lets me down or gives daft answers!'

'Why do we have to be at the back, miss?' asked White.

'In the hope the religious examiner won't notice you, that's why.'

A few minutes later, Mr Thomas entered the room with the religious inspector – a tall, fresh-faced young man who exuded enthusiasm from every pore.

'Let me introduce Father Mulhearn,' said Mr Thomas, addressing Miss Eager. 'Father is one of our more, shall we say, progressive thinkers with very modern, up-to-the-minute ideas on methods of inspection.'

'How do you do, Father,' said Miss Eager, all coy and simpering.

'Pleased to make your acquaintance,' said the great man, offering a limp hand.

The class waited in trepidation for the stranger to make the first move. Miss Eager sat at the side of the room with that peculiar, fixed smile frozen on her face. The priest's first words struck everyone – including the teacher – rigid.

'Let us imagine,' he began, 'that we are going to have a football match against the devil. Who shall we have on the devil's team and what position will they play?'

There was a long silence as the class tried to take this in. There was nothing in the catechism about the devil and his angels being allowed to play soccer. The smile on Miss Eager's face had changed and her expression was beginning to resemble that of Our Lady of Dolours.

Carrots Campbell was the first to respond.

'Lucifer in goal.'

'Mussolini and Hitler on the wings,' shouted Shacklady.

'Good. Good,' replied the priest.

'Dracula and Frankenstein in defence,' called Henry, joining in the spirit of the team selection.

Miss Eager sat frigidly at the side with a look that reminded the class of the Agony in the Garden.

'We need half-backs,' said the oddball cleric.

'How about Herod, Pontius Pilate and Boris Karloff?' suggested Billy, getting into the swing of things.

'Now the Evil Ones just need a good centre-forward,' said Father Mulhearn.

'I've got it,' shouted Stan White. 'Me dad. He'll play a blinder for the devil.'

'Right,' said the priest. 'That's the opposition. Now who are we going to have on our side? God's side. First who shall we put in goal?'

'Christ,' said Joey Duckett. ' 'Cos he's a Saviour.'

'Nah,' said Billy. 'Let's have one o' the apostles, 'cos as fishermen they'd be better in the nets.'

'Angels Gabriel and Michael on the wings,' said Henry.

'Holy Ghost as centre-forward,' said Campbell. 'He'd be much too tricky for 'em. Besides, they wouldn't see him 'cos he's invisible.'

'St Peter in charge of defence, as he'd thump anyone who tried to get past him,' said Shacklady.

'St Jude for lost causes and St Veronica as she'd wipe the floor with 'em,' threw out Billy, feeling that this football-team idea was ridiculous.

Miss Eager had gone into some kind of trance.

'Joan of Arc with St Peter in defence, and finally the Little Flower of Jesus as inside-right,' suggested Henry.

'Why the Little Flower?' asked the Father.

'Dunno,' said Henry. 'But I've allus fancied the Little Flower.'

By this time, the inspector was beginning to feel that his progressive approach had gone far enough.

'Very well,' he said. 'Enough of all that. Now let's see if you know your catechism. What are the twelve Fruits of the Holy Ghost? And don't say apples, bananas, oranges and so on.'

The class laughed politely. Miss Eager seemed to be coming back to the land of the living and looked encouragingly towards Billy and Joey Flewitt.

'Charity, Joy, Peace and Patience,' recited Joey.

Miss Eager nodded enthusiastically – now smiling brightly.

'Benignity, Goodness, Longanimity and Mildness,' said Billy.

Miss Eager positively beamed.

'Faith and Modesty,' added Henry.

Miss Eager smiled broadly, but then looked worried, for Stan White had put his hand up.

'Yes. Finish them off,' said the priest heartily, pointing to Stan.

'Please, Father. Incontinence and Ignominy.'

'That'll do for today,' said the visitor abruptly. 'Thank you so much, Miss Eager, for letting me take your class.'

After the inspection, Miss Eager said:

'White, see me after school! Flewitt and Hopkins come out here. For answering so well, a bag of toffees each and I hope you'll share them with your friends.'

She hugged the two boys to her shapely breasts – one each. Billy wasn't sure whether he liked it or not. Perhaps it was because he was having to share with Joey Flewitt.

A week later, Miss Eager spoke to the class:

'Only two boys are entering for the scholarship this year. That is not very good. What happened to you, Flewitt?'

'Please, miss, me mam and dad want me to leave school

181

at fourteen and help me dad on his second-hand stall on Bradford Road Market.'

'What a waste of a good brain! At the last test you were second in class, only one or two marks behind William. You could easily pass.'

'Me dad says there's good money in buying and selling second-hand things.'

'Very well,' she said. 'If that's what your dad thinks. Then we're left with just William and Henry, both from Honeypot Street.'

Little did Miss Eager suspect the planning, plotting and conniving which had gone into Billy's application form. At the weekend his dad had set his face completely against the idea.

'Shall we let our Billy take the scholarship, Tommy?' Mam had asked.

'Not bloody likely, Kate,' he'd said. 'He can bloody well leave at fourteen like the rest of 'em and start getting a good trade in his hands.'

'Look, all the others could have gone to college but for you, Tommy. You've been too fond of the bevvy. Our Billy's our youngest. Why don't we give the last kid a special chance?'

'I don't want no kid o' mine getting above himself. Getting too big for his boots. Our sort have got to stick together, 'cos we allus get the rough end o' the stick.'

'But one day he might become a doctor or a teacher – even a priest.'

'Then he'll start talking and acting posh. Giving himself airs and graces, being lah-de-dah and all that. Then he won't be one of us no more. He'll be a toff.'

'And what's wrong with that? You'll be proud of him, specially if he starts bringing in a bit o' money when you're old and grey.'

'If he becomes a toff he won't want to know us. Anyroad, he's not going to no college, and that's the end of it.'

But that Monday morning, Mam had come to Billy and said:

'I've been talking to 'er-next-door, and their Henry's going in for it, so I don't see why you shouldn't and all. So here's your form – Steve and Polly helped me to fill it in – all signed, sealed and delivered. You go and do your scholarship and never mind your dad. I'll see to him when the time comes, but it's best you say nowt to him for the time being. It'll be our little secret.'

'Who says I'll pass anyroad?' said Billy.

Once Susan Eager knew that Billy and Henry were entering the lists, she piled on the pressure. Both boys were kept back after school for extra coaching, and as if that weren't enough, she gave them masses of homework in sums, in punctuation, in composition, in problem-solving, in dealing with trick questions.

'Noses to the grindstone,' she insisted. 'Study Chapters One and Two of Fowler's *The King's English*, do all the sums on pages sixty and sixty-one in the London Arithmetic, and write a composition on "Keeping a Pet". I shall want them all by Monday morning.'

'But that means we can't go out to play, miss,' said Henry.

'Forget play,' she said. 'The honour of St Chad's is at stake.'

'But all work and no play makes Jack a dull boy,' said Billy.

'And an empty sack cannot stand up,' she said. 'And the devil finds work for idle hands. So get on with it.'

Billy began working and studying so hard that Dad

began to suspect something was going on.

'That lad's brain's going to explode one day,' he remarked. 'Doesn't he know that you never learn nowt from books?'

'Come on, our Billy,' said Mam. 'Stick at it. I'll see you get some more fish for your dinner tomorrer.'

Came the morning of the scholarship.

'Do your best writing, son,' said Mam. 'Wear these rosary beads round your neck and don't forget to use your blotting paper or you'll have smudges.'

Armed with a new ruler, a pencil, a sharpener, a new Waterman's fountain-pen – a present from Flo – a small bottle of ink and a large piece of blotting-paper, Billy met Henry and together they took the 62 bus to Heath Street Municipal School. Both lads were highly nervous and uncomfortable in their single desks in the strange surroundings – especially since there were no familiar faces, no holy pictures, no crucifixes and no statues.

The teacher came round with the test papers and soon they were so busy adding, subtracting, multiplying and dividing that they forgot where they were. The second paper was Problems, and they quickly became engrossed in calculating areas for wallpapering, volumes for bath-filling and finances for housekeeping. The afternoon was taken up with punctuation, spelling, grammar and finally writing a composition on the proverb 'All that glisters is not gold'. Billy had read a poem about a cat that fell into a tub of goldfish. He thought he would write about that. He remembered what Miss Eager had said about the tragedy of the cat being a lesson to everybody not to be taken in by false riches. He had a bright idea. He recalled what Mam had said about Auntie Cissie – 'Money doesn't allus mean happiness.' He began writing:

OUR KID

A few years ago, in the town of Salford, there lived
an old man and his wife but they were very unhappy
because they were always short of money. One day,
the old woman found a mangy stray cat and so she
took it home, fed it and looked after it. The next day,
she found that the kitten was really a fairy princess
who was so grateful for all the care the old woman
had given her, she granted her one wish.

'Please give me some more money so that we can
be more comfortable,' the old woman pleaded.

'Your wish is granted,' said the fairy.

The next day, her husband – the old man – was
knocked down and killed whilst on his way to work
and the old woman received thousands of pounds in
compensation. She now had so much money she
didn't know what to do with it. So she got drunk
every night in the pub with all her friends. But even
though she had so much money, she was very miserable and so she learnt the lesson: 'All that glisters is
not gold.' The End.

Henry and Billy went home with their heads spinning
after a full day of writing non-stop. But the big challenge
came the following day with the intelligence tests. At top
speed, the two boys tackled question after question on
opposites, analogies, sentence completion, deciphering
codes and reasoning.

It was dinner-time when the tests finished and they
returned to St Chad's, where Miss Eager conducted a
thorough post-mortem and inquisition.

'What did you put for this, and what did you put for
that?' she snapped. 'That sounds right! And that sounds
right! I do believe the both of you may have passed!'

That night the boys got back to Honeypot Street with

their brains in a whirl. There was only one cure! They went to the Rivoli to see Walt Disney's *Snow White and the Seven Dwarfs*. As they licked their giant cornet ice-creams, they both thanked God it was all over.

But was it?

A month later, both boys were invited to attend with their parents for interview at Damian College, Regina Park. Mrs Sykes and Billy's mam accompanied them on the bus ride across Manchester.

'You can only do your best,' said Mam to the two lads.

Before going into the interview, the youngsters were taken into a small examination room, where a brother in clerical cassock gave them a piece of paper and told them they had fifteen minutes to study the question and then write a short paragraph on the subject given.

'Bring your effort into the interview with you,' said the brother.

'Perhaps me dad was right,' said Billy to Henry. 'It's not worth all this trouble to get into this snooty school.'

He looked at the test paper which said: '*Write on what you understand by the sentence "Uneasy lies the head which wears the crown."*'

For fifteen minutes they wrote furiously.

Henry was called in first. Ten minutes later he emerged and gave Billy a big wink.

'Nowt to it.'

Billy was next. Heart thumping, he went into the office, where the head – a tall, white-haired brother, was seated at a desk with a lady and another cleric.

'Now, William,' boomed the head. 'Tell us something about yourself. How old are you?'

'I'll be eleven on the eighth of July, sir.'

'Good. And why do you want to come to this school?'

'Me friend David Priestley comes here, sir, and 'e says it's very good, sir.'

'Priestley? Priestley? Ah, yes. In Upper Four. A clever young chap. Nice to know he recommends us, eh! And tell me, William, what do you want to be when you grow up? Apart from being an adult, that is.'

'A writer, a teacher or a priest, sir.'

This appeared to be the right answer, for they smiled and nodded approvingly.

'Good. Very good,' said the white-haired head. 'Now we should like you to read us your effort on the subject we set you: "Uneasy lies the head that wears the crown." '

'Yes, sir,' said Billy, and he began to read his composition.

' "There was once a man called Dionysius who was made King o' Syracuse. The royal hatter measured him for a crown and said, "Six and seven-eighths, sire, is your hat size," and he made him a crown that was a perfick fit. As Dionysius sat on his throne, his subjects flattered him. "O great King, you are the greatest ruler of the world," they all said. The king became so swelled-headed that the crown began to hurt his head. The hatter came back to inspect and he said, "Your hat size 'as gone up to eight and a half, sire." And no one could get the crown off his head. He had to go to bed that night still wearing the crown. All his subjects said to each other when they retired, "Poor man! I wouldn't fancy being king tonight. Uneasy lies the head that wears the crown." '

'Don't be a teacher or a priest,' said the white-haired man in a fit of laughter. 'Be a writer! Tell your parents we'll let them know the results in July. Now good morning, William. Size eight and a half, eh? That's a good one.'

Chapter Nine

Red-Letter Day

On Saturday 8 July 1939, the day was bright and sunny and Billy had been up since the crack of dawn, as this was to be a big day – a proverbial red-letter day. Not only was it his eleventh birthday, but it was also the day of Capper's annual pub outing to Blackpool. What was more, the icing on the cake was that Mr and Mrs Sykes, along with Henry, had agreed to make up a little Honeypot Street party on the trip to the coast.

At eight o'clock the two families, wearing their specially bought summer outfits, met outside the pub along with the other day-trippers to await the arrival of the 'chara'. Suddenly from around the corner it came, a motorised magic carpet that was to transport them to the wonderland of Blackpool.

'It's here! It's here!' shouted the two boys, hardly able to contain themselves.

'Look at the size of it, Henery! It's massive!'

The golden Fingland coach pulled up outside the pub and the Queen's Arms regulars, along with a motley collection of relatives who had been kept hidden in various cupboards for most of the year, boarded the single-decker bus – all laughing and chattering in holiday mood. John

Capper, the landlord, ever anxious to slake the thirst of his patrons, loaded on his gift of three crates of ale and countless bottles of stout. Finally the white-coated driver in his peaked hat climbed aboard, turned the ignition key, and the great diesel engine roared into life.

Along Chapel Street they sped, leaving the murky factories and the grey streets of Salford behind. Billy sat with Henry, who had 'bagsed' the window seat. Behind them sat Mrs Sykes and Mam, whilst Mr Sykes and Billy's dad were in front.

As the coach ate up the miles, Henry and Billy were mesmerised by the ever-changing scenery, and places with foreign, strange-sounding names like Irlams o' Th'Height, Blackrod and Whittle-le-Woods. The two mothers behind them, however, were less interested in the ever-receding parade of houses, shops, pubs, fields and cows, and more concerned with matters medical. What Dad referred to as an organ recital.

'How have you been lately, Jessie?' Mam asked.

'Oh, not so bad, Kate. I've been under the doctor for the last three month. And he's told me if I don't pull meself together, I'll never get on top of it.'

'Why, what's been the trouble?'

'Me legs again. It's with having kids.'

'Ooh, I am sorry to hear about that. What's been wrong with your legs?'

'First,' she said, 'I had inflation of the veins which turned into bellicose ulcers. But, thanks be t'God, they're non-malicious.'

'Phlebitis?'

'Oh no, there's no fleas in our house. I've scrubbed it from top to bottom, I have. You could eat off my floor.'

'I weren't implying anything, Jessie. Not for a minute.

But you've been having a lot o' trouble with Harry there, and all, haven't you?'

'Oh, aye. He were in hospital for a bit. He was having terrible abominable pains. And they had to give him all sorts o' tests. They fed him one o' them there barium meals.'

'They're funniosities, these men. I'll bet if you'd given him that for his tea at home, he wouldn't have touched it.'

Billy caught these snippets of clinical conversation, but as most of them were lost on him, he turned his attention to the two dads sitting in front.

'I never thought Portsmouth would beat Wolves in the FA Cup, Tommy,' said Harry Sykes.

'They more than beat 'em, Harry,' said Dad. 'Four–one was more like a massacre, eh?'

'Aye, I reckon you're right there, Tommy. Talkin' of massacres, who do you fancy for the big fight on Monday?'

'I think it'll go to Len Harvey, Harry. He's got a better punch than Jock McAvoy. Len's one of our lads, y'know. Manchester born and bred.'

'Well, would you believe it?'

There was a temporary pause as the two men studied the fleeting Lancashire countryside. Then Dad said:

'That was a terrible thing what happened the other day to them sailors trapped in that submarine in Liverpool Bay, eh, Harry?'

'The *Thetis*? Terrible, Tommy. There was nowt anyone could do to get 'em out in time.'

'Poor buggers! They tapped messages in Morse code on the sides. Only eight got out alive. But seventy-one dead!'

'Horrible, Tommy. Just horrible! But you know there'll be a lot more than that killed if there's another war.'

'War! I tell you, Harry, I'm more worried about the

bloody IRA at the moment. Bombs in London and bombs in bloody letter boxes. It's not safe to post a bloody letter no more. Thank God they caught five o' the buggers last week.'

'Aye. They gave each of 'em twenty years in Strangeways for their trouble.'

'Twenty years! I'd have hanged the bastards if I'd had my way. Bombing us when we're facing those two bloody dictators in Germany and Italy.'

'You think there's gonna be a war then?'

'I don't think, Harry. I'm bloody sure. The signs are all round us. We've doubled the Territorial Army, we're digging shelters everywhere, we're turning out hundreds of planes every month, and we've even got plans for evacuating all the kids. There'll be a war all right, make no mistake.'

'But the new Pope, Pius XII, has called for all the leaders to meet him at the Vatican.'

'He might as well save his breath, Harry. Eh, did you see that they've banned throwing darts in Glasgow pubs. Too dangerous, they said. Either the Scotch gets are too pissed to see straight or they're throwing 'em at one another.'

'The best way to beat these German bastards,' said Harry Sykes, 'is to send in the Black Watch with a set o' darts each. And watch the Jerries run.'

'Or better still – send in the Beefeaters.'

Dad looked out of the window.

'There it is, everybody,' he called. 'The Tower! Over there on the horizon!'

Everyone turned their eyes to the distant view of Blackpool's famous landmark.

'Eh, do you know what that reminds me of, Kate?' called Dad.

'Never you mind what it reminds you of,' replied Mam. 'Keep that sort of thing to yourself.'

'I was goin' to say a salt cellar or a vinegar bottle in a chip shop,' said Dad. 'There's nowt wrong with that.'

'Aye, I know you too well,' replied Mam.

The Tower was the cue for the communal singing to start.

'*Oh, I do like to be beside the seaside,*' they all sang. '*Oh, I do like to be beside the sea.*'

Twenty minutes later the bus pulled into Bloomfield Road parking lot behind the football ground.

'This is it, folks – Blackpool!' announced the driver. 'And it's turned out proper nice for you. But I'd like y'all back here by seven o'clock as the traffic will be heavy on the way back. Now off you go and I hope y'all have a reet champion day.'

The laughing, carefree passengers disembarked and went their separate ways. The little Honeypot Street party strolled blissfully down Lytham Road, heading – as if guided by some primeval instinct – for the sea.

'Eh, Henery, just look at the tower now,' said Billy. 'Not so long ago it was just a tiny thing in the distance. Now it looks like something built from a giant's Meccano set.'

By the Manchester Hotel they turned the corner, and there it was! The sea, and miles and miles of Blackpool's legendary golden beaches.

'First thing we do,' said Mr Sykes, 'is get these two lads buckets and spades.'

They crossed the road and over the track, and nearly jumped out of their skins when a passing tram suddenly gave a loud, piercing shriek. They reached the promenade safely and Billy's mam said:

'Right, you two lads, stand there, breathe out and get rid of all that Manchester muck from your lungs. Now get snuffing up this good seaside air. That's what we've brought you for. Go on, snuff up!'

Billy and Henry stood there holding on with both hands to the promenade rail and taking deep breaths. When Mam judged that they had completed the lung-clearing exercise, then and only then did the party go down on to the sands.

'Last in the sea is daft,' called Dad, now in boyish mood as he took off his boots, peeled off his socks and rolled up his trouser legs. There was a mad, childish scramble not to be last, and five minutes later the six of them were paddling in the Irish Sea.

'That sun's very hot,' said Mam. 'You men had better cover up your heads or you'll get burnt. Especially you, Tommy.'

The four malcs tied knotted handkerchiefs around their heads, and the picture and their joy were complete.

'Doesn't the sand feel lovely under your feet – so soft and soothing, like,' said Mrs Sykes.

'And this salt water'll do your bunions a power o' good,' said Mam.

They returned to the spot where they had left their shoes and clothes. Whilst the adults just lay back, snoozed and generally enjoyed relaxing and doing nothing, Billy and Henry got down to the serious business of building a medieval citadel in sand.

After about half an hour Dad said:

'I wouldn't mind wetting me whistle over there in the Manchester.'

'Trust you to be thinking of booze,' said Mam.

'I think it's the best idea I've heard all day,' said Mr Sykes.

'Go on then,' said Mrs Sykes. 'After all, Kate, we are on holiday.'

'Right then, you two lads,' said Mr Sykes. 'Here's a coupla bob. Get yourself some ice-cream and we'll be back in two shakes.'

After their parents had gone, Billy bought two giant cones from Pablo's van and Henry and he settled down to licking them into extinction. Like two consultant engineers, they continued constructing a castle complete with bailey, barbican, keep, gatehouse and, most important of all, elaborate moat.

As they added more details, a shifty-looking middle-aged man approached them.

'That's a great castle you've built there, lads. It's got everything. If you're interested in castles, there's one on exhibition in the Tower. Have you seen it?'

'No, we haven't,' said Henry.

'Come on then,' the man said. 'I'll take you to look at it.'

'But our mams and dads will be back in a minute – they've just gone for a drink over there,' said Billy.

'Oh, you'll not be gone long,' said the stranger. 'We'll be back in no time. I've got my car parked up there.'

'I don't think so,' said Billy. 'Besides, that's me dad just coming across the sands.'

The man darted a quick look in the direction Billy had indicated and hurried off.

'Who was that man?' Dad asked when he got near.

'Some bloke who wanted to take us in his car and show us a castle in the Tower.'

'Listen,' Dad said. 'Never, never talk to strangers. Now let that be a warning to you. There's some right funny people in this world. Anyroad, the tide's almost in and it's dinner-time. What do you say to fish and chips in Woolworth's café.'

'Smashing, Dad,' said Billy. 'But first we want to see the tide go over our castle.'

The two boys watched their artistic handiwork, their city in sand, slowly but surely being enveloped and destroyed by the incoming tide.

'I can understand how old King Canute felt,' said Henry.

After a magnificent repast of fish, chips, bread and butter and a pot of tea, served up as only Blackpool could, the little group decided to spend the afternoon strolling along the Golden Mile.

'Have you seen the sign over that café?' asked Billy. 'It says "Jugs of tea for the sands". Seems like a waste of tea pouring it into the sand like that.'

'Stop talking daft, our Billy,' said Mam.

At a stall on the front, Mr Sykes bought hats for everyone – pirate hats for the boys, cowboy hats for the men and 'Kiss-me-Quick' sailor hats for the ladies. Dad bought a dozen sticks of rock and a bright-red carrier bag to take them home in.

'Isn't it marvellous how they get the name to go right through the rock?' said Mam. 'How do they do it, Tommy?'

'It's very complicated, Kate. You wouldn't understand it.'

'Oh, aye,' she said.

The first stop on the Mile was to have their photos taken for the family albums at the cut-outs of fat women with big bosoms.

'If you two go to Damian, I only hope the head doesn't see them photos,' said Mrs Sykes. 'Or he'll throw you out on the first day.'

The next stall was Gypsy Rose Lee, the fortune-teller.

'Go on, it's only a bit o' fun,' said Mam. 'Let's have a go.'

Mr Sykes went in first. After five minutes he came out,

shaking his head and chuckling to himself.

'Hey up, Jessie,' he said. 'You'd better watch out. She says I'm going to get married again, to a younger woman.'

'Over my dead body,' replied Mrs Sykes. 'Anyroad, who'd have you? You're just a rag-and-bone man.'

Mam and Dad went in together, and when they emerged she said:

'Good news for me, anyroad. I'm goin' to live to ninety-two, God help me!'

'A lot o' bloody rubbish,' said Dad. 'She said we're going to flit in the next two years. We've no intention of moving from Honeypot Street.'

Mrs Sykes reported next:

'She says me health is going to get better and I'll get over me asthma. But when I asked how long I was going to live, she said she didn't give predictions like that. Waste of half a crown, if y'ask me.'

'It's only a giggle,' said Mam. 'Let the two lads have a turn. Here's half a crown, our Billy, ask her to do the two for half-price.'

The two boys went into the dimly lit tent and could just make out the figure of the old gypsy in the gloom.

'Cross me palm with silver,' she said.

'Can you do the two of us for half a crown?' asked Billy. 'We're only young.'

'Very well. You pay half the price and I give you half of your future. You,' she said, pointing to Henry, 'will lead an exciting life in the next two years, but after that I see only clouds.'

'P'raps you're goin' to join the RAF and be a pilot, Henry,' said Billy.

'Or work in the CWS Tobacco Factory,' replied Henry.

'What about me, Gypsy Rose Lee?' asked Billy.

'You're a poet and don't know it,' said Henry.

'For you, I see a strange life,' said the gypsy. 'Many children and you live in Africa. That is all you get for half a crown.'

When they came out of the tent, Billy said:

'Daylight robbery! She says I'm going to have a lot o' kids and be a missioner in Africa. The Pope would never allow it, 'cos missioners can't get married.'

At the next stall, there was a man labelled 'The Memory Man' who could remember the past and tell the future for the price of a tanner a question. He offered a prize of a shilling if he couldn't answer.

Mr Sykes paid over his sixpence and asked:

'Who won the FA Cup in 1909?'

'Too easy,' answered the blindfolded oracle. 'Manchester United beat Bristol City one goal to nil.'

'What was the name of the woman who tried to stop the King's horse in the 1913 Derby?' asked Dad.

'The woman's name was Miss Emily Davison, aged forty, and she died four days after; the King's horse was named Anmer.'

'Bloody amazing,' said Dad. 'Go on then, for another tanner: will there be a war?'

'The war will start this year and it will last five years.'

'Righto,' said Billy's mam. 'I may as well have a tanner's worth. When will the world end?'

'The world will come to an end on the seventh of August 1945 in the biggest fireball the world has ever seen.'

'You're wrong there, for a start,' said Kate. ' 'Cos Gypsy Rose Lee has just told me I'm goin' to live till I'm ninety-two! So there! I want the shilling prize money.'

'You'll have to come back on the eighth of August 1945 for that,' said the voice.

'Bloody twister!' said Mam.

They spent the rest of the afternoon exploring all the different stalls and listening to the various spiels, each one extolling the virtues of the product in question and claiming it as the greatest discovery of the twentieth century. Tommy and Harry Sykes, however, seemed to get caught up at the newsagent's shop, which displayed hundreds of saucy postcards.

'Hey up, Tommy. Have you seen this one? She's saying, "You Union Men are all the same – sticking out until you get what you want!" '

'There's one here where the wife is saying to her husband, "Fancy being jealous of the milkman – he's in and out in five minutes!" '

'Are you two going to spend all day reading dirty postcards or what?' asked Mam.

'Right, Kate,' said Dad. 'I think we just about read 'em all now. All hundred of 'em. What we doing next?'

'Me and Jessie thought we might have a tram ride up to Cleveleys and have a look round up there and a bit o' tea whilst we're there.'

The rest of the visit was spent at Cleveleys. At six o'clock they took the tram back to Blackpool for the coach home. Too soon, their day trip had come to an end.

On the journey back, the weary holiday-makers were strangely quiet and subdued after such an exhausting, fun-filled day. The only sound to be heard was the gentle snoring of a few passengers who had dozed off, and the comforting throb of the coach engine. At Adlington, the chara made a last stop at an old coaching inn to allow passengers to empty and re-fill their bladders and to exchange stories of the day's events. Dad came out of the pub after five minutes.

'Here y'are lads, a bottle o' lemonade each and a packet

o' Smith's Crisps. Mind you don't eat the blue paper inside – that's the salt!'

When they set off again, the short stop seemed to have galvanised the passengers into action and given them a new lease of life, for they began a fresh round of community singing – working their way through their repertoire of 'The Man Who Broke the Bank at Monte Carlo', 'Cleaning Windows' and 'Leaning on a Lamppost', and finishing most appropriately with 'My Little Stick of Blackpool Rock'. The hat was passed round for the driver, and as Mr Sykes handed him his money, the trippers gave him a chorus of 'For He's a Jolly Good Fellow'. An hour later, the bus came to a halt outside the Queen's Arms.

'Harry and me'll just go in Capper's and have one for the road,' said Dad.

'Which road?' asked Mam. 'You've just finished with the road. It's the road to hell you're drinking for, if you ask me.'

'Don't spoil a nice day, Kate. We'll be home in 'alf an hour.'

Billy's red-letter day had almost come to an end. But not quite.

When they got back into the house, there, leaning up against the tea-caddy on the mantelpiece, was an official-looking letter. Mam didn't like receiving typewritten letters, and it was with a worried frown that she sat down in her rocking chair to read it. She hadn't got very far when she burst into tears.

'It's about Damian College,' she said.

'I've failed me scholarship,' Billy said. 'I just knew it.'

'But you haven't,' she said. 'That's just it. You start at the college on Monday the fourth of September!'

'Oh Mam,' exclaimed Billy. 'I can't believe it. Me at

199

Damian College! But what will Dad say when he finds out? He won't like it.'

'You leave your father to me,' said Mam. 'I know how to keep him quiet.'

'I must run and tell Henery!' said Billy. 'It's only half past nine; they'll still be up.'

'Henery, I've passed! I've passed!' he called excitedly when Henry opened his front door. 'What about you?'

But one look at Henry's face gave him his answer. A bit like Miss Eager's when Stan White had answered in religious inspection.

'I didn't make it, Billy,' he said simply. 'We've had a letter and all. So it's St Chad's for me and Damian for you.'

'It's all right, Henery. Just 'cos we go to different schools doesn't mean we can't still knock around together.'

'Dead right,' Henry replied.

But somehow they didn't believe each other.

Chapter Ten

Back To St Chad's

Day after day in that summer of 1939, the news bulletins talked about 'dark clouds gathering over Europe', but for Billy, in Manchester, there was nothing but blue skies and glorious sunshine. It was warm that August and there was a great chorus of birdsong from the rooftops – even in Honeypot Street. In this idyllic atmosphere, there was only one dark spot on his horizon, and that was the fact that Henry would not be accompanying him to his new school.

'Y'know, Henery, you must've just missed passing by a few lousy marks. I'm really sorry, I am, 'cos we could've travelled to school together every day. Now I'll have to go on me own and I won't know nobody there.'

'I know, Billy. And I only wish I'd passed. But I'm not bothered no more 'cos me dad says I can join him in the family business. There's a lot of money in the rag-and-bone trade.'

Throughout that month, Henry and Billy played together in Honeypot Street. Besides the usual games of kick-can, alleys, garfs, yo-yos and spinning tops, they had found a new challenge. Henry's dad had presented them with a large bike – the sit-up-and-beg type – commonly called a bone-shaker. Neither of them could reach the pedals from the saddle, but they had devised a way of riding side-saddle by placing the left foot on the pedal at the same time as sticking the right leg through the triangular gap under the crossbar. They had both become very skilled at propelling the bike by pressing the right foot forward and then back-pedalling with the left; so skilled, in fact, that they were able to attain a high speed up and down the street.

On her way back from Ormeroyd's corner shop one day, Mam had called out:

'That's very dangerous riding that bike side-saddle like that. If you break your legs, don't come running to me moaning about it.'

Their favourite activity, however, was sailing their model yachts on Queen's Park lake. This meant a whole day's outing, with lots of banana sandwiches, a large bottle of sarsaparilla and threepence for an ice-cream.

To get there they had to tramp across Barney's – stopping, of course, to chew the rag with Mad Jack, who was still in residence in his ramshackle oil-drum cabin. Then along Queen's Road to Hendham Vale.

'What a beautiful name!' remarked Billy to Henry.

From there it was but a short walk to Queen's Park. The scene which met them at the lake resembled a miniature Henley regatta, with throngs of noisy, excited youngsters all intent on launching and sailing a wide variety of models ranging from motorboats, catamarans, and steamers to square-riggers and three-masters.

Hurriedly removing stockings and plimsolls, which they hung around their necks for safe-keeping, Billy and Henry paddled through the cool, clear water pulling their yachts behind them like Gulliver hauling in the Lilliputian navies.

'If only it could be like this for the rest of our lives!' sighed Billy.

'This must be what paradise is like!' added Henry.

But such happiness could not last forever. It was on one of these joyous days that the letter arrived. Billy returned from Queen's Park lake to be confronted by his dad waving a piece of paper at him.

'We've had a letter from that there college of yours,' Dad shouted, almost triumphantly. 'It's all off!'

Billy's heart skipped a beat.

'How d'you mean, all off?'

'See for yourself,' said Dad, handing him the letter. With trembling hand, Billy took it and began to read:

Dear Parent or Guardian,

I write to you as parent of one of our new boys due to begin studies here on Monday 4 September. You will appreciate that, in order to maintain the high standards of the school, we expect our pupils to dress appropriately and to be furnished with all necessary equipment in order to be able to take full advantage of the facilities offered by the school. Overleaf you will find a list of essential requirements which we expect our boys to possess on the first day of term, together with the name and address of the school outfitters.

Yours most sincerely,
Adam McGrath, OD.
Headmaster

Frantically, Billy turned over the page to examine the school's requirements. When he saw the length of the list, he was filled with dismay. No wonder Dad had said it was all off – the list was formidable. It included a full school uniform, plus sports equipment – a complete football outfit, cricket gear, gym clothes. The inventory seemed endless. Further, the school outfitter was located in King Street, Manchester, notoriously the most expensive part of town. When he had finished reading, Billy knew it was hopeless.

'How much would it all cost?' he asked in despair.

'How much? How much?' Dad echoed. 'I'll tell you how much. About twenty-five quid! That's how much! If we can all do without food and not spend a penny for the next ten weeks, we could just about afford it.'

'It may as well be twenty-five hundred or twenty-five thousand then,' said Billy.

'The best thing you can do,' said Dad, 'is to forget these daft ideas of going to this lah-de-dah school. Go back to St Chad's; leave at fourteen and get a good job like our Sam's at Dobbin's, or apprenticeship at the Wallworks.'

Throughout this speech, Mam was strangely quiet and offered no comment.

She's as shattered as I am by this blow, thought Billy.

'There's one consolation,' Billy said at last. 'At least me and Henery will be going to the same school after the holidays.'

But Mam was more shattered than he thought, for she still said nothing. Instead she wore an odd look – one he'd never seen before – and she was counting her fingers on her chin as if involved in some bizarre mathematical exercise.

That night, Billy went to bed despondent. The dream of going to that posh college had been all very well, but it was time to come down to earth. How could his family ever afford such huge sums of money for uniform and sports equipment?

No, it was back to St Chad's for him. And in three years' time he could leave school and start bringing in some money, instead of taking it out. Perhaps a job like Sam's. It might be good fun riding up and down in a lift, announcing things. And then it would be nice to see Miss Eager again. She would be disappointed, of course, after all her hard work. But that was too bad. After all, that was what life was all about, wasn't it? He could still beat Joey Flewitt in class and it would be great to be going to school with Henry again. Now, whose class would he be in at St Chad's? Why, Mr Kinsella's! Only the most popular teacher in the school, that's all. That was good, wasn't it?

But if it was so good, why was he weeping as he went to sleep that night?

Chapter Eleven

Uncle To The Rescue

The next day it was raining heavily.

'What rotten weather!' Billy said aloud to himself. 'What a rotten day! And what a rotten life!'

He went downstairs and was surprised to find the house deserted. Everyone had gone to work, but Mam was usually there when he appeared for breakfast.

'Strange! I wonder where she's got to?'

He looked at the old clock on the mantelpiece and was taken aback to see it was ten o'clock, for he didn't normally sleep as late as that. He made himself a small pot of tea, and hacked into the loaf, producing a lumpy slice of bread over which he spread first a thick layer of margarine, then a liberal coating of raspberry jam.

'You always make a big mess o' the loaf when you cut into it,' Mam had said. 'And you can have either maggy-ellen or jam, but not both.'

Today, the way he was feeling, he didn't care. As he bit into his thick jam butty, he wondered what he and Henry could do with themselves on such a wet day.

The front door opened suddenly and in strode Mam.

'Right,' she said decisively. 'Get your best clothes on. We're going to town. As for the college – it's on again! I'll show your father what's what and who's who.'

'But where did you get the money from? Twenty-five quid!'

'Never you mind about that. I've just been talking to that Mrs Priestley, her-across-the-road, and she says you don't need half of them things on that list. For a start, there's no cricket until next summer; so that lot can wait. I won't have no son of mine losing his chance to make summat of himself just for a few quid. Hurry up and get changed. We're off to King Street.'

Billy ran upstairs to change into his Whit Friday clothes for the trip to the tailor's.

Where had she got the money?

Then it struck him like a bolt out of the blue. When he'd looked up at the old clock on the mantelpiece that morning, he'd felt somehow that something wasn't quite right, something was missing, but he couldn't quite place it. Now he knew! The family heirloom! Grandma's ship-shaped teapot! It was gone!

He went downstairs.

'What's happened to the teapot?' he asked.

'Gone to uncle's for safe-keeping.'

'Which uncle? Uncle John or Uncle Eddy?'

'Your Uncle Abie.'

That day in Wippell's of King Street, Mam spent £12 on equipping Billy with gym shorts and singlet, grey woollen stockings with blue turnovers, grey worsted shorts, two white poplin shirts, a silk blue-and-gold tie, a royal-blue blazer with the gold school crest on the breast pocket, and a matching cap with a metal badge just above the peak.

Billy gazed at himself in the full-length mirror and saw a strange, snooty-looking kid looking back at him.

'Is that really me?' he asked.

There were tears in the corners of Mam's eyes as she gazed at him proudly and said:

'It's you all right, our kid. And you really have joined the toffs! We'll show 'em.'

Next port of call was Timpson's shoe shop for new black, low quarter shoes – none of your boots this time – a pair of white galoshes and, strangest purchase of all as far as Billy was concerned, a pair of hard-toed football boots.

'While we're out getting fitted up and kitted out,' Mam said, 'we've got one last place to visit.'

Billy wondered what and where it could be, since they seemed to have everything. When they went into Cheetham Town Hall, he was even more puzzled. Then he saw the notice on the door:

OFFICIAL DEPOT FOR ISSUE OF GAS MASKS

Billy and his mam were given various gas masks to try on, but they found it impossible to refrain from laughing as the celluloid visor and the metal snout gave them an inhuman look.

'You look like a Martian, Mam.'

'And how do you know what a Martian looks like, since you've never seen one? Anyway, you look like a pig.'

The masks gave off a nauseating smell of rubber, and testing them by placing a card over the snout and then sucking in steamed up the visor and almost suffocated them.

'I think I'd rather be poisoned by the gas,' Mam said.

Toddlers were also being fitted out, with Mickey Mouse-type masks, whilst very young babies were being placed in huge black rubber contraptions which looked like divers' helmets and which terrified the lives out of the poor little things.

'There's nowt funny about this exercise,' said an official. 'Please sign for your mask and then read the notice on the wall. If there is a war, you must carry your gas mask everywhere with you.'

They did as they were told and started to read the notice:

POISON GAS:
If poison gas has been used, you will be warned by means of hand rattles. If you hear hand rattles do not leave your shelter until the poison gas has been cleared away. Hand bells will tell you when there is no longer any danger from poison gas.

'It's beginning to sound serious,' said Mam.

The school uniform and the other items were put away to await the fateful day when Billy would go to his new school. Meanwhile, he and Henry returned to their sailing pursuits and street games. Their latest craze was jumping down the stone steps in front of the house. Billy held the record of five, but Henry was always threatening to take it away from him by attempting six. That Sunday morning, Henry decided to have a go, and taking a deep breath he said:

'I'll do it. I'll do it. I'm not scared.'

'Go on then, let's see you. You keep saying you'll do it.'

Henry jumped. It was a mistake. He landed badly and bashed his forehead against the concrete gate post, and when he saw the blood, he let out a yell that could be heard several streets away.

'I'm bleeding to death,' he bawled, and ran inside to get help.

* * *

Billy rushed into his own house to tell Mam of Henry's mishap.

'Mam! Mam! Henery's cut his head open and . . .'

But he got no further, for his dad landed him a clout across the head and shouted:

'Be quiet, you daft little bugger!'

The family was gathered round, looking at the wireless set and listening to some miserable fella saying:

'. . . no such undertaking has been received and that consequently this country is at war with Germany. This is a sad day for all of us, and to none is it sadder than to me. Everything that I have worked for, everything that I have hoped for, everything that I have believed in during my public life has crashed into ruins.'

'He's not the only one it's a sad day for,' said Billy. 'Henery's just crashed into ruins as well by jumping down the steps.'

And everyone seemed to find it funny. Poor Henry!

Chapter Twelve

Scholarship Boy

Came the day that Billy had been dreading. His first day at Damian College! He donned his new uniform and felt very self-conscious in his new get-up. He looked new and he smelt new.

'Everyone will be looking at me, Mam,' he said.

'Nonsense,' she said. 'No one will even notice you. Besides, David Priestley said he'll go with you on your first day to show you the ropes. So stop worrying.'

For that first day, Mam had made up sandwiches and coffee in a new thermos flask. Billy brought out his new school set of pencils, pen, ruler, compass and protractor. He gathered everything together. It was then he made the discovery.

'We've forgotten to buy a satchel. What am I supposed to carry all these things in? A paper bag?'

'Oh, bugger it,' said Mam. 'I thought we'd got everything. It's the one thing we didn't think of. I'll get you one this week as soon as I get the time to go into town again.'

'But what am I going to do today? I've got all these things to carry, and there's my gas mask as well. Mustn't forget my gas mask.'

'Wait a minute,' she said. 'You can use that big strong

carrier bag what we bought on our trip to Blackpool.'

'But it's bright red, and on one side it's got a big picture of George Formby saying "Turned Out Nice Again" and on the other a dirty big Union Jack.'

'It doesn't matter just for a few days. No one will ever notice.'

'Oh, all right. If you say so,' said Billy doubtfully.

David Priestley called for him at half past seven and they set off together. On the 42 bus, the conductor said:

'What've you got in the bag, lad – your ukelele? If it's Blackpool you want, you're going the wrong way.'

'Take no notice,' said David. 'Come on, I'll show you where Regina Park and the school are. Don't be nervous, Billy. You'll be all right. I was just the same on the first day – as nervous as a kitten. But you'll soon pick up the new routine.'

They passed through two huge iron gates, not unlike those Billy had seen on the front of Strangeways, and into a large quadrangle. There it was – Damian College! A massive, towering, frightening red-bricked building with hundreds of windows. In the yard there was a great crowd of boys all dressed in school uniform – some obviously new like himself and looking very edgy and ill at ease. And a few looking petrified like the proverbial lambs. About the place there were also many adult-looking students in similar smart – but not so new – uniforms. The big fellows completely ignored the young ones. As they walked through the school gates, David Priestley glanced over towards his own form-mates, who were laughing and pointing at Billy's red carrier and at David, who had now turned the same colour as the bag.

'I'll leave you here, Billy,' he said abruptly. 'I have to join my own friends over there. You'll be OK now.'

Eventually, a master in a cassock appeared and blew a

whistle. They were shepherded – new boys first – into a large hall with a stage over which there was a giant shield with the school motto in large letters across the top: ASTRA CASTA, NUMEN LUMEN – which meant 'The stars my camp, God my lamp'. The new boys were lined up trembling with fear, caps in hand, satchels on backs – with the exception, of course, of one who carried a red bag. The rest of the school was brought into the hall and arranged in ascending order of age, with the big adult-types at the back.

On to the stage came the all-male staff, wearing black gowns.

'If they were hanging upside down from the ceiling,' said Billy to the tall, thin boy next to him, 'they could be a scene out of *Mark of the Vampire*.'

In unison, the staff sat down and Billy waited in trepidation for Bela Lugosi to appear.

He hadn't long to wait. On to the stage he swept – the star of the show. As he did so, the whole staff rose as one to its feet. He was a giant, majestic figure wearing thick, dark glasses, and more terrifying than Lugosi himself. Adam McGrath, alias Brother Dorian, OD, gazed down on the boys as if they were ants, and even though there were over three hundred boys in the hall, you could have heard the pin. The new boys watched the performance, hypnotised.

Brother Dorian took out a small silver snuff-box, sprinkled a little snuff on to the back of his wrist and sniffed the powder deliberately up each nostril. From somewhere deep down in the folds of his black cassock he extracted a huge silk handkerchief, into which he blew his nose with a deafening explosion. Looking like a human giraffe sniffing down his nostrils at the mortals beneath, he glared at his juvenile audience. Slowly and meticulously he proceeded to fold the handkerchief into a long sausage, which he used to polish under his nose with a side-to-side sawing movement. Lingeringly, he put the kerchief back into his cassock, removed the heavy spectacles, fixed his eyes solemnly upon his insect-like students and addressed them in deep, sepulchral tones.

'Be under no delusions . . .'

Thinking that a delusion might be some kind of sword of Damocles, Billy looked up anxiously at the ceiling to make sure he wasn't under one.

'The world is now poised on the edge of an abyss,' the silver-haired colossus continued. 'Yesterday, war was declared on Germany. One third of our school has been evacuated to Blackpool and you who remain here in Manchester must be prepared for the might of the Boche and Goering's Luftwaffe to be turned on us. It may not be tomorrow, nor even the next day. But make no mistake – come he will. We in this country must be ready for him. But I hear you ask . . .'

Billy looked round to see who had asked, but the school seemed to be listening stony-faced.

'Yes, I hear you ask,' continued Brother Dorian. 'How long can Herr Hitler and his group of wicked men whose hands are stained with blood and soiled with corruption keep their grip on the docile German people? It was for Hitler to say when the conflict would begin, but it will be for us to say when it will end. Today is not the end. Nay, it is not the end of the end. It is not even the beginning of the end or the end of the beginning. But of one thing you can be sure – today, we begin to begin.'

The staff behind him looked perplexed at this statement.

Billy was almost sure he had heard a song on the wireless with very similar words: 'When they begin the beguine' or something like that.

'Now let us pray,' said Brother Dorian.

After the prayers the school was dismissed, but the new boys were told to stay behind in the hall, where a roll-call was taken and they were allocated to their forms. Billy found himself in a form with the curious title of Three Alpha, and one of the bat-like masters – a particularly corpulent individual – herded them off to their form-room, with Billy making futile attempts to hide his conspicuous carrier bag. There, the master assigned each one of them to an individual desk and told them to print their full names on the cardboard badges which he had supplied.

'These badges must be worn on your lapels for the first month,' the fat man said, 'until we get to know you. Woe betide anyone who loses his badge.'

Carefully, the boys set to work. When the task was completed, the master addressed them again.

'My name is Ronald Puddephatt. If I see even a flicker of a smile on anyone's face at the mention of my name, they'll be for it.'

The boys sat staring ahead, poker-faced.

'For my sins,' he continued, 'I am your form master and your English teacher. Right, let's begin. Each of you will now introduce himself to the rest of us by giving his full name and telling us something about himself.'

'We shall start with you,' he said, pointing to a fair-haired, spotty-faced boy in the front row.

It was during this session that Billy came to a full understanding of how different this new school was from the dear, dear old St Chad's he had left behind.

'My full name,' said the boy indicated, 'is Rodney Arthur Potts, and I live with my parents and four older sisters in a detached house in Fallowfield. My father owns a chain of grocery shops in the Manchester area; you may have seen one or two of them about the place.'

'Next, Cash.'

Cash was an ugly, buck-toothed, thick-set, heavily built lad who looked a little older than the rest of the class.

'My full name is Robert Edward Cash,' he drawled. 'You will note that my name could be abbreviated to R. Eddy Cash. Ready Cash, do you see? My father thought this rather droll, as he is a financial consultant on the Royal Exchange.'

'Next, Hopkins. Aren't you the boy with that hideous red carrier bag? Where on earth did you get it from?'

'Yes, sir. P-please, sir, me dad got it with some sticks o' rock when we went to Blackpool in the summer.'

'Did he indeed! And why, may we ask, have you not acquired a satchel like the rest of the form?'

'Please, sir, me mam forgot to get one o' them satchels. But she says she's gonna gerra new one tomorrer.'

'Yes, all right. Go ahead. Tell us about yourself.'

'Please, sir . . .'

'And stop saying "Please, sir". You're not at your elementary school now.'

'Yes, sir. Me name's Billy 'Opkins and I come from Cheetham Hill and me dad's a porter.'

' "Hopkins" isn't a name," remarked Cash. 'It's some sort of disease, isn't it, sir?'

'You stupid fellow,' said the master. 'You're thinking of Hodgkin's disease. No, this name is altogether different. It's the name of a famous poet, but we can hardly call our new boy here "Gerald Manley", can we? Perhaps George Formby would be a more appropriate name, eh? Anyway, this poet wrote, *"Glory be to God for dappled things –/For skies of couple-colour as a brindled cow"*, but in that beautiful poem, Hopkins, your namesake makes no mention of red

216

carrier bags bearing the face of George Formby and the Union Jack.'

'Perhaps Gerald Manley was his grandfather,' volunteered Tony Wilde, another new boy.

'I doubt it,' said the teacher, 'since Gerald Manley was a Jesuit priest! But one thing is obvious, my dear Hopkins, we are going to have to do a *Pygmalion* job on you. Does anyone know what I mean by that?'

'Isn't that the name of a fillum, sir, with Wendy Hiller and Leslie Howard?' said Billy.

'It is indeed,' said the master. 'Has anyone here been to see it?'

'Not bloody likely,' said Billy.

'Get out here, Hopkins. You must be introduced to my method of dealing with unruly little boys.'

'But, sir,' protested Billy, 'I was only quoting a line from the fillum. I read about it in the *Evening Chron.*'

'The fact that George Bernard Shaw swears is no excuse for you to emulate him. Now turn your face over to the side.'

Mr Puddephatt made Billy stand by his side and then tilted his face at an angle, leaving him in that position.

'Excuse me, sir,' said Billy. 'That fillum was on in town but we can't go to see it now 'cos the gover'ment's closed down all the picture 'ouses in case the Germans drop bombs on 'em.'

'They won't remain closed forever, boy. Now keep your head tilted.'

The next boy, Robin Gabrielson, had a face resembling one of the angels painted on St Chad's altar. His head was a mass of black curls and his eyes seemed to dance when he spoke.

'Don't tell us you're the son of an archangel,' said Puddephatt after Robin had introduced himself.

'No, sir. My father is a tea merchant. He buys and sells tea in the Manchester district. We live here in Rusholme, not too far from the school.'

'Sounds very impressive,' said the master. 'Next boy!'

'Me name's Nodder, sir.'

Before Nodder could continue, however, Mr Puddephatt moved at lightning speed and delivered a stinging slap to Billy's face, which was still inclined at the angle where he had set it.

'That is known in the school as the Puddephatt Slap. Sit down and remember it! Now, Mr Nodder, you were about to enlighten us with a few details about yourself. Incidentally, I do hope you're not related to the infamous murderer, Frederick, who was hanged at Lincoln last year.'

'No, sir. Me name's Norbert – Norbert Nodder. Me friends call me Nobby. And me dad's a driver on the 95 bus with Manchester Corporation.'

'Neither the number of the bus nor the particular corporation he drives for is of any interest to us here,' said the teacher. 'But I trust, Mr Nodder, that you're not going to nod off to sleep in my class. Anyway, I shall call you Fred. Next boy.'

'Me name's Richard Smalley, but at me last school everyone called me Dick Smalley. And me dad's a cleaner for the LMS Railway.'

Not a muscle on Puddephatt's face moved as he said:

'Dick Smalley? Yes. Yes. A most interesting name. But in this class you'll be called Titch, which has a less phallic ring to it, I think.'

The boy sitting behind Titch had an even more unfortunate name.

'I'm called Oliver Hardy, sir,' he said apologetically.

With a menacing scowl, Mr Puddephatt quelled the roar of laughter which had been suppressed since Titch had announced his appellation. When the noise had subsided, he said:

'Go on, Olly.'

'My dad's got his own window-cleaning round and my brother's learning to be a priest at a college in London.'

'A window-cleaning round, eh? Another George Formby aficionado. Perhaps you should buy a bag like that of Hopkins.'

By break-time, Mr Puddephatt had managed to get round the whole form of twenty-five boys, hearing introductions, making what he thought were facetious comments and dishing out nicknames. Antony Wilde, a tall, thin boy, became Oscar, whilst a rather tubby, bespectacled boy named William Bunnell was awarded the sobriquet Bunter.

At the end of the session, Mr Puddephatt said:

'It is quite evident that a number of you are going to have to learn the King's English. For some of you, English is a foreign tongue. But remember this, to quote from Shaw's *Pygmalion*: "Your native language is the language of Shakespeare and Milton and the Bible", and I'm going to make sure you speak it correctly if it's the last thing I do. It is vital that you read and read and read. I shall insist that you get through at least one book per month. Now, here is your first piece of homework. You will begin by studying the first tale in this book that I am about to present to you, and I shall test you on it in our very next lesson.'

He pointed to Cash. 'I'm appointing you form monitor, as you seem to be the oldest and perhaps the most sensible boy here. Give out the books.'

'Yes, sir. Thank you, sir,' said Cash as he distributed copies of *The Arabian Nights* around the class.

'Secondly, by tomorrow – and not by tomorrer,

Hopkins – you will each write either a limerick or an epitaph based on one of the names of a member of this form. You may work in pairs if you wish. I look forward to hearing them. Class dismissed.'

As the boys filed out of the room, Cash mimicked Billy's introduction:

' "Me name's Billy 'Opkins and Ah coom from Cheetham 'ill and Ah bought me red bag in Blackpool, Ah did. And me dad's a porter." Good God, how have these working-class peasants got into one of our schools? And his father's a porter, don'cha know? I do hope he's not one of those black chaps who carry boxes on their heads for explorers like David Livingstone.'

He roared with laughter at his own joke. A few of the rich boys who were near him joined in, mainly to avoid becoming targets of his sarcasm themselves.

Robin Gabrielson overheard the jibes and immediately took Billy's side.

'Look, Cash, we're all new here today and we're all feeling edgy and nervous. We've got to make the best of it and try to make friends – not enemies. So lay off. And if you're so high and mighty, why didn't your father send you to a public school?'

'As a matter of fact,' said Cash, 'my father did consider Downside, but I preferred to remain at home.'

'S'all right, Robin,' said Billy. 'Cash don't worry me. I've dealt with tougher guys than him in me time. But what do you make of this Mr Puddephatt then?'

'Who does he think he is, making fun of our names?' said Tony Wilde, joining in. 'We're not even allowed to smile at his stupid name. I think I shall call him "Pussycat". '

'I think I'd rather have "Puppyfat",' said Billy.

The laughter which this suggestion occasioned decided the issue.

After the break there began what seemed like an endless procession of masters, each trying to sell his subject, rather like the stallholders on Tib Street Market – French, Latin, maths, physics, history, geography, art and physical education.

At the end of that first day, Billy went home with his head in a whirl and feeling distinctly unhappy.

'I don't think I'm going to like this school,' he said to Tony Wilde who, since he lived in Moston, used the same 53 bus home.

'I feel just the same,' said Tony. 'I don't think I can put up with Puppyfat for a whole year.'

When Billy reached home, Mam was waiting for him with a cup of tea.

'Well, how was it – your first day?' she enquired anxiously.

'I'm missing St Chad's, Miss Eager, Henry Sykes, Joey Flewitt and even Stan White already. And please, please, Mam, can we go out now afore the shops shut and buy a satchel?'

'No need,' she said. 'I've already done it!' and she produced the most beautiful leather satchel.

'Thank the Lord for Grandma's teapot!' he said.

The next day Billy went proudly to school with his new leather satchel firmly strapped to his back. He didn't feel quite so bad on this second day, as he now knew what to expect, and he had made a few tentative friends in Robin Gabrielson, Tony Wilde, Titch Smalley, Nobby Nodder and Olly Hardy.

Things could be worse, I suppose, he said to himself.

In the first lesson of the day, Puppyfat wasted no time.

'Right, yesterday I set you some homework. I hope for your sake that you've done it or it'll be the Puddephatt Slap for some of you. So let's hear your efforts. We'll start with you, Oscar.'

'Yes, Mr Puddephatt.

> *'An unfortunate lad, Rodney Potts,*
> *Was plagued by an outbreak of spots,*
> *Zam-buk he applied oh so thickly,*
> *Which made him look even more sickly,*
> *But won him the name "Join-the-dots".'*

'Quite good, Oscar,' said Puppyfat. 'And your reply, Potts?'

'Very good, sir.

> *'A beanpole whose name was Wilde.*
> *Said "No, it can't be denied,*
> *When challenged to fight,*
> *I take off in flight,*
> *And burst into tears like a child." '*

'Touché,' said the master. 'Now let's have your effort, Gabrielson.'

'Mine is an epitaph for Titch Smalley, sir.

> *'Titch Smalley's dead, and here he lies,*
> *Nobody laughs and nobody cries;*
> *Where his soul's gone, or how it fares,*
> *Nobody knows, and nobody cares.'*

'That's a very grave statement,' said Puddephatt. 'No doubt you have a reply to that, Titch?'

'Yes sir. I knew he'd written that and so I've written an epitaph for Gabrielson's tombstone.

> *'Here lies Robin who came from heaven*
> *And left this world in thirty-seven,*
> *Where he's gone, no one can tell,*
> *We only hope it isn't hell.'*

'You really are a bunch of malicious boys,' the master said happily. 'Your effort now, Cash.'

'Very good, sir. Mine's about Billy Hopkins.'

'Yes, I thought it might be,' said Puddephatt. 'Let's hear your masterpiece.'

> *'A slum-kid named like a poet,*
> *Was stupid and didn't even know it.*
> *He carried the flag,*
> *On the side of his bag,*
> *And thought he would hide it, not show it.'*

'I am not sure Gerald Manley would appreciate your wit, Cash,' said the teacher. 'Do you have a reply, Hopkins, to this onslaught?'

'Yes, sir.

> *'A lad by the name Eddy Cash,*
> *Thought he was really quite flash,*
> *But when faced with a fight,*
> *He quickly took flight,*
> *And broke the school's hundred-yard dash.'*

'And that's where I think we'll finish,' said Puddephatt. 'We'll hear the rest next week.'

* * *

As David Priestley had predicted, Billy soon fell into his new routine, and the days passed quickly. He travelled into school on the 42 bus with David, and at night he made the long bus ride home with Oscar Wilde on the 53. The days turned into weeks, and before he knew it, November had come round, and St Chad's and the scholarship exam seemed like ancient history.

At school, the learning went on relentlessly. He found geometry particularly difficult, mainly because of the bad teaching of Brother Campion, who had the rare gift of making the simplest proposition sound like Einstein's theory of relativity. Further, he had devised a cruel and inflexible means of punishing those who had the audacity not to understand his gobbledy-gook.

'Let me introduce you to Paddy-whack,' he said, flourishing a large gym shoe above his head. 'If you get two out of ten for your homework twice running, he will make his acquaintance with your backside.'

Billy had already had one two-out-of-ten for his attempt to answer a question he did not understand: '*Show that if the mid points of the sides of an equilateral triangle are joined, the resulting triangle is also equilateral. What fraction of the whole triangle is it?*' That weekend he made a superhuman effort to solve the problem and produced work of incredible neatness, but it was wrong again. On Tuesday morning he met Mr Paddy-Whack, and received two swipes on his rear which made it difficult for him to sit down for the rest of the day.

'There's only one thing for it,' he confided to Oscar on the way home. 'I shall have to get help at weekends from my brother-in-law, who's a draughtsman at Avro's.'

Indeed, it was Steve Keenan who gave Billy what little spare time he had to help him solve his problems and unravel the mysteries of Euclid's theorems.

Soon, classroom personalities emerged and two distinct groupings began to form. The Cash group, made up largely of fee-payers and well-to-do pupils, sneered at the other set, which consisted mainly of working-class scholarship boys. There was no doubt which of the two divisions Mr Puddephatt favoured.

One day towards the middle of November, the master was called out of the room by a telephone call.

'Cash, whilst I'm out, stand by my desk and take the names of any boys who make a nuisance of themselves.'

As soon as Puppyfat had left the room, Billy called out: 'Who do you think you are, Cash?'

'He thinks he's a teacher,' said Robin.

'He thinks he's rather flash, does Cash,' said Oscar, unable to resist quoting Billy's immortal verse.

'You think you're a teacher, Cash. Here's a piece of chalk for you!' shouted Titch, and he threw a small morsel at Cash's head.

'And another from me!' called Nobby Nodder.

At that moment Brother Dorian was walking by, and as he entered the room a deathly hush fell over the class.

'Where is Mr Puddephatt?' he asked sternly.

'He had to leave the room for a few minutes, sir,' answered Cash, 'and he left me in charge and told me to take the names of troublemakers.'

'And have you?' asked the head. 'I would very much like to know who was making all that row just now.'

'Yes, sir. I've taken down the names.'

Cash handed Brother Dorian his sheet of paper.

'Right, the following boys will now go down to the gym and wait for me. I will not tolerate such hooliganism in my school: Hardy, Hopkins, Gabrielson, Wilde, Nodder and Smalley.'

'I just knew there'd be trouble,' said Titch.

'Not many people know,' said Olly, 'that if you relax your whole body on the first stroke of the cane, you won't feel any pain.'

Trembling, the six boys made their way down to the gym. After five agonising minutes, Brother Dorian strode in swishing and testing out a long cane.

'Line up,' he said. 'Gabrielson, you first. Out here and touch your toes.'

Robin went forward and bent down as if about to play a game of leapfrog. The five waiting boys watched spellbound. Brother Dorian took up his stance, raised the cane high in the air, and brought it down with a loud swishing sound. There was a thwack as the cane bit into the flesh of Robin's bottom. The scream which started up from Robin's throat was quickly stifled. The torture continued, and as the second blow was on its way down, Robin reached instinctively to his backside and the cane struck him across the back of his hand, immediately raising an ugly, livid, purple weal.

'Stay down, boy,' called the head. Robin received a total of six strokes, and when he straightened up there were two large tears glistening in the corners of his eyes but he made no sound.

'Next, Hopkins.'

Slowly and fearfully, Billy went forward to take his punishment. No sooner had he bent over than the first blow landed. To his surprise, he heard the crack as it struck but he felt no pain. There followed five more strokes. Still no pain. He stood up, and it was then that a searing, burning sensation hit him, as if someone had applied a red-hot poker to his buttocks. The whole of his rump was aflame. He could hardly breathe let alone move out of the gym because of the agony. He forced the tears back and painfully made it to the door.

Outside, he waited with Robin for the others to emerge from the torture chamber. They heard the pistol shots of the stick as it struck buttocks, and the screams of torment as each in turn underwent his flogging. When all was over, the six boys climbed painfully back up the stairs.

'That theory of yours, Olly,' said Oscar, grimacing, 'about not feeling anything. Well, it needs looking at again.'

'That's what was claimed in the book where I saw it.'

As they re-entered the form room, a strange, unearthly silence fell over the class and looks of admiration followed their return to their desks. Cash, however, could not look the heroes in the eye.

Chapter Thirteen

What's In A Name?

At the end of November, Jim came home on leave. He had completed his initial course on the training ships *Exmouth* and *Drake*, qualifying him as a naval gunner, and the navy had finally posted him to the battle-cruiser *Renown*. Before sailing off, he had been given a week's furlough, and he intended to make the most of it.

When Billy saw him after so many weeks' absence, his heart filled with pride at the sight of this handsome hero-brother in smart, immaculate nautical uniform.

'He smells so clean and fresh and soapy,' he said to Mam.

'And he insists on ironing everything himself,' she replied.

Jim gave Billy the job of rolling his cigarettes. Billy would gladly have gone through fire or swum the Atlantic, let alone roll his cigarettes. He got down to it, delighted and honoured to have been entrusted with such an important task. He opened the sealed tin, releasing the pungent aroma of fresh Virginia tobacco, sprinkled the requisite amount into the little machine, inserted the Rizla paper, licked the adhesive strip, and lo and behold! A cigarette! He must have made almost three hundred in this way – enough to keep both Jim and Dad going for some considerable time.

Jim spent half his time at Auntie Cissie's shop, where the unorthodox lifestyle seemed to appeal to him. He spent the other half in the company of Jean Priestley, who had developed into a most beautiful raven-haired young lady. But he still had lots of time for his youngest brother.

'Well, our kid,' he asked one day, 'how's it all going at that new school of yours?'

Billy poured out all his sorrows about Puddephatt, about Brother Campion and his Paddy-whacker, about Brother Dorian and the flogging, but most of all about Cash and his snooty, mocking ways.

'But you've made some friends, I hope.'

'Yes, a few.'

'Then you're lucky, old son. Have they given you a nickname yet?'

'No, not yet. But Mr Puddephatt said he'd call me George, after George Formby.'

'When your mates give you a nickname – not this Mr Puddephatt – then you'll know you're in and that you've been accepted.'

'What's your nickname in the navy, Jim?'

'Oh, they call me the Champ, 'cos of my boxing. But when I first got there, it was just the same for me in Devonport Barracks. Everything was strange and unfamiliar. If you've got a few good mates, though, you can face almost anything and anybody. And things do change and get better in the end, you know.'

'Right now, I wouldn't mind going back to St Chad's and me old mates.'

'No, that's the one thing you cannot do. You can't go backwards. Forget St Chad's. There's only one solution to your problems, you know,' he said calmly, lighting up one of Billy's cigarettes. 'The question is: do you have the guts to do it?'

'Just tell me what to do and I'll do it.'

'Take on Cash and beat him.'

'You mean – fight him? Jim, you must be joking. He's older, he's bigger and he's about a stone heavier.'

'You know what we say in boxing: "The bigger they are, the harder they fall." Tell you what I'll do. I go back Sunday night, so on Saturday afternoon I'll give you some pointers. On Monday you challenge this Cash character to a scrap with gloves in the gym. Then you fix him good and proper.'

Jim was as good as his word, and on the Saturday afternoon he met Billy in the old familiar back yard.

'OK,' he said. 'We don't need Bennie the Dummy today. I'll move around the yard and when I stick out my glove, you hit it. Now take up your stance and your peek-a-boo style. Let's go!'

Together the two brothers danced around, and every time Jim showed an open glove, Billy struck it with the rapidity of a lizard snapping up a fly.

'You've lost none of your speed, and the way you hit, you've got golden hands,' said Jim. 'Remember to keep moving all the time, though. See, when you punch, your opponent concentrates on avoiding it. If you punch and move, by the time he gets set you're not there.'

'What about breathing?' asked Billy.

'When you're boxing, breathe fast and keep bobbing and weaving. You've got to get yourself fit by running and skipping; that's what I do.'

'And smoking?' chipped in Billy, unable to resist the jibe.

'Yeah, yeah, yeah. OK, St William. I hear you. But most important, watch your opponent's eyes.'

'Why his eyes?'

'Because they tip you off when he's going to try for a punch; there's a slight movement of the eye and that's your signal to make sure you're not there when he goes for it. And keep looking all the time for an opening.'

'He's a very big lad, Jim. What if he gets a punch in first? He'll flatten me.'

'Make sure he doesn't. Block him with your elbows, like this. And keep your defence up. When you've let out a punch, move quickly to the side, or duck and then let in a sneaky one-two-three. Look for his weakness all the time.'

'Right, Jim. I'll remember it. But I hope you'll send me some grapes if I end up in hospital.'

'You won't. You'll be too fast for him. He won't be able to get near you. Your best plan is to take it easy in the first round, watch his style and look for his weakness; in the second, give the poor lad a bit of false confidence; in the third, finish him off! Think at all times and keep your head.'

'That's the one thing I'll try to keep.'

'Right. Enough talking. Let's go for a run.'

And the pair of them set off across Barney's.

The end of Jim's leave came all too soon. On the Sunday evening, the whole extended family descended on Honeypot Street – Uncles Eddy and John, Aunts Cissie, Mona and Hetty, Steve and Pauline, who had left the children in the care of Steve's mother, and a few friends, including the beautiful Jean from across the street. The great crowd went off to Capper's pub to commemorate the send-off in Tetley's ale. At ten o'clock, they all returned with innumerable bottles of beer to the Honeypot Street home to tackle the mountains of tongue-and-pickle sandwiches which Mam had prepared beforehand.

Between bites of bread and swigs of ale, the gathering sang their way through their whole repertoire of nautical songs: 'The Sailor with the Navy-Blue Eyes', 'All the Nice Girls Love a Sailor', 'Sons of the Sea', 'The Fleet's in Port Again, Yo-Ho', 'The Fleet's In'. As time went on, the songs became more and more sentimental and sad: 'We'll Meet Again', 'Yours', 'If I Had My Way', and Jean Priestley gave a soulful rendition of 'I'll Pray for You While You're Away'.

Jim, as the centre of attention, sat there with a happy grin on his face, enjoying and savouring every moment.

For a brief moment the spotlight turned on Billy.

'Come on, our Billy,' said Dad. 'Time you was in bed! Up the Molly Dancers!'

'Hey, Tommy, don't be such a miserable old sod!' shouted Uncle Eddy. 'Leave the little bugger alone. He can stay up just this once, can't he?'

Dad, who was a little afraid of Uncle Eddy, deferred.

'Go on, then. Just this once.'

Uncle Eddy thrust half a crown into Billy's hand.

'Here, you clever little bugger,' he said. 'Tek it for your eddication. Grammar school, eh? What're they learning him at this bloody posh place then, our Kate?'

'Eeh, I tell you, our Eddy, he's that clever I get worried, I do. There's so much stuff going into his head. There can't be room for it all. I'm afeared that one o' these days his head's gonna burst like a sausage in a frying pan. And you should see the things they're learning him! Foreign languages and all! Hey, come here, our Billy, and say a few words in algebra for your Uncle Eddy.'

After the knees-up came the sad part. Quiet, unassuming Uncle John had gone on to Cheetham Hill and ordered two taxis – a thing almost unknown in that district. The assembly crammed into the cabs and escorted Jim to London Road station. There, at two o'clock in the morning at the main platform, stood a huge train crowded with sailors. The wooden signboards attached to the last carriage announced its destination: MANCHESTER– PLYMOUTH EXPRESS. How that signboard conjured up romantic pictures in Billy's mind! Of battleships with their massive fourteen-inch guns, cruisers, destroyers; of sea-battles with German pocket battleships; and of U-boats and E-boats being sent down to Davy Jones's locker.

Then came the parting.

Billy watched with a lump in his throat as his mam hugged Jim close to her and said quietly:

'Look after yourself, son.'

Dad took Jim's hand and was about to shake it, but he changed his mind and instead took him in a tight embrace.

'All the best, son. Take care.'

Billy looked at his brother's dear, beloved face, and realised that soon he would be gone.

'Come here, our kid,' Jim said, and gave Billy a big bear-hug. 'You look after Mam and see she's all right. And see you win that fight at school. Remember all I've told you.'

The family withdrew a short, respectful distance to let Jim be with Jean Priestley. He spent the last five minutes talking earnestly to her, and finally took her in his arms and gave her a long, lingering kiss.

'Goodbye, Jean,' he said quietly. 'I'll be thinking of you.'

He boarded the train and stood leaning out of the window. The train began to move off, taking him away. They watched him still grinning and waving as he got smaller and smaller, until they could see him no more. All around them were other relatives straining for a last glimpse of their loved ones – still waving their goodbyes to the hundreds of sailors disappearing into the distance.

Finally, the train was gone and the family and Jean Priestley were left alone – sad and deflated – to make their melancholy way back to Honeypot Street.

Billy was very tired the next morning and could hardly open his eyes. It made no difference. He still had to go to school.

The daily routine at Damian College ground on as usual until break.

'Good God!' exclaimed Cash. 'Just look at Silly Billy Hopkins. He looks like something the cat's dragged in! Can't you peasants in Cheetham Hill afford beds, Silly?'

His cronies around him rewarded him with the usual supportive guffaw.

'For your information, Cash, my name is Billy. You will either stop calling me Silly Billy or I shall be forced to take it out on your ugly face.'

This fighting talk attracted a small group of third-formers who were eager to enjoy the witty exchanges.

'My dear Silly, if you would only wash your neck, I'd wring it.'

'Cash, you're a dimwit, and furthermore, you've got buck teeth.'

'Who cares what his teeth cost?' said Titch, who was listening to the exchange.

Cash grabbed Titch's lapel and examined his name tag.

'Keep out of this, Smelley, or whatever your name is. It's none of your business. It's between Hopkins and me.

'Hopkins,' he continued, 'you're a nasty little insect, and if you're not careful, I shall stamp on you.'

'You'll either apologise for that remark, Cash, or I'll be

forced to teach you a lesson you'll never forget.'

'I can't believe my ears! Why, you little runt! As the Arabs say: "May the fleas of a thousand camels infest your armpits"!'

'You're not the only one who's read *Arabian Nights*, Cash. "May your left ear wither and fall into your right pocket"!'

'Hopkins, you are asking for a severe beating. Did anyone ever tell you that you have a face like a cake left out in the rain?'

'Cash, I would say the same about you if you had a face.'

'That's the last straw, you little pipsqueak. I can swallow you in one bite.'

'And if you did, Cash, you'd have more brains in your belly than in your head.'

'Are you looking for a fight, Hopkins?'

'Cash, everyone in the form knows you're all talk. Like an over-ripe banana – yellow outside and squishy inside.'

'Hopkins, you little tin-ribs, I challenge you to a fight in the gym!'

'You're on, Cash! Let's go and fix it up with Brother Brendan right now.'

The big fight was arranged for Thursday at 4.15 in the gym.

'Are you sure you know what you're doing, Billy?' asked Oscar.

'No, I'm not. But it's too late now.'

'What kind of flowers do you like?' asked Titch.

'I think Billy will pull it off,' said Robin. 'Brains will always triumph over brute force and ignorance.'

Every night until the fight, Billy skipped in the back yard and went for a run across Barney's.

235

'I must get myself really fit if I'm going to beat Cash,' he said to Mam.

The big fight had been well publicised. There were notices on the boards of 3A and 3 Alpha.

DON'T MISS THE BIG FIGHT IN THE GYM
THURSDAY 28 NOVEMBER AT 4.15
CASH, THE FIGHTING FINANCIER FROM
FALLOWFIELD
VERSUS
HOPKINS, THE BATTLING BARD FROM
CHEETHAM HILL

Brother Brendan had made a professional job of setting out the boxing ring. At four o'clock every place was taken and the atmosphere was at high voltage. Many third-formers had postponed going home, and a few of the teachers, including Mr Puddephatt, Brother Placid and Brother Campion, were there to witness the event. Robin, Oscar and Titch Smalley had agreed to act as Billy's seconds. Cash had Rodney Potts and a couple of other rich kids as his.

At 4.10, the two contenders, fully kitted out in shorts and singlets and wearing boxing gloves which seemed much too big for them, put in their appearance. There were loud cheers from all the spectators. Next to Cash, Billy looked truly diminutive, and the fight had all the hallmarks of a David-and-Goliath battle.

At 4.15, Brother Brendan announced the fight.

'For the boxing championship of the third forms, we have in the right corner, Ready Cash of Fallowfield.'

There were loud cheers from his supporters.

'Go on, Eddy, show him who's who.'

'Give him one for me, Eddy!'

'You're too strong for him,' shouted Potts.

Cash nodded his head and smiled in acknowledgement and agreement.

'And in the left corner,' the brother continued, 'we have the Bard from Cheetham Hill, Billy Hopkins.'

'Teach him a lesson,' said Oscar, none too convincingly.

'I'm sure you can do it, Billy,' called Robin confidently.

'You can only do your best,' said Titch dubiously.

'The contest will be fought by Queensberry Rules over five rounds,' announced Brother Brendan. 'When you hear the bell, come out fighting. Let's have a clean fight.'

The bell rang for the first round. Billy hardly heard the cries of excitement. Taking up his boxing stance and his peek-a-boo style, he walked to the middle of the ring.

'Weigh him up in the first round and find his weakness,' Jim had said.

Billy slid to his left and feinted. Cash's body moved to avoid the punch that never came. Billy moved to the right and jabbed. Once again Cash moved back to evade the blow. Billy was moving smoothly and was in control.

Cash rushed Billy, who moved back and made a rapid move to his left and feinted again. Cash's short arms moved to block the punch that should have come. But there was no punch. Billy, busily sizing him up, smiled at Cash, who went red with anger, rushed again and threw a wild left hook. But Billy was no longer where Cash thought he was. The rush sent Cash headlong on to the ropes.

Billy was already in the middle of the ring, and he beckoned to Cash to come and get him. Enraged, Cash lowered his head and rushed like a bull in a tournament, and Billy, with the graceful movement of a matador, danced to the side and instead of punching Cash propelled him into the ropes, where his head became entangled.

The bell for the end of the first round sounded. Billy had learned all that he needed to know about his opponent. Cash lost his temper easily, relied on brute force to win and occasionally lowered his guard.

As he sat in his corner, Robin Gabrielson wiped his brow with a wet flannel.

'You're doing OK, Billy,' he said, 'but don't let him land one of those vicious punches on you or you won't get up.'

'Keep ducking and diving, bobbing and weaving,' said Titch.

'You make it sound like a cotton mill,' said Oscar.

Over in the other corner, Cash's seconds were giving frantic advice.

The bell rang for the second round. Now what was it Jim had said about the second round? 'Give the poor lad a bit of false confidence' – that was it.

Billy danced to the middle of the ring. With a snort, Cash charged, and this time he landed on Billy's chest a lucky thump that was heard all round the gym, followed by an elbow in his opponent's face.

This is definitely not part of the plan, thought Billy.

Winded and gasping for breath, he could hardly move. As Billy panted and tried to regain his composure, Cash smelt blood and moved in for the kill. Like a man possessed, he swung stiff punches, each connecting with a different part of Billy's body. A right-handed blow sent Billy reeling against the ropes.

Brother Brendan approached anxiously.

'Do you want to throw in the towel, Hopkins? There's no shame. You've put up a very good show.'

'No, sir. Please, no towel. It's nearly the end of this round.'

Then his forehead started to weep blood. He tried to
stem the flow with his glove. Whatever happened, he had
to avoid those vicious swings of Cash's if he was to stay
on his feet. He danced around lightly, staying out of reach.
Cash moved clumsily like a great elephant, and so it was
not so hard. Cash kept up the pressure but Billy was an
impossible, moving, dancing target. Then blessed relief.
The bell rang.

'He's tired,' said Mr Puddephatt to Brother Placid.
'Hopkins should throw in the towel. Cash is much too
big and heavy for him. Our Cheetham Hill poet has done
awfully well for such a lightweight, but he should know
when he's beaten.'

'Give him one more round and then I think Brother
Brendan will have no alternative but to stop the fight.'

In Billy's corner, Robin was busy stemming the blood
with a wet flannel and styptic pencil.

'Are you sure you want to go on, Billy?' he asked.

'Look, Billy,' said Titch, 'be a pal. Throw in the towel.
I can't stand seeing you hit like that. Just 'cos he got us
the stick from Dorian – well, it doesn't seem worth it.'

'He's right,' said Oscar. 'Pack it in, Billy, and call it a
day.'

'The odds are against you, Billy,' said Titch. 'It's a well-
known fact that the heavyweight always triumphs over
the lightweight.'

'We're on your side, Billy,' added Oscar, 'but I think
Cash is too big and heavy for you.'

Billy noticed the purple weal on Robin's wrist; he
remembered the caning from Brother Dorian, the snide
remarks about his Blackpool bag, the insults to his
Cheetham Hill background and to his father's job.

'Oh, no!' said Billy. 'It's not over till the final bell.'

Third round.

With a smirk on his face, the over-confident Cash made his play and rushed at Billy like a tank. He wanted to hit and hit. His hands had become lower than before. Billy jabbed and crossed with a right. Though the jab was on target, the right cross missed. But it was enough. The leering expression on Cash's face had changed to one of utter amazement and consternation.

Billy recovered his posture and was in charge again. A jab. Another one. He moved back and threw in a one-two-three combination, and all three punches landed on Cash's head.

'Good jabs, Billy,' called Robin.

'Give it to him,' yelled Titch.

'Let him have it,' shouted Oscar.

'You've got him now,' called Robin. 'I knew you had it in you to beat him.'

Billy now moved like a ballet dancer, and as he pirouetted, he flicked left jabs on Cash's head. Cash was hurt and his legs started to wobble.

'Timber!' called Oscar.

'He's going down!' shouted Titch.

Billy moved in and delivered a right uppercut. Cash went down on one knee – shaking his head in disbelief.

Brother Brendan moved in quickly and signalled the end of the fight. He raised Billy's right hand above his head and said:

'The boxing champion of the third form. The Battling Bard from Cheetham Hill, Billy Hopkins.'

Then someone from 3 Alpha called:

'Well done, Hoppy!'

Billy turned round to face the speaker.

'Thanks,' he said.

Now he had his nickname.

Chapter Fourteen

Mind Your Language

Before that first term ended, Billy had a piece of good news and a piece of bad.

The bad news was that, in the terminal examination, he came twentieth out of twenty-five. This was a blow for a boy who had been accustomed to being first in class.

'*Could do better. Must try harder,*' said his report.

'There was never a truer word spoken,' Billy said, as he handed his card to Mam.

The good news was that Puddephatt had been called up into the army.

'I shall be taking the King's Commission,' he announced one morning towards the end of term, 'in the Royal Artillery.'

Not even Puddephatt could stop the cheer that went up.

'I take it,' he continued, 'that the cheer is because you appreciate that my contribution to the war effort will help bring hostilities to a speedier conclusion. And not because you are pleased to see me go.'

At the break, the boys agreed to take a collection for a parting gift. A set of bound copies of the works of George Bernard Shaw was decided on.

'But what can he do in the Royal Artillery?' asked Tony Wilde.

'I heard on good authority,' said Olly, 'that fat men in the army are put in the Pioneer Corps and employed on clerical duties.'

'They could fire him as a human cannon-ball on to Berlin,' said Robin. 'He'd wipe out the whole city.'

'Or they could tie a rope to him,' said Billy, 'and float him high in the sky as a barrage balloon – after they'd filled him with gas, of course.'

'No need for the gas, Hoppy,' said Titch. 'He's full o' hot air as it is.'

After Christmas, the study and hard work began in earnest and the procession of subject specialists stowed, stacked and stuffed their esoteric knowledge into the heads of their reluctant recipients. In Latin, the boys learned about the nominative, the vocative – O Chair! O Table! – the dative and the ablative; in physics about batteries, bunsens and Boyle's Law; in maths about powers, percentages and Pythagoras; in art about painting and perspective; in history about Perkin Warbeck and Lambert Simnel; in geography about cotton, coal and anthracite.

War or no war, the endless, relentless cramming process went on.

Not all was gloom in the classroom, however. French was taught by a bad-tempered brother called Placid. One day, Billy had to translate: '*Jean et Paul marchent sur le plancher; ils ne marchent pas sur le plafond; ils ne marchent pas sur les murs; ils ne marchent pas sur les fenêtres.*'

'John and Paul walk on the floor; they do not walk on the ceiling; they do not walk on the walls; they do not walk on the windows. But sir,' said Billy. 'Flies do.'

Which seemed to amuse all and sundry except Brother

Placid, who blew his top. But such was schoolboy humour. And then there was the case of the Rodney Potts translation.

'Translate the following sentence,' said Placid.

He wrote up on the blackboard: '*Non, merci, ma cherie. Je ne vais pas acheter un appareil cinematographique.*'

Poor Rodney did his best to make sense of this incomprehensible language, and read out his English version:

'No sherry for me, thank you. I'm appearing at the cinema.'

They played the 'Knock-knock. Who's there?' game in French.

'*Toc-toc. Qui frappe la porte?*'

'*Henri.*'

'*Henri qui?*'

'*Henri soit qui mal y pense.*'

Music was taken by a bumbling, absent-minded, slightly deaf middle-aged man, Brother Maurice, a brilliant musician. The boys loved him. He introduced them to his favourite traditional English folk-songs, with a few Irish, Scottish and Welsh thrown in. How Billy loved singing the various descants and rounds which the brother taught with great verve and enthusiasm.

It was in early 1940 that Tony Wilde revealed his talent for making up unauthorised versions of some of the songs. These compositions had to be quite subtle, in that they had to avoid arousing Brother Maurice's suspicions. The result was that the brother was never altogether sure that he'd heard aright. One of the most popular songs with the boys was 'Come Lasses and Lads'. The third verse was where Oscar had done his work, changing it from:

'You're out!' says Dick;
'Not I,' says Nick,
' 'Twas the fiddler
played it wrong.'
' 'Tis true,' says Hugh.
And so says Sue,
And so says everyone.

to

'Take out your dick!'
'Not I,' says Nick,
'The fiddler'll
play with my dong.'
' 'Tis true,' says Hugh.
And so says Sue,
And so says everyone.

No doubt the adults, had they discovered this ribaldry, would have found it disgusting. But Billy and his twelve-year-old companions thought that it was the funniest thing they had ever heard and considered their Oscar to be something of a genius.

The most momentous event in the school that year was the appointment of a middle-aged lady, a Miss Sybil Barrymore, to Puddephatt's English post. She was a gushing, bubbling bundle of energy and enthused about everything in sight.

'What a beautiful day it is today,' she rhapsodised at lunch to the brothers seated round their refectory table. 'I am so uplifted that I feel as if I'm floating on a little cloud. And how particularly crisp, green and lettucy the lettuce looks today!'

In her first English lesson with 3 Alpha, she gave out

copies of *Treasure Island* and prattled on about Robert Louis Stevenson whilst the form sat spellbound by this female phenomenon.

'What a great writer he was!' she babbled. 'And do you know, boys, he was ill with tuberculosis for most of his life? He wrote *Treasure Island* simply to amuse his stepson, and the book became a best-seller in the 1880s. Let us now read it aloud around the class. Each of you will take turns so that I can see how well you enunciate and articulate.'

The lesson went smoothly – each boy giving of his best in order to impress this elegant lady of letters.

When the last boy had read, she said:

'Excellent, boys. Really excellent. I can see many of you will get jobs with the BBC. Class dismissed. But would the following boys kindly remain behind: William Hopkins, Norbert Nodder, Richard Smalley.'

'We're in trouble again,' said Titch.

'I'd like to talk to you three about your English,' she said. 'Can you meet me here in the form room during the lunch break at, say, one o'clock?'

'But we allus play footer at dinner-time,' said Nobby.

'Then you must forgo your footer for once,' she snapped.

Just before the appointed time, the three boys waited for her in the form room.

'I wonder what she can want,' said Billy.

He didn't have long to wait, for at that moment Miss Barrymore sailed into the room.

'I shan't beat about the bush,' she said. 'I am concerned about your powerful Manchester dialects.'

'What's wrong with 'em?' asked Nobby.

'Oh, there's absolutely nothing wrong with them. All three of you speak the dialect perfectly. That's the trouble.

But I want to help you to do something about it. You, William, show a distinct talent for language. What a pity it isn't English.'

'I can't see nowt wrong with the way we talk,' said Titch.

'Eeh, I don't want to learn to talk posh,' said Billy. 'Me mam and dad wouldn't like it.'

'I'm not going to try to teach you to talk posh. On the contrary, I can teach you to speak not posh but properly, if you will give me the chance. In six months I can teach you RP.'

'You mean the language of the dead?' asked Billy.

'No, not RIP, but simply RP – Received Pronunciation – the accepted way of talking.'

'I can't see any point in it,' said Nobby. 'The way you talk doesn't matter.'

'That is where you are so wrong,' she said. 'The way you speak can affect your whole life, the kind of job you will get, the kinds of friends you will make, even the kind of wife you will eventually marry. The way you talk does matter, believe me.'

' 'Ow d'you make that out?' asked Billy.

'Listen,' she said. 'I'll give you an example. How would you like it if you went to the doctor and he said: "Hey up – chuck th'cap in, and coom in and get sat down. 'Ow've you bin, luv? Eeh bah gum, you do look proper poorly." '

The boys laughed at her mimicry.

'Doctors don't talk like that, miss,' said Titch.

'Exactly,' she said. 'I want to try a little experiment. Here's a list of occupations. I want you to tick the job you think best fits the way I read this extract from *Treasure Island*. In other words, what's the job of the person reading it. Ready?'

'Right, miss,' they said, enjoying the game.

'Number one: "Ah remember 'im as if it was yisterday, as 'e coom ploddin' to th'inn door, 'is sea-chest followin' be'ind 'im in an 'and barrer; a tall, strong, 'eavy, nut-brown man; 'is tarry pigtail fallin' over t'shoulders of 'is soiled blue coat; 'is 'ands ragged and scarred, with black, broken nails; and t'sabre cut across one cheek, a dirty, livid white." ' Her first reading was in a powerful Manchester dialect.

'Well?' she asked. 'Which occupation have you picked?'

'Comedian,' said Billy.

'Street sweeper,' said Nobby.

'Coalman,' said Titch.

'Now I'll read it again.'

This time, she did so in an exaggerated upper-class accent.

'Which occupations this time?' she asked.

'Prime Minister, but it sounded a bit like Cash and all,' said Billy.

'Duke of Windsor,' said Nobby.

'A butler,' said Titch.

Laughingly, she said:

'Now listen to the same passage read with Received Pronunciation.' And she read it in a clear voice.

'Teacher,' said Billy.

'Lawyer,' said Nobby.

'News reader on the wireless,' said Titch.

'So you see,' she said, 'how we associate certain occupations with accent and dialect. We'll finish this little session by reading a very short play I have written for you. William, you take the part of Herbert; Norbert the part of Henry; and Richard the part of Howard.'

The boys began to read her script.

Billy: 'Ello, 'Enery. 'Ello, 'Oward. 'Ow are you?

Nobby:	'Ello, 'Erbert. 'Ello, 'Oward. 'Ave you 'eard 'Arry 'Opkins 'as gone on 'oliday?
Titch:	'Ow 'appy for 'im. 'As 'e gone to 'Arrow again?
Billy:	Honestly, I 'aven't 'eard.
Nobby:	I 'ope 'e 'asn't gone 'untin' on 'is 'orse again.
Titch:	I 'ope not. Last year 'e 'ad an 'orrible accident.
Billy:	Yes, 'e 'ad it when 'is 'orse refused to jump a 'igh 'edge.
Nobby:	'E 'ad to go to 'ospital, 'adn't 'e?
Titch:	'Ow 'orrible!

'Thank you,' said Miss Barrymore. 'I rather think I 'ave taken on an 'ard up'ill task!'

The boys agreed to meet Miss Barrymore for half an hour every lunch-time, and gradually they began to slough off their unwanted dialects. She was a hard taskmistress and she believed in repetition – over and over again.

> *Moses supposes his toeses are roses*
> *But Moses supposes erroneously.*
>
> *Round and round the rugged rock,*
> *The ragged rascal ran.*

After countless sessions of reciting selected tongue-twisters, Billy learned how to aspirate.

'Say them ten times a day,' she said, 'until it's second nature to pronounce the 'aitch'. Push a lot of air out and do not let your tongue touch the roof of your mouth.'

But Billy had a further problem. He had to be very careful not to speak this new language at home.

'That little bugger's getting above himself,' said Dad. 'He'll be thinking he's better than us soon. You mark my words.'

'I don't think so,' said Mam. 'Anyroad, he's got to learn to talk proper if he's going to make summat of himself.'

As the nights became colder, Billy found he could no longer do his homework in the bedroom but had to tackle his geometry and his Latin and the myriad other subjects in the living room, where he had to compete with the wireless, constant chatter, and the numerous visits of friends, neighbours, relatives and customers for gloves and Cossack hats.

'Why can't we have a fire in the front room, Mam?'

'Because. That's why. You know very well we only have a fire in there at Christmas. D'you think we're made of money?'

Then there was Henry Sykes. He called one night in October.

'D'you fancy coming out for a game o' footer, Billy?' he asked. 'Me and the other lads are trying to get a bit of a team together to play Derby Street.'

'Sorry, Henery. I've got piles and piles of homework.'

'OK, Billy,' said Henry sadly. 'Be seeing you then.'

'Sometimes,' Billy said to his mam, 'I wonder whether all this learning's worth it.'

'It's worth it,' she said simply.

Chapter Fifteen

A Bit of Excitement

'Some war!' said Billy to Mam. 'Here we are, August the twenty-second, and nowt's happened.'

Dad overheard and, looking up from his paper, addressed the wireless set:

'Nowt's happened! Hitler's taken over all bloody Europe, we've had Dunkirk, we've had the Battle of Britain and Jerry's in Paris. And he says nowt's happened!'

'You know what I mean,' said Billy. 'All those things are taking place somewhere else. Here in Manchester there's been nowt exciting.'

'No, and we don't want nowt exciting, thank you very much,' said Mam. 'Don't tempt providence, our Billy.'

'Yeah, but at school they're making jokes, calling it the Bore War and saying Hitler's Blitzkrieg should be called his Sitzkrieg. Anyway, all the kids who were evacuated in 'thirty-nine are coming back home.'

'We've had our share of excitement in this house,' said Dad. 'Take last December. Look at the way our Jim in the *Renown* chased across the Atlantic to Rio after the *Graf Spee*. He made it scuttle itself in Montevideo, didn't he? And he helped to sink the French fleet last month. So what more d'you want?'

'I just feel sometimes that the war's happening to other people all the time, that's all.'

'Let's hope it stays that way,' said Mam.

Billy had spoken too soon, for on Wednesday 4 September, the Luftwaffe carried out night raids on twenty-one British towns, including Manchester. The RAF replied by bombing Berlin, causing fires that could be seen fifty miles away.

'We'd better get ourselves organised,' said Mam, as she sat with Billy in the dark cubby-hole in the coal cellar. 'We'll catch our death o' cold if we have to come down here every night.'

That first raid lasted only three hours and little damage was done in the centre of the town, but there was the promise of more to come. The next day, as Billy walked back from Ormeroyd's corner shop with Dad's Player's Weights and his *Evening Chronicle*, he read the front page headlines and reports:

HITLER PROMISES TO BREAK US!

In a speech yesterday to the German nation, Hitler said: 'The British will know that we are now giving our answer to the impudent raids of the RAF. If they attack our cities, we will erase theirs. We will call a halt to these night pirates. The hour will come when one of us two will break up, and it won't be Nazi Germany. If the British throw two or three thousand pounds of bombs, we will unload 150, 180, yes, 200 thousand . . .' Apparently he intended to continue the progression of figures, but the shouts of the crowd halted him.

'It looks as if our Billy's going to get his excitement after all,' said Dad when he read the headlines.

Blackout curtains were put up to the front cellar windows and a new mantle was fitted to the gas bracket down there. Mattresses were placed on the floor and the Hopkins family prepared to dig in. In fact, provision for only three was needed, as Flo was on permanent night work with the Dunlop Rubber Company, whilst Les and Sam were out every night on duty as ARP messengers.

Next door, the Sykes family had made similar preparations and were ready for the Blitzkrieg which Adolf had threatened. The two families were able to communicate with each other through the adjoining cellar walls. Billy had made a special 'knocking' hammer which was beautifully decorated and was most effective in calling their neighbours' attention.

'Are you there, Jessie?'

'Aye, we're here again, Kate.'

'Are y'all right, Jessie?'

'Not so bad, but being in this cellar's not doing me asthma no good.'

'Who's with you then?'

'There's just me and our Henery. Harry won't get out o' bed. He says if he's gonna die, he'd rather go in his bed than in the coal cellar.'

'Same with Tommy. He's still in bed too. He says, "What has to be will be and if your name's on the bomb it'll hit you no matter where y'are." '

'By gum, that's true. So why are we here in the cellar, Mrs Hopkins?'

'Well, you won't know your name's on it till it hits you, will you?' said Mam.

This philosophical poser seemed to stump Mrs Sykes, for she went quiet after that.

Billy often wondered himself about this notion of names on bombs. He could imagine some Luftwaffe corporal over there in Germany carefully chalking his name and address on the side of a large hundred-pound bomb: 'With love to Billy Hopkins, 17 Honeypot Street, Cheetham. Special Delivery. By Express Air Mail.'

'It's a frightening thought, Mam,' he said, 'to think that up there, floating above us in the clouds, there are some men trying to kill us.'

The raids began to increase in frequency and duration. Regularly at six o'clock, the siren sounded.

'There it goes. Moaning Minnie! You can almost set your clock by it,' said Mam. 'Come on, our Billy. Down we go. Bring your homework with you. You'll just have to do it down there.'

The raids usually lasted until dawn. Early on, Billy would get on with his Latin and geometry whilst the heavy bombers droned overhead. Around ten o'clock, after a cup of cocoa made during a lull, it was time for shut-eye on the mattress.

One night all was quiet and calm, a heaven-sent respite from the waves of bombers passing above. Suddenly they were awakened by the sound of heavy gunfire, which was so loud it seemed to be in the cellar with them.

'God help us!' cried Mam as she awoke with a start. 'That's near!'

Then they traced the source of the gunfire. It was their black cat, Snowy, walking gingerly across the upturned tin bath!

On Friday 29 November, the sirens burst out as usual at six o'clock, and Billy and his Mam took up their places in the front cellar. There was something different about this raid, though, for the deafening sound of gunfire – of the real kind – began almost immediately and the dull explosion of faraway bombs was heard within the first five minutes.

'It says on the wireless that the Jerries are giving London a miss tonight and heading up north,' Dad called down to them. 'Manchester's gonna get it tonight. I think I'd better join you two down there.'

'What about all that stuff about your name being on the bomb?' asked Mam.

'Aye,' he said. 'But there's no sense in me writing it meself, is there?'

The raid lasted twelve hours. All night they listened to the thud of bombs dropping somewhere to the north of the city.

'Some poor buggers have been getting it up there,' said Dad.

'I wonder how our Polly is,' said Mam. 'She lives up that way, doesn't she?'

'I'm supposed to be staying with 'em this weekend,' said Billy. 'I'm going up there after breakfast, so I can see how they are.'

He took the 62 bus up Cheetham Hill to Heaton Park and was unprepared for the sight which met him. As he stepped off the bus, he saw devastation everywhere. A great area of the new housing estate where Pauline, Steve and the two children lived had been flattened and left a smoking ruin. Billy ran to Pauline's lovely new house to find Steve nailing boards to windows and doors.

'Steve, Steve,' he cried. 'What's happened? Where's Polly and the kids? Are they all right?'

'They're all OK, but we've had one hell of a night, Billy. Jerry has well and truly plastered this area. God knows what he was after. Pauline's in the garden round the back trying to put a few things together.'

In the back garden, Billy found Polly and the two boys packing up a few suitcases of the belongings they had managed to get out of the house. She was weeping quietly.

'Oh, Billy,' she sobbed. 'We've lost everything, and we're all lucky to be alive.'

'Tell me what happened, Polly, for God's sake.'

'During the night the bombers dropped those aerial landmines – the ones that come down by parachute. Twenty-five people have been killed and I don't know how many injured.'

'Where were you during all this?'

'We were in our Anderson shelter for almost twelve hours. I suffered a dislocated jaw because of the blast but Steve seemed to know what to do.'

'I'm so sorry,' he said. 'But at least you're all OK.'

'We're not badly injured like a lot of other people. But we've lost our new home. It's unsafe to live there now as the foundations have been rocked by the explosions.'

'What'll you do now? You can always come to us in Honeypot Street.'

'No, we'll go to one of the emergency centres set up by the WVS, and then we'll be found a new home.'

'Is there anything I can do?'

'No, nothing. You'd best get back and tell Mam and Dad what's happened here. We'll come down to see them later today.'

As Billy turned away to go back to his bus, young Oliver said:

'Unca Billy. Make us laugh!'

But he couldn't, because of the tears in his eyes.

The air raids on Manchester did not let up. If anything they intensified, and a second evacuation of children from the big cities was being organised. This time Billy was included.

'You'll have a smashing time,' said Mam, trying to be cheerful. 'You'll be going to Blackpool of all places. You've allus been lucky; that comes of being a Sunday child.'

Towards the end of the Christmas term, Brother Maurice came round during the music lesson as the boys were singing 'Come Lasses and Lads' and, cupping his hand to his ear, listened to each boy individually.

'He suspects something,' said Billy to Robin Gabrielson.

At the end of the lesson the brother said:

'I should like to see the following boys before they go: Gabrielson, Hardy, Hopkins, Nodder, Smalley and Wilde.'

'Trouble again,' said Titch to no one in particular.

Billy could almost feel the pain again on his backside.

'Right, boys,' said Maurice. 'I've selected you to form a little choir for the school concert on the last day of term, Friday the thirteenth of December. It's bound to be a very lucky day.'

'Why is that, sir?' asked Billy.

'Because thirteen is my lucky number,' he said. 'We shall put in twenty minutes' practice every lunch-hour.'

'I wonder when we'll get time for dinner,' said Nobby to Billy.

'If you want to learn to sing and speak English, you'll have to do without dinner,' replied Billy.

For Billy, the school concert was a most unusual affair because not only Mam but also Dad had agreed to attend – his very first visit to the school. In the first half, the school orchestra, conducted by Brother Maurice, played, in its inimitable off-key style, various pieces of light classical music. At the interval Billy went back-stage to check a few details of their appearance in the second half. When he returned to the auditorium, he found Mam and Dad already engaged in conversation with Tony Wilde's parents.

'The fall of France was a disaster,' said Mr Wilde.

'Just terrible,' said Dad. 'And did you see the way Jerry went up Champs Elsie. Must've been a terrible sight for the French.'

'It's to be hoped the German SS brigades never get over here,' said Mr Wilde.

'You've never said a truer word,' said Dad. 'Them Gas Peter fellas would love to get their hands on Churchill.'

'Sorry, not with you,' said Tony's dad.

'Y'know, the SS fellas.'

'Oh, you mean the Gestapo. But you're too right there, Mr Hopkins. The SS seem to be without normal feelings – a bit like what we hear about the Japanese.'

'The Japs have already signed an agreement with Hitler. Mark my words, they'll be worse than the Jerries if they ever go to war against us. Y'know they worship their Emperor, Hi-de-hi, as God.'

'Hi-de-hi?'

'Y'know, that Mickey Doo fella.'

'Oh, you mean the Mikado?' said Mr Wilde.

'That's right. That's what I said.'

Mam, meanwhile, was chatting with Mrs Wilde.

'We've been having one or two air raids round our way,' Mam said.

'Oh, aye,' said Mrs Wilde.

'First they dropped them Fairy lights – the ones that make it all bright as day.'

'Oh, aye.'

'Then they dropped them there incondescet bombs to start fires.'

'Oh, aye.'

'And me daughter what lives in Heaton Park has just been bombed out. It was a good job she and her family was in one of them Hans Andersen shelters.'

'Oh, aye.'

Billy interrupted Mam's one-way conversation.

'How are you enjoying the concert so far, Mam? What did you think of the orchestra?'

'I enjoyed it – listening to 'em practising and tuning up their instruments. And when they get the tune right, I think they'll be very good.'

The second half of the concert was a tear-jerker. Five of the boys, looking like cherubs in altar boys' gear, hummed softly whilst the chief cherub, Robin Gabrielson, gave a heart-rending solo performance of Schubert's 'Who is Sylvia?'. But the item which had the mothers in tears and the fathers swallowing hard was the boys' *pianissimo* performance of Ivor Novello's 'Keep the Home Fires Burning' whilst a handsome sixth-former, dressed in full military uniform, rifle on shoulder, recited the lines from *Richard II*:

> *This royal throne of kings, this sceptred isle,*
> *This earth of majesty, this seat of Mars,*
> *This other Eden, demi-paradise,*
> *This fortress built by Nature for herself*
> *Against infection and the hand of war,*
> *This happy breed of men, this little world,*
> *This precious stone set in the silver sea,*
> *Which serves it in the office of a wall,*
> *Or as a moat defensive to a house,*
> *Against the envy of less happier lands.*
> *This blessed plot, this earth, this realm, this*
> *England.*

At the conclusion, Brother Dorian took the centre of the stage to deliver the final speech.

'My dear parents, this is a sad day for us all. The might

of Goering's Luftwaffe is now being turned on us civilians. Night after night, hour after hour, raider after raider dumps bomb after bomb upon us and our homes. We in Manchester have suffered, but I tell you now, we have not suffered one half as much as those poor citizens of Coventry who were bombed mercilessly on the night of the fourteenth of November. We are all in the front line now. I read in my newspaper today – and it may be of some comfort to you to know it – that it takes one ton of bomb to kill three-quarters of a person. At that rate, it will take Hitler many years to wipe out Manchester.

'But we must stand rock-like together, shoulder to shoulder, and when the blast of war blows in our ears, then we must imitate the action of the tiger, and go forward together as one man, a smile on our lips and our heads held high.

'And soon you must part from your children. They are our future, our seed-corn. Without them there is no tomorrow, and they must be protected from the evils of that guttersnipe, Shikelgruber. But rest assured about this: I shall try to love them all as if they were my own. Let us therefore look to the distant horizon, raise our eyes to the golden light on the hillside, and filled with confidence and courage, our resolve unshaken, we shall not fail.'

This moving speech was met by thunderous applause from the assembled parents.

'Ooh, he does sound like Winston Churchill,' said Mam on the way home.

'Where d'you think he got the bloody speech from?' observed Dad shrewdly. 'And how, I should like to know, are we supposed to stand rock-like together and at the same time go forward like bloody tigers with smiles on our bloody faces?'

* * *

The decision to send Billy to Blackpool was reinforced just before Christmas. Manchester suffered its worst blitz on the nights of 23 and 24 December when the centre of the city was almost blasted out of existence.

The sirens sounded at dusk on Christmas Eve right on time.

'Time, gentlemen, please,' said Mam. 'Here we go again.'

'You're just like the landlord o' the Queen's Arms,' said Dad. 'And you keep a good cellar.'

As soon as they had descended to the cellar, Billy knocked on the cellar wall with his home-made mallet.

'Are y'all right, Jessie?' called Mam.

'We're not so bad,' called back Mrs Sykes. 'We're all down here tonight. What a bloody way to spend Christmas, eh? I think we're for it again, Kate.'

Shortly after she had spoken, the fiercest anti-aircraft barrage they had ever heard began, as chains of shells burst high in the sky, creating a curtain of steel.

'Hey, Billy,' shouted Henry, 'there'll be tons of shrapnel for us tomorrow from that lot.'

They heard off in the distance the cracking explosions of bombs followed by a succession of staccato reports like machine-gun fire. From dusk to dawn there was hardly a period of more than two minutes when bombs were not falling on the city.

'The town's getting it tonight,' shouted Mrs Sykes. 'Look out your cellar window, Kate. Thompson Street goods yard's gone.'

They turned off all the gaslights and opened the window, and there across the railway sidings, silhouetted against the skyline, was their beloved city of Manchester – a raging inferno.

'The whole bloody world's on fire,' said Dad.

'It's like that scene in *Gone with the Wind* where the whole town is in flames and Scarlett O'Hara rides up in a carriage,' said Mam.

'If we had a fiddle, we could play it like Nero did when Rome was burning,' added Billy, showing off his classical knowledge.

'I'm just glad you're getting out of this next week,' said Mam. 'You'll be a lot safer in Blackpool.'

'Hey, Kate, it's Christmas Eve,' called Mrs Sykes. 'How's about a bit o' carol-singing?'

'Right, you're on,' Mam called back. 'What d'you suggest, our Billy?'

'How about a nice German carol – "Silent Night"?'

At dawn, the all-clear sounded, and Billy and Henry spent that Christmas morning collecting shrapnel, which they found in great abundance scattered in the cobbles of Honeypot Street.

Despite the pounding their city had received, the Hopkins family enjoyed a magnificent dinner on Christmas Day, thanks to Mam's culinary skills on the living-room range, and Dad's special connections in Smithfield Market. At three o'clock they gathered round the wireless set to listen to the King's broadcast to the Empire from Buckingham Palace. When he had finished, Dad said:

'After that rousing speech, what about cheering ourselves up and giving ourselves a good laugh. Let's have a listen to Lord Hee-Haw.'

Carefully, he fine-tuned the wireless set to 31 metres.

'Jairmany calling. Jairmany calling,' drawled a nasal voice. 'This is Reichsender Hamburg, Station Bremen on the thirty-one-metre band.

'Merry Christmas to all you British citizens, especially those of you living in the big cities. We do hope you enjoyed our little Christmas gift to you. No doubt you have finished your Christmas dinner of scraggy chicken and the few paltry rations your government allows you. Are you aware, people of Britain, that your well-fed Winston is at this very moment puffing away at a good Corona and sipping his Napoleon brandy after a lavish banquet with your stuttering King at Buckingham Palace? Hard luck on you working cheps, what?

'During the week, your Air Ministry announced that many German bombs were dropped at random. Honest injun, we do offer our special condolences to the denizens of that unfortunate city. Sorry we had to pick on your town, cheps, but there really is nothing left worth bombing in Coventry. And all you people of Manchester must be very busy sweeping up the mess our gallant Jairman airmen have left behind. By the way, do you know your Town Hall clock has stopped? We know that because we are the ones who stopped it. Sorry about that, old man. However, we here in the Jairman Reich do hope your Christmas goes with a bang. But in the words of your coloured singer, Mr Albert Yolsen, "You haven't seen anything yet". We conclude this transmission by wishing you all a Heppy New Year – even if it's a short one.'

'I do feel sorry for all them poor people what live in Random,' said Mam.

'That bugger Hee-Haw should be hanged,' said Dad.

So 1940 came to its close.

'Well, our Billy, I hope you've had all the excitement you was wanting. Let's hope 1941 is a quieter year for us all,' said Mam.

'I'll drink to that,' said Dad.

If only they'd known.

Chapter Sixteen

I Do Like To Be Beside The Seaside

During the Christmas holidays, the college had sent one of its letters listing the clothes it deemed essential for an evacuee, and for over a fortnight Mam had been busy washing, ironing, and sewing name tapes on the huge pile of garments the school insisted on.

'I've never had pyjamas before, Mam,' Billy said.

'It's not the only thing you've never had before. Looking at this list, anyone'd think you was going on safari to Africa. It's a wonder they've not asked for mosquito nets and a sun helmet. Anyroad, I've packed your bucket and spade as well, in case you go on the sands.'

'I'm not going on me holidays, Mam. I'm being evacuated.'

'I know that. I'm not daft. But take 'em just the same. You never know when they might come in handy. I'm also giving you some sandwiches, a bar of Cadbury's and a bag o' fruit in case you get hungry on the journey. Oh, aye, and when you meet your new "mother", make sure she gets your ration book, and here's a nice bag of chocolate biscuits to give to her when you get there.'

On that first Monday of 1941, they made the bus

journey across Manchester together – Billy loaded up with a satchel and his gas mask on his back, a small suitcase in his right hand and his red Blackpool bag in his left.

On the 42 bus, the familiar conductor said:

'Off to Blackpool again, then, eh, lad? I told you last time you was going the wrong way.'

'Not this time I'm not. Anyroad, I'm not supposed to say where I'm going; it's a state secret.'

'Do I look like a Jerry?'

'If your right ear was a bit bigger, you would definitely look like the Jerry we have under our bed.'

'Cheeky little bugger,' said the conductor good-humouredly. 'You should be on the music hall.'

Outside the college gates there was a fleet of six double-decker buses waiting to take them to Victoria Station on the first leg of their journey, and a great crowd of schoolboys with their tearful mothers issuing last-minute instructions and advice.

'Don't forget your gas mask!'

'Don't lose your money!'

'Change your underpants twice a week.'

Billy reported to Miss Barrymore, who ticked off his name on her clipboard. He gave her his ration book and she handed him a set of labels with his name printed on them.

'You look like a post-office parcel,' Mam said as she helped to tie the labels on to his raincoat.

'I don't mind – as long as they don't stick stamps on me face and sealing wax down me ears,' he said, trying to make a joke and keep the parting cheerful.

'Keep well lapped up, son. Have you got your hanky? Don't use your sleeve like that. Don't forget to wash your neck and behind your ears or you'll leave a tide-mark.'

'I won't. I promise.'

'And don't stick your head out o' the train window or you'll get it sliced off. And don't forget to write every week and let us know how you're getting on. You'll be all right with your pals.'

'Time to get on your bus, boys,' Miss Barrymore called.

'I'll have to go now, Mam.'

'I won't kiss you. Not in front of all your pals. And I won't cry neither,' she said, two big tears glistening in the corners of her eyes.

'Thanks, Mam.'

'But there's nowt wrong with a big hug for a smart guy and a tough kid,' she said, suiting the action to the words.

'Ta-ra, Mam.'

'Ta-ra, son. And look after yourself.'

Billy boarded the bus and went upstairs to join his pals. He watched Mam out of the window and could see her looking up so sad and forlorn as the bus pulled away from the kerb.

Five minutes later, they were moving rapidly along Oxford Road towards the railway station.

'Old Hoppy's brought his George Formby bag,' called Oscar, grabbing the carrier bag. 'And look! He's brought his bucket and spade for the sands. Isn't that nice?'

'So what!' Billy replied. 'We are going to Blackpool after all. In case you didn't know it, Oscar, there's a beach there. You might find a bucket and spade useful yourself.'

'The day I need a bucket or a spade, Hoppy, I shall hire yours for threepence.'

'Hey, look at Potts's gas-mask case,' shouted Titch. 'It's dead posh. That must've cost a bomb, Potts. Let's have a look at it.'

'My eldest sister bought it for me for Christmas,' said

Potts. 'It's got a red velvet lining and a little zipped pocket for my ear plugs.'

'And what about your teddy bear and your little drum?' said Titch. 'I hope you haven't left them behind.'

'My mother said I had to take no notice of boys who were rude and tried to make fun of me. So I shall ignore you, Smalley,' said Potts.

At Victoria Station there was chaos as thousands of children in crocodile columns each headed by a Pied Piper marched across the concourse to the 'Evacuation Specials', which stood ready and waiting to take them off to their rural and seaside destinations.

Guards' and teachers' whistles shrilled at the same time, adding to the confusion of both schoolchildren and train drivers. Amidst the hissing steam, teachers ran hither and thither through the whirling mass like sheep-dogs, trying to head stray children back into their designated places.

The Damian College contingent found their way to the Blackpool platform and a single blast of Brother Dorian's whistle gave the signal for them all to climb into the compartments of the non-corridor train. A final register check was taken by the form teachers and they were off, clattering out through Salford and Pendleton.

'This is a great adventure into the unknown,' said Oscar.

'I hope it's not an adventure into trouble,' said Titch.

Soon they were out into open country, doing at least ten miles an hour – crawling at a snail's pace through Lancashire's rustic regions.

'If we go any slower,' said Robin, 'we shall be going backwards.'

Then the train did start to go backwards, and a great cheer went up from every compartment.

'We're going back,' said Billy. 'Hitler's surrendered to our Beefeaters.'

Finally the train stopped, and there they remained for a whole hour. 'Why are we waiting?' sang the whole train, followed by an old First World War favourite, 'We're Here Because We're Here'. An inquisitive matronly cow came to the embankment fence to inspect them.

'There's one of Hoppy's brindled cows,' said Oscar.

'And there's a scarecrow in the field,' added Nobby.

'That's not a scarecrow, Nobby,' said Billy. 'That's the farmer.'

While they waited they made weak jokes to pass the time and to cover up their nervousness about what fate had in store for them. Eventually the train began to move, but oh so slowly.

'Why do we have to wear these stupid labels, I wonder?' asked Robin. 'I feel like a turkey with its weight and price tagged to it.'

'It's so people will know who we are,' said Titch.

'But we've got mouths and we can talk. Why do we need labels?' asked Oscar.

'In case we're killed and need to be identified,' said Titch gravely.

'Who'd want to kill us?' asked Billy.

'The Germans, of course. That's why our destination is kept secret,' answered Titch. 'They might want to machine-gun the train.'

'Might be true,' said Robin. 'Look at the way that evacuee ship was sunk last year. I forget what it was called.'

'The *City of Benares*,' said Billy. 'I read about it in my dad's paper. Over three hundred were drowned.'

'Many of the rich people have tried to get their kids out of the big towns,' said Oscar.

'That's what happened to Cash,' said Nobby. 'He went to boarding school in the end.'

'That wasn't because of the war,' said Robin. 'It was because Hoppy beat him in the ring.'

'Anyroad, if the Germans decide to bomb us,' said Titch, 'we're a sitting duck right at this moment 'cos we've stopped again.'

Someone in another compartment started up community singing again, and choruses of 'Ten Green Bottles' and 'Ten Men Went to Mow' rang out across the countryside.

Three hours later, they reached Preston.

'You know,' said Billy, 'I did this journey by bus last year and it took only an hour and a half all the way to Blackpool. Today it's going to be almost four hours.'

'I want to go somewhere,' said Titch, 'and there's no toilet on this train.'

'Pee out of the window,' suggested Robin.

'I can't make my thing reach that high,' he answered.

'I've got the same problem,' said Oscar.

'I've got the answer to our prayers,' said Billy. 'Do it first in my bucket and then chuck it out of the window. The pee, I mean, not the bucket.'

'Me first,' said Titch.

'Me second,' said Oscar.

'For you, Oscar,' said Billy, 'it's threepence. Remember?'

'I can see you were brought up in Cheetham Hill,' he said.

There was a loud yell from the compartment behind.

'Who the hell's throwing tea out of the window?' an angry voice enquired.

Titch popped his head out.

'Well, we haven't thrown any tea,' he called truthfully.

Just then, the sudden thunderous roar of a train going the other way made him jump out of his skin and pull his head back into the compartment.

'That were a close thing,' he said. 'I nearly lost my head. But blast it, I've got a piece of soot in my eye.'

One after another, using their handkerchiefs, they all tried to remove the dirt from Titch's eye, but to no avail. By the time they reached Blackpool's Central Station, his eye was red, swollen and watering and he looked like Tommy Farr after his fight with Joe Louis.

Outside the station, Miss Barrymore took another roll-call to make sure no one had run away. Then she ordered her form into the coaches for final allocation to their new homes and their new parents. Before they set off, three ladies from the WVS boarded the bus bearing lots of small carrier bags.

'We're very sorry, boys, to hear about the air raids on Manchester,' said the first lady.

'We're very sorry to see you taken from your homes like this,' said the second. 'But we have these little parcels of emergency rations – a tin of Spam, a tin of baked beans and a bar of chocolate – to tide you over the next few hours until billets are found for you.'

'We're very sorry we couldn't do more for you,' said the third, 'but we wish you all the very best of luck and we hope you'll be happy here in Blackpool.'

'They're very kind ladies,' said Nobby. 'But what does WVS stand for?'

'Didn't you notice,' said Billy, 'what each one said? WVS stands for "We're Very Sorry".'

'Oh, that explains it,' said Nobby.

The coach moved away from the station.

'Anyone got a tin-opener?' Billy called out.

No one had.

'Ah well,' he said. 'We'll just have to wait till we get one.'

Attention now turned to the business of finding new homes.

'This is the part which worries me most,' said Titch. 'With my kind of luck, I'm bound to end up with a couple of loonies or a mad scientist or something.'

'Stop being so cheerful,' said Billy. 'You might get someone really nice like Sweeney Todd or Boris Karloff.'

The bus wound its way slowly round the streets and avenues of Bispham, stopping every so often so that Miss Barrymore could match boys to billets.

The selected foster-parents waited anxiously at their doorways to see what they had let themselves in for, and what kind of kid destiny would deposit on their doorstep. Would he be thin, fat, tall, short, spotty or bespectacled? Cheeky or well-behaved?

'You two boys, go here,' Miss Barrymore said consulting her clipboard and choosing boys at random. 'And you three go over there.'

Nervously, the boys remaining in the bus watched and waited their turn, wondering what kind of folk fate would ordain for them.

'It's like a raffle or a lottery,' said Oscar.

'More like a cattle market,' said Robin.

Eventually the coach stopped outside a large, luxurious villa and an extremely ugly, cross-eyed lady wearing a pinafore and a hair-net emerged to collect her quota.

'One only here,' called Miss Barrymore.

Every boy tried in his own way to look invisible by avoiding eye contact: some gazed off into space, some looked at the floor, some became suddenly engrossed in the books they weren't reading.

'No volunteers,' she said. 'Then I must use my pre-rogative. I choose you, Hardy.'

'Aw, miss. Please pick on somebody else. Not me!'

' "Many are called, but few are chosen",' she replied. 'Be brave, Hardy, for that is what your name means, and you share it with the great sea-captain, Sir Thomas, who was Nelson's great friend.'

'Yes, miss, if you say so.'

'Also, Olly, remember your other great friend, Laurel,' said Oscar. 'And it looks as if you've gotten yourself into another fine mess.'

Slowly, the reluctant Olly, carrying his case and his gas mask, got up from his seat and, accompanied by his form mistress, dragged himself across the road to his new 'mother', who promptly embraced him and gave him a big kiss, which delighted the busload of boys, sending them into convulsions of laughter.

'Kiss me, Hardy,' Titch called.

The laughter, however, was tinged with a certain amount of relief at their lucky escape.

Two hours later, Miss Barrymore was down to the last five boys, who were now beginning to look tired and dishevelled. The bus drove on, passed a cemetery, turned left into Kincraig Avenue and stopped outside some small semi-detached houses. Billy noticed standing at the gate of number 1 a pretty, dark-haired girl of about twelve years of age who was studying the proceedings with great interest.

'I hope I'm billeted there,' said Billy. 'Now that is what I call a real foster-mother.'

'You should be so lucky,' said Robin.

'I have you five boys left and only four billets,' Miss Barrymore said. 'Come along and we'll see what can be done.'

Mrs Rivers at number 7 was a round, motherly woman with a kind face.

'I'll take two,' she said, as if ordering pints of milk.

'Thank you, Mrs Rivers,' the teacher said. 'It's much appreciated.'

She consulted her clipboard.

'Tony Wilde and Nobby Nodder – you're here with Mrs Rivers. Say good evening to your new mother.'

'Good evening, Mrs Rivers,' the two boys said.

'Come on then, lads,' said Mrs Rivers. 'Bring your things and we'll go inside.'

'Right, I have just you three boys now and then I'm finished, thank the Lord. Let's go and see if we can persuade Mrs Mossop at number 9.'

Mrs Mossop was a serious-looking, unsmiling woman, aged about forty-five. She wore steel-rimmed glasses and her hair was arranged in a bun. She waited impatiently at her door.

'I asked for two girls,' she said. 'Not all these boys.'

'I'm afraid we have only boys in stock today,' said Miss Barrymore. 'Girls are being billeted on the South Shore. But these are three very nice boys.'

The boys did their best to look nice, which wasn't easy since they had been on the road for over eight hours. Robin put on his best angelic expression. Mrs Mossop seemed unimpressed.

'I used to be a nurse,' she said. 'And I can tell you – they don't look very nice to me. That little squidgy one there looks as if he has conjunctivitis, which is very, very contagious. And I have two children of my own to think of. The other two don't look too clean either. They don't have nits or anything like that, do they?'

'I'm sure they don't,' said their teacher. 'They were all medically examined and certified clean before we let them out of Manchester. As for young Smalley there, he's got some dirt in his eye, that's all.'

'What about bed-wetting? I hope they don't wet the bed. I wouldn't stand for that. I've heard some terrible stories from other landladies.'

'These boys have all passed their scholarship – besides which, they're all over twelve years of age. But even if they did wet the bed – which they don't, I can assure you – you would get a special enuresis allowance on top of all the allowances you'll already be getting for three.'

'Aye, but boys eat more than girls, don't they?'

But the mention of money seemed somehow to have done the trick and changed things a little, because Mrs Mossop said:

'Oh well, I suppose I've got no choice. I really did want girls but these three'll have to do. All right then, I'll take them.'

Miss Barrymore entered the details on her pad and then heaved a great sigh of relief.

'Now perhaps I can see to my own accommodation,' she said. 'Best of luck, boys. I'll see you at our new school tomorrow.'

The bus drove off and the boys were left with their new mother.

Inside the house, they saw two young children – a podgy boy who looked a little overweight for his age, and a rather tubby girl who was studying them closely. Mrs Mossop said:

'This is my daughter, Beryl, who is now eight, and this is my darling little boy, Neville, who is six. Say how-do-you-do to our visitors, children.'

'How do'y' do?' said Beryl with a strong, adenoidal twang.

'How do you do,' said Neville, like a trained parrot.

273

'I'm Billy,' said Billy, taking the initiative, 'and this is Robin and Titch. Is Mr Mossop in the army?'

'I can see you're a nosy boy and no mistake,' she said. 'But no, if you want to know, my husband, Donald, is on war work at Salford Docks. He gets home leave every six months or so. Now are you satisfied?'

'Yes, thank you, Mrs Mossop.'

'Anyroad, yours is the back bedroom,' she said. 'It's a bit small but I'm sure you'll be all right. The three of you will have to share the double bed, as I only expected two evacuees.'

'Fine, Mrs Mossop. We'll be OK,' said Robin, his usual optimistic self.

'You can take your things up now and unpack. Go and get a wash in the bathroom but don't make a mess. I hope you brought your own soap and towels with you. When you've finished, come down and I'll give you something to eat.'

'Yes, Mrs Mossop, we brought soap and towels. And we've got some food to give you as well – tins of Spam from the WVS and some chocolate biscuits from my mother in Manchester,' said Billy.

'Well, I'm glad somebody appreciates all that we're doing for you here in Blackpool.'

Upstairs they shared out the wardrobe and drawer space and began putting their things away – which was not a very big job as they hadn't brought all that much with them. They had been occupied in this way for about ten minutes when young Beryl knocked at the door and said:

'I have a letter here for William.'

'A letter for me?' said Billy, perplexed. 'I don't know anyone here.'

'But someone knows you,' replied Beryl. 'It's from

274

Doreen Aspinall who lives at number one.'

'That must be the girl I saw leaning on the gate,' said Billy. 'How does she know my name?'

'I told her,' said Beryl proudly.

Billy took the letter, which was sealed in a blue envelope and addressed in a large hand 'To William'.

'Very odd,' he said.

'Maybe it's a proposal of marriage,' said Titch.

'You're not very far out. Listen to this,' said Billy, reading the letter. ' "*Darling William, I am sorry to hear that you have been bombed out. Will you go with me? I love you. From Doreen Aspinall. P.S. We are having a game of Truth or Dare outside my house tomorrow night and you and your friends are invited.*" '

'Talk about fast worker! How come she loves you and not us?' asked Titch.

'I thought I was the one with the film-star face around here,' said Robin.

'You are. You are,' said Billy. 'But we didn't say which film star.'

'How's about Charles Laughton as the Hunchback of Notre Dame?' suggested Titch.

'Anyway, for Doreen Aspinall it must have been love at first sight,' said Billy.

'Ah, she probably just feels sorry for you 'cos you look so pathetic,' said Robin. 'Are we going to accept?'

'What do you think?' said Billy. 'Of course we're going to accept. I haven't played that game since infant school but I think I can still remember the rules. I suppose they're the same here in Blackpool. Come on, though, we'd better go down and eat.'

Downstairs, Mrs Mossop had prepared a meal of mashed potatoes and cabbage.

'I'm sorry, Mrs Mossop,' Billy said. 'I don't eat cabbage.'

'Can I have yours, Hoppy?' asked Titch.

'And why, may I ask, do you not eat cabbage?' enquired Mrs Mossop.

'It's ever since I saw a whole load of caterpillars on some cabbages. You can't be sure they've all been washed off.'

'On second thoughts, I won't have any cabbage either,' said Titch. 'Could we have some of the Spam, Mrs Mossop?'

'You'll have none of that Spam today. I've put that in the larder for a rainy day. And you'll all have to get used to eating what's given to you. Don't you know there's a war on?'

As they tucked into their mashed potatoes, she stood over them and said:

'We'd better get a few things straight as long as you're in this house. First, I am the one to say what food we'll eat – not you. Secondly, you do not help yourself from my kitchen; in there I'm the boss, d'you understand?'

'Yes, Mrs Mossop,' they chorused.

'We share our food with you and so it's only right that you should share any food you get with us.'

'Yes, Mrs Mossop.'

'And you can stop calling me Mrs Mossop. Call me Auntie – it's more friendly.'

'Yes, Mrs Mossop – Auntie.'

'I've got some other rules as well. I don't want you in this house during the day. During the week don't come back here before five o'clock. As I said, the house is a bit small; we have only this kitchen, a lounge and three small bedrooms and so I can't have you cluttering up the place.'

'What do we do about dinner when we're at school?' asked Billy. 'Do we take sandwiches?'

'I haven't time to be making sandwiches. Besides, I

can't afford them on the allowances I get. You can take any toast that's left over from breakfast. I'm sure you can get by on that.'

'Yes, Auntie. What about weekends?' asked Robin.

'I'll try to make a Woolton Pie on Sundays.'

'Woolton Pie? What's that, Auntie?' asked Billy.

'It's a pie made of carrots, turnips and potatoes.'

'Sounds like good fodder,' whispered Robin.

'And at weekends I don't want you under my feet either – so you can play outside.'

'What if it's raining, Auntie?' asked Titch.

'Then you can go to the garden shed and play in there.'

'Maybe we could keep out of your way by going into the bedroom,' suggested Titch.

'You may not. You must not go upstairs until it's time for bed. And you must never, never go into my bedroom or the children's. Is that clear?'

'Yes, Auntie.'

'I didn't ask for three boys, as you know. So the best thing you can all do is keep right out of my road.'

'You mean "seen and not heard",' said Robin.

'No,' she said. 'I mean both. Not seen. Not heard.'

'What about the bathroom?' asked Titch. 'Are we allowed in the bathroom?'

'There's a toilet out in the garden which you can use during the daytime.'

'What about baths?' asked Robin. 'What do we do if we need a bath?'

'There's not enough hot water for all of us. My back boiler's not big enough. You must take your bath after me and the children have finished.'

'You mean in the same water?' asked Billy incredulously.

'I do, young man. We've got to save water and energy.

Don't you know there's a war on?'

'I think we're beginning to realise it,' said Billy.

'Anyway,' she said, 'I hope you'll all be very happy here. If you're not, it'll be your own fault, because I'll do my very best to make you feel at home.'

'Are we allowed to go out for a walk now?' asked Titch nervously.

'I don't mind what you do as long as you don't come bothering me and as long as you're back by nine o'clock.'

'Thank you, Auntie,' said Robin. 'Right, boys, let's go.'

As soon as they got outside, Billy said:

'The bloody old battleaxe. We may as well be in Strangeways. And we've not even committed a crime.'

'And there's no bail,' said Robin.

'I knew we'd be in trouble as soon as we left Manchester this morning,' said Titch. 'I felt it in my bones.'

'You thought we were going to be machine-gunned by German planes,' said Billy.

'Living with this Mrs Mossop is nearly as bad,' said Titch.

'I'm still hungry,' said Billy. 'Let's see if we can find a shop open and buy a bar of chocolate.'

'A bar of chocolate!' said Robin.

'Don't you know there's a war on?' they chorused.

Chapter Seventeen

Keep A Diary

The next day, the boys reported to school, which had been accommodated in a domestic science college. There they sat between the gas cookers, the sink units and the baking tables whilst Miss Barrymore tried to inspire them with a love of Shakespeare and an appreciation of *Julius Caesar*.

' *"Let me have men about me that are fat"*,' she intoned. ' *"Sleek-headed men and such as sleep o' nights."* '

'She won't find any of those if they come from Mrs Mossop's place,' said Titch.

At the end of the English lesson, Miss Barrymore said:

'Last night I had a brilliant idea for all of you. A famous lady once said, "I always say, keep a diary and some day it'll keep you." '

'Who said that, miss?' asked Oscar.

'A certain Mae West in a film called *Every Day's a Holiday*.'

'But why should we keep a diary, miss?' asked Robin.

'We are living in such an exciting time in history, you should try keeping a record of all that is happening to you. You can also note down all your secret ideas. Who can tell? One day you might be studied by future generations just as we today study Samuel Pepys. If you're interested, you couldn't do better than begin reading an exciting sea-story entitled *Two Years Before the Mast,* by R.H. Dana.'

'If you wrote secret things in it, miss,' said Billy, 'someone else might read them.'

'Oh, no, never,' she answered. 'A diary is a very private thing indeed and no one should ever read another person's secrets. Anyway, it's just an idea. It'll give you food for thought.'

'Talking of food, miss,' said Titch. 'Do you think we could ever have dinner here in the school?'

'I'm afraid not,' she said. 'There are complications with ration books, and although it's a domestic science college, they don't have the facilities to provide food for big numbers. Besides, we are allowed here in the mornings only, as they require their premises back in the afternoons.'

'Does that mean we have only half-day schooling then?' asked Oscar.

''Fraid so,' she said, 'but we have to be grateful we've been given even the mornings, because this place was designed to teach cooking, baking and the other culinary arts.'

'Fancy being taught in a domestic science college!' said Robin. 'The smell of all this grub around the place will drive us mad.'

'Water, water everywhere,' said Titch, 'and not a drop to drink.'

'What I wouldn't give for a piece of my mam's apple pie right now!' said Billy.

At break-time, the boys swapped horror stories with their friends.

'Your Mrs Rivers looked nice and friendly, Oscar,' said Billy.

' "Looked" is the right word. She hasn't spoken to her

husband for two years because of some argument they had about who should wash the pots,' answered Oscar.

'How do they manage?' asked Robin.

'They talk through their young daughter, Mavis,' said Nobby. 'She's a cracker, about our age, by the way. Mr Rivers says, "Mavis, tell your mother there's too much salt in this porridge", and Mrs Rivers says, "Tell your father to like it or lump it." '

'What happens then?'

'He lumps it,' said Oscar.

'What about you, Olly?' asked Billy. 'How are you getting on with your beauty queen?'

'I think I must've got the best billet of you all,' said Olly. 'She's a very rich widow, she's got a car, a chauffeur and everything. She has no kids but she's always wanted a son. So now she's got one, and I'm it!'

'Trust you to be lucky,' said Titch. 'If it were raining soup you'd have a big bowl and I'd have a toasting fork.'

'It's not quite so straightforward,' said Olly. 'She has some peculiar habits.'

'Like for instance?' asked Oscar.

'She smokes a pipe for one thing, and for another, she keeps cuddling and kissing me. Last night she tucked me in and sang me nursery rhymes. It's a well-known fact that women who smoke pipes are not to be trusted.'

'There's nowt so queer as fowk,' said Billy.

'The best billet of the lot,' said Rodney Potts, who'd been listening to their conversation, 'is mine.'

'I suppose you landed up in the Imperial Hotel,' said Titch.

'No,' he said. 'I'm in Brother Dorian's bungalow at Cleveleys along with Miss Barrymore, two other teachers and twelve boys. The food is great and we're well looked after.'

'I'll bet it was your dad pulling strings,' remarked Nobby.

'Or pulling out his wallet,' said Oscar.

'Rubbish,' said Potts. 'It was the luck of the draw.'

'Maybe,' said Titch. 'But first you've got to have the money to buy a ticket.'

In the afternoon, after their meal of cold toast, the three boys wandered along the promenade. The gold of the Golden Mile had turned to grey. The stalls which had so recently been the occasion of so much happiness and gaiety were now boarded up and lifeless. On the beach there were miles and miles of barbed wire to keep potential German invaders at bay. There were airmen everywhere, particularly Polish pilots, who could be distinguished by the small silver eagles chained to their lapels. Even the Tower had had its tip lopped off as it had proved a danger to the many aircraft buzzing around the skies. Even as they strolled along that afternoon, Bolton Paul Defiant fighters zoomed at head-top height along the beach, swooping over the piers at dizzy, breathtaking speeds.

'One of these days, one of those crazy pilots will have a nasty accident,' remarked Billy.

Then, drawn by the sound of a juke-box playing 'Tumbling Tumbleweed', they went into an amusement arcade.

'Anyone got any money?' asked Billy. 'I'm still hungry.'

Between them they managed to raise three penny pieces.

'What's the money for?' asked Robin.

'Over there there's one of those machines with little cranes for lifting toys and things out. And that one has bars of Fry's chocolate. Let's try our luck.'

Billy inserted the first penny and, sticking out his

tongue to aid his concentration, manoeuvred the crane until it picked up a small chocolate bar. Just as he thought he had grabbed it, it slipped out of the grip and fell back amongst the other trinkets.

'Damn and blast it,' he said.

'Here, let me try,' said Titch.

He could do no more than steer the chocolate a little nearer to the edge.

'This requires a professional touch,' said Robin, putting in the last penny.

His efforts left the bar balanced precariously and tantalisingly just over the outlet.

'That's the last coin,' said Robin. 'What do we do now, Hoppy?'

'Confucius he say, "When fate not go your way",' said Billy, narrowing his eyes, ' "give fate little nudge." '

As he spoke, he hit the machine with his backside and the chocolate rolled out.

'Hoi, you lot,' shouted the attendant. 'I saw that. Bring that bloody chocolate back.'

Too late, they were gone. As they walked along the front eating their prize, they were joined by an English airman.

'I saw all that, boys,' he said. 'Are you hungry? Is that it?'

'You're telling me,' said Titch.

'Come on,' said the airman. 'I'll buy you some food.'

'Food?' said Robin. 'What's that?'

Together the four of them went into the self-service restaurant above Woolworth's store.

'That's right,' said the airman as they slid their trays along the bar. 'Enjoy yourselves. Chips and fish, bread and butter and a pot o' tea for the three of you. Just what the doctor ordered. My name's Kevin, by the way.'

To say the boys ate heartily would be the understatement of the year. They pitched in and devoured the meal as if they hadn't eaten properly for a couple of days – which they hadn't.

Kevin watched them with an amused smile.

'I thought you were hungry when I saw you trying to capture the chocolate in the arcade. Look, I can't stay now. But I like your company. You remind me of my young brother at home. Would you like to go to the pictures with me tomorrow? I'll pay. They're showing *Stagecoach*, starring John Wayne, at the Regent.'

'That'd be fantastic,' said Titch, 'because we're going to be free every afternoon.'

'OK, Kevin,' said Robin. 'It's a deal. See you tomorrow.'

'Right,' said Kevin as he got up to leave. 'I'll meet you outside the cinema at two o'clock tomorrow.'

'At last, a friendly face,' said Billy.

When they got back to their billet at five o'clock, Mrs Mossop had prepared a meal of baked beans – their own – on toast. They tucked in ravenously despite the fish and chips earlier.

'I knew it,' she said. 'Boys just wade in and shovel it down. I don't think I can afford to feed you lot on the pittance they're paying.'

'Sorry, Auntie,' they said.

After tea they went upstairs to prepare for the game of Truth or Dare. Billy spent much time trying to tame and flatten an errant lock of hair which insisted on sticking up like a feather on an Indian brave. Feeling happy, nervous and excited, they went downstairs.

'I know where you three are going,' Mrs Mossop said. 'You're going out swapping spit with those girls in the avenue.'

'Hope so,' Robin whispered to Billy.

'I wonder if it's the same game as I used to play many years ago,' said Billy.

'We'll soon find out,' said Titch nervously.

They called next door for Nobby and Oscar. Nobby appeared immediately.

'Let's go,' he said.

'What about Oscar?' asked Titch.

'I dunno,' said Nobby. 'He says he's not interested in girls. He prefers to stay in, reading.'

'Maybe the love bug hasn't bitten him yet,' said Billy.

Outside the gate of number 1, four girls were already waiting.

'Hello, William,' said Doreen of the long black tresses. 'This is Mavis, who lives next door to you; this is Sally, who lives opposite; and this is Ruby, who is fourteen and works at the Milady toffee factory.'

Mavis was a fair-haired girl with bright, clear blue eyes and a freckled complexion – obviously the healthy, outdoor type – whilst Sally was an auburn-haired beauty with dark-brown eyes and a ready smile. Ruby was also pretty, with a friendly face, but what distinguished her from the others was her grown-up figure with its definite shapely bust – which the boys weren't slow to notice.

The evacuees smiled and nodded shyly.

'I'm Billy but everyone calls me Hoppy; and this is Robin, Titch and Nobby. But Mavis and Nobby already know each other as they live in the same house.'

'Right,' she said. 'It's nice to have some boys from Manchester as a change from all the lads here in the avenue. Do you know how to play this game?'

'I played it a long time ago,' said Billy, 'and I think I can remember it.'

We all stand in line against the fence – first a boy, then a girl, then a boy again, like that.'

The participants arranged themselves according to the instructions, and Doreen started off the proceedings. In the first round, everyone cagily opted for Truth.

'Hoppy, is it true you've never kissed a girl?'

'No, it's not true. I once kissed a girl when I was in infant school.'

'Mavis, is it true you like boys a lot?'

'Yes, it's true.'

When Doreen had gone round everyone with her questions, Billy said:

'It *is* the same game that I used to play years ago, when I was a mixed infant.'

'Then you've not learnt very much,' said Ruby. 'We'll have to see if we can teach you a thing or two here in Blackpool. I'll start the second round.'

Doreen opted for Dare.

'I dare you to show Hoppy what a real kiss is like by giving him a film-star kiss.'

Doreen wrapped herself around Billy, put both hands behind his head and gave him a long, lingering kiss as she had seen Katherine Hepburn do with Cary Grant.

'Wow! When's the wedding?' asked Titch.

Having seen what happened with a Dare, Robin thought he'd better play it safe and chose Truth.

'Coward!' said Ruby. 'Is it true you've never felt a girl?'

'True!' said Robin, turning bright red under the streetlamp.

Courageously, Titch selected Dare.

'I dare you to put your right hand on Sally's breast.'

Titch did as he was instructed.

'But there's nothing there,' he said. 'It's as flat as a billiard table.'

'Thank you very much,' said Sally. 'Don't you be so cheeky. There is something there.'

When it came to Sally's turn, Ruby said:

'I dare you to feel Titch's thing.'

Sally placed her hand at the strategic place.

'But there's nothing there,' she said, getting her own back. 'It's as flat as a pancake.'

'What do you expect,' said Titch. 'After all, my name is Dick Smalley.'

Nobby was next in line.

'Let's see how daring you are. I dare you to put your hand here,' said Ruby, indicating her breasts.

Nobby put his hand on his own chest and said:

'Nothing to it.'

That night in Blackpool, the boys' sex education had begun. The second lesson was the very next day.

As the boys were leaving their classroom at lunchtime the following day, they passed the wing where a lesson in baking was just about to finish. As they listened to the teacher, their mouths watered.

'So, girls,' the teacher was saying, 'always keep pastry light and fluffy. The secret is in the amount of fat you use and the method of rolling. Our efforts today at shortcrust mushroom pie should be ready in about ten minutes. We'll have a short coffee-break and then finish. Now remember where you left your dish in the oven, as we don't want to get them mixed up, do we?'

The class laughed politely at the thought of this happening.

'Dear me no,' said the teacher. 'We don't want to go home with someone else's pie, do we?'

No sooner had the class filed out to the common room than Billy said:

'This is where my Cheetham Hill training comes in handy. Quick, boys!'

With the speed of lightning, they whipped into the classroom, opened the oven doors, helped themselves to a mushroom pie each and were out of the room before the cookery students had even poured their coffees.

They walked along the front, munching voraciously at the stolen pies.

'Do you realise that a hundred and fifty years ago we'd have been sent to Botany Bay for this?' said Titch.

'It would be worth it for these pies,' said Robin.

'Yes,' said Billy. 'But there's something worrying me.'

'What's that?' asked Titch anxiously.

'That teacher was right. These pies needed another ten minutes.'

Just before two o'clock, the boys arrived at the Regent cinema to find Kevin already waiting. He paid for four seats in the stalls, and as they settled down – Kevin on the outside of the row next to Billy, with Titch and Robin on the inside – offered round a bag of sweets.

'Chocolate eclairs,' he said. 'Only the best is good enough. And this should be a really exciting film.'

'We're really looking forward to it,' said Robin.

'Let me see your hands,' Kevin said, taking Robin's right hand into his own. 'They're so soft. I'll bet none of you has ever done a real day's work. Look at mine.'

Titch examined the palms of Kevin's hands.

'They're rough,' he said. 'You must do very hard work for the RAF. Look at my hands; they're soft like Robin's and Hoppy's.'

Kevin examined Billy's hands as well.

'It's time you three did some work for a living,' he said.

The big picture began and soon the three boys were transported to Monument Valley as the stagecoach bearing its five passengers made its hazardous way across Indian territory. Soon the passengers were joined by the Ringo Kid in the person of John Wayne.

'Gosh, isn't this exciting?' said Kevin, taking hold of Billy's hand. 'Don't worry, though. John Wayne will look after them.'

Billy became completely engrossed in the action of the story, which began to reach a climax when the Indians attacked the coach and it was only because of the Ringo Kid's bravery that the day was saved. As the coach rolled into Lordsburg escorted by the cavalry, Billy felt the imprint of a button on his hand and became aware that his right hand was being used to massage Kevin's testicles.

He snatched his hand away, got up, and said:

'I'm just going to the toilets and also to see the manager.'

Two minutes later he was back with the manager, but Kevin's seat was empty.

'Where's he gone?' he asked.

'Dunno,' said Titch. 'When you went to the toilet he got up very quickly and walked out. What did you say to him, Hoppy?'

'Whatever it was,' said Robin, 'we just lost our meal-ticket.'

'Worse things happen at sea,' said Billy.

Later on that night, when they were in the bedroom, he told them what had happened. For hour after hour they plagued him for further details.

'Eh, what was it like?' asked Robin and Titch over and over again.

'The nearest thing I can think of,' said Billy, 'is a peach. It was like massaging a large soft peach.'

'Eh, was it heck. What was it really like, eh? What did it really feel like, eh? Did it? Did it heck!'

When news of the event got round the school, Billy was a celebrity for some time afterwards as the whole schoolboy body latched on to the catchphrase.

'Eh, what was it like, eh? Like massaging a peach? Was it heck! What did it feel like, eh? Did it heck!'

Boys continued to trot out the phrases long after the event which had occasioned them had been forgotten.

Psychologists have claimed that somewhere between the ages of eleven and thirteen a young boy experiences a gradual awakening of his dormant sexual desires, which grow in strength until they amount almost to an obsession. Under normal circumstances, this might be true, but for our three boys at number 9, Kincraig Avenue in 1941, circumstances were far from normal. They did, however, have one obsession – food! They spoke of and thought of little else.

The subject even invaded their dreams, and they had nightly visions of Christmas turkey, roast potatoes and plum duff.

'Last night,' said Titch, 'I dreamt of a bakery and tray upon tray of hot, crusty bread soaked in creamy butter. It was so real you could even smell the grain and the flour.'

'That, I suppose,' said Billy, 'is what is called a wheat dream.'

Billy even began to eat cabbage.

'What about the caterpillars?' asked Titch.

'Good protein.'

Ideas far removed from the topic of food became immediately associated with eating.

'Fancy going for a stroll?' asked Robin one evening.

'Sure,' replied Billy. 'But where are we gonna buy a roll at this time of night?'

'What's that book you're reading, Hoppy?' asked Titch.

'It's a book about spies.'

'What kind of pies? Apple or rhubarb?'

They tried every way they knew to supplement Mrs Mossop's meagre fare. Doreen stole food for Billy from her mother's larder, Sally became Titch's provider, and Ruby brought bags of Milady toffees for Robin. The boys' two-and-sixpenny postal orders which arrived from home every Friday became their lifeline.

'I'm beginning to feel like that music-hall singer, G.H. Elliott,' said Robin one Friday as they came out of the sweet shop. 'You know, the one they call the chocolate-coloured coon.'

'Me too,' added Titch. 'I've eaten so much Cadbury's I look like the chocolate soldier. We've been here now for three months and I think we're suffering the torture of slow starvation.'

'It's time we did something,' said Billy. 'I didn't want to bother my mam and dad at home 'cos they've got their own troubles, what with the bombing and all that. But I think I'll write them a letter.'

'You mean complaining?' asked Robin.

'No, not so much that,' said Billy. 'I could ask them to send us some food or something. My dad can get fruit in Smithfield Market.'

'That would be really fantastic,' said Titch.

One day, two weeks later, they got back to Kincraig Avenue from one of their frequent visits to the amusement arcades at about four o'clock.

'We're not allowed back in until five o'clock,' said Titch. 'What about a game of cricket against the lamppost?'

'Great idea, Titch,' said Robin sarcastically. 'What do we use for a bat or ball, since they're up there in the bedroom.'

'What're you so scared about?' said Billy. 'She can't

stop us going to get our own things. I'll go up and get them. I'd like to see her stop me.'

Boldly he went into the house by the back door. As he crossed the threshold, he was met by the most delicious whiff of meat stew, and there at the kitchen table sat Mrs Mossop with her two children tucking into a meal of Lancashire hotpot complete with golden pastry crust.

'What do you mean bursting in on us like that?' she screamed. 'You're not allowed in until five o'clock and you know it.'

'Sorry, Auntie,' he said. 'Just want to get our cricket things from the bedroom.'

'Hurry up and get out,' she yelled.

Billy did as he was told but not without a backward glance at the meal, which was still steaming on the table.

That night the boys were given their usual meal of bread and jam. When they went to bed, Billy wrote furiously in the diary which he kept locked in his case under the bed:

'*Came home early today. Entered house at four o'clock. Found Mrs Mossop having secret meal of Tater Ash. She was very angry as she was CAUGHT IN THE ACT!*'

'Did you ever hear from your mam and dad about the parcel you wrote for?' asked Titch.

'I had a letter from them to say they had sent some fruit. Jaffas, my dad said. Eat them slowly, my Mam wrote, 'cos they're like gold. But they never arrived.'

'They've gone astray,' said Robin. 'A lot of things have gone missing because of the war.'

'More like one of those thieving temporary postmen,' said Titch, always ready to look on the bright side.

'Well, parcel or no parcel,' said Billy, 'I don't intend letting Mrs Mossop starve us. We'll wait our chance.'

Their chance came on Friday night.

* * *

It was one of those rare occasions when Mrs Mossop was going out for the evening – on the town! During the day she had been to the beauty salon for a hair-do and a facial. She had removed her glasses and looked almost pretty.

'I shall be back about ten thirty,' she said. 'I'm leaving you boys in charge and you are on your honour. Look after things whilst I'm out, and maybe tomorrow you'll have a nice omelette for dinner.'

'Real eggs?' asked Billy. 'Or the dried variety?'

'Dried, of course,' she said. 'What else is there?'

Whilst she was out, the boys and her two children played a game of Monopoly with much cheating and much arguing about rents, mortgages and going to gaol, until it was time for bed. At ten o'clock the two young ones were duly retired and the three boys were installed in their double bed top and tail. The five youngsters filled the house with the singing of all the patriotic songs they knew, beginning with 'God Save the King', through the Polish national anthem and 'Rule Britannia', and finishing with 'There'll Always Be an England'.

'Did you notice,' said Robin, 'in that last song, there's no mention of Scotland and Wales?'

'Perhaps they've had their chips,' said Titch.

'Are you going to read us a bedtime story before we go to sleep?' shouted Neville.

'OK, just one,' called Billy. 'And then it's time for shut-eye.'

He went through to their bedroom and read them the story of 'The Frog Prince' by the Brothers Grimm.

'That's it for tonight,' he said, as he got up to go. 'Time for sleep now.'

As he was leaving, he noticed some very tiny blue

stickers on their dressing-room mirror. 'Jaffa', they read.

'Where did you get these?' he asked.

'Mummy said it's a secret and we weren't to tell. But they were on the big oranges she gave us.'

'I see,' said Billy. 'You were very lucky to get a Jaffa orange. Don't you know there's a war on?'

That night he made another entry in his diary.

At about eleven thirty Mrs Mossop came home, and she wasn't alone. The boys were still awake and they heard the sound of a man's voice – a foreign voice.

'Do you think it's a spy?' said Titch. 'Do you think Mrs Mossop works for the Germans?'

'Grow up, Titch, and don't ask daft questions,' said Billy. 'Of course she does.'

Half an hour later, Mrs Mossop went into her bedroom. And so did the man.

'Now's our chance,' said Billy, 'to get some food. Titch, you listen at her bedroom door and give the word if you think she's coming out. Robin and I will go downstairs and see what's in the pantry.'

The three of them listened at her door to make sure she was fully occupied, but all they could hear was the creaking of bed springs and Mrs Mossop moaning as if in pain.

'Whatever she's doing,' whispered Titch, 'she doesn't sound as if she's enjoying it.'

Robin and Billy went down to the kitchen, where they noticed a Polish pilot's tunic draped on one of the chairs.

'It's nice to know that Auntie is doing her bit for the war effort,' whispered Robin.

They managed to filch a good piece of cheese and a hunk of bread. As they lay in bed consuming their feast, Billy said:

'Another entry for my diary. At this rate I'm going to need a bigger book.'

In the afternoons, the trio continued to frequent the arcades, looking for coins which punters might have dropped on the floor or left in the slots of the apparatus. Over the months they had become extremely skilful at manoeuvring prizes out of the crane-grab machine and other tests of mechanical skill. They had also come to know every tune in every juke-box: the Ink Spots' 'I Don't Want to Set the World on Fire', Flanagan and Allen's 'Let's Be Buddies', Tommy Trinder's 'All Over the Place' and many others.

They had also invented an extremely dangerous game called 'Race Against the Sea'. The game was most exciting when the sea was rough and choppy, and required good timing as it involved running down the wooden promenade steps when the tide receded and then running back up to beat the returning wave. The winner was the one who could run furthest down the steps, and the game was made more hazardous by the fact that the steps were wet and slippery. On one of these occasions Billy ran down almost to the bottom, but as he turned to come back, he skidded on the greasy surface. The sea showed no mercy and a great wave enveloped him, soaking and almost drowning him in the process.

There was nothing for it but to find shelter in the warmth of Woolworth's café, where they found they could just about afford one cup of tea with the twopence they had left. Completely saturated and dripping sea-water everywhere, Billy sat huddled near a radiator.

'We can't go back until five o'clock,' said Robin. 'So you'd better make that cup of tea last.'

The hands of the clock moved extremely slowly and it seemed like eternity before it was time to go back to the billet. When they finally got there, there was more trouble waiting. Mrs Mossop was on the warpath. As Billy went into the house, shivering and sneezing, she was standing there, hands on hips.

'I've just been cleaning out the bedrooms and I've found this,' she said ominously, indicating Billy's diary.

'But that was in my locked case under the bed,' he managed to stammer between sneezes.

'Well, you left it open this time,' she yelled. 'And just what do you mean by "Caught in the Act", you cheeky little bugger. If you were my child, I'd give you a bloody big slap in the chops.'

'You have no right to pry into my things,' said Billy. 'That diary was private.'

'And so is my life,' she bawled. 'Who I choose to get in bed with is my business, not a little snotty-nosed evacuee's. How dare you write in your diary, "Tonight, Auntie brought home an airman and together they went climbing and exploring the North Pole." And later there's this: "Where did Auntie get the Jaffa oranges?"'

'Well, where did you get them from?' asked Robin, joining in the fray.

'I bought those from Thomas Talbot's Fruit Market on Waterloo Road.'

'And I suppose they went over to Palestine to get them,' said Titch.

It was then that Billy collapsed in a heap, shivering uncontrollably.

'Why, he's ill! Quick! Help me get him to bed,' exclaimed Mrs Mossop, her nurse's instincts coming to the fore.

Billy remained in bed for ten days, suffering from a severe bout of influenza. During that time, Miss Barrymore came to visit him:

'You have been very ill,' she said, 'and you have lost a great deal of weight.'

'I was already a tin-ribs to start with, miss,' he said.

'This is the billet where the lady was most reluctant to take you, isn't it? I feel partly to blame for all that's happened. I should have been along to see how you were getting on much earlier than this.'

That afternoon, Billy and his form teacher had a long heart-to-heart about the billet and the treatment they had received at the hands of 'Auntie'.

'I'm not sure about that idea of keeping a diary, miss,' said Billy.

'It's a good idea,' she said. 'But you must always make sure it's kept under lock and key. You never know, one day you might include some of the details in a book.'

A week later, Mrs Mossop was requested to attend at the school to meet Brother Dorian. The trio were called out of class to go to his office. There they found Auntie, wearing a smartly cut suit, and a hat with a veil, but looking distinctly uncomfortable. She was left in no doubt as to whose side the head was on.

'Come in, the little soldiers,' boomed Brother Dorian.

There followed not so much a trial as an inquisition.

'Tell me, Mrs . . . cr . . . Messup. What do you give these young growing boys for tea? Perhaps muffins with butter, or crumpets? Perhaps eggs, cheese, meat, that kind of thing?'

'Well, no,' she said falteringly. 'I make them a nice tea of bread and jam or lemon cheese.'

'Yes, yes, I see,' he said, making Auntie's food sound like Oliver Twist's workhouse gruel. 'And what about supper? Perhaps hot-milk chocolate or cocoa with a biscuit or two?'

The three boys exchanged 'is-he-kidding?' glances.

'Well, no,' she said. 'I don't give my own children anything before bed. Besides, we couldn't afford all those

297

things on the allowances you pay to us landladies.'

'No, no, quite,' he murmured. 'Talking of allowances, I notice on the returns you have been submitting that you have been claiming the special enuresis allowance. Which of these boys wets the bed?'

Mrs Mossop had turned red.

'I can't really say. But I did once find the bed slightly wet,' she said.

'Quite. Quite,' he said. 'Well, thank you for coming, madam. I think I have the picture now.'

Turning to the boys, he said:

'Wait outside the door now, you brave little soldiers. England should be proud of you.

'Now, Mrs Messup, I am going to take the three boys away from you.'

'Mossop, sir. Very well, then. But perhaps you could send me two nice girls in their place?'

'Be under no delusions, madam. Under no circumstances would I even contemplate such a thing. I do not consider you a fit person to take care of young evacuees.'

'Well, I must say! I did my best for them. I looked after them, I did.'

'Tell me, madam, do you consider half-starving them was looking after them? Do you consider keeping them out of the house until five o'clock every day in all kinds of weather to be looking after them? I am in two minds whether to advise the evacuation authorities to prosecute you for falsifying the returns you made.'

'I don't know what you mean.'

'You claimed the enuresis allowance when you knew perfectly well it was false,' he roared angrily. 'These young boys are away from home, and they come from good homes, let me tell you. They are young and vulnerable and it is an easy thing to take advantage of them. The generous allowance you received was for their sustenance, not your profit. Now I advise you, madam, to go before I change my mind about prosecuting you. I shall find a new billet for them this very day. Good day, madam.'

'Well, I've never been so insulted in all my life!'

Mrs Mossop stormed out of his office and glowered at the three boys, who had heard every word of the discourse, as Brother Dorian had intended.

'Now, my young warriors,' he said. 'I want you to go back to your billet with Miss Barrymore and collect your things. I am moving you all to my bungalow at Cleveleys. I think you will find the fare we provide a distinct improvement on what you have been used to with that wretched woman. Go along and I shall send Miss Barrymore to you immediately after lessons.'

'Oh, thank you, sir,' they said together.

'At last things are looking up,' said Robin when they got outside. 'According to Potts, we've got the best billet in Blackpool.'

'About time too,' said Billy, 'after the lousy time we've been having with Auntie. Going to live with Brother Dorian is bound to be better.'

'You know,' said Titch, 'whenever I hear you two talking happily like that . . .'

'It makes you feel happy too, I suppose,' said Robin.

'No,' said Titch. 'That's when I feel most worried.'

'You're just a born Jeremiah,' said Billy.

'Not at all. I just feel that if things are going to get better, it's only because they're going to get worse later on.'

Chapter Eighteen

Out of The Frying Pan . . .

In the spacious living room of Martindale Bungalow, the three boys, feeling distinctly ill at ease, sat stiffly together on the edge of the *chaise-longue*. Brother Dorian was standing, whisky and soda in hand, with his back to the fireplace.

'You three young, brave warriors have come through the fire, and now you must become hardened like tempered steel, ready to face up to all the trials and tribulations that you will meet on the road of life. Are you ready for such challenges?'

'Yes, sir,' they said, not altogether sure exactly which challenges he was referring to.

'One of our generous old boys,' he continued, 'has kindly given us the lease of this magnificent bungalow together with all its elegant period furniture for as long as we require it. I feel it is our solemn duty to so bear ourselves that should we be here for a hundred years, men will still say, "Neither the furniture nor the residence had a single mark upon them." Do you agree with these sentiments?'

'Yes, sir,' they chorused enthusiastically.

'You will sleep in the main house, and I have reserved

for this purpose the top attic room, which has a truly panoramic view of the sea. I trust you will find this to your satisfaction.'

'Yes, sir,' they chanted eagerly.

'I have also arranged for all our boys to eat and spend their leisure hours in the capacious garage at the back of the house. In charge there we have a most worthy fifth-former in the person of Pablo Garcia, who has my full authority and acts on my behalf. You will find him firm but fair and you must obey him in all matters. Do you agree to this arrangement?'

'Yes, sir,' they sang in unison – at the same time wondering what would have happened if they had said 'No, sir, these arrangements are unacceptable.'

'You will find the food here plain but wholesome and a great improvement on that provided by your Mrs Massey.'

'Mossop, sir,' said Billy. 'She was called Mossop.'

'Mossop, Moscrop, Mossman, Mussell – no matter. You will find our comestibles a distinct improvement. We have an excellent cook in Brother Brendan, who will make sure that your need for sustenance is well met. Does all this meet with your approval?'

'Oh, yes, sir,' they said fervently.

'Very well. I shall conduct you to the garage and introduce you to Pablo.'

The garage was large enough to accommodate a fleet of cars. The far end had been converted into a mini games area with a small billiard table and a darts board, whilst at the near end there was a large oak dining table with monks' benches at either side and a large carver chair at the head.

'This is Pablo Garcia, our head boy at Martindale,' said Brother Dorian, indicating a tall, dark, heavily built youth. 'Three more for you, Pablo. That gives you a total of fourteen. Can you cope?'

'No problem, Brother,' Pablo replied. 'I can cope.'

'Then I shall leave you now in the capable hands of Pablo, who will show you our facilities and explain our routines. Good afternoon, boys.'

'Good afternoon, sir, and thank you, sir,' the three boys said.

When he had gone, Billy turned to his two companions.

'We're going to be OK here,' he said. 'It's much better.'

'I just knew things were going to get better,' said Robin. 'Everything has turned out for the best.'

'I hope you're right,' said Titch doubtfully.

No sooner had he spoken than Pablo took out a large scout knife and threw it at the garage door just behind Billy's head, missing him by a hair's breadth.

'I did not say you could speak,' he said with a most peculiar smile on his face. 'In this place, I am boss and you speak when I say so. Do you hear me?'

'Yes,' they mumbled.

'Louder!' he cried. 'Say, "Yes, Pablo, we hear you."'

'Yes, Pablo, we hear you,' they shouted together.

'Told you there'd be trouble,' whispered Titch.

'Did you speak then?' demanded Pablo, recovering his knife from the door.

'Not me,' replied Titch. 'Not a word.'

'Understand this,' said Pablo. 'If you want to play darts or billiards, you ask permission and then you sign the book. Got it?'

'Got it,' they said.

'At mealtimes, I bring the food from the main kitchen. You eat when I say so. Got it?'

'Got it.'

'You step out of line and you don't eat. Give me cheek – you don't eat. Break any of the rules – you don't eat. Say, "Yes, Pablo." '

'Yes, Pablo.'

'May we please play darts and billiards this afternoon, Pablo?' asked Billy.

'Yes,' said Pablo. 'But first, you go down on one knee – all three of you – and say, "May we please, Pablo?" '

'May we please, Pablo?' they asked from the kneeling position.

'Very well,' he said. 'You're getting the idea. Now sign the book, join the others at the back and wait your turn. I have to go into Blackpool for Brother Dorian's snuff and I shall be gone for a couple of hours.'

'Thank you, Pablo,' the three boys said.

'Bassett, I'm leaving you in charge and I'll want a full report when I get back.'

When Pablo had gone, there was an audible sigh of relief – a cork-out-of-the-bottle effect – as the fourteen boys tried to make up their daily quota of conversation like Trappist monks suddenly released from their vows.

As the trio played a game of '301' at the darts board, Billy said:

'Thought you said this was a good billet, Potts. That Pablo is a bloody big bully.'

'Not so,' said Potts. 'He sounds tough but he's always very fair. You'll see.'

'It's more like a gaol,' said Robin. 'We just need a couple of warders, a few Alsatians and a solitary confinement cell, and we're there.'

'And James Cagney and George Raft,' added Billy, 'and don't forget the electric chair.'

'We could try digging a tunnel,' said Titch, 'but with my kind of luck it'd come up in Brother Dorian's bedroom.'

'Anyway, the food here is good,' said Potts. 'You'll see at dinner tonight.'

'Dinner at night?' said Billy. 'What kind of weird place is this we've come to? Next thing you'll be saying supper is tomorrow morning.'

Dinner was at seven o'clock in the evening, and the fifteen boys – all with good healthy appetites – were standing around in anticipation of the 'off' signal. In front of Pablo's place at the head of the table, the soup plates and the thick 'paving-stone' slices of bread were piled up ready for the feast.

'Come and get it!' called Brother Brendan from the kitchen in the big house.

'Right. Bassett and I will bring the food across,' said Pablo. 'The rest of you wait at your places.'

The trio sat down at one of the benches in readiness.

'If he catches you sitting down,' said Potts, 'you don't eat. You have to wait until Pablo gives the word before you sit down and before you can begin.'

Pablo and Bassett soon came back carrying between them a large, double-handled cauldron of hot, delicious-smelling soup.

'Make way! It's fish soup!' called Pablo as they set the heavy dish down at the head of the table.

The diners stood at their places, their tongues hanging out, their mouths watering at the prospect of getting that lovely concoction inside them.

'First – grace!' announced Pablo, throwing his scout knife quivering into the table. 'For what we are about to receive, may the Lord make us truly thankful.'

'Amen!' they all replied impatiently.

'Sit!' he ordered.

Then, skilfully and carefully, he ladled the soup into the plates, which were then passed from hand to hand down the table. Next came the slices of bread, and when all had been distributed, he said:

'You can begin!'

Fourteen spoons were lifted and were about to descend as one when suddenly Pablo called:

'Wait! There's one slice of bread left.'

'You have it, Pablo,' said Potts ingratiatingly. 'You've earned it.'

'No,' he said. 'Justice must not only be done, but must be seen to be done.'

Wresting his knife from the table, he cut the slice into fifteen small squares – each about the size of an Oxo cube – and distributed one each to the assembled company.

'Never let it be said,' he stated, 'that I, Pablo, took more than my fair share. Now, once again – you can begin.'

It was then that Billy saw the fish eyes floating on the surface of his soup. He thought for a moment of caterpillars and cabbage. He hesitated. He closed his eyes and made a decision.

Bugger it! he thought I'm too hungry to worry about it.

The boys fell into their new way of life, and although they found it difficult at first to adjust to Pablo's hard manner, they found that Brother Dorian's early assessment of him as 'firm but fair' was about right. They weren't too keen on his knife-throwing exercises, but these were severely curtailed after an incident one Saturday morning.

'See that small round mark on the door, Hoppy,' he said, pointing to a knot about the size of a penny.

'Yes, I see it, Pablo.'

'Throwing underhand, I'll get the knife right into it. Watch!'

He threw the knife low down, but instead of hitting the mark with the point of the blade, he struck it with the hilt. The knife bounced out of the door and embedded itself in his shin. Pablo uttered no sound. He looked in surprise at his leg, reached down, calmly removed the knife and went off to get a plaster. Billy noticed that after that there was a definite reduction in knife-throwing.

Not so spartan was Rodney Potts. On the same Saturday morning, Potts came into the garage, holding his hand to his forehead and grimacing in pain as he approached Pablo.

'I have the most terrible headache, Pablo. May I please be excused from football practice this afternoon?'

'Come off it, Potts,' said Pablo. 'You're making it up. You're like a shy bride on her wedding night.'

'Honestly, Pablo, it's true. I do have a headache.'

'S'probably a brain tumour,' said Titch cheerfully.

'Yes, that's what it looks like,' said Robin. 'Why, there's even a big bump at the back here.'

'Nonsense,' said Billy. 'That's where his mother dropped him. Or maybe it's proof that he comes from the apes. You're the missing link, Potts.'

They came home from football later that day and were sitting around the table waiting for their cream of onion soup.

'So, then, Pottsy,' said Titch. 'How's the brain tumour?'

'Cut it out, Smalley,' he said.

'I would, if I were a surgeon,' said Titch.

'Don't worry, Pottsy,' said Robin. 'We'll see you get a good funeral.'

'Or he could give his body for medical research,' said Billy.

'If you're not careful, Pottsy,' said Titch, 'people will start to call you big-headed.'

'Anyway,' said Pablo, 'you missed the football, Potts, and in my book that means death. Which do you prefer – burial or cremation?'

'Just stop it – all of you!' cried Potts, rushing away from the table.

Later that night, Billy realised that they had over-stepped the mark with the hypersensitive Potts when they found him kneeling by his bedside, his missal open, reciting the prayer, Litany for a Happy Death.

'*O Lord my God, I now, at this moment, readily and willingly accept at Thy hand whatever kind of death it may please Thee to send me, with all its pains, penalties and sorrows.*'

'Listen, Potts,' Billy said. 'It was all a daft joke. No one really meant it. You'll live till you're a hundred.'

'No,' said Potts. 'I'm ready to die and I shall phone my dad tomorrow and tell him to arrange the funeral.'

'Don't be so stupid, Pottsy,' said Robin.

'It's all gone wrong,' said Titch. 'There'll be trouble.'

Titch was right. For once his pessimistic prediction came true.

The following night when Billy, dressed only in pyjamas, was coming out of the downstairs lavatory, he saw in the main hallway a small knot of boys, with Brother Dorian towering in their midst. He was brandishing a long cane above his head.

'Pull the chain and close the lavatory door, boy,' he bellowed. 'Then come over here.'

Shaking with fear, Billy joined the little assembly.

'Now, this evening,' began Brother Dorian, 'I have had a most distressing telephone call from Potts's father. He accuses you, Hopkins, of persecuting and tormenting his son. Is this so?'

'Yes, sir,' said Billy, now paralysed with terror.

'He claims that you have convinced his son that he is about to die of a tumour on the brain. Is this true?'

'It's not true about the tumour, sir, but Potts did think he was going to die.'

'Did you think you were going to die, Potts?'

'Yes, sir. He asked me if I wanted to be buried or cremated.'

'I cannot allow this kind of thing to go on under my roof,' roared Brother Dorian. 'I am going to give you, Hopkins, a thrashing you will never forget. Bend over.'

As Billy was in the act of touching his toes, he thought back to the last time he'd had the stick – to the agony, to the purple weals left on his backside. This time would be infinitely worse, as he was wearing only thin cotton pyjamas. His fingers reached his toes.

'Stretch tighter, boy. Tighter.'

Billy winced, steeled himself and waited for the first stroke to descend.

'Wait, sir,' said a voice. 'I cannot allow you to do this.' It was Robin.

'Cannot allow! What on earth do you mean, boy?' raged the brother.

'Everybody here present was involved,' said Robin. 'So you must punish us all.'

Titch and the other boys exchanged glances on hearing this. They did not look altogether happy about Robin's suggestion.

'Explain yourself, Gabrielson.'

'It was just a prank, sir. A joke that went wrong. We had no idea that Potts would take us seriously.'

'I support Gabrielson, sir,' said Pablo. 'We were all involved. You must punish us all.'

'I see. I see,' said Brother Dorian. 'Get up, Hopkins.'

His heart still thumping, Billy straightened up.

'Now, Potts. Why did you name Hopkins if so many others were involved?'

'His was the first name to come to mind,' said Potts.

'Potts, you are a great sissy!' boomed the brother. 'A girl! A spoiled brat! It's time you grew up and faced up to the world. As for the rest of you, these games must stop. I shall overlook it this time. Now be off with all of you before I change my mind.'

'Oh, thank you, sir. Thank you, sir,' they all murmured as they began climbing the stairs.

'Wait a moment!'

They froze.

'Tell me, Potts. What did you decide in the end? Burial or cremation?'

'Burial, sir.'

'That's good, Potts, since cremation is forbidden by the Church.'

Back in their room, Titch said:

'That was a close shave. I like the way, Robin, you volunteered us all for the stick. That was very brave of you. If you ask me, you've spent too much time reading all that public school stuff in *The Fifth Form at St Dominic's*. Next time, volunteer your own backside. If you want to be brave, let it be your own funeral, not ours!'

'I owe you one, Robin!' said Billy. 'What courage! What bravery! What madness!'

In the warm spring of that year, there was little to remind them that a major world war was being fought in far-off lands, and that only a few miles away Goering's Blitzkrieg continued unabated. The air above them was filled with friendly aircraft and the boys had become expert in aircraft identification: Avro Ansons, Bothas, Paul Defiants, Hurricanes and Spitfires – they could recognise them all with hardly a second glance.

After the brain tumour incident, the trio became more friendly towards Potts and began to include him in their activities.

'He's spent too much time in the company of women,' said Robin. 'Remember, he's got four older sisters at home, molly-coddling him.'

As Potts was drawn into their games, he in turn became less selfish and less turned in on himself. One day, he even told them a joke.

'This man met a girl at a party and he took her into a dark corner and asked her for a kiss.

' "No, I won't," she said.

' "Why not?" he asked.

' "Because I've got scruples," she said.

' "That's all right," he said. "I've been vaccinated." '

'Is that it, Pottsy?' they asked.

'That's it,' he said anxiously, searching their faces.

The three boys all laughed, perhaps over-long.

'That's not bad, Pottsy,' said Billy. 'Not bad at all.'

Sometimes they walked around the superb golf course at the back of the bungalow, looking for lost golf balls. Occasionally, when their searches were proving fruitless, they hid in the bushes and waited for the odd ball to come bouncing over the horizon – its arrival thoughtfully announced by a distant figure calling out, 'Fore!' Then they would snatch the ball up and run for all they were worth to the beach, leaving the unfortunate golfer to drop another ball at the cost of a penalty stroke.

Most of their evenings were spent on the beach, constructing masterpieces in sand, and now that there was a team of fifteen working on the projects, whole cities were shaped rather than single castles. The joy of building their town was only exceeded by the sheer ecstasy of destroying it in an imaginary raid over Berlin. Holding Titch aloft like an aeroplane, Billy and Robin carried him over the unsuspecting city.

'Target in view, skipper.'

'Roger, Titch, old boy.'

'Starboard a little, skipper. Now port a little, skipper. Steady! Steady-y-y! Bombs gone!'

A brick would be dropped mercilessly on a building which had taken all of two hours to create, and the fantasy air-raid would continue until the city had been razed. Then the boys would break out humming the RAF march-past as the young bombers headed home to their well-earned celebration in the local pub and the love and admiration of their WAAF girlfriends.

One day – out of the blue – Billy had a letter written in an almost illegible scrawl from his dad – a rare event indeed, since Tommy found it inordinately difficult to put pen to paper, having left school at the age of ten.

Well, Billy, so you have moved in with Brother Dorian so I am coming over to see how you are getting on next Saturday with a special present for him I will be on the nine o'clock train from Manchester so please meet me hoping this finds you as it leaves me.

Your loving Dad.

Billy hadn't seen any of his family for over three months, and so it was with great eagerness that he went down to Central Station to meet him. The train was only one hour late and then there he was – Dad, dressed in his funeral best, complete with pot hat, hurrying down the platform to meet him. He was clasping a large brown paper bag to his chest.

'How do, son,' he said. 'I won't give a hug or anything like that as I've got summat precious here for you and your Brother Dorian.'

'How do, Dad,' said Billy, falling into the vernacular. 'S'great to see you again after all these months. But what've you got in the bag?'

'Shhh!' he whispered. 'Eggs! Three dozen of 'em! Eggs! Like bloody gold. In fact better'n gold 'cos you can't eat that stuff.'

'I haven't tasted an egg since God knows when,' said Billy. 'They're scarce, aren't they?'

'Scarce! Scarce!' Tommy said, appealing to the unseen listener he seemed to carry on his shoulder for moral support and confirmation of his arguments. 'I should bloody well think they are. They're worth more than a bloody penny-black. They queue up for hours in Manchester just to get one.'

'Then where did you get 'em from, Dad?'

'Ah!' he said, tapping his nose with his finger and addressing his phantom audience. 'He wants to know where we got 'em from. But what we say is "Ask no questions and you'll get told no lies." Anyroad, come on, let's get out o' this station.'

'It's too early to go up to Cleveleys,' said Billy. 'They'll still be having their dinner up there – what they call lunch.'

'Then what do you say to a plate of fish and chips and a pot o' tea at Woolworth's?'

Billy's heart turned over with joy, not only at the prospect of the promised meal, but because it was so good to see Dad's simple manner and to have him around again; he seemed so normal after all the bizarre experiences of the previous few months.

In later years, Billy might have enjoyed grander meals

– champagne dinners and the like – but there was never anything to equal the feast of that day in Woolworth's – eaten to the background music of Deanna Durbin singing 'Waltzing, waltzing, high in the clouds'.

Whilst they were tucking in, Billy took the opportunity to catch up on family news.

'Our Jim's been given another ship – HMS *Fiji*, a new type of cruiser,' said Tommy. 'Our Sam's joined the Marines. He got fed up going up and down in that lift. Les's still in the ARP messengers and our Flo's still at Dunlop's. Oh, aye, and she's got herself a fellah at last – a sergeant in the army. Polly and Steve have another house in Cheetham Hill – not as good as the one that was bombed. But beggars can't be choosers, can they?'

'And what about Mam?'

'She keeps us all going in spite of some terrible air raids we've been having. We get down to the cellar quick now – and no messing.'

'Tell her ta for all those postal orders she's been sending me. I'd have starved without them. One of these days I hope to get back to Manchester again.'

'You're best stopping where y'are with the raids we've been having. There's hardly any of the town left.'

After dinner, they strolled together – father and son – along the front towards South Shore.

'Is there anything you need here, our Billy?'

'I don't think so, though one thing that would be useful would be a bike; it would save a lot of tram fare. My two pals have both got bikes and we could ride together. Maybe Mr Sykes could find a cheap one that we could do up.'

'I'll see what I can do.'

They reached Tommy's favourite Blackpool pub, the Manchester, and the tempting smell of XL ales was too much for him.

'Wait outside a moment, Billy,' he said. 'I'll just pop in and have a quick one.'

After a minute he came out again.

'No,' he said. 'I've changed me mind. I won't go to see Brother Dorian with the smell of beer on me breath.'

They continued their walk until they reached the Pleasure Beach.

'Most of it's closed up for the duration,' said Billy.

'But not all of it,' Tommy said gleefully, now in boyish mood. It seemed to be the effect that Blackpool had on him. 'Come on, our Billy. Let's have a go on this.'

He bought two tickets and together they clambered aboard a car to ride the Big Dipper. At a crazy, breakneck speed they hurtled around the roller-coaster, leaving their stomachs behind at every turn and every sudden, precipitous plunge into empty space.

'Wheee!' squealed Tommy in delight, now a young child again, but still clutching his precious cargo of eggs.

After their suicidal ride round the perimeter of the Pleasure Beach, they took the promenade tram-car to Cleveleys.

As the tram lurched its way northwards along the front, Dad seemed to get more and more jumpy.

'This is like going to see the bloody Pope or King George,' he said. 'I need a drink for this kinda thing but I can't even have that. Anyroad, I've brought me peace offering.'

'Don't worry, Dad. You'll be all right. Just be yourself. He's only human like the rest of us.'

'That's just what he's not. Human like the rest of us. He's a brother. Doesn't smoke or drink or do any of the things that make life worth living. Anyroad, what do I do? Do I shake hands with him or kiss his ring, or what?'

'He's not a bishop, Dad. Just say good afternoon.'

'And he talks like Winston Churchill. He's probably a friend of his.'

'Give him the eggs. That'll keep him quiet.'

The tram passed the Norbreck Hydro.

'For a minute there, I thought you lived in that bloody big castle. It wouldn't have surprised me.'

'No, that's been taken over by Lord Woolton. That's where they do all the work on the ration books for the whole country.'

'Then the Germans should drop a bomb on that bloody place for a start. That lot in there are starving us to death with their coupons for this and coupons for that.'

They reached Cleveleys and the bungalow and Billy took his dad up to the front door and rang the bell. Dad removed his pot hat and held it in his right hand whilst he held the bag of eggs in his left. The door was opened by the great man himself.

'Good afternoon, sir,' said Billy. 'This is my father who has come from Manchester to have a word with you.'

'Delighted to make your acquaintance, Mr Hopkins. An honour and a privilege,' boomed Brother Dorian.

'Very happy to shake your hand, sir,' said Dad. 'And I've brought you a little gift for your dinner table, sir.'

'How generous of you! How magnanimous of you! And how appreciated it will be! What is it, by the way?'

'Three dozen eggs, sir.'

'Three dozen eggs!' echoed the brother, taking the eggs quickly before Dad could change his mind. 'I can't believe it, Mr Hopkins.'

He inspected the eggs.

'Why, these are almost as valuable as Fabergé eggs.'

'These are the best new-laid,' said Dad with a puzzled frown. 'Where do these Farberjay eggs come from?'

'They're from Russia,' said the brother.

'Oh, I see,' said Dad, relieved. 'These are from English Leghorns. We don't deal in foreign eggs at Smithfield Market.'

'Yes, I see,' said Brother Dorian, equally puzzled. 'William here is a fine young chap and we all think very highly of him. He gets on very well with all his school companions, don't you, my boy?'

'Yes, sir,' said Billy dutifully.

'Anyway, come along into the drawing room, Mr Hopkins, and we'll have a chat. William, take the eggs to Brother Brendan, there's a good fellow.'

The two men went into the drawing room and were in there for over half an hour. Billy tried to overhear what they were saying but in vain – the door was too thick. Eventually they emerged.

'So nice to have met you, Mr Hopkins, and so interesting to hear about your family, especially your son on HMS *Fiji*. We must listen out for news of him. I am sure he will distinguish himself again as he has obviously done aboard HMS *Renown* with the vital part he played in the sinking of the *Graf Spee*. Good afternoon, Mr Hopkins, and if you are ever in the area again, don't hesitate to call. And thank you so much for the eggs. I'll make sure the boys get the benefit of them.'

'Thankee, sir,' said Dad. 'And God bless you and all you're doing for these lads.'

Billy accompanied his dad to the tram stop.

'The old bastard,' said Dad when they got outside the door. 'He was drinking Guinness and smoking all the time we was talking, and the old get never offered me a bleeding drink or a bleeding smoke. The bloody old skinflint. Then the bastard says he'd rather have bleeding Russian eggs. Well, I hope them good English eggs bleeding choke him. Make sure you get some of 'em from the bastard, our Billy.'

'I will, Dad. Don't worry. Ta-ra, Dad,' Billy called as the tram pulled away. 'Love to everyone at home. Make sure you get a drink on the way back.'

'Have no fear on that score, son. I will,' he shouted. 'And I'll see Mr Sykes about a bike for you. Ta-ra.'

He was gone. Billy walked sadly back to the bungalow. Neither he nor any of the boys got to see a single egg on their dining table.

Chapter Nineteen

Blitzkrieg

About a month after his dad's visit, Billy was playing a game of pontoon with Robin when Brother Dorian made an entrance into the garage. An immediate hush fell over the room, reminiscent of a scene in a cowboy film when the stranger walks through the swing doors and up to the saloon bar.

'William,' he said. 'I should like to see you in the drawing room; it's a personal matter.'

'Trouble,' whispered Titch.

Billy wondered what the matter could possibly be. When Brother Dorian summons you, he said to himself, it usually means something's wrong.

'You have a brother serving on HMS *Fiji*, do you not?' asked the brother. 'Only the ship has been in action at Crete and it, along with a number of other ships, has been sunk. Let us listen to the news bulletin.'

He switched on the wireless.

'*This is the BBC Home Service,*' said the announcer. '*Here is the news and this is Wilfred Pickles reading it. Crete has been evacuated and more than fifteen thousand troops have been withdrawn to Egypt. The losses inflicted on the enemy's troops and aircraft have been enormous but we regret*

---

to announce the loss of the two cruisers HMS Gloucester *and HMS* Fiji *and also four destroyers including HMS* Kelly, *commanded by Lord Louis Mountbatten, who is reported to be among the survivors now in Alexandria.'*

Brother Dorian switched off the wireless.

'I am sorry you have received such bad news, William. We can hope and pray that your brother is amongst the survivors now in Alexandria. I shall get everyone here to say a special prayer for him.'

'Yes, thank you, sir,' said Billy, bewildered and over-come at the thought that Jim might be dead.

He returned to the garage and told his friends of his news.

'I'm sure he has been saved, Billy,' said Robin. 'From what you've told us about him, he sounds as if he's a lucky type.'

'You'll see,' said Titch, untypically hopeful. 'He'll be at Alexandria with all his mates.'

All that week, Billy could think of nothing else. His mind went back to the 'skenny-eyed kid' days, to the 'daft and potty' letter to Sam, to the boxing lessons in the back yard, to the games of pitch-and-toss and the rides in the big tyre, to the send-offs at the end of Jim's furloughs, to the way he waved goodbye from the train at London Road. And as he reflected on all the good times in the past, he wept for the brother who might be lying at the bottom of the Mediterranean.

'Cheer up,' said Pablo. 'Remember – no news is good news.'

Then the letter from home arrived. With shaking fingers, Billy tore open the envelope. He scanned the first page of his mam's writing – hungrily, desperately.

Everything was all right! Jim had been saved and was amongst the survivors at Alexandria. Furthermore, he was being sent home on compassionate leave and would be in Manchester within a fortnight.

A fortnight is only two weeks, or fourteen days, but that particular fortnight in 1941 seemed like forever.

'Do you think time can stand still?' Billy asked Titch.

'Depends,' said Titch. 'If you're watching a good film it flashes past, but if you're in a lousy Latin lesson it doesn't move.'

Billy went about his daily routines – working in lessons, eating Brother Brendan's thick soups, doing homework, playing on the beach and on the golf course, cheating at cards in the evenings; still the days went by at a snail's pace.

But time runs through the longest day, and one Friday afternoon the endless period of waiting came to an end.

He came cycling up to the gate – on a Raleigh bike. Jim! He hadn't changed – same stupid grin and in the same immaculate uniform, except now it was decorated with all kinds of service stripes, gunnery emblems and war ribbons. His brother! They shook hands and then grabbed each other in a powerful bear-hug.

'How've you been?' asked Jim.

'OK,' said Billy, his eyes glistening. 'And what about you?'

'Not bad,' he said. 'I should be OK. After all, I've just come back from a sea cruise – with a tour of the Greek islands thrown in.'

'Whose is the bike?'

'It's yours,' he said. 'I brought it on the train and cycled up from the station. Dad bought it for you from Mr Sykes for a couple o' quid.'

By this time a number of the boys had appeared and were looking curiously at this brotherly scene.

Pablo came forward deferentially and asked:

'Are you the brother who served on the *Fiji*?'

'That's right. That's me.'

Billy stepped back and simply basked in the reflected glory. Brother Dorian and a couple of the other brothers came out and enquired if he was *The* brother. When it was confirmed that indeed he was, Brother Dorian said:

'We are honoured to have you here. Let there be no misunderstanding that we citizens at home fully appreciate the suffering, the conflict and the sacrifices which you and your shipmates have so recently undergone.'

'Thank you, sir,' said Jim politely.

'Won't you come into the drawing room and tell us exactly what happened at Crete?'

'Certainly, sir,' said Jim. 'But it would be nice if all these young boys here could come too, as I'm certain that they would be interested to hear.'

'Of course they may,' said the brother. 'Come along, boys. Everyone into the drawing room. It's not every day we get the news straight from the horse's mouth.'

All the residents crowded into the drawing room and all eyes were on Jim as he told his story.

'The destroyer *Greyhound* was sunk first. The *Gloucester* and the *Fiji* were ordered to pick up the survivors. But the *Gloucester* was hit, set on fire and started to sink fast. We had to leave her or we would have lost contact with the rest of Admiral Cunningham's fleet. We managed to survive nearly twenty bomber attacks before we ran out of ammunition.'

'What kind of plane attacked you?' asked Pablo.

'We were hit by bombs from Messerschmidt 109s, but there were also many, many Stuka dive-bombers coming at us.'

'What kind of gun do you operate?' asked Brother Brendan.

'I was operating a Pom-Pom, with my mates, of course. I tell you, when the Stukas came screaming down at us, we could almost see the eyes of the Jerry pilots.'

'What did they look like?' asked Titch, shivering.

'They looked as if they had been drugged.'

'And tell me, James,' said Brother Dorian, 'what happened next?'

'I spent over twelve hours in the sea, clinging to wreckage, until me and my mates were picked up by the destroyer *Kipling* and taken to Alexandria.'

As Jim related his experiences to the admiring group, Billy looked on, his heart filled with pride – as much pride as he had felt when Jim had given the skenny-eyed kid his come-uppance. Now he could see from the glances he was receiving from his fellows that his own status at Martindale Bungalow had taken off into the ether.

When Jim had finished relating his adventures, Brother Dorian said:

'On behalf of us all, I must express our deepest appreciation and gratitude for a truly fascinating account of the action off Crete. The glorious defence which our forces put up can only command admiration in every land. If we in this island can keep up the same spirited defiance, it can only result in the annihilation of the savage Hun.'

After this ringing, stirring speech from the headmaster, the group broke up.

'I have a favour to ask you, sir,' said Jim.

'Ask away,' said the brother.

'If you could agree, sir, I should like to take my young brother back to Manchester with me, as we shall be having a family gathering to celebrate my homecoming.'

'Why, certainly,' he said. 'By all means. We shall expect to see him back here after the Whitsun holiday.'

322

When he heard this, Billy's cup overflowed. Had he been able to look into a crystal ball, however, he might not have been so happy.

The party for Jim's home-coming was a grand affair. All the uncles and aunts, plus the beautiful Jean Priestley and the Sykes family, gathered together for the customary booze-up in Capper's and the sing-song and sandwiches back at Honeypot Street. Dad even made a speech.

'I'd just like to thank y'all for coming tonight to celebrate our Jim's safe return. A lot o' sailors was killed at Crete and he's very lucky to be here with us tonight, and I thank God for sparing him.'

'You mean his time hasn't come,' said Auntie Cissie.

'His name wasn't on the bomb,' said Mam.

'P'raps that bugger Hitler didn't know how to spell it,' said Uncle Eddy.

'Anyroad, Jim's here with us tonight and I raise me glass to him and say: good luck to you, son, and God bless you and I'm proud of you.'

Overcome with emotion, Tommy had to sit down.

'Come on, our Kate, give us a song,' called Uncle Eddy.

After much protesting, Mam was persuaded to sing her favourite song, 'Keep Right on to the End of the Road.'

'Go higher! Go higher!' Dad kept calling proudly as she sang.

'What about a song from you, Dad?' said Billy. 'Give us "Dolly Gray".'

'Y'can have her,' he said. 'Bloody hell! How old d'you think I am? That song's from the Boer War. I won't sing that, but I will sing this.'

In his high, cracked voice, he gave his rendering of

'Don't Dilly-Dally on the Way', with the crowd joining him in the chorus. This seemed to encourage other would-be soloists, for after that followed versions of 'Miner's Dream of Home', 'Nellie Dean' and 'Goodbye!'.

Whilst all this was going on, Billy managed to exchange a few words with Henry, his old pal.

'How's it goin', Henery?'

'Not so bad, Billy. I leave school next year.'

'Great. What are you gonna do?'

'I'm gonna work with me dad on the rag-and-bone cart. Me dad says I can earn nearly two quid a week.'

'Lucky you, Henery. Me – I've got to go on studying at school till I'm sixteen.'

'How're you getting on there?'

'Not so bad now. I didn't like it at first but I'm getting used to it. Right at the very beginning, I was nearly last in class.'

'You last!'

'Yeah – well the work was so different. But at the last exam I came twelfth out of twenty-five, so I'm getting better.'

'If I know you, Billy, you'll be near the top before long.'

'And if I know you, Henery, you'll be a millionaire before you're thirty.'

'I should live so long!' he said, imitating their Jewish neighbours.

The next day was Sunday, and in the evening Billy and his mam and dad took Jim to London Road station for a quiet send-off.

'Not like the old days, Jim,' said Dad, 'when we poured you on to the train in the middle of the night.'

'Thank God for that,' said Jim. 'We used to have terrible

hangovers when we got back to the ship. Hardly a fit state to fight a war.'

'Anyroad, you're not going back to fighting for a bit,' said Mam.

'Will you get another ship, Jim?' asked Billy.

'No, I don't think so. After Crete and all that time I spent in the water, it won't be long before I get my ticket.'

'You mean – leave the navy?' said Billy.

'That's right,' he said. 'I'll get an honourable discharge.'

'What'll you do then?' Billy asked.

'I could join the Merchant Navy or something like that, but I'll cross that bridge when I come to it.'

'Ta-ra, son,' said Mam. 'Now you look after yourself, d'you hear?'

As the train pulled away from the platform, Mam said:

'I'm not kidding. I've said ta-ra that many times to that many people, I'm beginning to sound like a record with its needle stuck.'

At ten o'clock that night, Billy went up to bed, leaving his mam and dad downstairs listening to Sandy Macpherson at the organ; Les was out as usual on ARP messenger service. As he lay there in the darkness, he heard way off in the distance first the gentle hum-hum of aircraft engines, then the very faint whistle of bombs, followed by muffled explosions. There had been no air-raid warning and so Billy wondered if he were hearing things. Hardly daring to breathe, he listened again. There was no mistake – the sounds were still there.

'Mam,' he called, 'I think you'd better come up here and listen to this.'

She did so cupping a hand to her ear and straining to listen.

'By gum, you're right,' she said. 'I can hear 'em. It's a raid.'

She called downstairs.

'Tommy, they're here. The Germans. A raid. Come up here and listen. It's the bombers.'

Billy got up quickly, dressed and went into the cellar. Soon afterwards, Mam joined him.

'Best to get under the stairs,' she said. 'It's the part of a house that's always still standing after it's been bombed.'

They sat together in the dark on the cold stone steps. Thirty minutes later the sirens sounded and Dad joined them.

'They're a bit bloody slow in sounding the warning tonight,' he said.

'I must have a word with her-next-door,' said Mam.

Billy knocked on the wall in the customary manner.

'Are y'all right, Jessie?' called Mam.

'Aye, we're all right, Kate,' she answered. 'I think they're after the railway tonight, the bombs are that close.'

'Look after yourself, Jessie.'

'Aye, you and all.'

'Are y'all right, Henery?' Billy yelled.

'I'm OK,' replied Henry. 'You remember that fortune-teller in Blackpool?'

'Yeah, so what?'

'I think I can see them clouds she was talking about.'

Billy and his mam went back to their place on the steps.

The bombers came closer and closer, louder and louder, and the guns all around the district opened up with their distinctive '*Crump! Crump!*'

'I wonder where our Les is,' was all Mam could say.

Then the air attack really began. Deafening explosion after explosion. The bombs whistled with the shriek of death as they hurtled across the rooftops, detonating on the nearby Red Bank sidings.

'It's the railway they're after all right,' said Dad. 'The bastards know it's the main line between Manchester and Sheffield.'

'Tommy! Tommy!' cried Mam hysterically. 'We'd better get out to the big shelter afore we all get killed here.'

Dad was on the step above him, and Billy could hear his slippered foot trembling near his head. The thunderclaps and the bangs now bursting around them became louder than a dozen storms rolled into one. The three of them passed beyond fear and resigned themselves to death.

'By God,' Dad shouted. 'We'd better get out or we're dead. I'll put me shoes on!'

He got up and went upstairs into the living room. At that moment, there was a hellish, terrifying screeching across the house and there followed the mother of all explosions. The whole world shuddered – the house seemed to lift up and sway over to one side. Then came the overpowering, nauseating smell of cordite, filling their mouths, throats, nostrils with choking, suffocating soot and dirt.

'God help us, Tommy, we've been hit! Are you all right? Are you still there?'

'I'm all right, Kate,' he yelled. 'I was saved by the kitchen door. Never mind me bloody shoes! Let's get out afore the whole bloody place falls on us!'

During the short lull they got out of the ruined, devastated house and hurried towards the public shelter. They were not prepared for the horror outside.

'It's a bloody nightmare!' Dad shouted.

It was a fitting description of the ruins which were now all around them. It was still dark, but in the moonlight they could see that the shape, the landscape, the very geography of the district had been transformed in a few short hours. They struggled through the debris, clambered over crumbled walls and the remains of buildings until they reached the comfort, if not the security, of the large shelter under a raincoat factory.

There they found mayhem – a scene like that of the trenches in the First World War – with corpses and wounded lying higgledy-piggledy about the place. One man sat on the floor moaning and holding his face, which had been gashed and torn by flying debris; another lay with his face bleeding from the glass of his spectacle lenses which had been blown into his eyes. Others sat staring, bewildered – in a state of shock.

At dawn the all-clear sounded. The survivors emerged from the basement like moles blinking in the light. There was a pall of smoke hanging over the area, and some of the houses were still burning. Everywhere they looked, there was destruction and desolation.

The family walked back to the place where their house had been and found only a heap of rubble and charred timbers. Sitting nearby on a low wall was Mr Sykes.

'They're both gone, Mrs Hopkins,' he said flatly.

'Good God! What's happened?' she asked.

'During the night, I heard screams of women and children and I went out to see if I could help. It was then that that bomb – the one which has wiped out your house and mine – hit us. A direct hit, as you can see. Jessie, Henery. Both gone. They were in the cellar. They couldn't have known a thing. Blew them to smithereens. The ambulances have taken what was left of their bodies away.'

He continued to stare off vacantly into space. No tears. No emotion. He was mesmerised and unable to take in the enormity of the disaster which had befallen him.

Heartbroken at the loss of his old pal, Billy took off his woollen scarf and wrapped it around Mr Sykes's neck, but the man didn't seem to notice.

Dear old Henry – dead! Henry, who'd shared so many games, so many exploits, so many dreams!

'No career in the rag-and-bone trade for Henry,' Billy said tearfully to Mam.

'And Jessie's had her asthma cured good and proper,' replied Kate sorrowfully.

'We've lost our home and our good friends all in a few short hours,' said Dad. 'If that bomb had fallen just a couple of yards shorter, it would've been us taken away in them ambulances.'

'Somebody up there must like us,' said Mam. 'Either that or our name wasn't on that bomb.'

As they left Honeypot Street, Billy glanced back. The last view he had of the place where he had spent such a happy boyhood was Mr Sykes sitting expressionless and alone on that low wall.

The family moved to an Emergency Rest Centre to await re-housing. Back safely from his ARP duties, Les found them two hours later and gave an account of the hair-raising time he had had during the night, cycling around the district which had been disintegrating and falling about his ears.

'You'd best get back to Blackpool,' said Dad to Billy. 'You'll be safer out of this lot. You never know, Jerry might be back tonight.'

It was a very sad farewell when Mam went with him to Victoria Station.

'Ta-ra again,' she said. 'One o' these days, all this lot'll be over and I might find myself saying hello just for a change. And here's a photo of the Sykes family I found in me handbag. You might like to keep it to remind you of happier days.'

As he sat on the train, Billy looked at the photograph and his eyes filled with tears. It was a picture of the two families posing together in the cut-outs on Blackpool promenade – oh, so long ago, before the horror of war had rained death from the sky. He recalled how he and Henry had run away to join Mad Jack's army on Barney's, how Jim had pushed them home in the big tyre, their boat-sailing adventures on Queen's Park lake, how they had sat the scholarship together and the look of bitter disappointment on Henry's face when he found he hadn't made it, and how he had defended Henry against Stan White's bullying in the schoolyard. Well, Henry wouldn't have to worry any more. This time, though, there had been nothing Billy could do to save Henry from being blown to bits by a German bomb. But for a quirk of fortune, a slight deflection of the wind, it would have been him, and not Henry, lying on that mortuary slab in Monsall Hospital. How cruel was fate, which seemed to pick its victims so mercilessly and so haphazardly. As the thoughts went through his mind, the tears ran down his cheeks.

A WAAF sitting opposite him in the compartment regarded him with concern.

'Are you all right, son?' she asked.

'Yes, thank you,' he replied. 'Just sad at having to leave home.'

'I know the feeling,' she said. 'Only too well.'

When he got back to Cleveleys, Billy reported to Brother Dorian all that had happened.

'Oh, you poor boy,' said the brother, embracing him. 'And your poor family. Tomorrow at morning prayers, I shall tell the school about your tragedy.'

He was as good as his word.

The whole school was assembled in the large hall of the domestic science college.

'Out of the depths I have cried unto you, O Lord,' intoned Brother Dorian.

'Lord, hear my voice,' responded the school. 'And let Thine ears be attentive to the voice of my supplication.'

'Eternal rest give unto them, O Lord,' said the brother.

'And let perpetual light shine upon them,' replied the school.

'May they rest in peace.'

'Amen,' chorused the school.

'And now I have to give you solemn news concerning one of our boys. William, would you please come up here on the stage where we can see you?'

Billy walked slowly and reluctantly on to the stage.

'Let this boy be an example to us all. He returned to the bosom of his family, believing it was safe to do so, but behold the disaster which has befallen him. Last week, Hitler's Luftwaffe flew over Manchester like vultures looking for carrion and rained down havoc and annihilation on the houses beneath – destroying this unfortunate boy's home and killing the family of his neighbours. Be under no delusions. Death can strike at any time. Consider Snake Hips Johnson in the Café de Paris, which is deep under a cinema – so deep that the noise of an air raid above does not even reach the revellers below. There he was, Snake Hips . . .'

Here the brother did a hula-hula dance.

' . . . swaying his hips from side to side in lecherous gyrations, thinking he was safe and immune from the conflagration which raged above. But the bomb searched him out all right. Snake Hips was killed along with thirty-two others and with over sixty injured.

'Stay here in Blackpool, boys, where you are safe from harm and under our care. Very well, William. You may return to your place.'

Shortly after the bombing, Billy wrote a poem for the school magazine.

SIRENTIME

The sirens burst out on a sleeping town
And people withdraw to shelters deep down.
The buzz of a plane is heard in the sky
And innocent people get ready to die.
Thud! Thud! Thud! drop the bombs with a quiver
And children in cellars start to tremble and shiver.

Soon the city's aglow with buildings on fire
And for some folk out there, it's their funeral pyre.
Crump! Crump! Crump! goes the sound of a gun
And so it goes on till the rise of the sun.
But we must pray hard for a glorious end,
Therefore to God, all our prayers do we send.
O please, please God, grant us a boon,
Let the end of this havoc come very soon.

Life ticked over peacefully and uneventfully at Martindale Bungalow until a certain day in August 1941.

One evening when all the boys were occupied with their various games, Johnny Bassett burst into the garage with astounding news.

'The old bugger's started giving us baths. I've just had one and he spent an awful long time washing my balls. There's a roster on the bathroom door, so you lot can check when it's your turn!'

The trio rushed into the house to consult the list and to find out when they were due for the treatment.

'Bloody hell,' said Robin. 'You and I, Hoppy, are down for tomorrow.'

'My name isn't down,' said Titch.

'Perhaps he doesn't fancy you,' said Billy.

They listened at the bathroom door, and over the sound of splashing water they could hear – if somewhat muffled – Dorian's deep, sonorous voice.

'How's that, my boy? Do you like that, boy? Let me wash under there, boy.'

'My God!' Billy said. 'What are we going to do?'

That evening, dressed only in pyjamas, Robin went down to see the brother to tell him that he had a touch of the flu and wished to be excused baths for the time being. It seemed to work, for five minutes later he was back.

'I've been excused for a week,' he said, 'but if you're going down to see him, Hoppy, for God's sake watch your step. He's gone off his head.'

Also dressed only in pyjamas, Billy went down to see the head.

'I have a very bad cold, sir. I think I must've caught it from Gabrielson, sir,' he said.

'And I suppose you want to be excused baths too. Is that it? That will be no problem, William. You just get off to bed.'

Brother Dorian stood up and caught him in an embrace, hugging him close and at the same time cupping his hand under Billy's genitals.

'Good night, my boy. What beautifully shaped testicles you have. Would you like to take hold of me there?'

'No thank you, sir.'

'Very well, my boy. Perhaps tomorrow, then.'

Billy escaped to his room, where Robin was waiting for a report.

'Did he try it on?'

'Yes, he did. And with you, I suppose.'

'Yes. What are we going to do?'

'I don't know what you and Titch are going to do, but I'm off.'

'How do you mean, "off"?' asked Titch.

'I'm going back to Manchester now – tonight!'

'But how . . . ?'

'I've got my bicycle with a dynamo and I reckon I can ride it to Manchester in about four or five hours. I'll get my dad to write to Brother Dorian and tell him I'm not coming back to Blackpool. That I'm needed at home. Anything.'

'Why not go tomorrow and I'll come with you,' said Robin.

'No fear,' said Billy. 'Dorian wants to see me tomorrow. I'm going before he puts sex education on the timetable and makes the practical part compulsory.'

'Right, I'm coming with you,' said Robin. 'I've got lights on my bike too.'

'What about me?' said Titch.

'He's not asked to see you – yet,' said Billy.

'It's only a matter of time,' said Titch. 'I'm so small, he hasn't seen me. But wait till he notices me and I've had it.'

'You haven't,' replied Robin. 'But you'll get it.'

'Then I'm coming too. The three musketeers!'

At midnight, when the house was quiet, the three boys sneaked downstairs. As they passed the head's bedroom, they could hear him snoring loudly. He turned over and snorted. The boys froze. Billy put his finger to his lips and pointed downstairs. Hardly daring to breathe, they tiptoed down to the hallway and into the kitchen, where they helped themselves to a few provisions for their journey.

'I reckon the old bugger owes us this food,' said Billy,

'for all those eggs we didn't see.'

They crept out to the garage and retrieved their bikes from the small shed at the back, then very, very quietly wheeled them out on to Briarwood Drive.

'Let's go!' whispered Billy.

Through the night they pedalled. Kirkham – Preston – Leyland – Chorley – Horwich – Bolton – Salford – Manchester.

They rode and rode through the darkness until their legs seemed to belong to other people. The journey took not four hours but eight, and they finally cycled into the centre of their beloved Manchester at eight thirty the next morning.

'God knows what my dad'll say,' observed Titch.

'Same here,' the other two said.

'Are we all agreed,' said Robin, 'that we say nothing about Brother Dorian to our parents?'

'Agreed,' said Billy. 'There's no point. They probably wouldn't believe us anyway.'

'Agreed,' said Titch. 'There'd have to be a big inquiry and it would land him and us in big trouble.'

'Anyway,' said Billy, 'I'm going home to a new address somewhere in Crumpsall, and first I have to find it. It sounds really posh – forty, Gardenia Court! I can hardly wait to see it.'

Chapter Twenty

Gardenia Court

'Gardenia Court' Mam had written, '*off Smedley Road, off Queen's Road.*'

Billy rode down Queen's Road, checking off various landmarks: bus depot, Harrigan's Dance Academy, Clifton Street, Smedley Road.

'At last,' he said aloud. 'This is it.'

He pedalled down the road and there, at the end, he beheld what seemed like a whole city of tenement blocks: Hyacinth House, Hazlewood House, Hawthorn House.

What lovely-sounding names, he said to himself. What a pity they're all slums.

He freewheeled down Hazelbottam Road and then he saw it – opposite a large shirt factory – a dirty, dilapidated building all on its own. GARDENIA COURT, the sign said. He turned left into the approach road and was attacked by a pack of snarling mongrel dogs, which barked furiously and determinedly at his back wheel.

He dismounted and walked a few yards along the pavement. There, sitting on a low wall, was a buxom girl in her early twenties, singing to herself.

'Baa baa black sheep,' she mumbled, saliva gathering on her lips.

'Excuse me,' said Billy. 'Do you know where the Hopkins family live?'

'Ockins,' she babbled. 'Ockins.'

'Right,' said Billy, getting the picture. Then, more kindly, 'What's your name?'

'Annie,' she sputtered.

He walked a little further into the cul-de-sac which ran by the side of the tenement block. He looked up at the filthy grey building with its mean, ugly verandas, which seemed to be used mainly for hanging and draping out the washing. Sitting at the bottom of one of the stairways were two shabbily dressed boys, about his own age, playing cards.

'Excuse me,' he said. 'Can you tell me where I can find number forty?'

'Oh, h'excuse me,' replied one of them, mocking his accent. 'Well, h'aren't we posh, then? Whadda y'think we are – a bleeding information desk?'

'Try the next hovel,' said the other lad.

'Hovel?' said Billy. 'What's that?'

'Are you bleeding daft or wha'?' said the first one. 'Hovel. The stairway. The entrance.'

'Right, ta,' Billy said.

He hoisted the bike on to his shoulder and entered the stairwell. 'Hovel' was indeed the right word. The first thing that hit him on the ground floor was the vile stench of stale urine and pickled herrings. On the first floor his nostrils were assailed by a second, more powerful smell – that of sour cabbage mixed with onions cooking. The third floor was worse, with its stink of rancid cheese and human excrement.

'Shut your bleeding mouth, yer stupid cow!' roared a gruff male voice from number 38.

'Don't you bleeding well talk to me like that or you'll

337

get this bleeding frying pan on yer 'ead,' screeched a female voice.

Finally, he reached number 40 on the top floor. He gave a rat-a-tat-tat with the brightly polished knocker.

Mam came to the door and gazed at him uncomprehendingly.

'Yes?' she said. Then she recognised him.

'It's our Billy. What in the name of God are you doing here? You should be in Blackpool.'

'Well, I'm here now,' he said. 'I'll just bring my bike in and I'll tell you all about it.'

Once inside, and after a breakfast of bacon and dried-egg omelette, Billy said:

'Many of the boys are coming back from Blackpool now that you're not getting as many air raids. Not since Hitler's been kept busy in Russia. We can't see the point in being evacuated any more.'

'I see,' she said. 'But it's a bit sudden, like, isn't it? I mean, why didn't you write and tell us you was coming?'

'I couldn't,' he said, continuing the lie. 'Me and me pals decided to come back to start the new term in Manchester. Half of Damian College is still here, remember. You'll have to get Steve Keenan to write a letter to the school explaining how I'm needed at home.'

'Oh, I see. Well, I just hope you and your pals know what you're doing.'

'What about this terrible place we've come to, Mam? It's worse than the dwellings in Collyhurst. The Priestleys got themselves a nice house in Wythenshawe.'

'I know, they was lucky. We didn't have no choice after being bombed out. We was just told to take it or leave it. So we had to take it. It's a bit small, I know, but we do have a little bathroom and we've got hot water for the first time in our lives.'

'But what a rotten district! And who was that funny girl I met coming in?'

'Oh, that would be Annie. She's bit simple, like, but harmless enough.'

'Then there were those lads playing cards in the next hovel. They looked a right pair.'

'That'll be Mick Scully and Vinny Buckley. You'd better keep well away from them two or you'll have your father after you.'

'Why, what's wrong with 'em?'

'They've both been away in Borstal for the last three years – that's what's wrong with 'em. They've only just come back.'

'Planning their next job, I suppose. What about that couple underneath us? He's bawling his head off and she's screeching like a lunatic. Her voice is worse than Auntie Cissie's.'

'That's Mr and Mrs Pitts, and she *is* a lunatic. They're allus at it – fighting like cat and dog all the time. She's either screeching at him or the kids or both. It's worst on Friday nights when he's had a drop too many. But not all the neighbours are as bad as that, thank God. On the bottom floor there's a very nice family – the Weinbergs.'

'That explains the smell of pickled herrings I got a whiff of as I came up. But you know, Mam, we're back where we started in Collyhurst. And there at least we had a view of the Cut and the railway. Here, from that veranda, we're just looking at another block of flats.'

'There's allus the view at the back.'

'Oh, aye, a great view of the Smedley Shirt Factory.'

'Well, our Billy, we'll just have to grin and bear it, won't we?'

'We'll bear it, but it doesn't mean we have to grin about it as well.'

* * *

After a year of bearing it, the family became resigned to their lot and to their wretched existence in the squalid tenement block. How they looked back wistfully to those wonderful days in Honeypot Street before the war when, despite the lack of bathroom and hot water, they had had space and privacy.

'Life is like a game of snakes and ladders, Mam,' said Billy. 'Just as you think you're getting somewhere, down a snake you go.'

'But then there are always ladders just around the corner,' she said.

'That's not what I've found up to now. You go down one snake only to find it leads to an even longer one.'

'You are an old grumps.'

Misery makes strange bedfellows, and the occupants of the Gardenia Court block were a miscellaneous set of people ranging from the respectable to the criminal, the reasonable to the insane. The one thing they all had in common was their joylessness.

If anything, though, when it came to misery, the Weinbergs on the ground floor were in a class of their own, for not only were they poor, they were Jewish into the bargain. This combination made life intolerable for them. Successful Jews had long since moved on to the affluent northern suburbs of Manchester, such as Heaton Park or Prestwich. To make matters worse, the Weinbergs had three daughters they had to find husbands for. The girls were pretty enough, but in their straitened circumstances, how were they going to capture nice Jewish boys with well-paid jobs if they couldn't offer a decent dowry? The whole family went about with permanently melancholy expressions and they rarely spoke to or even acknowledged the existence of anyone else on the block.

During that first year, Billy spent much of his time looking out from the veranda at the flats opposite and the people walking below.

One afternoon, he saw Vinny Buckley and Mick Scully sitting on a wall opposite the flats.

'Hey, Billy,' called Vinny Buckley. 'Come down here. We wanna talk to you.'

Having nothing better to do, and being a little curious, Billy went down and joined them.

'There's bugger-all to do round 'ere,' said Mick Scully. 'If you get bored just looking out from your veranda, why don't you come out on a job with us? We'll show you how to have a good time round 'ere.'

'Yeah, it's dead belting,' said Vinny Buckley. 'Anything for a bit of excitement.'

'Better not,' said Billy. 'I don't want no trouble with the coppers.'

'Neither do we,' said Mick Scully. 'We just make sure we don't get caught.'

Billy's dad was going past on his way back from work.

'Billy,' he shouted, waiting at the foot of the stairway, 'come over here quick.'

Billy did as he was told.

'Get upstairs,' Dad said. 'And don't let me see you talking to them two again, d'you hear? They're both up to no good and they'll drag you down with 'em if they can. You think on what I've said.'

But Billy was thoroughly dejected at the cramped conditions they had to put up with and the dismal district which surrounded them and hemmed them in. Nobody seemed happy. Nobody smiled. To while away the time, he took to spitting out the stones of the beautiful, plump plums his father had so abundantly supplied, to hit marked objects on the pavement three floors below. Like the game of 'Bombers over Berlin' on the Cleveleys beach, he pretended to be on a raiding mission with the RAF over a German city:

'Left a little, skipper. Now a little more. Steady-y-y. Bombs gone!'

Then he spat with deadly accuracy.

When feeling particularly fed up, he generously tried to share his despondency with the neighbours below by hitting the tops of their heads with the odd plum stone, and then withdrawing his own head inside quickly so that they were never sure where it had come from. On one occasion, when the Weinberg sisters were looking especially glum and down in the dumps, he tried to cheer them up by unselfishly releasing a large, succulent Victoria, which landed plumb on target. The bombing diversion had to stop, though, when Mrs Weinberg complained to his mam.

'I'm not kidding, our Billy, you must be going off your chump dropping plums on the poor people underneath. It's time you grew up.'

'It was only a bit of fun.'

'And talking of growing up, it's time you got out of them short trousers and into long pants. You're beginning to look like a big scoutmaster. And another thing – I think I can see a few hairs on your chin. It's time you tried having a shave.'

'Me? Shave?'

'Yes, you! Ask your dad tonight if you can borrow his razor.'

'What! You shave!' Dad exclaimed that evening. 'I didn't think you were that grown-up. But aye, you can borrow me razor. D'you know what to do?'

'I think so, Dad. You work up a lather with your brush and your shaving stick and then you scrape it off with that Gillette thing.'

'That's it,' he said. 'A good lather is half the shave. Should come off easy. That there fuzz on your face is only bum-fluff.'

Billy went into the bathroom and carried out the whole operation meticulously. He manufactured a great mountain of soapy lather, which he then worked into his face with his dad's shaving brush. He scraped off the foam very carefully and dried his face. The fuzz was still there! He repeated the whole operation, applying even more soap the second time. Again he scraped. No joy! He went out of the bathroom.

'Dad, this razor of yours doesn't work. Look, the fuzz is still there.'

'That's funny,' Dad said, examining the razor. 'Wait a minute, though, you little daft bugger. You've forgotten to put a blade in the holder.'

Early in 1942, Les was called up into the army.

'Everyone seems to be in uniform except me,' said Billy to his mam one day.

'If this war goes on, you'll be called up as well – just like our Les. Anyroad, what do you want to be in uniform for?'

'I want to do my bit for the war effort.'

'I think it's the girls you're thinking of. I suppose you think you'll have 'em all running after you.'

As usual, Mam was right. The following week Billy joined the Air Training Corps and was given a uniform.

Feeling somewhat self-conscious in his blue tunic, he set off one evening. On his way he passed Buckley and Scully at the foot of the stairway.

'Don't forget what we told you, Billy. Any time you want to join us, just let us know. We'll show you the ropes. You'll find it a bit more exciting than playing at soldiers or whatever you do at that ATC rubbish.'

'Better not,' answered Billy, hurrying off. 'I've got to get to the Training Corps parade.'

A couple of weeks after donning his uniform, he got a girlfriend by the name of Phyllis Hood. She was an extremely tall girl with a figure like a broomstick, but she had the most beautiful, doll-like face. For hour after hour he stood with her at the bottom of her hovel, talking, romancing and serenading her, though in order to reach her lips for a kiss, he had to stand on a higher step. The affair came to an end after a month when she found another boy who didn't have to stand on the step.

Apart from the uniform, Billy enjoyed his time in the ATC. How proud he felt when their commanding officer called out, 'Squa-a-a-dron . . . 'Shun!' It was almost like the real thing. Training involved parades, march-pasts, visits to airfields and, on one memorable occasion, a flight over Cheshire in an Avro Anson. There were also aeronautical studies – Morse code, radio technology and, most important, navigation. It was in this last subject that Billy acquired a deep interest and a fairly high level of competence. He learned to calculate precise latitude and longitude on a map, magnetic north, angles of deviation, wind speeds, and how to plot a flight path.

'I hope this war lasts long enough for me to get into it,' he said. 'I'd like to be a navigator in a bomber.'

'Well, I hope it doesn't,' Mam said. 'Anyroad, you've done enough bombing with them Victoria plums on the Weinberg girls.'

Not long after Billy had joined the ATC, Jim was given his honourable discharge from the navy. At first he was cheerful and happy at the idea of being back in Civvy Street, but as the weeks went by, he became more and more restless.

'I miss the navy and the sea,' he said one day. 'If ever

you get the chance, Billy, when the war's over, you should join the navy. You'd love it.'

'I want to be a navigator in the RAF. It's always struck me as a miracle the way our bombers set off in the dark and arrive over their target – Hamburg, Dusseldorf, Berlin – right on time. I want to be the navigator who gets them there.'

'Better to be a navigator aboard a ship. If you were really good and got all your qualifications, you could end up as captain of your own vessel. Imagine that!'

'How would I get to be ship's navigator then?'

'You'd have to study very hard at a college of navigation to get your Board of Trade certificate. There's a college at Southampton and one at Liverpool.'

'You make it sound really great. Maybe after I've finished at Damian College, I could go to one of them.'

For the umpteenth time in his life, Billy knew what he wanted to do and what he wanted to be.

'Right now,' said Jim, 'I miss the adventure and the excitement, but most of all I miss my ship-mates.'

'Why not join the Merchant Navy, like you said some time ago?'

'That's exactly what I have done. I've signed on, but it's not easy to get a berth.'

'But I always thought the Merchant Navy was crying out for men.'

'Yeah, but the best berths on the best ships are snapped up by the old hands who are well in with the masters. I can always get a place on a tanker, though.'

'Why is that?'

'See, it's like this. In a convoy, the tankers are the most dangerous ships to be on, 'cos the U-boats pick 'em out for special treatment. If they get torpedoed when they're fully loaded, they go up in flames like a Roman candle.'

'Best to avoid them then.'

'I'll say. I'd have to be pretty desperate to sign on for one of those. Anyway, I've managed to get some work on a coal boat that's sailing from Liverpool to Cardiff tomorrow. It's a pretty dirty job but it's better than just hanging around the house all day long.'

He was away for nearly a fortnight. When he returned, he was black with coal dust from head to foot.

'Just look at the state of you,' Mam said. 'I'm not kidding, anyone'd think you'd been down the mines, never mind on a coal boat. Get all them clothes off, our Jim, and I'll give 'em a good scrubbing. If you wasn't so big, I'd give you one and all. You used to be so particular when you were in the Royal Navy. No wonder that Jean Priestley found another fella. Why did you go on a coal boat?'

'Finding a ship isn't easy,' said Jim. 'You have to take what you can get. As for Jean, I haven't seen much of her since they moved to Wythenshawe. Might be as well – she was getting too serious for my liking.'

'But she was such a nice girl.'

'I'm not denying that. But the family's very religious. One brother training to be a priest; a sister training to be a nun. And Jean was that holy, I felt as if I was going out with a saint.'

It was two days after Jim's return that everyone started scratching. Under the arms, around the groin and, most especially, between the fingers.

'I think this itching is gonna drive me up the wall,' said Mam, scratching madly at her stomach.

'It's that bloody Jim that's brought this into the house,' said Dad. 'I've got them bloody red spots all round the top of me legs, and when I'm at work in the market I can't even reach down there for a scratch or all the other porters'll think I'm bloody well playing with meself.'

'It's in between my fingers where I find it's worst,' said Billy. 'You can even see the little mites in the tiny white lines where they've burrowed in.'

At the surgery, the doctor took one look between Billy's fingers.

'Scabies,' he announced. 'Your whole family, Mrs Hopkins, will have to go to the Infectious Diseases Hospital at Monsall to be treated.'

'Even me husband?' asked Mam anxiously.

'I said the whole family,' said the doctor. 'Furthermore, all your bedding and clothes will have to be disinfected.'

'Oh, bloody hell,' Mam said. 'He's not gonna like this.'

The treatment at the hospital involved first a very hot bath, after which a nurse, wearing rubber gloves and a rubber apron, covered them from head to foot with a foul-smelling sulphur ointment. Billy's dad moaned all the way there and all the way back.

'He's picked up these bleeding bugs aboard that bleeding coal boat and passed them on to us. I tell you, Kate, I'm not gonna stand for it. He'll have to go.'

'Give the lad a chance, Tommy. It's not his fault. It could've happened to anyone.'

That night, Jim came home with a shipmate at two o'clock in the morning after a night's revelry in the town.

Billy was awakened by the sound of voices being raised.

'What the bleeding hell d'you think you're doing, cooking chips at two o'clock in the morning?' he heard his dad yell.

'I've just come back with an old shipmate and we were hungry – that's all.'

'Listen, Jim, I've just about had enough of you. You sit round the house all day making us all miserable, then you give us all bleeding scabies, and now you're waking up the whole bloody house, making chips. Don't you know I've got to be up at four in the bleeding morning to go to work. It's hardly worth me going back to bed.'

'You've been at my bloody throat ever since I came back from the navy, turning your back on me and making those bloody hissing noises,' Jim shouted back.

'Listen, if you can't keep decent hours like other people, you can bleeding well sling your hook.'

'I'd better go,' said Jim's nautical friend. 'I'm not bothered about any chips. Be seeing you, Champ.'

'Wait,' said Jim. 'I'll come with you. I'm not stopping in this dump.'

Jim went into the bedroom and switched on the light.

'Sorry to disturb you, our kid, but I want to pack a few things and then I'm off.'

'Don't go, Jim,' said Billy. 'Stay. He'll get over it. He always does.'

'Nah, not this time,' Jim replied. 'Anyway, come on, give me one of your bear-hugs before I go.'

Billy held him in a strong clinch, at the same time patting his back.

'I wish you'd stay. What am I gonna do when you've gone?'

'You'll be OK, and anyway, even if I did stay, it wouldn't be for long. I've got myself a ship.'

'That's great news, Jim. What's its name?'

'*Empire Light.*'

'What kind of ship?'

'A tanker,' he said. 'I got fed up waiting.'

Billy's heart froze.

'For God's sake look after yourself, Jim.'

'The same goes for you, our kid. Be seeing you. Right, Judd.' He turned to his pal. 'Let's go. Sorry to leave on this note, Dad. Hope you get to work on time. Ta-ra.'

Billy heard the front door pulled to and Jim was gone.

He never forgot that Tuesday when he came home from school. He turned the key in the lock, and the moment he entered the flat he sensed that something was wrong. There was usually somebody talking or the wireless was on, but today it was ominously quiet. He opened the living-room door and took in the scene.

Dad sat at the table, chin in hand, the picture of misery, and Billy could see that he had been crying. Before him there was a mug of cold tea – untouched. Mam sat bowed before the electric fire, weeping silently. Billy felt a tightening of his stomach and his throat, and his hair seemed to stand on end.

'Oh, God,' he said. 'Please. Not that. Not Jim.'

'We've had a telegram,' Dad managed to say between sobs. 'The *Empire Light* has been sunk. Jim's missing.'

It was a Sunday afternoon in March when the *Empire Light* had been torpedoed. The captain wrote Mam and Dad a lovely letter explaining how the tanker had got it in mid-Atlantic on the way across to America. The sea had been rough and choppy and, as the ship had started to sink, most of the crew had got into the lifeboat which, for some reason or other, had broken away and was unable to get back to the ship. The captain and another officer had searched the ship for injured survivors but there were none. A destroyer had broken away from the convoy and had come as close to the ship as it dared, and the two officers had managed to jump on to its deck. RAF Coastal Command had scoured the sea for many hundreds of square miles but no trace of the lifeboat or any survivors had been seen.

'*It is with the deepest regret,*' concluded the captain, '*that I have to tell you that your son, James, must be presumed to be lost.*'

A few days later they received another letter, this time from the King.

BUCKINGHAM PALACE

The Queen and I offer you our heartfelt sympathy in your great sorrow. We pray that your country's gratitude for a life so nobly given in its service may bring you some measure of consolation.
GEORGE RI

'I can't believe he's dead,' said Mam. 'I could accept it better if they'd found a body. But we'll never know what really happened to him at the end.'

'It's best not to think about it, Kate,' said Dad. 'I only wish I'd never had that bloody row with him, all over such a daft thing as cooking chips late at night.'

'Maybe he's not dead,' said Billy. 'P'raps he's landed on some desert island and he's not been able to contact us.'

'No,' said Dad, his voice flat and final. 'He's dead all right. We may as well face up to it.'

Eyes overflowing, Mam began going through Jim's things in the wardrobe.

'Remember this green suit, Tommy? The one that drove us round the bend,' she sobbed. 'I only wish he were here now to wear it again.'

'Stop punishing yourself, Kate,' Dad said, very near to tears himself.

'And here's his boxing gloves and all his boxing things,' she grieved. 'You may as well have 'em now, Billy.'

'I don't want 'em, Mam. He might want 'em himself when he comes back.'

But in his heart of hearts, Billy knew Jim wasn't coming back. Jim, his beloved brother, was at the bottom of the sea.

As he lay in bed that night, he wept silently and sorrowfully at the thought of Jim dying in an open boat somewhere in the Atlantic Ocean. He had seen Noel Coward's film, *In Which We Serve*, and he wished that he hadn't, for only too graphically had it painted the picture of what could happen to men lost in an open boat at sea. Possibly a slow, agonising death from hunger, thirst and exposure. How long had it taken for them to die? How long had they waited to be rescued? How long had it been before they had lost all hope? He prayed that death had come to Jim and his mates with merciful swiftness.

Then his mood changed from sorrow to anger as he thought about the deaths in his lifetime and all that had happened since Chamberlain had made that fateful speech in 1939. Young Teddy Smith – drowned in the Cut. His pal, Henry – dead. His hero brother – dead. Their Honeypot Street home – gone. Steve and Pauline's happiness – gone. The world was an evil place with people like Mrs Mossop, Kevin the airman and Brother Dorian in it.

What a rotten, rotten, rotten world we live in, he raged silently. Very well, God, if there is a God, if it's part of your plan that I spend my life in this lousy, filthy hole here in Crumpsall, if I am to live in a slum with the mad and the criminal, I'm gonna start acting like 'em. Up to now, God, I've taken everything you've thrown at me with no complaints. But tomorrow I begin getting my own back. So watch out, God! Bugger the war! Bugger Hitler! Bugger Churchill! Bugger Damian College! Bugger the ATC! Bugger navigation colleges! Bugger the savage, heartless sea! Bugger everything and bugger everybody! Tomorrow morning, I'll go and see Vinny Buckley and Mick Scully and see what they have in mind.

Chapter Twenty-One

When In Rome . . .

'Hiya Billy,' said Vinny when Billy called at the Buckleys' ground-floor flat. 'I knew you'd come round to our way of thinking in the end. Come in a minute, will ya, and I'll be ready in two ticks. Then we'll go and get Mick.'

Billy went inside and was nearly bowled over by the stench of stale sweat and urine, which he traced to the steaming, wet nappies draped all round the fireguard. A snotty-nosed, bare-bottomed toddler sucking on a dummy gazed at Billy curiously and then greeted him by throwing a small metal toy at him, which fortunately missed the mark. Vinny's mother, a hundred per cent sourpuss, was breast-feeding a mewling, puking infant. She looked up from the baby to Billy but did not acknowledge his presence with even so much as a nod or a grimace. With practised ease, she switched the baby over to her other pendulous breast.

'If you're going out with that bleeding Mick Scully again,' she squawked, 'don't go getting into bleeding trouble with the rozzers again. We've got enough on our bleeding plates with your father in Strangeways without you joining him.'

'Awright! Awright! Stop bleeding going on at me,'

answered Vinny. 'Come on, Billy, let's get out o' this bleeding hole.'

When they were outside, he said 'Bleeding old cow! She's allus going on at me.'

'I didn't know your father was in Strangeways, Vinny.'

'Oh, him! The old man! He's in and out o' clink all the time. Got done this time for house-breaking. He's that well known in Strangeways, they invite him to the staff dances. What about you, Billy? Are y'off school today?'

'Yeah – I decided to take the day off. I'm sick to death of all that Latin, French, geometry and all that crap. I'm gonna start enjoying meself.'

'That's the idea. We'll show you how it's done. Just stick with us and you'll be awright. Let's go and get Mick. He's a right card, is Mick. Doesn't give a bugger for no one.'

It took Mick all of five seconds to make up his mind when they called.

'I'll get me coat,' he said. 'Right, let's go. First off – we need some fags.'

'I've no money on me,' said Vinny.

'Neither have I,' said Billy.

'Who said anything about money? Did you hear me mention money?' said Mick. 'Come with me.'

He led them to a car park outside a large biscuit factory.

'If you want the very best fags, always try the good cars first.'

He went along the row of cars, trying the door handles.

'Locked! Locked! Locked! Not locked!'

He opened the door of the Daimler and there, in the leather pockct in the door, spotted three twenty-packets of Player's Please!.

'We're in luck,' he said. 'And so early in the day! Must be Billy here – he's a lucky charm. Right, lads, cop for these!'

He threw each of them a packet of cigarettes, then took out of his pocket a brand-new Ronson and lit everyone's fag.

'See this,' he said, indicating the lighter. 'Got this on me last house-breaking job. Somebody carelessly left it out for me.'

Puffing arrogantly on their cigs, the three renegades walked up Hazelbottom Road, looking for fresh adventure and fresh quarry.

'This is more like it,' said Billy. 'Much better than wasting me bleeding time learning a lot of French irregular verbs.'

'I should bleeding well think so,' said Vinny. 'No one ever got rich reading a book.'

They came to a row of shops.

'OK,' said Mick. 'We're going into that toffee shop to see what we can knock off. Right, Billy. You watch me and Vinny – two master craftsmen at work.'

They entered the shop and a middle-aged lady came through a door at the back, ready to serve them.

'Good morning, lads,' she said. 'What can I get you?'

'Could I have a quarter of them boiled sweets on the top shelf?' said Vinny.

She climbed up her little step-ladder and turned her back for a moment, and in that instant Mick Scully helped himself to a big handful of Caley's Double Six.

'Which ones?' asked the lady naively.

'No, not them,' said Vinny. 'I mean the humbugs in the jar next to them.'

The lady turned to get the jar down and Mick moved to take his second handful – this time Mars Bars.

The shopkeeper weighed and bagged the humbugs.

'That'll be threepence,' she said.

'Oh, heck,' said Vinny, feeling in his pockets. 'I've left

me sweet coupons on the table at home. Just save them humbugs for me, missus, and I'll be back in a minute.'

Outside the shop, Mick took out his spoils.

'Let's see,' he said. 'Four bars of Caley's, five Mars. Not bad, eh, Billy. And all free!'

'Bloody fantastic!' said Billy.

'But wait,' said Vinny. 'You were so busy watching Mick at work, you didn't see me grab these.'

Vinny produced three packets of sherbet, two bags of Pontefract cakes, and three Cadbury's Milk. Billy began to feel that he had found his true calling – a life of crime with all its attendant excitement and thrills, not to mention the haul.

After eating all their loot, they developed a monumental thirst.

'S'not so easy to swipe bottles o' pop; they're too big and bulky,' said Mick. 'It's best to get a drink at the fountain in the park.'

'That's OK,' said Vinny, 'as long as you don't use that cup on a chain. You never know who's been using that.'

After quenching their thirst, they made their way to the pitch'n' putt course which, at that time of the day and year, was deserted and unattended.

'Fancy a round of golf, old chaps?' asked Mick, indicating the locked hut.

'Why not, old boy?' replied Vinny.

Mick picked up a largish stone from a nearby rockery and tapped it gently on the window of the hut, breaking the pane. Another small tap and he began removing slivers of glass until he was able to put his hand in and open the catch. After that, it was an easy job to get inside, and Mick began handing golf irons and balls through the open window.

The trio processed through the park, whacking golf

balls for all they were worth across the spacious lawns, until they were out into Delauneys Road, where they continued their madcap game. They chortled in delight and triumph with every successful stroke until Billy hit a glorious drive straight into someone's front window, showering glass on the poor, unsuspecting occupants.

An irate householder appeared, shaking his fist.

'You stupid lot o' bastards, you. I'm gonna set the bloody police on you. You should be locked up, the bloody lot o' you.'

'Run! Run like hell, Billy!' Mick shouted. 'Or you've had it.'

They ran like the wind until they arrived, panting breathlessly, at Woodlands Road, where they chucked the golf gear over a hedge.

'So far today,' said Mick, 'we've had fags, chocolates and a game o' golf. But what we need is money.'

'So what do we do?' asked Billy.

'We do a house, that's what we do,' he answered. 'Are y'on, Vinny?'

'On,' he said.

'This is the plan,' said Mick. 'Can you whistle, Billy?'

'Yeah, I think so,' he replied, giving a demonstration.

'That's bleeding smashing,' said Mick. 'As good as Al Jolson. You can be the dog-out while me and Vinny do that house over there. If you see anyone coming, do your Jolson bit and give us time to make our getaway. Got it?'

'Got it.'

The two youths went across the road and rang the door bell several times. There was no answer and so, using a small brick, Mick broke a pane of the leaded-light window in the corner of the door, reached in, turned the Yale lock and within a minute they were inside. Aware of his responsibility, Billy kept vigil, looking alertly up and down the road, but there seemed to be no one about. Five minutes later, the two were out again.

'Eight quid,' said Mick. 'Left in a box on the dressing table. Daft buggers they are, leaving money about.'

'Told you it was easy,' said Vinny. 'Money for jam.'

'Right, Billy. That's two quid for you for dogging-out, and three for me and Vinny for doing the job. Fair enough?'

'Fair enough!' said Billy, thinking it really was the easiest money he'd ever earned.

'I think I'll call it a day,' said Mick. 'Not a bad haul, eh, lads?'

'Fancy going to the pictures tonight, anyone?' asked Vinny.

'Not me,' said Mick. 'I'm doing another job later with my older brother. We're gonna do a warehouse and we've even got a van to carry the stuff.'

'Understood, Mick,' said Vinny. 'What about you, Billy, fancy the pictures?'

'Yeah, why not?' said Billy.

When he got home that night, Mam said:

'Have a good day at school, son?'

'Not bad. I learned a lot. One day I'm gonna be rich and play golf, you'll see.'

'What next, I wonder? They're learning you some funny things at that school of yours.'

'I'm going to the pictures tonight,' he announced suddenly.

'No homework, then?'

'Not tonight,' he lied.

At six o'clock he called for Vinny again. There was the same smell of sweat and urine, but now there had been added the smell of baked beans, which made the stink even more obnoxious.

They decided on the Temple picture house, which was showing a Boris Karloff horror. They paid for their tickets, swaggered down the aisle and pushed their way along the row to two vacant seats, treading on toes and a six-inch layer of monkey-nut shells. They slouched back in their seats, put their feet on the seats in front, lit up their fags and were ready to make nuisances of themselves. Their chance soon came.

In one of the shorts, the Mills Brothers were crooning something about dry bones and how they connected.

'Rag bone connected to you,' Billy shouted out in the same rhythm.

This witticism seemed to cause amusement to most of the cinema except the usher, who came rushing down the aisle.

'Any more of that and you're out,' he said, flashing his torch at them.

'You wanna fumigate this bleeding place,' Vinny called out to him. 'The bugs are taking it over. I came in here with a pullover and I'm going out with a jumper.'

During the big picture, the hero said to his girl: 'I love you darling but I have only one worry.'

'Me glass eye might fall out,' shouted Billy.

Later the handsome hero was saying: 'There is only one thing I desire in life.'

'Ten Woodbines and a box of matches,' Vinny yelled.

'But that's two things!' Billy called out.

'That's it,' shouted the usher. 'You two, out! And don't bloody well come back!'

They found themselves on Cheetham Hill Road.

'It's only nine o'clock,' said Vinny. 'Let's go to Lorenzelli's Milk Bar and see if we can pick up a coupla birds.'

Lorenzelli's was crowded that night.

'Two hot Vimtos!' Vinny ordered.

They took their drinks and sat down next to two girls, about fifteen years old, one blonde and one brunette – both of whom were chewing gum and wearing long, dangling ear-rings. Vinny looked them up and down.

'Wharra you lookin' at?' Blondie said. 'Whadda you want – a photograph or summat?'

'Wouldn't mind a bit o' summat if you've got any to spare,' said Vinny. 'Anyroad, evening, girls, nice weather for this time o' the year.'

'Bloody hell,' said Blondie. 'He'll be asking if we come here often next.'

'Well, do you?' asked Billy mischievously.

'Do we wha'?' asked the brunette, who was the less pretty of the two.

'Come here often,' he replied.

'Depends what you mean by often,' she retorted.

It looked as if the conversation might continue on this semantic level for some time, but Vinny changed its direction.

'Wanna fag?' he said, offering his packet of twenty Players.

'Don't mind if we do,' they both said with alacrity, removing the chewing gum and sticking it under the table.

'I say, we *are* posh, smoking Players. Me and Doris can only ever afford Woodbines.'

'What do you both do, then?'

'We both work at Woolworth's. She's Toys and I'm Toffees. She's Doris and I'm Elsie.'

'Billy and Vinny,' said Vinny. 'Pleased to meet you. And if ever I wanna buy summat under a tanner, I'll know where to come.'

The chatting-up process continued on this level until ten thirty, when the milk bar closed.

'We'll see you both home,' said Vinny.

'You don't half fancy your chances, don't you?' said Elsie. 'All right, then. Wait outside and me and Doris'll just go to the toilet.'

Whilst they were waiting outside, Vinny said:

'Elsie's mine and Doris is yours. See, I think this Elsie fancies me.'

'Thanks, Vinny,' said Billy. 'So I get the ugly one.'

'You know what they say about not looking at the mantelpiece.'

The two girls reappeared and Vinny said:

'I don't know what it is you girls do in the toilet but you both look smashing. Fancy a walk in Manley Park or wha'?'

'Don't mind if I do,' said Doris, linking her arm into Billy's.

They found their way to Manley Park shed and the four of them sat there smoking Players, blowing the smoke across the glowing cigarette ends.

'Whadda you say we stay out all night?' suggested Vinny.

'I'm game if you are, Doris,' said Elsie.

'Awright, then,' said Doris. 'It'll be a bit of a laugh. But what about work tomorrow, Elsie?'

'Oh, bugger work,' she said. 'I'm fed up with the bloody job anyway. Let the supervisor try serving just for a change.'

So it was decided. But no one, except Billy, noticed that Billy hadn't been consulted. It looked as if he were outvoted anyway.

Vinny moved with Elsie to a dark corner of the shed, and Billy could hear lots of furtive fumblings, which lasted the whole night with murmurs of, 'No, don't, Vinny. Don't do that. I don't allow it on the first date.' Then, 'Ah, Vinny, that's better.'

As for Billy and Doris, they sat most of the night smoking Billy's fags.

'You can put your hand here,' she said, placing his hand on her breast. 'I don't mind.'

'Thanks very much,' he said.

He remained in that position for most of the night, his right hand round her shoulder and his left hand on her breast over her dress. He could feel nothing but a hard lump and the unyielding material of a strongly built brassière. He was tempted to go further but didn't because it was much too cold, the wooden seats were too hard and uncomfortable, and besides, he didn't fancy her. He would have preferred the blonde and he was annoyed that Vinny had simply assumed that he could automatically have the prettier girl.

They watched the dawn come up, and feeling utterly washed out, grubby and dishevelled, they parted company.

'Billy,' said Doris, 'I think you're a real gentleman. Anyone else would have tried it on, but I liked the way you kept your hands to yourself. I don't believe two people should go too far on their first date, do you?'

'Dead right, Doris,' Billy said. 'That's the way I feel.'

'Or, in your case, Billy, didn't feel. Anyroad,' she said, 'I hope we see each other again in Lorenzelli's.'

'Hope so, Doris.'

On the walk back home, Billy said:

'Eh, Vinny, I've found out two things about girls tonight. First, why do you think they wear brassières?'

'To stop their tits from falling down, I suppose.'

'That's one reason. The other is to give 'em a suit of armour so a lad can't get his hand in there. You'd have needed an acetylene lamp to get into that Doris's bra.'

'What's the other thing you found out?'

'The less you want them, the more they want you. And

the more you want them, the less they want you.'

'That gives us a problem, then,' said Vinny. 'It means we can only ever have it off with the girls we don't want it with.'

'That's right. So if we don't want it with 'em, we won't have it with 'em.'

'You've got me bleeding beat there, Billy. All this bleeding education stuff is over my head. I just hope that you're wrong.'

They got back to Gardenia Court at six o'clock in the morning, and Armageddon in the shape of his dad was waiting for Billy.

'Where the bleeding hell do you think you've been all night?' he bawled as Billy opened the front door.

'Just sitting in a park shed with Vinny Buckley,' he mumbled.

'You stupid bleeding get,' he said, striking Billy across the head with each word. 'Do you know we've had the police out looking for you? Do you know I've lost a day's work today because of you?'

'We haven't done any harm,' stuttered Billy.

'Haven't done any harm! Haven't done any harm! I told you to keep away from that bleeding Buckley family. They're bloody riff-raff and they'll take you down with 'em. After we've encouraged you to go to college to make summat of yourself, you want to end up with that bleeding lot who'll have you in Strangeways afore you know where you are. You've worried your mother out of her mind all night. Haven't we had enough trouble, being bombed out and losing our Jim, without you going off the rails and all? Anyroad, you come with me.'

He took Billy by the scruff of the neck and forced him down to the Buckley flat, where he banged noisily on the door.

Vinny opened the door.

'What the bloody hell . . . !'

Before he had finished his sentence, Billy's dad had grabbed him by the shoulders.

'If ever I see you near my son again, I'll belt the bleeding living daylights out o' you. I'll bleeding swing for you, d'you hear?'

'Yeah, Mr Hopkins. But we haven't done nowt wrong.'

'Whether y'ave or y'aven't, I don't care. Just keep away. And as for you, our Billy, get up to bed afore I really lose my temper.'

A week later, Mick Scully was arrested with his brother for burglary and sent to Borstal for five years. One month after that, Vinny Buckley was caught house-breaking and sentenced to three years in the same institution.

Dad's punishment was bad enough, but Mam's was infinitely worse. For a whole week, Billy got the fish-eye treatment and his mother became stony-faced whenever he tried to speak to her. For a whole week she froze him out with that glassy-eyed stare of hers, and if she spoke to him at all, it was in monosyllables.

'I'm very sorry about last week, Mam,' he said.

'Oh, aye,' she said, not taking her eyes off the potatoes she was peeling.

'I didn't mean any harm and it won't happen again.'

'So you say,' she said, slicing up the potatoes for chips.

'A funny thing happened today at school, Mam.'

'Oh, aye,' she said, without looking up from the stove.

'During the PT lesson, a lad threw a fit.'

'Oh, aye,' she said, all her attention on the chips.

'He was foaming at the mouth and talking a funny language.'

'I dare say,' she said, concentrating hard on the frying pan.

'The teacher had to hold his tongue down with a ruler.'

'Oh, aye,' she said, moving the chips around the pan.

'Then they sent for the ambulance and he was taken away to Prestwich Asylum.'

'Oh, aye,' she replied, focusing on the loaf of bread she was cutting up.

By the end of the week, Billy was almost climbing up the wall to get her attention.

'If I stand on my head and sing "I'm an Old Cow-Hand" will you forgive me and talk to me?'

She almost smiled.

'Come on, Mam, give us a smile. It won't happen again. Honestly. I promise. I've been in Coventry for a week and I can't stand any more.'

'Oh, very well, you daft little bugger. Come here.'

She gave him a big hug.

'Just make sure you behave yourself in future. Anyroad, what happened to that lad they took to Prestwich Asylum?'

'Oh, him. They found he was all right in the end, after his mam started talking to him again.'

'I'm not kidding, our Billy, you are a daft bugger. Sometimes, I think you *should* be in a bloody asylum.'

'As long as you don't freeze me out like that again, I'll be all right.'

'What you need is an interest apart from all that studying you do at that school. Where were you in class last time?'

'Eighth, Mam. And that's without killing meself. If I really got my head down, I could be in the first five.'

'I'll have to see if your father can get you some more fish from the market. Talking of your father, why don't you go and give him a helping hand sometime? He'd like that, and maybe you and him can get back on friendly terms again.'

* * *

The following Saturday, Billy was up at three o'clock in the morning to go and help his dad in Smithfield Market. He dressed quickly and Dad made a quick brew before they set off.

'I don't know how you do this every morning, Dad,' Billy said. 'I feel as if I've just gone to bed.'

'You get used to it. Anyroad, come on, we can't sit here all day. We've got work to do. And remember there's no buses at this time in the morning.'

They strode swiftly the four miles to Smithfield Market – Billy hardly able to keep up with Dad's rapid stride. They arrived at four o'clock, and even at that early hour the market was already a hive of noisy, bustling, chaotic activity as the giant lorries discharged their loads of fruit and vegetables brought in from every corner of England.

Dad unlocked his cart and pushed it to his normal pitch in the centre of the market, where he sat on it waiting for custom. He hadn't long to wait.

Ely Entwistle, Choice Fruiterer and Greengrocer of Bury, approached him.

'How do, Tommy. Can you pick up me order for me?'

'How do, Ely. Aye, go on then. What is it?' asked Dad.

'Six cod at Holbrook's, ten taters, five cabbage, four caulies at Deakin's, eight apples at Smith's, seven strawberries at Keegan's, nine plums at Blundell's. Awreet?'

'That's a seven-an'-a-tanner job, Ely. Leave it to me,' replied Dad. Billy noticed that he wrote nothing down.

Like Stanley Matthews streaking down the wing, Tommy dodged and weaved his way through several bottlenecks of vehicles, whose drivers hooted and swore at one another in frustration.

Within an hour, Dad had loaded up all the orders and, with the strength of a donkey, pulled the heavily weighted cart along the cobbled market road.

'Push, Billy! Push!' he called to Billy at the back of the cart.

A few minutes later they found Ely's lorry parked on the edge of the market.

'You're a bloody good worker, Tommy,' said Ely. 'Here's ten bob. S'worth every penny. Will y'have a few things to tek home?'

'Aye, ta,' said Dad, helping himself to some fish and a selection of fruit and veg which he put into a canvas shopping bag hanging on the back of the cart.

'See you on Monday then, Tommy,' shouted Ely.

Billy and his dad then returned to his pitch to await further customers. They worked in this way all that Saturday morning – hard and fast – until eleven o'clock, when at last the pace began to slow down and the market became relatively quiet, by which time Billy was dropping with exhaustion.

'Here y'are, Billy, here's half a crown for you. You've earned it. You go on home and take these few things to your mother. I'll go and have a quick one or two in the Hare and Hounds afore I finish.'

'I never knew until now how hard your work was, Dad.'

'It gets easy when you've been at it for over forty years.'

Billy caught the 62 bus and made his weary way back home, carrying the canvas bag laden with fish, fruit and vegetables. As he walked through the door, he sang:

'*Show me the way to go home, I'm tired and I wanna go to bed.*'

He collapsed on to his bed and was asleep in ten seconds.

* * *

Shortly after that, following his mam's suggestion about taking up an interest, Billy decided to go for piano lessons. In fact he had taught himself to play by ear – mostly out of tune – on his sister Pauline's upright, driving the young Keenan family out of their minds in the process. His favourite piece was a distorted, discordant rendering of Rachmaninov's Prelude, complete with melodramatic commentary about a man buried alive in his coffin – which sent delicious shivers of horror down the spines of his two young nephews, Oliver and Danny.

> *'Now he's banging on the lid of the coffin.*
> *Now he's squirming, trying to get out.*
> *Now he's yelling for someone to help him.*
> *Now he's weeping quietly – almost given up.*
> *Now he's getting weaker.*
> *Now he's given up hope.*
> *Now he's dead.'*

'You could get a job in a pub playing that,' said Pauline.

'He'd soon empty it,' said Steve. 'They could use him at closing time instead of calling "Time, gentlemen, please." Just get him to play that piece and he'd clear the pub in thirty seconds flat.'

Billy thought it was time he learned to play properly, and it was with this in mind that he knocked on the door of Miss Lois de Lacy, LRAM.

'Do you give piano lessons?'

'I do, but I usually take on toddlers – just starting. How old are you?' said Miss de Lacy.

'I'm nearly fifteen but I'd like to start from the very beginning.'

'Very well, then. But I warn you, I'm more accustomed to teaching five-year-olds.'

At the first lesson, Miss de Lacy, all lace and dangly bits of jewellery, announced brightly:

'This is a piano!'

Acting the fool, Billy deliberately approached the sideboard.

'What – this?' he asked.

Miss de Lacy didn't blink or smile, thinking perhaps that she'd taken on a moron.

'No, this,' she replied, pointing to the piano.

'Got it!'

'These are the low notes,' she said, playing a bass chord. 'They sound like big bad bears, don't they?'

'And these are the high notes,' she said, playing a rippling arpeggio at the top of the keyboard. 'They are like little fairies tripping through the forest.'

'Got it.'

At the end of this introductory lesson he was given his first pieces of homework to practise. The first item required the playing of crotchets on one note – middle C – to the words of a song entitled 'Crunchy Flakes'.

'*Crunchy flakes! Crunchy flakes!*' he sang. '*Give you all – that it takes!*'

He played this over and over again as Miss de Lacy had instructed until he could execute it perfectly. Whilst he was practising and singing thus, Pauline decided quite suddenly and without any warning or explanation to take the children for a walk. When she returned, Billy had progressed to his second piece – a much more challenging number, entitled 'The Woodchuck'. The performance of this composition demanded singing and accompanying himself on two notes – middle C and G.

'*If a woodchuck could chuck wood,*' he trilled and played. '*How much wood would he chuck?*'

'If there's any chucking to be done,' said Pauline,

368

interrupting him, 'I suggest you chuck up learning to play the piano before you drive us all bonkers.'

'I can take a hint,' said Billy. 'But I like music, and as you know, we're not allowed to play musical instruments in the flats. If you'd let me practise here I wouldn't mind taking up the trombone or a trumpet, or maybe drums.'

'No, no,' she said hurriedly. 'Try something a bit quieter, like soft-shoe dancing. Wait a minute, I've got it! Ballroom dancing! That's it!'

And that was how Billy got himself into the world of Victor Sylvester and Harrigan's Dance Academy on Queen's Road.

Chapter Twenty-Two

Dancing In The Dark

Towards the end of 1943, things began to happen. General Eisenhower announced an armistice with Italy; the big three, Churchill, Roosevelt and Stalin, met in Tehran; Marine Sam Hopkins landed at Naples and had Mussolini on the run; young Les Hopkins, accompanied by the rest of the Eighth Army, fought his way up the boot of Italy; the bombing of Manchester ceased and the Blackpool evacuees, including the incorrigible Brother Dorian – as dictatorial as ever – returned to Manchester, the funny business at the Martindale bungalow forgotten; Flo at long last got her man and married Sergeant Barry Healey; and Billy learned to dance.

'Forward left foot – side right foot – close. Forward right foot – side left foot – close,' recited Billy, book in hand, as he practised his steps down the lobby of their flat.

'What is it you're doing now, our Billy? You're allus up to summat,' Mam said.

'Dancing, Mam. I'm learning the waltz from this book, *Ballroom Dancing Made Easy*. Forward left foot – side right foot – close. Wait a minute. I'm right up against the wall. What do I do now? This book doesn't tell you what to do when you come up against a solid object.'

'You'll never learn how to dance from a book, you daft ha'porth. You need to be learnt properly by a teacher, you need music, and most of all, you need a partner.'

'You're right, Mam. Lend us a coupla bob and I'll try Harrigan's Dance Academy on Queen's Road tonight.'

At seven o'clock, Billy turned up at Harrigan's and paid over his two shillings to a little old lady in the box office.

'Your two shillings covers the lesson and the dance afterwards,' she explained. 'Monday's the waltz, Wednesday's the slow foxtrot and Friday's the quickstep.'

'And Tuesdays and Thursdays?'

'They're for advanced only – South American dances, tango and rumba.'

Billy went through and saw several groups of men and women each being taught by different teachers.

'Over here!' called a giant of a man who, judging by his misshapen nose and his cauliflower ear, had once been a boxer.

Billy went over and joined a group of five other men.

'I'm Lofty O'Malley,' said the giant, raising both arms above his head. 'Your dance teacher. Tonight we're gonna learn the waltz. Get behind me and do just as I do. Ready! And – forward left – side right – close. Forward right – side left – close.'

Lofty waltzed forward gracefully and lightly like a butterfly whilst the six learners followed behind, walking stiffly like men trying out artificial legs.

'Watch yourself in the mirrors,' Lofty called over his shoulder, indicating the large wall mirrors which surrounded them.

Billy caught a glimpse of himself and was taken aback to see a tall, lanky boy of fifteen dancing behind Lofty.

'Gosh – is that really me?' he said aloud. 'I look so skinny and my nose looks as if it's outgrown my face.'

'That's you all right,' said Lofty. 'Don't worry about being on the thin side, though. That can only help your dancing. Look at Fred Astaire. Don't know about your nose, though; you'll have to wait for the rest of your face to catch up. But I'll swap noses with you any day.'

The rest of the lesson was taken up practising. Lofty took the girl's part, and he and Billy made a strange sight indeed as they waltzed round together – a gawky youth and a seventeen-stone bruiser.

After the lessons, old Mrs Harrigan, the lady from the box office, who looked even smaller standing up, announced through the microphone:

'And now you will have a chance to practise all that you've learnt this evening with our instructors, who are waiting in the centre of the floor to welcome you. We begin with the waltz. I'll come round and allocate the ladies and Lofty will do the same for the men.'

'Miss Lucy!' Lofty called, holding Billy's arm above his head like a referee declaring the winner of a boxing match.

Soon, calls of 'Miss Rosy!' 'Mr David!' 'Miss Joyce!' 'Mr Philip!' echoed all round the maple-floored ballroom until all the instructors had a learner each. The four-piece band struck up with the 'Fascination Waltz' and they were off.

Lucy was a young, slim sixteen-year-old with a pretty face, light-brown hair tied back with a ribbon, and a little attractive, turned-up nose.

'I hope I don't stand on your toes,' he said. 'I'm an absolute novice – so you'll have to be patient.'

'That's OK,' she smiled. 'That's what we're paid for, and I'm wearing me special steel-capped dancing shoes. First, place your right hand under me left shoulder blade.'

'Like this?' he said.

'That's it. No need to be shy about it. We're only dancing – you're not making love to me or anything like that. Now, take my right hand in your other hand and lift your arm to shoulder height. Does that feel comfortable?'

'Strange but OK.'

'Now, we move. Ready . . . in time to the music . . . And – one – two – three. Forward right – side – close. That's it.'

Together they began to move around the ballroom – Billy somewhat awkwardly, Lucy easily and gracefully.

'There's a big difference between dancing with you and dancing with Lofty,' he said.

'About ten stone difference,' she said. 'You know, you move quite well for a novice. You're quite light on your feet.'

'Well, like you, I'm not exactly a heavyweight. I used to do boxing and that teaches you to be light on your feet.'

'I think you could make a very good dancer if you put your mind to it. You never know, you might be another Fred Astaire.'

'Funny you should say that. Lofty just said I looked like him – a regular bag o'bones.'

'Well, that's a start anyroad.'

'You dance beautifully,' he told her. 'How long have you been at it?'

'I started just after leaving school. So it must be about two years now.'

'I wish I could reach your standard.'

'Nowt to stop you if you work hard enough at it.'

When the waltz had finished, Billy returned to his place and spent the rest of the evening simply observing.

'Now we have a demonstration of the slow foxtrot by Miss Lucy and Mr Lofty,' Mrs Harrigan informed everyone through her microphone.

Admiringly, Billy watched the couple glide across the floor so elegantly and so effortlessly to the tune 'I'll Be Seeing You'. As they floated by, Lucy gave Billy a broad smile which he returned with a surreptitious wink.

One day, he vowed to himself, I'll be the one doing that demonstration.

At the end of the evening, he met Lucy as she was about to leave.

'Which way do you go?' he asked, politely.

'I live in the flats.'

'So do I! Not Gardenia Court?'

'No, Hazlewood House.'

'Is it OK if we walk back together?'

'All right, I don't mind.'

'I'd love to be able to dance like you,' he said as they made their way along Queen's Road. 'You must have had private lessons, surely?'

'No, I didn't. I learned all me dancing in my spare time at Harrigan's.'

'I don't think I can afford to go to Harrigan's three or four times a week.'

'It is a bit dear, though not as dear as having private lessons with the top professionals like Frank Rogers or Archie Lamont. Don't you have a job?'

'No. I'm still studying at school. But I could look for a part-time job, I suppose.'

'Still studying at your age? I'm surprised anyone stays on after fourteen. Me, I hated school. Just seemed like a waste o' time. I could hardly wait to leave.'

'What do you do now, Lucy?'

'I work at the biscuit factory; it's a bit boring packing biscuits all day – that's why I took up dancing. At least I have summat interesting in my life. And the money I earn is good – it's helped me to pay for my lessons at Harrigan's.'

'I've got another year before I leave school.'

'You're lucky, if you're good at schoolwork. Not like me, a bit thick.'

'I'm sure you're not thick, but why do you say I'm lucky?'

'Well, if you go on to college, you'll end up in an interesting, well-paid job. Not like me – a skivvy in a biscuit factory.'

'But sometimes, school and all the studying I have to do seem like a waste of time. I'm always desperately short of cash and it's then I'm tempted to leave and take a job.'

'Don't talk daft. If you've got the opportunity to do summat useful with your life, don't throw it away. You could end up in a really boring job like mine.'

'It's just . . . well . . . when I see you dancing . . . like I did tonight, I'm tempted to jack it all in and start enjoying life a bit.'

'Look, dancing is the one and only thing I've got in my life. It's what helps me to get by. At work, we're like a bit of the machinery, having to keep up with it all the time. But at night, after I've got away . . . well, it's then I come to life. Dancing gives me a chance to express meself . . . to be me and not just part of a conveyor belt.'

'Still, I wish I could dance half as good as you.'

'Look,' she said suddenly, 'if you're really serious about wanting to learn, I could teach you at weekends.'

'Honestly? That'd be great. But where?'

'Why not on the rooftop of the flats?' she said, warming to the idea. 'I used to go up there sometimes in the nice weather – sunbathing. There's plenty of room for dancing – it's even bigger than Harrigan's dance floor. I could bring my portable gramophone and some Victor Sylvester records.'

'Lucy, you're marvellous. But why're you doing it? What do you get out of it?'

'I like teaching, that's all. And you never know, I might get Fred Astaire as a partner.'

'Thanks a lot, Lucy.'

'There's just one thing, though,' she said, turning serious. 'I mean dancing only, and no trying it on with me or anything like that.'

'Sorry, I'm not with you.'

'You know what I mean. Getting fresh and that.'

'Promise, Lucy. Cross my heart.'

They reached Hazlewood House.

'This is where I live. What's your name, by the way?'

'Billy or William – take your pick.'

'Billy's a nice name. I'll take that. See you on Sunday afternoon. Call round at two o'clock. I live at number ten.'

'It's a date,' he said. 'Good night, Lucy.'

'Good night, Billy. Be seeing you. Remember, though – just dancing and no messing about. No hanky-panky.'

'Hanky-panky? Never crossed my mind.'

'Not even once?'

'No, not even once.'

'Well, then I feel slighted and insulted,' she said, laughing.

'I'll never understand girls. Good night again, Lucy.'

Billy went home that night with a light step, a song in his heart and a whistle on his lips.

'How did you get on at Harrigan's, son?' Mam asked.

'It was great, Mam. I danced with a seventeen-stone boxer and a girl called Lucy. And I think I'm in love.'

'Oh, aye,' she said. 'Who with? The boxer or the girl?'

'Don't be funny, Mam. I think I know now what I want to do with my life.'

'You keep changing your mind every five minutes. One minute it's a boxer, then a writer, then a teacher, then a navigator. What is it today?'

'Professional ballroom dancer.'

'What next! Don't be so daft, you'd never earn a living as one o' them fellas wearing tights and prancing about the stage showing all they've got.'

'That's ballet, Mam. This is ballroom, and I'll tell you summat – it's a lot more interesting than all that boring stuff we're doing at school.'

'If you're going to be a teacher or a writer like you say, you'll have to stick it out at school and pass your exams. If you like dancing, keep it as your hobby. Anyroad, where are you going to get the money to keep going to Harrigan's?'

'Well, for a start, Lucy's going to teach me for nothing on Sunday afternoons. But you know, Mam, I get really fed up always being short of money. I think I'd be better leaving school, finding myself a job and getting a bob or two in my pocket.'

'You do talk barmy sometimes, our Billy. What was the point in us making all them sacrifices, pawning Granny's teapot and all that, if you're going to throw it all away just when you're nearly finished and the end is in sight?'

'Do you realise, Mam, that just at this moment I haven't got two ha'pennies to rub together?'

'I know. I know. I can't afford to give you any more. It's hard enough finding your bus fare every day. I know you don't like being without money in your pocket, but you could stop smoking for a start.'

'I smoke three Park Drive a day. That costs about tuppence ha'penny. I haven't even got that for tomorrow

377

unless I walk the six miles to school.'

'There's a few empty mineral bottles in the cupboard. You could take them back. That'd give you tuppence ha'penny.'

'Right, thanks, Mam. That'll give me a smoke tomorrow, at least.'

'Why don't you look for a part-time job?'

'I could start chopping wood again, or deliver papers, I suppose.'

'No, I don't mean that. You could help your dad in the market on Sat'days. That'd give you a couple bob.'

'But don't you see, Mam? It's just scrimping and scraping all the time. Cadging a penny here and a penny there just to keep going.'

'Well, no matter what you say, our Billy, you're not leaving school and that's that. Why don't you ask that pal you're allus going on about – Robin what's-his-name – if you can help him and his dad delivering tea on Sat'days?'

'You know, Mam, that's the best idea I've heard all week. I'll ask him at school tomorrow.'

Chapter Twenty-Three

Hands Across The Sea

The next day, Billy made a point of finding Robin at the mid-morning break.

'I'm looking for a part-time job, Robin,' he said. 'Any chance of me helping you and your dad with tea deliveries at weekends?'

'Funny you should say that, Hoppy. My dad just made a big delivery to the new American Red Cross canteen they've opened in St Anne's Square for American servicemen from Burtonwood, and the manager was asking him if he knew of two likely lads for an evening job shining shoes in the men's barber shop.'

'Sounds interesting. What's the deal?'

'Hours four thirty to seven o'clock. No pay – tips only. But they should be pretty good as the Yanks are very well paid. Our troops are always saying they're over-sexed, over-paid and over here.'

'They're just jealous. I don't know about over-sexed and all that, but as for being over-paid, I read somewhere that a Yankee private is paid five times as much as one of ours, and that an American sergeant gets more than a British captain.'

'Do you fancy giving it a try then, Hoppy? Or do you

think cleaning boots is stooping too low?'

'No, I don't mind cleaning boots as long as I don't have to lick 'em. What about homework?'

'We get at least two private study periods a day. So we should be able to do homework then.'

'You seem to have thought of everything, Robin. We'll go down together and apply for the job.'

The two boys presented themselves to the GI barber shop after school and got the job on a trial basis.

'A smart khaki uniform complete with GI hat goes with the job,' the head barber said. 'The Yanks like their employees to look smart – and that goes for even the shoe-shine boys.'

'In uniform at last,' said Robin. 'And look at these swish shoulder flashes saying "American Red Cross" with the Red Cross emblem underneath.'

'People are going to think we're a coupla surgeons, Robin.'

'In a way we are. Foot specialists.'

The next night, the two of them turned up for their first stint of duty. The music being played through the PA system was Bing Crosby's 'Shoe Shine Boy'.

'Why, they're playing our song, Robin,' said Billy.

'That's OK, Hoppy, as long as it's not "Lazy Bones".'

It wasn't long before they got their first customers – two GIs in the Army Air Force.

'Hi, there,' one of them said, sitting in the raised chair. 'I'm Tex and this is my buddy Rick. How's about a shoe-shine, boys?'

'Sure thing,' said Robin, adopting the American idiom. 'I'm Robin and this here is my pal, Hoppy. We're both students.'

'Stoodents, eh? Working your way through college.

That's what we Americans like to see. Get-up-'n'-go. I hated school myself. Didn't seem to get the hang of it no-how. Now, every time I pass my old high school, I nearly matriculate. You hear what I'm saying?'

They placed their feet on the shoe-stand. Billy and Robin took one look at their boots and their spirits plummeted, for both soldiers had size 10s richly encrusted in thick mud. The two apprentice shoe-shiners took in a deep breath and began scraping off the mud.

'We just flew down from doing manoeuvres in the Scottish hills,' said Rick. 'Boy, that Scotland is some place, I tell ya. What kinda language do they talk up there? All that "och aye" and "hoots mon" stuff. Sure beats me – just Double Dutch.'

'It sure is good to get back to Lancasheer where we talk the same lingo, eh, Hoppy,' said Tex.

'We're two great nations divided by a common language.'

'Say, that's pretty cute,' replied Tex. 'Whadda you two guys studying?'

'Oh, the usual stuff,' said Robin. 'Maths, languages, English literature, Shakespeare – that kind of thing.'

'Oh, Shakespeare, you mean all that "Hey nonny, nonny" crap?' said Rick.

'That's right,' said Billy, now beginning to apply brown shoe polish to Rick's footwear. 'We're studying *The Tempest* and *Julius Caesar.*'

'Ah tell ya,' said Tex. 'Last month in London, Ah was shacked up with this real classy broad. She took me to the theatre to see this Shakespeare guy. *Hamlet, Macbeth* and then *King Lear*. Boy, did those guys have problems! By the end of each play, everyone was mincemeat. Worse than Al Capone's St Valentine's massacre, Ah tell ya. Y'know what I'm saying?'

'I reckon this Shakespeare guy is over-rated,' said Rick. 'Ya see one of his plays, you've seen 'em all. Say, I once knew one of these high-brow dames in New York – crazy about opera, she was. She took me to the Met to see an opera called *The Valkyrie* by a guy called Wagner.'

'Oh, yeah. What was that about, Rick?' asked Tex.

'Don't rightly know, Tex. But there was this big fat guy wailing something in German and some huge, big-assed broad, as big as a house, with a kinda kettle on her head screaming the same thing over and over again. Sounded like "I-will-I-won't-I-will-I-won't".'

'A guy told me that them operas last a real long time.'

'Long? Well, I tell ya, Tex. The show started at seven o'clock. Three hours later, I looked at my watch. It was seven-fifteen. You unnerstand what I'm saying?'

'Yeah. So I guess we'll just stick to the good old movies – Bogie and Edward G. Whatcha got planned for tonight, Rick?' asked Tex.

'Ah got myself a whole pack o' rubbers and I'm gonna get myself laid until I've used up the whole pack. Either of you two guys got any sisters?'

'Sorry,' said Robin. 'Can't help you there, fellas.'

'I've got two,' said Billy. 'But they're both married.'

'Hell, that don't matter none,' said Rick. 'I'd be willing to keep 'em both happy and satisfied if their husbands are away. Come to think of it – even if their husbands ain't away.'

'Sorry, can't help you there, Rick.'

The shoe-shining operation was in the final stages and both boys began cracking their polishing cloths and buffing the shoe leather for all they were worth.

'Well, Hoppy,' said Rick. 'You've made a darned fine job o' my boots. Why, you can see your face in 'em. How much is that, now?'

'That'll be threepence, Rick,' said Billy.

'Here,' said Rick, tossing over a half-crown. 'Keep the change, son. You've earned it.'

'Gee, thanks, Rick,' said Billy.

'I never could figure out this funny money o' yours,' said Tex. 'But the same goes for you, Robin. Keep the change and put it towards your studying.'

'Gosh, thanks a million, Tex,' said Robin.

The two soldiers got down from the stand.

'Be seeing you, guys,' said Rick. 'And remember, Hoppy, if them sisters o' yours ever need any special comforting, you let me know, you hear?'

When they'd gone, Billy turned to Robin and said:

'I think I'm gonna like this job. If we keep up this rate of earning, we'll be rich by seven o'clock.'

'Yeah,' said Robin, 'and I like the way these GIs talk to us as if we're adults. It makes me feel all grown-up.'

The music over the PA changed to Irving Berlin's 'My British Buddy'. The next two soldiers were already waiting.

'I'm Ev and this here ugly-looking guy with the cigar is Bob. Maybe you could fix him up with a new face. If not, we'll settle for a shoe-shine.'

'I'm Hoppy and this is Robin. Shoe-shines a-coming up right away – sir!'

Without preamble, the cigar-smoking Bob handed Billy a photograph, as if giving him a visiting card.

'Is this your family?' asked Billy in amazement.

'Yep, it certainly is, young sir,' Bob replied. 'That there's my wife, Lee, and that's young Robert junior, aged ten. The old guy is my pop. Ain't they a swell-looking family?'

'They sure are, Bob,' replied Billy, getting down to the mud-removing business.

'You said your name's Hoppy. Any relation to Hopalong Cassidy?' asked Ev.

''Fraid not,' said Billy. 'But I'm a distant relation of Buffalo Bill.'

'You don't say,' said Ev. 'How's about that? You hear that, Bob? This guy's related to William F. Cody. Good job you ain't doing the barbering around here, Hoppy, or you'd be taking a few scalps, I guess.'

'I heard what you were saying just now to Tex and Rick about us having a different language and all,' said Bob, 'and I reckon you've certainly got something there. I just came back from my hotel and when I asked the desk clerk to give me an early call, she asked me what time I wanted to be knocked up. I tell ya, don't know about knocked *up*, you could've knocked me *down* with a feather.'

'Here in Lancashire,' said Billy, 'we have a man who goes round the streets very early in the morning with a long pole just knocking people up. He's called a knocker-upper.'

'You don't say! Now that's what I call a real man's job. And this guy's got a very long pole, you say. I reckon he needs one with a job like that.'

'You know,' said Ev, 'we've been given a little booklet explaining things about you Limeys, Hoppy. Lemme read a little bit from it: "If British civilians look dowdy and badly dressed, it is not because they do not like good clothes . . . All clothing is rationed . . . Don't make fun of British speech. You sound just as funny to them." Do we sound funny to you, Hoppy?'

'Not funny, but different,' answered Billy tactfully. 'We pronounce words differently. For example, you say ske-dule and we say she-dule.'

'So instead of saying, "It's our scheme to be scholars

384

in school", you guys would say, "It's our sheme to be sholars at shool." '

Billy and Robin laughed.

'It just goes to show,' said Billy, 'how crazy our pronunciation is. But apart from that, we also use words differently. Look, I'll say a word and you tell me what you understand by it. Ready? Bum.'

'Hobo,' said Ev.

'For us, that means backside or arse,' said Robin.

'For "arse",' said Bob, 'we say "butt" or "fanny".'

'For the English,' said Billy, ' "fanny" is on the other side of the body. Try this – petrol.'

'Gas,' said Ev.

'That's indigestion or idle chatter for us,' said Robin.

'What about "sidewalk"?' said Bob.

'To us,' said Robin, 'that's the pavement.'

'And for us,' said Ev, 'pavement's the middle of the road. That could lead to really disastrous consequences given the wrong instructions.'

'Try this sentence,' said Billy. ' "I'm mad about my flat." What does that mean to you?'

'That means,' said Bob, 'I'm darned angry 'cos my automobile has a puncture.'

'For us,' said Billy, 'it means that I'm really excited about my apartment. So you see what I mean about two languages. You just used the word "Limey", Ev. What does that mean?'

'Why, that's a word we use to mean someone British. Comes from the time when the British used to drink lime juice to fight against scurvy on board their ships. We Yanks just called 'em Limeys, I guess.'

'And that word "Yank", that's a funny word as well,' said Robin. 'What's it mean? Anyone know?'

'There's an argument about that word, Robin,' said

Bob. 'Some say it means "Janke", or Dutch for "Johnny", from the time when the Dutch ruled over New York. It was called New Amsterdam then. Others claim that "Yankees" is the Red Indian way of saying "English". No one really knows.'

'Say, what is this?' said Ev. 'Some kinda college or a shoe-shine stand? I'm learning fast. But what gets me is the way you Limeys have everything the wrong way round. You pile all your food on to a fork with your knife. We just need a fork.'

'I must admit you've got me there,' said Billy.

'Yeah,' said Bob. 'And you go into a shop to buy something and everybody keeps saying thank you the whole time. I bought a candy bar in a store yesterday and had to say thank you four times before they'd let me outa the joint. And whenever I ask for directions, the guy always says, "You can't miss it." '

'Say, Hoppy,' said Ev, 'why do you British like bathtubs? Who wants to sit in his own dirty water? We Americans always like to take a shower. Don't you think it's more hygienic?'

'Well, we British like to make sure we're clean before we take a bath – then we just like to sit there and soak all our cares away.'

At this point the GI boots were being given their finishing touches with the polishing cloth.

'That's what I call a shoe-shine,' said Ev, handing over a half-crown to Robin. 'I learned a lot from you two guys tonight. Thanks a lot. One last question, though. Exactly what is the name of this country of yours? Is it England? Britain? Great Britain? Or just plain United Kingdom?'

'None of those,' said Billy. 'It's just plain United Kingdom of Great Britain and Northern Ireland.'

'How about that!' exclaimed Ev.

'That really is a great shine, and it's been most interesting talking to you, Hoppy, and to you, Robin,' said Bob, tossing a half-crown in payment for his threepenny shoe-shine. 'Keep the change, Hoppy. Worth every cent. Here's a coupla Hershey bars and a packet of rubbers.'

And he stuffed the items into Billy's top pocket before he could protest.

'Thanks for the Hershey bars, Bob. Don't know about the rubbers, though.'

'You mean you're still a virgin, or you don't use 'em?'

'Both, Bob.'

'It's about time you tried, boy. All you need is a pair of nylons and you're away.'

'Never wear 'em, Bob.'

'Huh, funny guy, eh? Tell you what I'm gonna do for you, Hoppy. Next time I see you, I'm gonna let you have a pair of nylons so's you can get yourself a piece o' tail.'

'Gee, thanks, Bob. You're a pal,' said Billy.

At seven o'clock, the barber shop closed up, and the two boys did a final count of the night's take.

'Thirty-seven shillings and sixpence,' announced Billy. 'I'm as rich as Rockefeller, and this is only one night!'

'Thirty-five for me,' said Robin. 'I'm off to order my Rolls Royce tomorrow morning.'

The boys parted company in a happy, jubilant mood. Billy arrived home at 7.30.

'Well, Mam, how much do you think I made?' he asked triumphantly.

'I don't know. Five shillings?'

'Nearly right,' he said, pouring out all his takings on to the dining-room table.

'I hope you haven't been out pinching money,' she said. 'How much is there?'

'All honestly earned by the sweat of my brow. Over thirty-seven shillings for one night's work. By the end of the week I should have about eight or nine quid. And here's a coupla American candy bars for you.'

He said nothing about the rubbers tucked away in his back pocket.

'Eeeh,' she said. 'That's a lot more than your dad's earning in the market.'

'We're in the money! We're in the money!' he sang, dancing round the table. 'First thing, I pay you something towards my keep after all these years. Next thing I buy will be a pair of really good dancing shoes – those with the shiny patent leather – and I'm really going to learn how to dance. You'll see.'

At the end of the week, his total earnings came to over ten pounds, and Billy felt that he had at last found his niche.

'You know, Mam,' he said, 'I like the idea of having money in my pocket. It makes a big difference to life. Without money, you're nothing. What's more, the people I work with treat me as an adult instead of a child as they do at school. I wouldn't mind leaving and getting a full-time job.'

'Look, Billy,' she said, 'I've said it till I'm blue in the face. You're not leaving school – not before you're sixteen. And you're wrong. Money isn't everything. "The greatest wealth is being content with a little." Your health and strength are much more important. And don't you forget it.'

Chapter Twenty-Four

A Little Learning

All that term, Billy worked as he'd never worked before. At school he studied Caesar's *Gallic Wars* in the original, Shakespeare's sonnets and Palgrave's *Golden Treasury* of poems; mechanics, magnetism and electricity; Tudor architecture; the short stories of Guy de Maupassant; quadratic equations, Euclidian geometry and a lot of other useful subjects. His academic progress over the last year had been good and he was vying with 'Oscar' Wilde for fifth place in class, but at maths he was in a class of his own.

His shoe-shining activities were so profitable that he had managed not only to buy his dancing shoes and pay for lessons at Harrigan's, but to save some money as well, and by the end of November, he had accumulated the princely sum of twenty-five pounds.

But it was in the field of dancing that he made the greatest strides and the greatest progress, moving up from novice to accomplished amateur in the space of three months. After work in the barber shop, he attended Harrigan's every night, including Saturday, learning the basic steps and the many beautiful variations in every dance. He moved through the waltz, the slow foxtrot and

the quickstep, and on to the more advanced South
American dances – the tango and the rumba. He mastered
most of the subtle movements and absorbed the tech-
niques of the natural and reverse turns, double reverse
turns, the feather, the whisk and the chassé, the drag
hesitation and the backward lock. At home he studied
and practised all the advice and exercises given by Alex
Moore in his standard work on ballroom dancing. Billy
lived and breathed dancing until his movements became
smooth, graceful and effortless.

The master class, however, was held every Sunday
afternoon on the rooftop of Hazlewood House by Lucy,
who took all the skills he had acquired at the dance
academy and tuned and refined them to the highest level,
until Billy was beginning to feel that he had been dancing
all his life. As she had insisted from the start, the
relationship with Lucy was strictly dancing and nothing
else. On their third meeting in September, Billy had
presented her with two Hershey bars.

'A GI gave me these candy bars, Lucy. They're all
yours.'

'Are you sure? Good chocolate is so hard to get
nowadays.'

'That's OK. He also gave me these.'

He showed her the packet of rubbers.

'Oh, yes,' she said, frowning when she saw what they
were. 'So what? I do hope you're not getting any funny
ideas.'

'No, no. I just thought you might be interested to
know what these Yanks are like, that's all. That's not all he
gave me.'

He showed her the nylons that Bob, as good as his
word, had given him.

'Take 'em. I have no use for them.'

'Look, Billy, I thought we had things straight from the very beginning. I like you and I think you're very nice-looking and all that. But if you think you can buy me with a pair of nylons, you'd better think again, that's all. I'm not like that. I may work in a biscuit factory but I'm not crackers. Dancing only, and nothing more, remember?'

'OK, Lucy. But keep the nylons anyway, as a kind of fee for these lessons.'

'All right, I'll take 'em as sort of payment. Wait till the girls at work see 'em; they'll scratch my eyes out. Right then, so I'd better start earning them. Let's get to work! Slow foxtrot! My favourite dance! I want to see long, gliding, smooth steps from you. Try to make it look sort of lazy and easy.'

She switched on Victor Sylvester playing 'As Time Goes By' and they danced across the rooftop.

'Keep up on your toes on the feather step and don't forget what I told you about contrary body movement. It's a bit like you on your bike when you turn right. Sway over to the right a bit and stay relaxed. That's it. I've never known anyone to pick up dancing so quickly and easily.'

'What do you expect from Fred Astaire?'

'And I've never known anyone so modest, either.'

'My modesty's the thing I'm most proud of.'

Billy moved rhythmically across the floor, lightly and easily.

'Slow, slow, quick, quick, slow,' chanted Lucy in time to the music. 'Now the impetus turn. Move the left foot ever so slowly to your right and forward left. That's beautiful. We'll make a dancer of you yet. You'll see.'

Sunday after Sunday she added more and more refinements to his movements, until one day towards the end of November she announced:

'I think we're ready.'

'You mean for lovemaking, Lucy?'

'Stop acting the goat, Billy.'

'Huh! Very funny!'

'We're ready to enter a slow foxtrot competition at Harrigan's next Saturday. I think we're moving together quite nicely. It's amazing, really, to think that you began dancing only a few months ago.'

'That's me, Lucy. When I go for something, there's no half-measures. It's all or nothing at all.'

On the evening of Saturday 27 November, Billy put on his new dancing shoes and donned his dark-blue suit – which he had paid all of ten pounds for at Reid Bros in Market Street – a white silk shirt and a spotted tie. He spent a good deal of time Brylcreeming his hair until he had the quiff just right, and another ten minutes practising throwing his cigarette into his mouth from waist height until he got it on to the edge of his lip every single time.

'You handsome devil, you,' he said to his reflection.

'You remind me of that film star,' Mam said when she saw him.

'Which one?' he asked, throwing a fag nonchalantly into his mouth. 'Humphrey Bogart?'

'No,' she said. 'The one who's allus with him. Edward G. Robinson.'

'Stop taking the mickey, Mam. I need all my confidence tonight for this dance competition.'

At Harrigan's that night, there was a good crowd and it looked as if everyone was entering the competition.

'Don't be nervous, Billy,' Lucy said. 'Half this lot'll get knocked out in the first heat. Most of them ladies can't even do a proper heel turn.'

'And some of the men move like elephants,' said Billy

to boost his own self-confidence.

'The only pair to worry about is Freda Pritchard and Duggie Diggle over there, but I think we've got them licked.'

At nine o'clock promptly, Mrs Harrigan made her announcement through the mike.

'And now we come to our foxtrot competition for our regular patrons. Only those who have taken lessons with us are eligible. Please attach your numbers to the gentleman's back and take the floor for heat one.'

Billy and Lucy were given the number 17.

'My lucky number,' said Billy. 'We used to live at number seventeen, Honeypot Street, Red Bank.'

'I hope you're right,' said Lucy. 'I thought that's where you got bombed out.'

The Saturday-night five-piece band struck up with the song 'I Remember You' and the competition began. Billy and Lucy glided smoothly and effortlessly round the floor in perfect time to the music, Billy displaying a light feather step and a reverse wave with lots of contrary body movement. Freda and Duggie, numbered at 8, also swept beautifully around the room, making full use of the available space.

At the end of heat one, only six couples were called back – Lucy and Billy and Freda and Duggie among them. In heat two, Billy and Lucy began to show off their steps: the telemark, the open telemark, and the natural hover telemark, which brought a burst of applause from the spectators. Meanwhile, Freda and Duggie were giving a lovely display of light feathery dancing which brought gasps of admiration from their supporters. At the end of heat two, only three couples were brought back: Freda and Duggie, Rita and Roy and Lucy and Billy.

'At least we're in the first three,' said Lucy. 'But to win,

Billy, you'll really have to pull out all the stops.'

The band began to play 'It's a Lovely Day Tomorrow' and the three couples started to float their way around the ballroom, demonstrating the most intricate and subtle steps of the slow foxtrot.

Lucy and Billy put out all their best movements which they had practised so hard and so patiently all those Sunday afternoons. Billy performed the weave, the top spin and the outside swivel with grace and elegance. He and Lucy wore easy, relaxed smiles – 'the happy face' – as they flowed around the floor. Billy finished with a beautifully executed impetus turn followed by hover and on into the feather step and a reverse wave. Then it was all over.

Mrs Harrigan and Lofty went into a huddle for an eternity that was all of five minutes. The crowd waited tensely for the decision. Mrs Harrigan went to her mike.

'Here are the results of our slow foxtrot competition. In third place, number seven, Rita and Roy. In second place . . . number eight, Freda and Duggie. And our winners tonight . . .'

Her voice was drowned in the cheers of the spectators, while Billy found himself being hugged to pieces by an ecstatic Lucy.

'WE DID IT! WE DID IT!' she yelled. 'Billy, I think you're marvellous.'

'Ah know Ah am,' he said in his best Lancashire accent. 'Ah've 'ad a reet good teacher. And come to think of it, you're not so bad yourself, lass.'

The three couples went forward to receive their awards: a pair of small dressing-table mirrors for third, somewhat larger mirrors for second, and two superb gold-plated statues of a dancing couple for the winners.

'Congratulations to all of you,' said Mrs Harrigan. 'And Billy, could I see you for a moment after this dance?'

For Billy and Lucy, the rest of the evening was somewhat confused, as if they were in a dream come true – which they were. Lucy clung closely to Billy in every dance.

'I can't believe it's happened,' she said. 'After all our work! It's paid off! And as for you, Billy, I've never known anyone to pick up dancing so quick.'

'Right at the beginning, you told me I could be another Fred Astaire. I tell you this, Lucy. School, Caesar's *Gallic Wars* and quadratic equations seem a million miles away.'

'Remember what I told you, Billy? Your education's more important than dancing. Get yourself qualified and get a good job with good money and one that's interesting as well. How many more times do y'ave to be told, you daft devil? You can allus keep up dancing as your pastime. But don't end up like me in a lousy, monotonous job.'

'OK! OK! Keep your hair on. It's just that . . . well . . . I'm so happy that we pulled it off. It's all down to you, Lucy, and your teaching on the rooftop.'

Towards the end of that wonderful night, he went to see Mrs Harrigan in her office.

'Billy, you've made such astounding progress in dancing, I'd like to offer you a part-time job as instructor/ host on the staff. The pay is three shillings per evening, and naturally, your admission to all dances would be free. Are you interested?'

'Interested? I'll say, Mrs Harrigan. When do I start?'

'You can start on Monday if that's OK with you.'

Billy and Lucy were so preoccupied, so full of their triumphant win that evening, that they failed to notice the glamorous and beautiful young girl who watched all their excited reactions with a curious, faintly amused smile on her lips. If they'd known what she had in mind, they might have paid her more attention.

* * *

On Monday evening, after his shoe-shining duties, Billy managed to reach Harrigan's just in time to start his dance-instructor job. Pretty soon he was absorbed in teaching a group of novices the steps that he himself had learned only a few short months ago.

The usual practice session followed the lessons.

'Mr David! Mr Duggie! Mr Roy!' Lofty called out as he circulated the room, allocating ladies to the male instructors. It sounded so strange and it took Billy a little by surprise when he heard his own name being called: 'Mr Billy!'

It was even more of a surprise when he saw walking towards him the most beautiful girl he had ever seen outside the cinema screen. She had obviously modelled herself on Rita Hayworth, for she had the same hairstyle, the same cheekbones, the same dreamy, come-to-bed eyes and even the same kind of sultry expression.

'Good evening, Billy,' she said softly, with a charming smile. 'My name's Adele.'

'Hello,' said Billy, gulping, his eyes popping out of his head. 'Nice to meet you.'

The band struck up with 'Sleepy Lagoon' and the couples began to waltz around the floor.

'One thing is obvious,' said Billy. 'You're no novice. You move beautifully.'

'Why, thank you,' she said. 'I have been dancing for a number of years, as a matter of fact.'

They danced on for a while. She really was exceptionally good – like a feather in his arms.

'I specially asked for you tonight,' she said.

'Oh,' he said, puzzled. 'And why was that?'

'I watched you in the slow foxtrot competition last Saturday. I think you're pretty good.'

'The compliments are really flying around tonight.'

'Notice I said "pretty good". But you could be outstanding if you went about it the right way.'

'You think so? What is this "right way" you're talking about?'

'Look,' she said, 'I hope you don't think I'm being too forward, but I came here tonight just to see you. Could we talk at the interval, after the quickstep?'

'OK,' he said. 'Fine.'

Lucy waltzed past with her novice partner.

'Catch you later, Billy,' she said, eyeing Adele suspiciously.

'Right,' said Billy. 'See you after this dance.'

'Who's that girl?' asked Lucy when they met between dances.

'Dunno,' said Billy, 'but she certainly knows how to dance.'

'Watch your step,' said Lucy ominously. 'She's set her cap at you.'

'How can you tell that, Lucy?'

'We girls can tell. Believe me.'

At the break between dances, Billy invited Adele across to the ballroom snack bar. As they sat together talking over a cup of tea, he noticed from the corner of his eye that Lucy was engaged in earnest conversation with Roy on the other side of the room.

'Sounds very mysterious, Adele – this wanting to talk to me,' he said.

'Nothing mysterious, Billy. I'll come straight to the point. I broke up with my dancing partner a couple of weeks ago and I'm looking for a new one. I wondered if you were interested, that's all.'

'But you are obviously a much higher standard than I am – in fact, semi-professional, I'd say.'

'You would soon reach the same level if you had private lessons with the right teacher.'

'Who would that be?'

'Frank Rogers at the Deansgate Dance Academy is one of the best in the country. He's the north of England professional champion. I've been going to him for over two years.'

'Everybody knows about Frank Rogers, but he must be very expensive.'

'You have to pay if you want the best,' she said. 'Look, I'll be here tomorrow night, and if you decide to accept my proposal, you could let me know. I should warn you, though, that when I see something I want, I go after it until I get it.'

'You mean me?'

'You got it – first time.'

After their chat, Adele went to the cloakroom, collected her coat and left.

When all the practice sessions for the evening were finished, the band packed up and went home and Mrs Harrigan put on Victor Sylvester records for the last half-hour. It may have been merely coincidence or the fact that Mrs Harrigan was a keen observer of her staff's behaviour, but the record she put on as Billy and Lucy danced a last slow foxtrot was 'Won't You Change Partners and Dance with Me?'.

On the way home, Billy told Lucy about Adele's proposal.

'And are you going to take it? To be honest, I didn't like the look of that girl,' she said petulantly.

'I'm very tempted, Lucy. After all, Frank Rogers is one of the top teachers in the country. And you can't condemn the girl just because she's glamorous.'

'You may not agree with me, 'cos you're just an

innocent little boy. But us girls can tell a baby-snatcher from fifty paces.'

'Who're you calling a baby, Lucy?'

'You are, Billy, when it comes to girls.'

'I think you're just jealous.'

'Me? Jealous! Right, that does it, Billy! You can bugger off with this glamour-puss.'

'Very well, I will, if that's the way you feel.'

'It's bloody unfair that after all my efforts on the rooftop, you should go off with this man-chaser.'

'But that was our agreement, Lucy, remember? Business only. Dancing only. This could be my big chance to get into the big ballroom competitions – not just the local hop.'

'Then you can bloody well get lost, Billy. You can piss off. And don't come crawling back to me if it doesn't work out with Miss Glamour Pants.'

Lucy stormed off and Billy wondered if he had done the right thing, for he'd only decided to accept Adele's offer when Lucy had pushed him into answering.

'Would you do something for me?' Adele asked at their first private lesson with Frank Rogers.

'Sure. Just name it, Adele.'

'It's your name. Change it. "Billy" reminds me of the tin kettle we used when camping in the Girl Guides. It also sounds like the name of a plumber or a bus conductor, not a successful ballroom dancer.'

'What do you suggest?'

'How about Edwin, or Grant? Wait a minute . . . I've got it . . . Julian! That's a lovely name. From now on, for me, you're Julian.'

'OK, if that's what you want. Julian it is.'

The lesson began. Billy had thought he could dance – until, that is, he had his first session with Frank Rogers at his dance academy.

'The very first thing we have to teach you, Julian, is how to walk,' said Frank.

'But I learned that when I was eighteen months old.'

'That was toddling. This is walking rhythmically. Let's try it in slow motion. Swing the left leg forward from the hip – heel skimming the floor, toe slightly raised. Good.

'Now, as the left foot passes the toe of the right foot, release your left heel so that it just touches the floor. Lower your left toe so that the foot is flat on the floor.'

'There's more to it than I thought,' said Billy.

'Let's try it with your partner. Place both hands on Adele's shoulders and walk together across the floor. Excellent. Lightly. Move from the hips.'

The lesson continued in this fashion. Frank worked them both very hard and certainly earned the high fee of ten shillings an hour that he charged.

Towards the end of the first lesson, he said:

'We'll try walking together with close hip contact. Hands behind your back. Right, Julian, see if you can guide Adele around the room using hips only. Ready now. Push your hips, Adele, as if resisting. Push forward, Julian. Excellent. Now we'll try it to music. No hands! Hips only!'

He switched on Victor Sylvester playing 'Once in a While' and Billy and Adele moved around the room with both hands behind their backs.

'I'm finding this hip-to-hip business very sexy, Adele,' whispered Billy when they were out of earshot of Frank Rogers.

'I felt as much, Julian,' she whispered. 'Behave and concentrate on the dancing.'

'One final thing before we pack up,' said Frank. 'I'd like to check out your hold.'

They took up their position.

'Good,' he said. 'You're just the right height for each other. You're going to look great when I've finished with you both.'

He fastened an elastic band around Billy's right hand.

'You have a slight tendency to splay the fingers. That elastic band should keep them together. Keep your left wrist straight. Perfect. Now let's see your slow foxtrot.'

He switched on the record and Billy and Adele glided smoothly round the studio.

The weeks went by and Billy fell into a very busy routine – school, shoe-shining, dancing. As for Lucy, she soon recovered from her initial anger with Billy, as she found her new partner, Roy, to be a skilful dancer and an amenable person. Despite that, however, she never forgave Adele for the way, as she put it, she had snatched away her partner and protégé from under her nose. Adele joined Harrigan's staff. The two ladies were at daggers drawn every night as they stood together in the middle of the floor, waiting for novices to be allocated to them.

'Eaten any more men lately, Adele?' hissed Lucy.

'Why, are you offering, Lucy?' spat Adele. 'That new partner of yours looks quite tasty.'

'You keep your thieving eyes off him,' Lucy snapped.

'I will, Lucy, if you'll tell him to keep his big goo-goo eyes off my breasts.'

'My dear Adele, it's no wonder he's staring at 'em. It's that bloody dress you're almost wearing.'

'Why, thank you, Lucy, I'm sure,' Adele cooed. 'I'm so glad you like it. And that C & A dress of yours is lovely too – it's dyed really well.'

'But not as well as your hair, Adele,' Lucy sniffed.

'You bloody bitch,' Adele rasped as, adopting her fixed

401

Cheshire cat dancing smirk, she moved off with her stiff-legged, robotic partner.

'Yes, yes. Come on! Come on! That's it,' she grunted to the unfortunate learner. 'Forward left, side right, close. Forward right, side left, close.'

'Good. That's very good,' Lucy said encouragingly with her best ballroom Mona Lisa smile to her beginner. 'And . . . one . . . two . . . three. One . . . two . . . three.'

The two couples hadn't got far when they collided unceremoniously.

'You clumsy bitch! You did that on purpose,' Lucy snarled, all vestiges of her smile gone.

'Piss off, you stupid sod,' Adele hissed through clenched teeth, the Cheshire cat now turned to a tigress.

Each night the ladies bickered in this fashion, but meanwhile, Billy's private lessons with Frank Rogers began to pay off and the standard of his dancing improved by leaps and bounds. One evening, Mrs Harrigan called Adele and Billy into her office.

'I've noticed that you two are looking very good on the floor. I want to ask you to become our demonstrators of the slow foxtrot on Wednesday evenings; it would show our novices just how it should be done.'

'I vowed that this would come off one day, Adele, and at last it's happened,' Billy said.

'But only after a lot of very hard work and determined effort,' she said.

That first Wednesday evening, Mrs Harrigan announced:

'And now we have a demonstration of the slow foxtrot by two members of our teaching staff, Miss Adele and Mr Julian.'

They went into their routine – Billy now a very confident performer. As they danced around the floor, they could hear the admiring remarks of the novice spectators:

'See that lovely heel turn.'

'That's an impetus turn. I've just learnt that tonight.'

'Did you notice the CBM in that reverse wave.'

'She made a clumsy heel turn there, Roy. Did you notice?' Lucy said happily in a loud stage-whisper.

Despite Lucy's bitchiness, Billy was ecstatically happy that evening, dancing with a beautiful girl to the admiration of the crowd. The flattering remarks were meat and drink to him and he thought how perilously close his life had come to taking off in a different direction with Mick Scully and Vinny Buckley.

At the interval, he and Adele sat close together in the bar, enjoying the tea, the cakes, and the adulatory glances which were cast in their direction.

'Good demonstration, you two,' Duggie Diggle called light-heartedly from the other side of the room. 'If ever you get fed up with him, Adele, I'm without a partner. So you know where to come!'

'Gercha!' said Billy genially.

'No chance, Duggie. What happened to Freda?' said Adele, laughing.

'The usual story,' replied Duggie. 'She's found somebody new.'

'I enjoyed your demo, Julian,' gushed a young female fan as she ordered a tea at the counter. 'You and Adele look fantastic together.'

'Why, thank you,' said Billy.

A dark-haired, well-built youth approached.

'Here comes another admirer, Adele,' said Billy.

'I don't think so,' she said. 'It's Cyprian, my ex-partner. Watch him, Julian. He's dangerous – has a fierce temper.'

'You – Julian?' sneered the ex.

'That's right,' said Billy.

'My name's Reggie,' he snorted, 'but she renamed me Cyprian. Didn't like the name Reggie. "Not good enough. Too common," she said.'

'You're pissed, Cyprian,' Adele said, 'as usual.'

'I want to warn you, Julian, or whatever your bloody name is. Have a care. She's all top-show. She'll give you a new name and a new image, but as soon as she's had enough of you she'll throw you away like an old sock.'

'Get back to the pub where you belong,' Adele snarled. 'It was the best bloody day's work I ever did – dumping you.'

'Same goes for me, Adele,' he growled at her. 'You used me – took me for a ride. Well, promised me a ride, anyway, but never came across with the goods. Watch yourself, Julian – she'll have a ring on your finger and one on your nose if she gets her way.'

'I've heard enough,' said Billy. 'Get the hell out of here. Insulting Adele and causing trouble.'

'Or we'll call Lofty to deal with you,' added Adele.

'Oh, call the bruiser, would you?'

'Just bugger off,' said Billy. 'You drunken sod.'

'Why, you bag o' bones – you streak o' piss, I've half a mind to clobber you one.'

'That's it,' said Adele. 'Lofty! Lofty! Can you come over here, please?'

Lofty detached himself from his seat near the bandstand and strode over.

'Trouble?' he enquired.

'Trouble?' said Cyprian/Reggie. 'She's the bleeding trouble. Miss Prick-Teaser there.'

'Right, pal. On your way,' said Lofty, frog-marching the unlucky Cyprian to the door. 'And if I see you near this dance studio again you'll go home with a black eye and a thick ear. Now – git!'

Cyprian was helped through the door with a shove that sent him sprawling outside on to the asphalt path.

'You can see now,' Adele said, 'why I dumped him. He was just a brute.'

'You were well rid of him, Adele,' Billy said.

From that night, their romance developed apace and their necking sessions in her front room became hotter and hotter and dangerously close to getting out of control.

Adele's front room was directly under her parents' bedroom.

'You'll have to whisper,' she said, as they went into a close embrace on the settee.

They settled down to several minutes' passionate kissing which threatened to carry them both away to never-never land.

'I'll love you till the end of time,' she said.

'I'll love you till each mountain disappears,' he sighed.

'I'll love you till the wells run dry,' she murmured.

'Till hell freezes over,' he breathed in her ear.

'Till the deserts bloom,' she cooed.

Billy was beginning to run out of unlikely eventualities to love her till, and so thought it best to change the subject.

'My mother stopped breast-feeding me too early and put me on the bottle,' he said.

'How do you know that?' she asked softly.

'I've been trying ever since to get myself off the bottle and back on to the breast,' he replied plaintively.

'You're a clown,' she said. 'But a lovable one.'

'I've always had one big problem, though,' he continued.

'And that is?' she whispered.

'I've never been able to get the hang of these brassières,' he said, opening the buttons of her silk blouse.

'There's no problem here,' she said, cuddling into his shoulder. 'I never wear one.'

After ten minutes, there came a knock on the ceiling.

'It's getting late, Adele. Time to say good night,' her dad called.

'OK, Dad,' she called back sweetly. 'Just coming.'

Given the excitement of Adele and the dancing world, all the academic stuff Billy was learning at school seemed boring and irrelevant to life and having a good time. He vowed to leave school at the first opportunity, get himself a well-paid, interesting job and continue with the lifestyle to which Adele had made him accustomed.

New Year's Eve. Billy had big plans for celebrating this particular festivity. Everything in the garden was looking rosy. Flo's husband, Sergeant Barry Healey, was home on leave and staying with them in the spare bedroom; at Harrigan's there was to be a big shindig, ticket-holders only, and all their crowd would be there. At the GI barber shop, he worked until 7.30 that night, and the tips were unbelievable as the doughboys unloaded some of their dough. He had bought Adele's ticket and his own – never mind the cost of five shillings a head, he could afford it. He had arranged to collect her around 8.30.

When he got back after work to the Gardenia Court flat, though, he sensed that something was amiss. Flo and Barry were getting ready to go out, but one look at his dad and Billy knew immediately what it was. He'd been on the booze – probably all day in the Hare and Hounds – as his way of bidding farewell to the old year. He had spent the afternoon and early evening sleeping it off and had awakened in a foul temper.

By eight o'clock, he was suffering from a mammoth hangover. Eyes glazed and bloodshot, face haggard and drawn, he sat hunched at the fireplace with his back to everyone. He hated visitors at the best of times and he made no bones about showing it. But when he was in his cups anything could happen, and the family had found it best to make itself scarce. Every so often that New Year's Eve he muttered incomprehensible curses and strange incantations, accompanied by weird hissing, shushing noises which sounded like a tyre being let down.

'Bleeding strangers in the house,' he mumbled to himself. 'Hiss-ss. Shush-sh-sh.'

'No bleeding peace,' he grunted. 'Hiss-ss. Shush-sh-sh.'

Eventually Flo and Barry were ready to go out.

'We're going to visit Barry's married brother, Mam,' said Flo. 'We'll be back about one o'clock.'

'Righto, Flo,' said Mam.

'Bleeding nuisances,' growled Dad. 'Hiss-ss. Shush-sh-sh.'

Billy knew there was going to be trouble. He busied himself grooming and primping himself up for the big dance. He washed and shaved carefully, having showered previously at the American Red Cross Club, applied his aftershave, dressed in his Reid Bros suit and his best white shirt. He was ready to depart to collect Adele.

Then all hell broke loose.

'You drunken swine! You bloody great bully, you!' Mam screamed at his dad. 'You've been hissing and muttering to yourself all bloody day.'

He turned his bloodshot eyes on her.

'Who the bloody hell d'you think you're talking to?'

'Hitler! Hitler!' she yelled.

'Hitler? Calling me Hitler?' he snarled, thumping the table with his fist.

'You drunken pig!' she shouted, her blood up.

He stood up and thrust his face at her.

'S'no wonder I get drunk. A man's house is no longer his own. Bloody strangers everywhere I look.'

The conflict was reaching fever pitch. They were both seething and spitting hatred at one another.

'It's the same every holiday,' she cried, now in tears of rage. 'You stink the whole house out with your drinking. I'm ashamed to have visitors in the place.'

'Then you can piss off out and sling your hook,' he bawled.

He came at her then, grabbed her by the shoulders and thrust her up against the wall. She screamed and fought to get free from his grip. She put her arm up for protection as he raised his fist to strike her.

'You stop that, d'you hear! Don't you dare hit her!' said a disembodied voice.

To Billy's amazement, he found that the voice belonged to him.

Dad's fist froze in mid-air. He turned and gazed at Billy in amazement.

'Who the bloody hell do you think you're talking to, yer cheeky little bugger?' he growled.

But his hand was stayed.

Mam let out a long moan of utter anguish and began sobbing and wailing uncontrollably – sounding like Aunt Mona when Uncle Eddy had assaulted her. Released from the bully's grip, she opened the front door and ran outside, still crying.

'Wait, Mam, I'll come with you,' Billy shouted, all hopes of collecting Adele and all thoughts of the big dance now banished from his mind.

He sat with his mam on a low wall at the corner of Gardenia Court. She was shivering from the cold and, racked with misery, she continued to weep, tears overflowing. Billy put his arm round her to warm her and comfort her.

'Don't worry, Mam, don't worry,' he said. 'It was the drink talking.'

'I've had enough living with this pig,' she moaned. 'It's the same every holiday time. He comes back from the pub stinking the place out with his beer, and hissing and snorting like a bull. I can't stand no more of it, Billy. I'm gonna chuck meself in Union Street Canal.'

'It's OK, Mam. It's OK,' Billy consoled. 'He's drunk. He doesn't know what he's doing or saying. He'll be better tomorrow.'

'It's no use carrying on, Billy. I've had to put up with him for years. Tonight's the last straw. I'm gonna do away with meself. Don't bother about me, you go off to your dance.'

'No, Mam, forget the dance. I'm staying with you. I can always go dancing some other night. Adele will understand.'

They stayed there for over two hours, the two of them, sitting on that low, bottom-freezing wall. The moon was up and the tenements were bathed in a great white light. They sat watching the silent, smiling moon gliding through the silver-tipped clouds. In some of the flats they were holding noisy, festive parties, and Billy and Kate could hear the sounds of singing and revelry as the residents of Gardenia Court gave a liquid welcome to the New Year. At twelve o'clock, ships' hooters and car horns sounded off in distant parts of the city, and the party-goers began their drunken rendering of 'Auld Lang Sync'.

'Nineteen forty-four, Mam. Happy New Year!' he said, kissing her on the cheek.

'Same to you, son. Let's hope we have a better year ahead of us than the one behind. And let's hope this drunk you've got for a father mends his ways.'

'Come on, Mam,' he said. 'We're going back in. He'll have gone to bed by now, I should think. If not, and he starts again, he'll have me to deal with.'

'What a way to see the new year in, eh, Billy!' she said. 'Almost as bad as the Blitz in 1940.'

'Well, there's one thing about being here tonight. I'll be the first one to open the door and I've got dark hair. So that should bring us good luck.'

Next morning, it was the old, old story. Dad had sobered up and was all humble and contrite, trying to win back her love – in fact, everybody's love.

'Happy New Year, Kate,' he said softly. 'And I've bought you this big box o' chocolates, luv.'

But he had blown it and was due for his punishment. Sentence – one week's fish-eye treatment. Billy hoped he would be man enough to take it on the chin. Mam looked through him with that stony-faced, unseeing stare of hers.

'You eat 'em, Hitler!' she said.

Once again, Billy began to feel sorry for his dad. He knew what it felt like; he'd had some of this glassy-eyed, non-person torture after the stopping-out-all-night incident with Vinny Buckley.

'Happy New Year, Dad,' he said when he saw him.

'And the same to you, son. Sorry about last night,' Tommy said quietly. 'I've got you this box of fifty Players.'

'Thanks, Dad. I don't know where you get them from with this cigarette shortage. They're like gold.'

'Oh, I have my little ways,' he replied, winking.

'You do and all, Dad,' Billy said under his breath. 'You daft bugger. You do and all.'

And even though Billy consulted a map of Manchester, he never did find out where Union Street Canal was.

* * *

He saw Adele at the New Year's dance later the following night and apologised for his failure to turn up.

'I understand, Julian,' she said. 'Don't worry about it. I managed to take a taxi to Harrigan's and I danced with Duggie Diggle most of the evening. He took me home. I hope you don't mind.'

'No, I don't mind, Adele.'

He was lying, of course.

Chapter Twenty-Five

Schooldays: Dear Old Golden Rule Days

It has been claimed – though the actual authority is never quoted – that most men have a brief sexual thought every six seconds. This means, of course, that there must be at least five seconds when they're *not* having a sexual thought. For the smokers' club of the Upper Fifth at Damian College – not so. They thought about sex all the time. Constantly. Even when doing maths, it was sex. English – sex. History – double sex. Physics – more of the same. None of the members had actually had it. Full sex, that is. Though Nobby Nodder claimed to have got very near it with a girl called Ronnie in the Regal cinema.

At dinner-time, the six foundation members of the club – Billy, Robin, Titch, Nobby, Oscar and Olly – plus the more recently accepted Pottsy took their daily constitutional through the back alley adjoining the school. They lit up their fags – Park Drive on a poor day, Lucky Strike if Billy or Robin had struck lucky at the American Red Cross. The topic of conversation was the same each day and they took a prurient interest in examining the numerous condoms left behind from the previous night's copulations.

'Just look at all these Durexes,' said Oscar, poking the

abandoned contraceptives with a stick. 'There must have been a lot of shagging going on down here last night.'

'Well, the Government is always saying there should be mass production,' said Nobby.

'Mass seduction's more like it,' said Oscar. 'There are so many bags, they must have had the pros lined up against the wall – like an assembly line.'

'And why not?' said Olly. 'Didn't Herbert Morrison say, "Give us the tools and we'll finish the job." Did you know that over ten million a week are sold in Britain?'

'Half of them seem to be here,' said Pottsy, 'judging by all these Durexes.'

'Surely,' said Billy, the Latin scholar, 'the plural of Durex is Durices. It goes like radix – radices – and matrix – matrices.'

'As far as I'm concerned,' said Titch. 'They're just bags.'

'That's a very oversimplified view,' said Robin. 'There are subtle differences between them. The Yanks call them "rubbers" and they claim their models are ten inches long.'

'Oh, come, come,' said Nobby, 'that's stretching it a bit far.'

'Why do they have little teats on the end?' asked Pottsy.

'You mean you don't know, Pottsy?' asked Oscar.

'No, honest.'

'Then you must ask one of your sisters,' said Robin.

'I don't think they'll know,' he said. 'We're not allowed to say the word S-E-X in our house. It's taboo.'

'Not many people know this,' said Olly. 'The erect penis varies in length from five inches to ten inches.'

'Well, I certainly didn't know that,' said Pottsy.

'Some African tribes,' Olly continued, 'make their young boys go about with weights hanging from their things to make them longer.'

'I trust,' said Oscar, 'that they take them off when they're adults and are on the job.'

'Let's hope so,' said Billy, 'for the sake of their womenfolk.'

'I read,' said Nobby, not to be outdone in the display of sexual knowledge, 'that they have now begun manufacturing different coloured bags.'

'Green for beginners, maybe,' said Pottsy.

'And, I suppose, red, white and blue for the patriotic,' added Titch.

'Red for hot sex,' said Robin.

'The nearest I've ever got to hot sex,' said Oscar, 'is having a wank in the bath.'

'That's a very dirty way of doing a clean thing,' said Titch.

'Or a clean way of doing a dirty thing,' added Billy.

'Hey, fellas, I was told by a GI,' said Robin, 'that you can now buy banana-flavoured bags as well.'

'What next?' commented Pottsy. 'How does the woman get to taste it, I wonder?'

'Use your imagination, Pottsy,' said Olly.

'I still don't get it,' said Pottsy.

'But the woman does,' said Oscar lecherously.

The Upper Fifth studied nine subjects and the curriculum of the school was heavily weighted towards formal academic teaching. The boys did their utmost to make the dry educational programme more entertaining by introducing witty, comical comments. With some masters this was well-nigh impossible, as they interpreted these attempts as challenges to their authority.

One such was Brother Sebastian – the geography master – who developed an immediate antipathy towards Billy from the word go. The brother walked into the classroom each day and began his lesson with a routine opening:

'And . . . er . . . the meaning of "hinterland" is, of course, er . . . er . . .' A smacking of his lips. 'Hopkins!'

'Hinterland, sir, is a region lying inland from a coast and served by a port city and its facilities. For example, Lancashire is the hinterland of Liverpool.'

'Right,' grunted Brother Sebastian, sounding somewhat disappointed that he had failed to catch Billy out.

On another occasion, when Billy was feeling somewhat out of sorts, the master strode into the room and began in the accustomed way.

'And . . . er . . . the meaning of "irrigation" is, of course, er . . . er . . .' Smacking of lips. 'Hopkins!'

'DON'T KNOW, SIR!' replied Billy defiantly.

'Why, you blasted, blithering idiot,' Sebastian bawled, making a beeline for him.

Before the master had reached his desk, Billy managed to blurt out:

'Irrigation is the supplying of dry land with water by means of ditches, pipes or streams, so making the land fertile.'

Sebastian stopped and listened to the definition, then said grumpily:

'Oh, so you do know then.'

Brother Zachary was another master it was best not to try it on with. He taught maths and Latin and he took his subjects very seriously. Billy was one of his favourites, as he was always first in maths and second or third in Latin. On only one occasion did they clash, and this was so rare an occurrence that Billy was deeply upset by the encounter. It happened that he was translating a Latin unseen from Horace.

'Caesar, as a young boy,' he translated, 'would often visit the home of his . . .'

Billy stopped at the word *avus*, not knowing it meant 'grandfather'.

This surely means 'bird', he said to himself, thinking of the Latin word *avis*. I can't possibly say: 'Caesar used to visit the home of his bird.' It'll bring the house down and everyone will roar with laughter at me.

'Sorry, Brother Zachary, it doesn't make sense,' he said.

'Yes it does, William. Go on,' Zachary urged his favourite.

Billy was now determined not to become the butt of everyone's ridicule.

'Sorry, sir, it doesn't make sense to me.'

'It makes perfect sense, you chump!' Zachary said angrily.

Billy blushed to his roots and his eyes filled with tears, for Zachary and he had a close mutual-admiration relationship. Fortunately, it was the one and only time that the two did not see eye to eye.

The most popular master in the school was Brother Ambrose, a dark-haired, olive-skinned master from South America who had a ready wit, a keen sense of humour and an unwavering sense of discipline. He could cause chaos and wild horseplay one moment and then quell it in an instant with one stern, forbidding look. He was another not to be messed with.

He invariably began his French lessons with:

'*Ouvrez toutes les fenêtres*. Open all the windows – there's a terrible smell in here!'

'There wasn't till you came in,' replied Oscar.

'Oh, is that so, Wilde?' Ambrose said slowly, with ominous good-humour.

There then followed a wild rough-house, with Ambrose chasing Oscar around the room with a cricket bat and the students clambering over desks to protect their friend. After everyone had let off steam, Ambrose simply turned to the class and in a quiet, menacing voice said:

'OK, that's enough now. Let's get down to some work. Start exercise ten.'

The proverbial pin could be heard.

Physics was taught by a Bart Jarvis, an absent-minded scientist who had no class control whatsoever, despite his breaking several long, scientific rulers on the bottoms of his badly behaved, unwilling learners. It was in one of their early attempts to introduce sexual implications into physics that the smokers' club members came to grief.

Bart was demonstrating the expansion of iron and had to set up his apparatus to show how the coefficient of this metal was arrived at.

'It's definitely got much bigger,' said Oscar.

'And longer,' said Billy.

'And thicker,' added Robin.

'Look at the bulbous bit on the end,' said Nobby.

'It looks like a poker,' said Titch.

'And can you see all that stuff bubbling and spurting out,' said Olly, indicating the boiling water in the retort flask.

Bart ignored the ribald comments and continued with the experiment. At the end of the lesson, however, he looked up from his notes and said:

'Class dismissed, but would the following remain behind: Gabrielson, Hopkins, Hardy, Nodder, Smalley and Wilde.'

'Uh-oh,' said Titch. 'Trouble.'

'I want all of you to know,' said Bart, 'that I understood every disgusting reference you made during my lesson. If it ever happens again, I shall report you to Brother Dorian and you will probably be expelled.'

Bart had no more trouble.

It was in English and history that the club extracted most of its fun and entertainment.

English was taught by a little, elderly, dull-eared brother, nicknamed 'Baldy' for obvious reasons, who seemed out of touch with all that was going on around him. When he had first made his appearance, the whole class had broken down in paroxysms of suppressed laughter and heads had disappeared under desks for a good five minutes.

'I'm going to test your knowledge of grammar,' he snapped, slapping his elbow to his side. 'Give me an example of an adjectival clause.'

Oscar raised his hand immediately.

'The bag which was found in the alley had not been used.'

'Excellent,' he said, chalking it up on the blackboard with a noisy sucking-in of his breath with every word that he wrote.

The class watched, hardly able to contain its delight that he had fallen for it.

'Next, a noun phrase as subject of a sentence.'

'The survival of this country depends on the high quality of its seamen,' offered Nobby.

'Very good indeed,' said Baldy, putting it up on the board with his loud siphoning noises. 'Now, can anyone give me a sentence containing an adverbial phrase of place?'

'In the forest, the two boys espied two beautiful big tits,' said Olly.

'Excellent,' exclaimed Baldy. 'I'm glad to see that you all know your grammar and your parts of speech. What about figures of speech? Give me an example of a hyperbole.'

'The boy tried to hide his secret but it stuck out a mile,' said Robin.

'Good. I can see that I am going to get on well with this class.'

He seemed to have but one method of teaching, which could be termed 'reading round the class', for he rarely attempted any explanation or exposition. The method might have worked had it not been for the farting noises and the snorting sounds of suppressed laughter which accompanied every reading. Titch found particular difficulty, as he was a giggler and the slightest suggestion of a snort was enough to set him off.

'Enter certain niffs,' announced Billy, substituting his word for 'nymphs' in the stage directions of *The Tempest*.

Titch, reading the part of Ariel, was unable to continue – much to Baldy's perplexity and annoyance.

But it was the attempts to read the poetry in Palgrave's *Golden Treasury* which were the real test of strength and character. Billy found himself having to tackle those lines in Gray's 'Ode to Vicissitude':

> *See the wretch that long has tost*
> *On the thorny bed of pain.*

He could get no further, however, for all round him the snorts and the snuffles started up. And poor Titch, as luck would have it, landed up with the poem 'Willy Drowned in the Yarrow' and was completely stymied and unable to read beyond 'Willy' before the stage-whispers of 'Willy? Willy 'Eck!' were being called all about him.

Pottsy was not normally a provoker of laughter in the form, since he did not altogether understand the subtle allusions or the clever innuendo – the pace was too fast for him. But came the occasion when the naive Pottsy was an occasion of loud guffaws. During a reading of *The Tempest* he was due to say the line: '*Are we to be cheated of our lives by drunkards?*' Instead he confounded Baldy and the whole class by reading: '*Are we to be cheated of our lives by seventy drunkards?*'

'Yes, Potts,' said Baldy. 'But how do you come to the conclusion that there were seventy of these inebriates?'

'Because it says so in my book,' said Pottsy.

It was Oscar who saw it first.

'The number seventy is the number of the line on the left-hand side of the page!'

A great guffaw went up from the class at this stupidity, and Baldy himself almost smiled. Pottsy wasn't the only one to make a *faux pas*. One afternoon, during a poetry-reading exercise, Billy was disconcerted when his answer to a sudden question fired at him from Baldy was greeted with great howls of mirth and derision.

The class was reading 'The Bard' by Thomas Gray and had reached the lines:

> *Hark, how each giant-oak,*
> *O'er thee, oh King!*
> *their hundred arms they wave.*

Billy was preoccupied thinking about Adele and their next dancing date when Baldy suddenly asked:

'Hopkins, what's got a hundred arms?'

Billy was nonplussed for a moment, then answered:

'Why, a centipede, sir.'

Even Baldy joined in the laughter.

But the finest hour in the Baldy saga belonged to Oscar, who agreed, on payment of threepence per head from everyone in the class – giving a total prize of over six shillings – to faint during the lesson. Billy was elected stake-holder. Throughout the reading of *The Tempest*, Oscar issued instructions.

'Move your desk a little further forward, Hoppy. Titch, a little to the left. Robin, give me a little more space.'

Billy, in the role of Caliban, was just saying:

Be not afeard: the isle is full of noises,
Sounds and sweet airs, that give delight, and hurt not

when Oscar put a hand to his head, gave a loud moan and keeled over.

For a moment, Baldy was stumped. Then he reacted.

'Give him some air. Loosen his collar,' he bawled, slapping his elbow to his side. 'I'll get some water for him.' And he shot out of the room.

As soon as he'd gone, Oscar opened his eyes.

'Has he gone? Right, Hoppy, that's six shillings and threepence you owe me.'

Billy paid up just before Baldy got back.

'Here you are, Wilde, drink this water,' the master said, holding Oscar's head. 'Do you think you're going to be all right?'

'Yes, sir, I think so,' said Oscar weakly, pretending to come round.

'You'd better get some air,' said Baldy, helping him to the door.

After ten minutes or so, Oscar reappeared.

'I think I'll be all right now, sir,' he said, full of self-pity.

'No, you'd better go home, I think,' Baldy said, not relishing the thought of having to deal with yet another fainting fit, or even, horror of horrors, vomiting.

'Yes, I think you may be right, sir,' said Oscar feebly, at the same time seizing the opportunity to give the class a big, broad wink.

Oscar left – much to the annoyance of the rest of the form, who had to remain and plough their way for the umpteenth time through *The Tempest*. They were even more annoyed when they learned later that he had gone off to the Odeon cinema on their money.

The choicest sexual observations, however, were reserved for the history teacher, a dedicated young lady with the unfortunate name of Edith Dunn, a graduate straight from university, who had little realised when she took the job on that she would have to work in a cage of lions and a pit filled with venomous snakes. The form just about broke her heart. She had no discipline whatsoever, and from the moment she walked through the classroom door, there was chaos.

'Quiet! Sit down! Turn round! Put that down! Stop that!' she screeched before she had even crossed the threshold. 'Make less noise or we'll all write up notes.'

No one took a blind bit of notice of her.

'Right! That's it!' she yelled. 'Start writing notes! Now!'

She turned to the blackboard and began scribbling furiously on the board. Detailed notes on the Congresses of Vienna, the foreign policy of Palmerston, Kitchener's action in the Sudan, the Jameson Raid and the Boer War. Nobody even bothered to read the incomprehensible jargon she was chalking up so energetically. Most continued with their own activities.

In the front row, Robin Gabrielson was acting out the grunting of the Nile boatmen as they towed Kitchener's barge down the river; Billy was playing Hangman with Oscar; Olly was compiling a dictionary of swear words and, having reached 'B', was finding that letter as fruitful as 'A', which he had completed during Edith's last lesson with words like 'abuse', 'adultery', 'anus' and 'arse', along with compound words derived from these like 'arse-kisser' and 'arse-licker'.

At some point in the lesson, Oscar began asking his historical questions.

'Miss, is it true that during the Sino-Japanese War the Japs forbade the importation of Chinese prose?'

The question he was most proud of was:

'Miss, yesterday, you were talking about the Boer War. Can you tell us please who's Krujer?'

And Miss Dunn would naively begin answering his question:

'You mean Paul Kruger, I think. Well, of course, he was the Afrikaner leader and president of the Transvaal.'

'Ah, now I see, miss. The Afrikaner leader. He's Krujer. Thank you, miss.'

Finally, as she was leaving at the end of the lesson, Oscar would call out to her just as she reached the door:

'Miss, when's your next period?'

But even Edith Dunn spotted the *double-entendre* and obligingly blushed for the class. If only she had taken a leaf out of Bart Jarvis's book and threatened them with Brother Dorian, she would have solved her problems in one go.

June the sixth 1944 was D-Day. A terse, low-key announcement from General Eisenhower's HQ told the world that the long-awaited invasion of Europe had at last begun: 'Allied naval forces supported by strong air forces began landing Allied armies this morning on the northern coast of France.'

It was also D-Day for the Upper Fifth. The School Certificate examination of the Northern Universities Joint Board began.

From the beginning, it soon became obvious that the

exam was to be a travesty. The students were ill-prepared not only by the final year's course but by the whole period of their grammar-school education, which had been completely disrupted by a world war.

Apart from this major factor, there were one or two local practices which did not stand up to scrutiny. In art, for example, Billy's sketching and drawing skills were extremely limited – but not so those of his exam neighbour, Robin, who possessed a genuine talent in this direction. The subject for the drawing-from-memory part of the art exam that year was an inspirational one – a shovel resting across a bucket. The two friends sat at the same exam table. A quick switch of drawing boards, a quick switch back again, and lo! Billy had a most beautiful, accurate representation of the subject on his drawing sheet. The architecture section of the tests followed, and the art teacher invigilated the students – checking to see that there was no hanky-panky. As he circulated the examinees, he stopped at the occasional desk.

'No, Wilde, you've got that buttress wrong,' he murmured. 'It should look like this. Here, let me show you.'

And he executed a quick, skilful sketch on Oscar's exam paper.

He moved on, reached Billy's desk and looked over his shoulder.

'That Tudor chimney isn't quite right. Don't you recall doing it last month? This little drawing should help you remember.'

He left his crib on the desk for Billy to copy.

'I'll be back in five minutes to collect my drawing,' he said softly.

But Billy wasn't only a recipient, he was also a giver, and with his friend Robin he had a quid pro quo arrangement.

'What did you get for number six, Hoppy?' Robin asked in the algebra exam.

'Um . . . x = 69 and y = 73,' whispered Billy.

And in the French and Latin exams, Billy was a ready source of information for vocabulary.

'What's the French for "nest"?'

'*Le nid.*'

'What's the Latin for "The boys were hurrying"?'

'*Pueri festinabant,*' Billy whispered.

Two minutes later, Robin called his attention again.

'Psst! Hoppy, quick! That sentence *Fraus est celare fraudem*. What's it mean?'

' "It is a fraud to conceal a fraud",' said Billy in an undertone.

Thus ended Billy's grammar-school education.

The results of the examinations were published in July. Taken as a whole they were mediocre, as were Billy's but he was the only one to pass in all nine subjects – including geography.

'Blame the war,' everybody said.

At the final meeting of the smokers' club in the back-street alley, the members strolled along, puffing ruminatively at their fags and kicking away the odd condom.

'Well, boys, that's the end of the year,' said Oscar. 'See you next September in the sixth form.'

'Not me,' said Billy. 'I've had enough.'

'But don't you want to go to college?' asked Robin.

'No thanks,' replied Billy. 'I can't see the point in any of it. I've just completed five years' grammar-school education. Some education! The whole thing has been a mockery and a sham. What have I learned? How to fend off a randy headmaster and how to cheat at exams. In addition, my brain has been crammed with a lot of useless facts. I know about the Congresses of Vienna, how to copy a Tudor chimney from a crib and how to conjugate irregular verbs in French and Latin. Indispensable bits of knowledge to survive in the modern world.'

'But you were top in maths, Hoppy. Surely you're not going to waste all that?' said Titch.

'Maths!' Billy said. 'I know about quadratic equations, how to solve problems about filling baths and papering rooms, and, oh yes, that any two sides of a triangle are greater than the third, so I cross a field diagonally, but then the village idiot does that.'

'What will you do then?' asked Nobby.

'I'm not coming back to school for more of the same old stuff, that's for sure. I'll look for a job.'

'What sort of job?' asked Oscar.

'Dunno,' said Billy. 'I'd like to try my hand at being a writer. Maybe a job on a newspaper is the answer.'

Chapter Twenty-Six

Gopher On The Guardian

The middle-aged, bespectacled man behind the desk at the Juvenile Employment Bureau studied Billy's job application card whilst Billy studied his face, thinking how much he resembled Dr Crippen with his small moustache and his wire-framed specs. The clerk looked up.

'What kind of job are you looking for, Mr Hopkins?'

'What kind are you offering today?'

'Well, let's see now.'

He consulted his box of tricks.

'Here's one. Lift operator at Dobbin's.'

'No. My brother tried that. We all felt he was getting a bit above himself.'

'A comedian, eh? I notice that under 'previous experience', you've put down 'shoe-shining'. How would you fancy a job in a shoe shop?'

'No thanks. I've had enough of the shoe trade.'

'There's a job here at Atherton colliery. What about a career in mining?'

'After a grammar-school education, I think that's a bit beneath me.'

'Your jokes are killing me. Let's be serious for a minute.

First I need to know if you're manual or non-manual.'

'I thought I'd like to be a writer.'

'Ah, at last. Now we're getting somewhere. A writer? I see. A pen-pusher. That's non-manual.'

'I would have thought pushing a pen was manual.'

'Look, don't try to tell me my job.'

'Sorry. I don't just want to push a pen. I want to write imaginative stories; stories that I've made up out of my head.'

'Ah, then you'll want a job on a newspaper.'

'I'd love one if you have one.'

'The best way to go about it is to start on a little paper like the *Cheetham Gazette* and write about local events, like football matches or what's on at the local flea-pit.'

'Good idea. I'll take it.'

'But unfortunately, we don't have any jobs like that just at the moment. I see you've written "ballroom dancing" as one of your hobbies. Why not a job writing about that on a paper like *The Dancing Times*?'

'Sounds great. Right up my street.'

'However, we don't have any such job on our books.'

'Look, this is ridiculous. What jobs do you have on your books?'

'There's one here working on the *Manchester Guardian*.'

'But that's the best quality newspaper in the country. Well, second, anyway, after *The Times*. I'm not ready to write for that yet.'

'Oh, it's not as a writer.'

'Well, what is it as?'

'A copy boy – a sort of messenger boy. But you'd be mixing with the top journalists in the land. Maybe you could work your way up the ladder.'

'If there's a chance of getting on the staff some day, I'm willing to start at the bottom. What's the deal?'

'Pay, thirty-five shillings a week,' he said, reading from the card. 'Hours five p.m. to one a.m. And you get Saturday night off.'

'I'll give it a go. But that's my ballroom dancing gone for a Burton.'

'Good. The job's yours. Take this card of introduction and ask for Mr Fogg, who's head of the post-room and will clear up any questions you may have. And good luck.'

Frank Fogg was a short, disabled old man with a pro-nounced, bouncing limp and a withered left arm.

'Are we pleased to see you,' he said. 'We've been short-handed for weeks now. It says on this paper that your name's William Hopkins. But that's much too formal. What do we really call you?'

'My friends call me Hoppy.'

'Then Hoppy it is,' he said, 'though I'm the one you should be calling Hoppy, eh?'

He pointed to the other copy boy sitting at the table in the centre of the room. A tall, handsome, fair-haired youth about eighteen years of age, he was impeccably dressed in neatly pressed flannels, white silk shirt, dark tie and smart sage-green jersey; well groomed right down to his manicured fingernails, and probably his toenails as well.

'This is Miles Harrison, your opposite number; you two will be working very closely together.'

'Hi, Hoppy,' said Miles, smiling and extending his hand. 'Good to know you.'

'Hi,' replied Billy shyly.

'Our job,' said Mr Fogg, 'is to act as a communication centre between the writers and the printers. We are their go-betweens.'

'You mean messenger boys?' said Billy.

'That's another way of putting it, I suppose,' said Mr Fogg.

'It's a crude way of putting it,' said Miles. 'We are essential cogs in the production machine. We are the conduit which facilitates the flow of communication and information between the various parts of the network structure.'

'What happens,' continued Mr Fogg, 'is that the tele-printers upstairs chatter out the news on every conceivable subject. It's then dropped down a chute to us and we make sure it reaches the right sub-editor, who then writes it up in King's English. Show him how it's done, Miles.'

Miles collected all the strips of news items from the table and placed them between different fingers.

'Home – Parliament,' he listed, 'Sport – Entertainment – Foreign – Local Government – War – Science. See, I have eight items in eight finger spaces. Now follow me.'

Miles led the way into a large room – quiet, with an atmosphere like a reference library – in which numerous sub-editors, eye-shades on their foreheads, were busily writing up the day's news.

'We now collect their finished copy,' Miles whispered, 'and we send that up on a pulley to the compositors working upstairs on their linotypes.'

Billy examined a piece of finished copy and found it a mass of strange wiggles and hieroglyphics.

'Is this in code, Mr Fogg?' he asked when they were back in the post-room.

'It is a kind of code between the sub-editors and the compositors – they seem to understand it well enough, though.'

'And that's all there is to the job?' asked Billy. 'Carrying bits of papers to and fro.'

'Oh, no,' said Miles. 'Along the main corridor – we call

it the Holy of Holies – there are all the VIP leader-writers
– the editor, A.P. Wadsworth, the Miscellany writer,
Gordon Phillips, the deputy-editor, J.M. Pringle and other
big writers like Wainwright, Derek Senior, Crozier and
the features editor, Miss Linley.'

'And what do we have to do with them?' asked Billy.

'We collect their leaders and so are privileged to be the
very first in the whole of Britain to read what the
Manchester Guardian has to say about current events.'

'Big stuff, eh? And is that it?'

'There's more,' said Miles. 'A.P. Wadsworth and
Gordon Phillips always consult me and ask my advice as
they're writing their main leaders. I'll show you later on
in the night.'

'That reminds me, Miles,' said Mr Fogg. 'Isn't it time
to collect those items from Miss Linley?'

'Oh, yes, Mr Fogg,' said Miles. 'Perhaps Hoppy could
collect them as his first assignment.'

'Be glad to,' said Billy, anxious to contribute and be
accepted as one of the team.

'Right then,' said Mr Fogg. 'Ask Miss Linley, who's in
the fifth office along the corridor, if you could have the
long stand and the big weight.'

'Rightaway,' said Billy, eagerly.

He soon found Miss Linley's office. He knocked lightly
on her door.

'Come!' she called.

'Good evening, miss,' he said. 'Mr Fogg asked if you
could let me have the long stand and the big weight.'

Miss Linley was a middle-aged lady with greying hair.
She had obviously been very pretty when younger. She
smiled happily.

'You're new here, aren't you?' she said. 'What's your
name?'

'Yes, Miss Linley. New here tonight. Everyone calls me Hoppy.'

'Welcome aboard, Hoppy. I'm expecting an important phone call from London any moment now. If you could just stand outside and wait for a while, I'll be with you shortly.'

Billy took up his stance outside her office door. Half an hour passed by . . . nothing happened. He stood his ground. Another quarter of an hour. Nothing.

'Strange,' he said aloud, shaking his head. Then the penny dropped. He knocked on her door again.

'Come!' she called.

'Thank you for the long stand and the big weight, miss.'

'You're welcome, Hoppy,' she said, laughing.

Back in the post-room, Mr Fogg and Miles were waiting. When Billy appeared, they both roared with laughter.

'What kept you?' chuckled Mr Fogg.

'Now we'll go and have a conference with the editor and the Miscellany writer,' said Miles, still chuckling.

'No tricks!' said Billy.

'No tricks, honest.'

They arrived outside the office of the big white chief, A.P. Wadsworth, and Miles tapped gently on the glass door.

'Yes,' barked Wadsworth. 'Come in.'

'I've come for the usual consultation, sir,' said Miles.

'That's the new copy boy, eh?' said the editor. 'Welcome to the *Manchester Guardian* staff. Right, Miles, what're you waiting for? Fire away, then.'

'Pies are on the menu for supper tonight, sir. Cheese and onion, meat and potato, steak and kidney, plus the usual veg.'

'Yes, yes. What do you recommend?'

'Cheese and onion looks good, sir.'

'Very well, then bring that for me. Oh, and collect tonight's editorial, will you?'

'See what I mean about the editor consulting me before he submits his editorial?' said Miles.

As they walked back to the post-room, Billy read the editorial hot from Wadsworth's typewriter.

'*Five years!*' it said. '*We look back today upon five years of the sternest struggle which the British people have ever fought, a war for our national survival, for the rights of free peoples and for the life of civilisation itself . . .*'

'This is pretty good stuff,' said Billy. 'I think he deserved the steak and kidney instead of that cheese and onion.'

'Right,' said Miles. 'But we must make sure there's some of that left for us at twelve o'clock.'

So Billy joined the staff of the *Manchester Guardian*, and it was not long before he had the routine practices of the job at his fingertips. After he'd been there over a month, he began to wonder when he might get the chance to write something.

'When I joined the staff here, Mr Fogg,' he said one day, 'I hoped to become a writer.'

'Yes,' said Fogg. 'I thought that might be the case. But you know, Hoppy, you're going about it the wrong way. You wouldn't believe it to look at me, but I too joined the staff here over thirty years ago with the same idea.'

'What happened, Mr Fogg?'

'Well, about twenty years ago my bicycle and I got into an argument with a GPO van which left me like this. But before that, I had big ideas about becoming the next C.P. Scott. And then I found out the truth.'

'And what's that?'

'All the writers on this paper, even the reporters, are time-served journalists. Most of them have honours English degrees, many of them Oxbridge. Working your way up from the rank of copy boy isn't on. Look at me – aged sixty and still a copy boy after all these years. The only thing I've got to look forward to is retirement, a gold watch and a nursing home. Do you really want to become a writer?'

'I really do, Mr Fogg – it's my one great burning ambition in life.'

'Then go and study for a degree. Become an expert in something so that you can write with authority and knowledge. Don't let anyone or anything distract you from that purpose. When you're young, you'll find all kinds of temptations around you trying to pull you off your chosen path. Don't let them. Stick with your goal. Don't stay as a copy boy all your life, taking restaurant orders from the leader writers and acting as a go-fer for the rest of the staff. Start as a door-mat – and you'll end up as a door-mat.'

'So there's no chance for me to become a writer on this paper?' said Billy miserably.

'Sorry to be so blunt, Hoppy. You may have some talent for writing but you'll never develop it as a messenger boy. I'm sorry for you, but it's for your own good. I'm really doing you a big favour telling you all this.'

'What about Miles? Have you told him the same thing?'

'Don't talk to me about Miles! He has delusions of grandeur and is living in cloud-cuckoo land. His real name is Harry Miles but he's switched the names around to Miles Harrison. Says it sounds posher and more impressive. That's Miles to a T. All image and no substance. He goes home at night looking more like the editor than the editor.'

This statement about Miles was true. Billy had taken to accompanying him on the same all-night bus after work. For these public appearances, Miles wore an immaculately tailored military-type raincoat, and a smart trilby; he carried a leather attaché case with the words 'MILES HARRISON: MANCHESTER GUARDIAN' blocked in gold letters on the side for all the world to see. When they boarded their bus, they each carried a fresh-smelling copy of the next day's paper straight from the presses, and talked to each other about the night's events as if they had written and produced it personally.

'Before APW sent up his copy to the compositors tonight, he asked my advice,' said Miles in a voice that all the bus could hear, 'and I told him the first option would be the one least likely to give him ulcers.'

'Yes,' said Billy, 'and I thought the Low cartoon tonight was particularly apt, so I told the illustration editor that she ought to go ahead with it.'

At that point, the bus conductor came round collecting fares.

'My son was hoping to become a reporter,' the conductor said, addressing Miles. 'What would you advise, sir?'

'Tell him to drop me a line with a small example of his work. That's me,' he said, pointing to his name on his case.

'Thank you, sir. Oh, no, never mind the fare. Have this one on me,' he said, giving a broad wink.

In fact, the idea of a copy boy writing for the great newspaper was not entirely barmy. Gordon Phillips welcomed stories for the tailpiece of his Miscellany column and a payment of ten shillings was made for a successful entry. Billy managed to get one published during his time there.

FEROCITY AT THE THEATRE

Emerging from the Opera House the other night after a performance of *King Lear*, two theatre-goers were overheard to say:

'Some say Wolfit takes the cake but is Giel-gud!'

'Yes, and some say Gielgud takes the cake but you should see Donald Wolfit!'

'Rather a ferocious contribution, I think,' said Gordon Phillips after he'd read it. 'Nevertheless, I'll accept it. You write rather well, by the way. Shows promise!'

This from the great man himself! God had spoken!

It was about this time that Adele began to make her feelings known.

'Look, Julian,' she said, 'if we're going to continue as partners, we need more practice. The odd afternoon session at the Ritz and the Saturday-evening hop at Harrigans – well, they're just not enough if we're going to get anywhere.'

'But it's my job, Adele,' he said.

'Some job! A glorified messenger boy! Sometimes you even dress like one. We need to get a decent suit and maybe change our hairstyle. Then we'd be getting somewhere. But I really do wish we would change our job. Can't we get one with decent hours so that we can spend more time together? And not just for dancing either. The settee and I are wondering when you're going to come back to us.'

'Funny you should say that, Adele,' said Billy. 'I've been thinking exactly the same myself. And as for my job, I had hopes of becoming a writer one day but there's no chance of coming up through the ranks. Not on the *Manchester Guardian*, anyway.'

'It's just a dead-end job for dead-beat characters,' she

said. 'You can get a job with better pay and higher status if you really look. My dad's always telling me that without money, you're nothing in this world and nobody'll respect you. And anyway, I don't want my friends saying I go round with a messenger boy.'

'Dead right, Adele,' he replied. 'At the *Guardian* I've learned how to carry bits o' paper between my fingers, carry messages, read out the menu every night till I can say it in my sleep. "And what would you like tonight, sir? Steak and kidney, meat and potato or cheese and onion? Yes, sir. Yes, sir. Right away, sir. Three bags full, sir." And all for thirty-five bob a week. I can see myself still doing it at sixty, like old Mr Fogg.'

'Now you're talking sense,' she said. 'So what are you going to do about it?'

'The only way to become a writer and to get on the writing staff of a paper like the *Manchester Guardian* is by going to college or university.'

'I hope you don't,' she said quickly. 'There's no money in books, study and all that. Besides, that would take you away from me. It's here that I need you – partnering me on the dance floor.'

'And on your front-room settee as well.'

'Trust you to think of that.'

' "In the spring a young man's fancy lightly turns to thoughts of sex", Tennyson said that.'

'And in your case, not only in the spring.'

'I think you're beginning to understand me at last,' he said.

At Christmas that year, Billy reached the end of his tether as general dog's-body and glorified waiter. Early in the New Year he handed in his notice at the newspaper and began to look for another job.

Chapter Twenty-Seven

It Takes Two To Tango

'Everyone thinks the tango is difficult,' said Frank Rogers, 'but it's actually easier than the other dances.'

'I love the tango music and rhythm,' said Adele, 'and I just adore the jerky head movements.'

'She loves South Americans,' added Billy. 'But where do the jerky movements come from, Frank?'

'The tango came from Cuba in the late nineteenth century,' said Frank, 'via Argentina, Spain and France. Unlike the flowing dances – the waltz, the foxtrot and the quickstep – it is a kind of static, stop-start dance with aggressive movements.'

'Why jerky movements, though?' asked Billy.

'The jerky movements are reminiscent of a strutting cockerel asserting his authority. But enough of the lecture, let's check your hold. Right arm further round Adele.'

'With pleasure,' said Billy, holding Adele on his right side.

'Behave, Julian,' said Adele.

'Bring your left hand slightly in towards yourself, Julian, and lower it slightly. Good. Now, let's try it all to music.'

He switched on 'La Cumparsita'.

'Ready – now!'

Adele and Billy began to dance the tango with perfect rhythm and expression, like two professionals.

'Remember all I've told you,' Frank called. 'Staccato movements. Crisp walk! Keep it sharp! Eyes . . . look at each other! That's it! Change direction – now! Body sway . . . good! Rock turn! Back corté! Promenade – turn! Outside swivel and sway!'

'That felt good,' said Adele.

'You know,' said Frank, 'you two are looking better on the floor each time I see you. You've got good appearance, excellent technique and fluent movement.'

'Do you think we're ready for competitions yet, Frank?' Adele asked.

'I've taken you both as far as I can,' he said. 'Now you need the experience of competitive dancing. You may not win straight off, but it would be good if you had a shot at it.'

'We're ready, Frank, as soon as you give the word,' said Billy.

'There's the Manchester Amateur Tango in a coupla weeks' time at the Ritz ballroom. That'll be the time to get you two launched.'

'Then I'd better start thinking about my dress,' said Adele. 'All those thousands of sequins to be sewn on. It's going to be hard work.'

'Yes, for your mother,' Billy said. 'I suppose I'd better start saving for the hire of my Moss Bros suit.'

Later, after Harrigan's Saturday-night ball, Billy and Adele got down to their regular snogging session on the front-room settee.

'Don't get carried away, Julian,' she whispered. 'Keep your self-control.'

'It's not me you should be talking to,' he said. 'It's JT down there.'

'JT?'

'John Thomas – he's got a mind of his own. Nothing to do with me what he decides.'

'That's the beast in you.'

'On the contrary, he always behaves like a perfect gentleman.'

'How do you make that out?'

'He always stands up in the presence of a pretty lady.'

'Sometimes I think you're crazy.'

'Yes, Adele. Crazy for you. When are we two really going to get it together? These necking sessions are driving me wild. You can't go on teasing me like this.'

'I don't want to go too far, Julian. If you made me pregnant, it would ruin everything.'

'We could always use something.'

'You mean a Durex. I've seen them advertised in the chemist's. I don't know how anyone could have the nerve to ask for them.'

'No need. I've got some left from the time I worked in the Red Cross. American rubbers.'

'I don't know. I don't really trust those things.'

'Look, Adele, we've got to do something or I'll end up as a babbling idiot.'

'Oh, I'm still not sure about it. But . . . well . . . look . . . I'm not promising anything, Julian, but sometimes my parents go out on a Saturday night to the Queen's Park Hipp. Maybe we could . . . maybe that'd be our chance . . . maybe . . . I'll let you know.'

'I'll love you, Adele, till the world stops turning.'

'I'll love you, Julian, till the stars lose their glory.'

'Till the birds fail to sing.'

'Do you have a handkerchief handy, Julian?' she whispered into his ear.

'It's late, Adele,' said the voice from the ceiling.

'Julian's just on his way, Dad,' she said.

'Back again already!' said the Juvenile Employment Officer. 'So what happened to our budding young Charles Dickens at the *Manchester Guardian*?'

'It wasn't Charles Dickens they wanted. It was Joe Muggins to run their errands and carry their messages.'

'And now I suppose you'd like me to find you another job? What kind would you like this time?'

'Anything that doesn't involve night work.'

The officer consulted his box and flicked through several cards.

'Do you have a good hand?' he asked. 'Only here's a job offering thirty-seven shillings a week for a good hand.'

'As a matter of fact, I've got two good hands. Does that mean double pay?' Billy said, holding out both hands as evidence.

'I remember you now,' said the officer. 'You're the one with the funny sense of humour and the ballroom dancing.'

'That's me summed up in two phrases,' said Billy. 'Does this job require special knowledge or anything like that?'

'No, it simply requires good penmanship, calligraphy – handwriting to you. You don't make blots or anything like that, do you?'

'No, I've tried to keep my copybook clean. I'm not an ink-spiller, provided I don't have to use a quill pen. Who's the job for – Dombey and Son?'

'Listen, Tommy Handley,' the man said. 'Show a bit more respect. The job is with the Inland Revenue. They're switching over to the Pay-As-You-Earn system and there's an urgent need for clerks to write up their new filing cards. Hours nine to five.'

'I think I can push a pen with panache,' said Billy. 'I'll take it.'

'Very well, then. Take this introduction card to District Three, Sunlight House, and ask for a Mr Albert Fiddler.'

'Fiddler? Inland Revenue. You must be joking!'

'Your corny sense of humour should take you a long way,' said the clerk. 'A long, long way.'

Billy found Sunlight House on Quay Street and took the lift up to the eighth floor. He went through the office door leading to the Third District of the Inland Revenue. There was certainly no sunlight there – not even fresh air. The office was a large, smoke-filled room with a great number of desks at which sat several wan, sad-looking tax officers studying mountains of paper and puffing away at their fags. There was an air of doom and gloom about the place.

Billy presented himself at the counter.

'May I please see Mr Fiddler?'

'What's your tax problem?' said the shrivelled-up old man on counter duty.

'No tax problem. I'm the new clerk.'

'God help you!' said the old man, shaking his head. 'Come this way.'

Albert Fiddler, a sour, sallow-looking individual, was the most miserable bloke Billy had ever set eyes on outside Gardenia Court. His mouth turned south at the corners, giving him a perpetual expression of disapproval. Strangers in the street put it down to a bad case of indigestion but the permanent frown frozen on to his features was more the result of a lifetime spent poring over ledgers and unravelling the financial affairs of countless would-be tax-dodgers than problems with his metabolism.

Let it be understood then – Albert Fiddler was not a happy man. He could never understand why his fellow-citizens seemed so unwilling to pay their taxes with a smile, as he himself did.

Billy wasn't the only recruit that Monday morning. There was also a young, fair-haired boy eagerly waiting to be instructed in his duties.

'We start here at nine o'clock prompt,' recited Fiddler in a bored monotone. 'If you're late, your pay gets docked fifteen minutes for every five minutes or part thereof that you are behind time. You get one hour for lunch and the same rules apply if you come back after one p.m. Any questions so far?'

'No, Mr Fiddler,' the two youths replied.

'Now, Hopkins and Fernley, as you were no doubt told at the Labour Exchange, we are changing over our whole system to PAYE. Your job will be to copy out the names and addresses from these big ledgers and transfer them on to con-cards.'

'Just that, Mr Fiddler? Names and addresses?' said Billy brightly.

'Yes, just that, Hopkins,' he sighed wearily. 'Our qualified tax officers will do the rest, the brain-work – sorting out code numbers, et cetera. You print the surname at the top followed by the other names, in legible handwriting. Addresses should be printed neatly under-neath. Do you think you can manage that?'

'I think so, Mr Fiddler. How many names and addresses are there?'

'This first batch is the whole of the GPO in our catchment area. About five thousand, I believe. But when you've finished them, we have the rest of our district taxpayers, about thirty thousand in toto.'

'Yes, Mr Fiddler.'

'To avoid you getting bored, you can arrange the con-cards in strict alphabetical order when you've finished writing them up.'

'Yes, Mr Fiddler.'

Billy surveyed the waiting ledgers and the huge pile of blank con-cards, and his spirits plunged.

'My God,' he said to the other lad. 'The labours of Hercules.'

'His jobs were easy,' said Cliff Fernley. 'He had it cushy – killing a monster or two and cleaning out a few stables. Look at us, we've got thousands of cards to fill in.'

'And Hercules was made immortal at the end, whereas we just get thirty-seven shillings a week. No use moaning about it, though. We may as well make a start.'

After an hour, Billy said:

'In the Catholic Church, we have a prayer, "O God, send me here my purgatory." I think the prayer's been granted.'

'Who said this is purgatory? More like hell, if you ask me,' whispered Cliff.

Billy began singing softly to the tune from Gilbert and Sullivan's *HMS Pinafore*:

> *'When I was a lad, I served a term*
> *As office boy to an Attorney's firm,*
> *As office boy, I made such a mark*
> *That they gave me the post of a junior clerk.*
> *I served the writs with a smile so bland*
> *And I copied all the letters in a big round hand,*
> *I copied all the letters in a hand so free*
> *That now I am the boss of District Three.'*

'No singing whilst on duty!' said Fiddler, scowling.

Hour after hour they sat there, the two young men, copying, copying, copying until their hands ached. After ten days they finished the GPO staff, only to be given the employees of several large firms in the area. The days became weeks and the weeks became months and still they sat there, copying out the names and addresses from the big ledgers.

'My God, my God!' Billy cried out one day in anguish. 'Why hast Thou forsaken me? Cliff, this is worse than a term in prison. I'd rather be on a chain gang – at least they're out in the fresh air. This task we've been set is like writing out the London telephone directory. What have we done? What have we done to deserve this?'

'Perhaps we were murderers in a past life,' said Cliff, 'and this is our karma.'

'If you're right,' said Billy, 'then we must have been mass murderers to merit such a punishment. I'll say a prayer that this torture will come to an end soon.'

St Albert Fiddler must have heard him, for the next day he came to them.

'You two have done very well. You have completed more than twenty thousand con-cards between you. Time for a change. We don't want you becoming bored, and so I'm giving you a new task. I'm putting you on a creeping check.'

'Oh, thank you, thank you, Mr Fiddler,' exclaimed Billy. 'But what's a creeping check?'

'In the filing room, we have over thirty thousand files. Sometimes they get put back in the wrong order. Your job for the next few weeks will be to check through them all and make sure they're in the correct sequence. If they're not, put them right. It'll make a change from all those con-cards, anyway.'

'You've been praying to the wrong saint, Hoppy,' said

Cliff Fernley after a week of it. 'I'd rather be back on the con-cards. Look at the cuticles of my fingers, torn to ribbons.'

That night, when he got home, Billy said to his mam:

'I don't think I can stand much more of this job, Mam. I'll end up in Prestwich Asylum if I have to spend my life filling in con-cards and doing creeping checks.'

'Everybody has to work, son. And you can't expect to like your work. That's what you get paid for – for doing summat that you don't like doing. Otherwise they wouldn't pay you, would they? Stands to reason.'

'There are two things keeping me sane at the moment, Mam. One is my dancing. If it weren't for that, I think you could send for the yellow van.'

'And what's the other?'

'Reading and studying. I've started reading Plato's *Republic* just so's my brain won't seize up.'

'And what about your ideas of becoming a writer or a teacher? I hope you haven't given them up.'

'Just about, Mam. I've dug myself into a deep hole and I can't see any way out.'

'You never know, son, you never know. Life's funny that way. Sometimes when you're least expecting it, opportunity knocks at your door. What I allus say is – what has to be will be.'

'That's a very helpful saying, Mam, I must say. You're a fatalist. It means I may as well stop trying.'

'It means nowt o' the sort. It means that if it's meant to happen, it will, that's all. And I'm not that thing you just said I was – that fatalist thing. I'm a Catholic and proud of it.'

'Anyroad, as I was saying,' Billy added, 'it's being so cheerful as keeps me going. That, Plato and my ballroom dancing.'

* * *

'You look very smart, sir, if you don't mind me saying so,' said the man at Moss Bros. 'A perfect fit. Tailor-made for you, in fact.'

'Nice of you to say so,' said Billy.

'That'll be thirteen pounds altogether, sir,' he said as he folded up and packaged the outfit. 'Three pounds for the hire of the dress suit and ten pounds deposit – returnable if the goods come back undamaged.'

Billy came out of the shop carrying his precious parcel as if it contained the Crown Jewels. All the way home on the 62 bus, he nursed it like a baby, and managed to reach the flat without mishap.

'Well I never,' said Mam when she saw the evening suit hanging up in the wardrobe. 'Our Billy's joined the toffs.'

'That there is the uniform o' the Tories,' said Dad. 'Didn't I say a long time ago that he'd be getting ideas above his station?'

Billy could hardly eat his omelette-tea that Friday night because of the excitement.

'This is a big tango competition, Mam. The best amateurs in Lancashire will be at the Ritz tonight.'

'I hope you win, son.'

'Oh, we don't think we'll win anything, Mam. We've not got the experience and it'll all depend on what the judges are looking for.'

'Then why go in for it?'

'For the experience. If we get any recalls, that'll be a big success.'

'Oh, I see.'

When Mam said 'I see' like that, it meant that she didn't.

'Anyroad, Mam, I'd better start getting ready. I've ordered a taxi for seven o'clock and I'm picking Adele up at quarter past.'

'A bloody taxi! What next!' said Dad.

After a long bath, a close, careful shave and a thorough sprucing-up, Billy emerged in full array.

'Bloody hell!' said Dad. 'He looks like a waiter at the Midland Hotel. He's bloody well gone over to the enemy.'

'Eeh, I'm right proud o' you, son,' said Mam. 'In them tails you look just like Astaire in that picture, *Top Hat*. All's you need now is a cane, a big hat and Ginger Rogers.'

'Wait a minute, then,' he said and ran into the bedroom.

A minute later he emerged wearing Dad's pot hat and carrying his walking stick under his arm, began to waltz around the flat giving his best imitation of Astaire singing and dancing.

Then he took his mother in his arms and began dancing around the table with her. 'You're as light as Ginger Rogers, Mam,' he said.

'Get off with you,' she said. 'You daft ha'porth.'

There was a loud knock at the door.

'That'll be my taxi,' Billy said. 'Better not keep it waiting.'

'Best o' luck, son,' Mam called. 'Do your best! And put these rosary beads round your neck and tuck them under your shirt so's they can't be seen. You got them beads at the infants' school for answering your catechism. D'you remember? And they've been blessed by the Bishop o' Salford. They'll help you to win summat, you'll see. And try not to let the neighbours see you as you go out. We don't want them thinking we're getting stuck-up and above ourselves.'

'Aye – do your best!' said Dad, looking out of the window. 'But some hopes of the neighbours not seeing you. Nosy buggers are looking out already.'

'And you're looking out o' your window looking at

them looking out of theirs,' said Mam.

'Aye,' he said, 'but it's our Billy's taxi, not theirs.'

A taxi at Gardenia Court was a rare event. A small crowd had gathered round the black cab when Billy got to the foot of the stairwell. There were three or four bare-arsed, snotty-nosed toddlers with the inevitable dummies stuck in their mouths. A mongrel dog raised its hind leg and pissed on the rear wheel of the waiting car.

'Sod off!' yelled the taxi-driver, aiming a kick at it.

'Ockins! Ockins!' simple-minded Annie sputtered when she saw Billy.

'Evening, Annie,' Billy said.

'Bleeding hell!' screeched Mrs Pitts from her veranda. 'It's the bleeding Duke o' Windsor.'

'More like a bleeding tailor's dummy,' said Mr Pitts, who was standing next to her.

Billy ignored all the comments and waved to his mam and dad, who were gazing down at him from the top veranda.

'All the best, our kid,' called Mam.

'To Clifton Street, please,' Billy said to the driver.

Five minutes later the taxi pulled up outside the terraced house which was Adele's home. Billy rang the bell; the door was opened by her mother, a small, kindly, round woman in her mid-forties.

'She's almost ready, Julian,' she said. 'She'll be down in a minute.'

'Plenty o' time, Mrs Lovitt,' he said.

'I'm really glad you're taking her out like this,' said the woman. 'Adele is our only child and she gets a bit turned in on herself sometimes. A bit depressed, like.'

'I didn't know that, Mrs Lovitt.'

'She can also have a bit of a temper if she's rubbed up the wrong way. I know me and George have got to tread carefully sometimes. She's looking really lovely tonight, though, you'll see. Mind you, she ought to be. She took the day off work and has been dolling herself up all day.'

'What exactly does she do, Mrs Lovitt?'

'Why, hasn't she told you? She's on the cosmetics counter at Kendals.'

'Ah, that explains her skill with make-up.'

'She's always been fussy about her appearance and that. Oh, here she is now.'

Adele appeared and Billy's heart skipped a beat. She had excelled herself in her preparations. She looked like a fairy princess – a vision in pale-blue tulle with sequins and pearls sparkling on the fitted bodice of her dress and shimmering in her light-brown hair, which she wore tied back to emphasise the beauty of her face and neck.

'You look stunning,' he gasped. 'You take my breath away. I can't believe that you are actually going to the ball with me.'

'Why, thank you, kind sir,' she said. 'And why shouldn't I be going with you, Mr Astaire?'

'Best of luck to both of you,' said her mother. 'You make a beautiful couple when I see you together like this.'

'Don't wait up, Mother. We may be quite late.'

'No, I'll wait for you to help you off with the dress.'

'I said don't wait up, Mother,' Adele flashed, 'and I mean it!'

'Temper! Temper!' said Mrs Lovitt.

'You just make me so bloody mad sometimes, Mother, you do, honestly,' Adele snapped, 'always fussing.'

'Don't spoil all your nice make-up, dear,' said Mrs Lovitt.

'Oh, come on, Julian,' Adele said impatiently. 'Let's go.'

* * *

The Ritz ballroom in Whitworth Street was crowded that Friday night with exquisitely dressed, glittering competitors, along with their supporters and spectators. The twenty-two-piece orchestra struck up and began playing in strict tempo the sweet-sounding melodies of the day – 'I'll Buy That Dream', 'Laura', 'You'd Be So Nice to Come Home To' and 'Who's Taking You Home Tonight?'. What a wonderful, magnificent scene as the radiant couples arrayed in full feather glided across the polished maple floor of the spacious ballroom. And what a glamorous, romantic night for Adele and Billy as they merged into the crowd of whirling, elegant dancers.

'I hope we get at least one recall after all our efforts,' he said.

'Don't worry, Julian,' she said confidently. 'We shall. We've got Frank Rogers sitting over there ready to give us support and advice. Also, we've been given the number twenty-eight – the year of our birth. It's bound to be lucky.'

'I only hope it doesn't mean we're going to come twenty-eighth,' he replied.

'And now we come to the main event of the evening – the one you've all been waiting for – the Manchester Amateur Tango Championship!' the Master of Ceremonies announced through the PA system. 'There will be three heats in all. So would competitors now kindly take the floor for heat one.'

'This is it,' said Billy nervously.

The band began to play 'Temptation' and the thirty competing couples took to the floor. The three judges, clipboards in hand, stood at different points in the ballroom jotting down notes as the dancers swished past them.

Adele and Billy gave it everything they'd got,

remembering all that Frank had taught them. Smooth, flowing, skimming steps – then crisp, staccato changes of direction capturing the elusive tango atmosphere. They felt completely at home on the floor and almost forgot they were in a competition. Ten minutes and heat one was over.

'Well done, you two,' said Frank when they joined him at his table. 'Couldn't have done it better myself. I'm sure you'll get a recall into heat two.'

He was right. They found themselves called back along with eleven other couples.

'I just can't believe it,' cried Adele. 'A recall on our first attempt. I knew my instincts were right, Julian, when I first saw you at Harrigan's all those months ago.'

'Watch your timing, Julian,' said Frank. 'Remember what I said about rhythmic expression – steal a little time from one step and add it to the other – that's what makes it fascinating to watch. And Adele, when you turn your head in a change of direction, make it sharp and brisk. Now go on and make me proud of you.'

'Right, boss,' said Billy.

The band began to play 'Jealousy' and the twelve couples went into their routines.

Adele and Billy danced the tango as they'd never danced it before. They skimmed across the ballroom with flair and panache, every movement, every step, clean and crisp, every variation performed in fine, graceful style: the fall-away promenade with outside swivel and brush tap, progressive link, twist turn, and a flourishing bow as the music came to a close.

'That was superb, Julian,' whispered Adele.

'You were pretty good yourself, Adele – everything depends now on what the judges thought of it.'

They hadn't long to wait. Adele gripped Billy's arm

nervously when the MC began making his announcement.

'For the final heat, the judges have selected the following six couples: numbers six . . . nine . . . fourteen . . . seventeen . . . twenty-four . . . and twenty-eight!'

'OH, JULIAN! JULIAN!' Adele shouted excitedly, clutching even more tightly at his arm. 'I CAN'T BELIEVE IT! WE'RE IN THE FINAL!'

'I had a hunch you two were going to get in,' said Frank. 'That last performance was the best I've ever seen you do. But now you're up against the very best amateurs in the north-west. You'll need to pull out something really special. Remember the cockerel and the jerky movements!'

'We can only do our best,' said Billy, touching the outline of the rosary beads under his dress shirt.

At that moment he glanced around him and it was then that he saw them. Sitting up in the spectators' balcony. He couldn't believe his eyes. There was his mam and his two sisters watching the whole performance. How had they got there? They must have taken a taxi! They must have had it all organised secretly. He gave them a big smile and a cheery wave of recognition, to which they responded with an encouraging thumbs-up.

'We'd better do well now, Adele,' he said. 'I've got half my family up there in the visitors' balcony.'

'Oh, God! Here's hoping,' said Adele, as the music struck up with 'La Cumparsita'.

They gave a repeat performance of the tango, but the knowledge that the Hopkins women were now eyeing his every step lifted Billy's efforts to a new level. This time, their presentation surpassed even that of heat two in brilliance and finesse. In quick succession, one subtle variation followed another, giving a sparkling, lively interpretation of the Argentinian dance. Footwork, body turns, head movements, facial expressions – all combined to produce a fluent, streamlined performance which brought spontaneous applause from the onlookers. As the music finished, Adele, smiling happily for the judges, timed her final curtsey to perfection.

'Out of this world,' Billy whispered to her. 'The best yet.'

'Same goes for you, Julian. You were fantastic.'

'If you two don't make the first three, I'll eat my hat,' said Frank Rogers. 'You excelled yourselves there. What happened to you, Julian? I've never seen you dance as well as that – ever.'

'Fear, Frank, fear. With the women of my family watching every move, I just had to pull something out of the hat.'

'And now, here are the results of our 1945 tango competition,' announced the MC. 'In third place, couple number twenty-eight; in second place, couple number six, and in first place, and the Manchester tango champions . . . couple number fourteen!'

It took a moment or two for them to take it in.

'OH, JULIAN! OH, JULIAN! WE MADE IT! WE MADE IT!' Adele cried ecstatically, throwing herself into Billy's arms. 'You great big wonderful Fred Astaire, you!'

'I knew all along we'd do it,' he said with pretend nonchalance. 'Otherwise I'd never have paid three pounds for the hire of this suit.'

'You wonderful, crazy boy,' she said. 'I love you.'

'I'm proud of you both!' called Frank enthusiastically. 'It's moments like this that make the job of dance instructor worthwhile. Well done!'

They went forward and collected their engraved silver medals to the applause and whistles of the crowd.

'Come on, Adele,' he said, pointing to the balcony.

'Come and meet the Hopkins women.'

'I hope they like me,' she said anxiously.

'How could they not?' he said as they made their way through a congratulatory crowd of spectators.

'Adele,' he said when they'd found them, 'I'd like you to meet my mother and my sisters – Pauline and Florence.'

'Pleased to meet you, I'm sure,' said his mam. 'And I think your dancing was lovely – just lovely.'

'Nice to meet you, and congratulations,' said Polly.

'Likewise,' said Flo. 'You both looked marvellous on the floor. I think you two should've come first, though.'

'Thank you all so much. It's so nice to meet all of you,' said Adele, shaking hands with each of them in turn. 'Isn't Julian an absolutely wonderful dancer?'

'Julian?' Mam asked. 'Who's Julian when he's at home? My son here is called Billy – not Julian.'

'S'all right, Mam,' he said. 'It's Adele's pet name for me, that's all.'

'Pet name? What are you – a dog or summat? And what's wrong with the name you were christened with, I should like to know? I don't understand all this changing o' names. Polly is now Pauline; Flo is Florence; and now our Billy isn't Billy any more – he's Julian.'

'But Julian's a lovely name, Mrs Hopkins,' said Adele.

'I'm sure it is,' said his mam. 'For someone else – but not our Billy.'

'Anyroad,' said Billy, anxious to get out of an awkward situation, 'we'll get back to our dancing, Mam, and then I'll be taking Adele home.'

'Good night, everybody,' said Adele. 'Hope to see you soon.'

'Good night, Adele,' said the Hopkins sisters.

'Good night, Adele,' said his mam. 'And good night, our Billy!'

'Good night, Mam,' Billy called.

'Julian . . . bloody daft name . . .' Mam muttered.

After the last waltz, Billy took Adele home by taxi.

'It's after midnight, Adele,' he said at her doorway. 'So I won't come in. But thank you for the most exciting night of my life.'

'And thank you, Julian,' she said, kissing him on the lips. 'It's all been like a wonderful dream and I don't want to waken up. I never thought for a moment we'd win anything.'

'I did all along,' he said, opening the buttons of his shirt and showing her the rosary. 'I think these beads I've had round my neck all evening might have helped a little.'

'Rosary beads?' she said, frowning. 'Who gave you those to wear?'

'My mother told me to wear them for success and good luck.'

'I see,' she said. 'Sorry, Julian. I don't believe in all that hocus-pocus, that mumbo-jumbo stuff. And talking of your mother, I had the distinct impression tonight that she doesn't like me. She objects to me calling you Julian. I'll bet you find her a bit awkward to deal with. And I'm sure of it – she doesn't like me.'

'Oh, she's not so bad, Adele. And I'm sure that you're wrong about her not liking you. But never mind all that about my mother for a moment – you won't have to dance with her. What about us? When are we two going to . . . you know . . . get together, like?'

'I think I'd rather like to have some sort of ring on my finger before we thought about that.'

'We're a bit young for rings and things, Adele – we're only seventeen, for God's sake.'

'I don't mean a wedding ring – an engagement ring for a start would do.'

'I'll start saving tomorrow. But in the meanwhile, we've still got JT to consider.'

'Oh, him! I'd forgotten about him. The gentlemanly JT. Look, they don't know it yet – but my parents are going to the Queen's Park Hipp tomorrow night. I'll see what I can do. Call for me about seven o'clock.'

'But how do you know in advance that your parents are going to the Hipp?'

'Oh, I have my little ways of persuading them. They usually do as I tell 'em. You can rely on it – they'll be on their way out just before seven.'

'I'll count the hours, Adele. And JT has just heard what you said and has begun to act like a gentleman again. We'll both see you tomorrow. Good night, Adele.'

'Good night, Mr Astaire.'

Her front door opened and her mother appeared.

'I thought I'd better help you off with the dress, Adele,' she said.

'Look, Mother,' Adele rasped. 'I told you not to wait up. I can damn well get the bloody dress off myself. I'm not a little girl, you know.'

Billy heard this little exchange as he walked away, but it didn't really register. Perhaps he didn't want it to.

The next morning was Saturday and Billy returned the Moss Bros outfit to the shop in St Anne's Square and got back his ten pounds deposit. He spent the rest of the morning browsing through Sherratt and Hughes bookshop, but his mind was on other things – certainly not books, except maybe for the one or two he found in the health section. He picked one out entitled *Family Health*.

'*Priapism*,' it read, '*a persistent erection that cannot be made to subside. If you have an erection that persists for no apparent reason, do not waste time trying to get it down with cold compresses or other home remedies. Go to the nearest hospital at once.'*

What a thing to have, he said to himself. Suppose a ballet dancer got it. He'd have problems all right.

He looked furtively around the shop and put the book back hurriedly in case the prim middle-aged female shop assistant had seen him reading it. He selected another called *Guide to Better Living.*

'Condom,' it said, *'made of thin rubber and unrolled over the erect penis. Should be used in conjunction with a spermicide. Reliability: 2–15 per cent get pregnant. Disadvantages – can break or leak.'*

Best not to read these things, he thought, returning the book to the shelf. Anyway, where am I going to buy spermicide in Manchester on a Saturday morning? And when it says 'can break or leak', it probably means British-made. I'm sure the Yanks make their things stronger.

As he left the health section, the lady assistant eyed him suspiciously and he was glad to get out of the shop. He spent the afternoon in a state of feverish excitement. He lay on his bed reading, trying to concentrate on following the convoluted arguments between Socrates and Glaucon on the meaning of justice, but they held no appeal for him. Would it never be seven o'clock? The hands of their mantelpiece clock seemed to have stuck at four.

He unlocked his private drawer in the dressing table to check. Yes, they were still there in his wallet, along with the ten one-pound notes from Moss Bros. The packet containing three new pink Yankee condoms.

They won't be new for long, he thought salaciously.

The clock hands moved slowly, but oh so slowly, round to five.

'Switch the immersion on, Mam,' he said. 'I think I'll have a bath.'

'But you had one last night,' she said. 'Why so many baths? You haven't got scabies again, have you?'

'Don't be daft, Mam. I just want to relax for a while, that's all.'

'I'll bet you're going out with that girl again. The one that was calling you Julian. Bloody daft name. I just didn't take to her – I don't know why. You be careful of her, that's all. Don't go doing anything you shouldn't or she'll have you walking down the aisle afore you know where y'are. Anyroad, I'm sure too many baths can't be good for you – they ruin the pores of your skin.'

After a long soak, Billy shaved and applied liberal quantities of stinging aftershave to his face and body, primped up his hair and dressed in his best bib and tucker.

'You stink like a bloody brothel,' said Dad.

'Here, how do you know what a brothel stinks like?' Mam asked.

'It's just a way of speaking, Kate, that's all,' Tommy said humbly.

'I should hope it is,' she said.

'Anyway, he does stink a bit, you've got to admit,' he said. 'Where's he off to then? Chasing the girls, I'll bet.'

'Just 'cos I'm all spruced up and smelling nice for a change, everyone in this house thinks I'm up to summat. I'm just going dancing at Harrigan's, that's all.'

At 6.45 p.m., Billy stationed himself in a secluded spot at the top of Clifton Street, from where he had a clear view of Adele's house. He patted the back pocket of his trousers to make sure he had not forgotten the rubbers. No, they were still there. He was now trembling with excitement and anticipation at the thought of what lay ahead and what she had agreed to. A little before seven o'clock, the front door opened and her parents appeared.

'We'll be back around ten, Adele,' her dad called back. 'If you go to Harrigan's tonight, don't be back too late. It was well after midnight before you got to bed last night.'

He pulled the front door to and strolled down Clifton Street with his missus linking him. Billy waited a good five minutes and then, with heart pounding, knocked softly at the door. Adele appeared almost immediately.

'Come in, Julian,' she said. 'They've both gone off to the theatre.'

'I know,' he said. 'I saw them go.'

'I hope you've not been up in a tree watching them like a sniper.'

'No, I saw them from the end of the street. I've been waiting all day for this moment, Adele. Look, I'm trembling like a leaf. Is it still on?'

'I suppose so, if you insist,' she sighed. 'Did you get the American thingies?'

'I've got 'em here. Three of 'em.'

'You'll not need three unless you're Errol Flynn. All right, we may as well get this over. Give me a minute.'

She left the room and went upstairs, and Billy took the opportunity to remove his clothes. He sat naked on the settee. In a moment, she was back.

'I see JT is the perfect gentleman again,' she said. 'Better turn off the light, and lie down on the fireside rug.'

She switched on the electric fire.

'Right then,' she said, 'let's get on with it.'

'What about the rubber? We have to put that on first.'

'Oh, all right, come here. I'll do it. It's like rolling on a silk stocking.'

'Have you done this before?' he asked.

'No. Like you, it's my first time.'

She lay back and lifted her skirt.

'OK, I'm ready. You can do it now.'

'But I can't do it without some help from you. Guidance, like.'

'You'll have to find your own way in, Julian. No hands. I'm not helping you.'

Adele lay back, her body tense and unyielding, whilst he made several unsuccessful stabbing attempts.

'You're making a pig's ear of it, Julian. You've no idea, have you? You've lost your way.'

He tried again – and again – but could find no way in.

'Look,' she said after a while, 'this isn't going to work, Julian. I don't think you're doing it right.'

By this time, he had begun to fear she was right and that he really did lack the necessary skill.

'Remember, this was all your idea, Julian, not mine,' she said.

'Sorry, Adele. Maybe it wasn't such a good idea after all. What do you say we abandon it for the time being? Maybe try it some other time. I'll read a couple o' books on the subject.'

'That'd suit me fine, Julian. Some other time. I don't think this is the time or the place.'

They both stood up. JT was no longer behaving like a gentleman.

'It's a relief anyway to know I haven't got one of those priapism things,' he said.

'I'll slip upstairs and replace a few garments,' she said. 'Then I suggest we go out to Harrigan's to do the thing we're really good at – dancing.'

'Agreed,' he said.

As they walked together down Queen's Road, Adele's arm through his, Billy sensed that, somehow or other, it was the beginning of the end.

'When we're engaged, Julian,' she said, 'then I'll give

you the help you were asking for. But you really boxed it up tonight, didn't you?'

'Suppose so, Adele. But JT really does need help. After all, he doesn't have an eye down there to see where he's going.'

'If we were to announce our engagement, I think you'd find JT would be able to see where he was going.'

'You think so?'

'Mind you,' she continued, 'after we were married, we'd have to clear up one or two things.'

'Like, for instance?'

'Well, I wouldn't want to see you wearing any of those funny things, those rosary beads that you had on the other night, and I definitely wouldn't want any of those crucifixes and holy pictures I've heard you Catholics hang on the walls.'

'Right. Now I'm beginning to get the picture.'

'My dad said that you lot worship statues and other holy objects you have round the place. Is it true?'

'Of course it's true. Every night I talk to the statues, and sometimes they talk back. I've found I've had the best results from talking to a teapot or a cup and saucer.'

'Now you're mad at me. I can tell.'

'No. Didn't your dad tell you? Us lot never get mad at anyone. It's against the fifth commandment.'

'I'm only thinking of what's best for us, Julian. You know, when we're married. I can see it now. A nice little house and maybe two lovely children – a boy and a girl would be nice. I wouldn't want a house full of dozens of kids like I've heard some Catholics have, would you?'

'Not really,' Billy said grimly. 'But one thing you'd better start doing from now on.'

'Oh, and what's that?'

'Stop calling me Julian and start calling me Billy. And

another thing. I do not hang holy pictures and crucifixes, but if I married you, the first item on the agenda would be to book you and me a nice pilgrimage to Lourdes, where I'd buy the biggest statue of the Virgin, the biggest picture of the Sacred Heart and the biggest crucifix I could find to hang in our bedroom. Then I'd have a great big painting of the Pope done on the ceiling so that you'd see it every time we were on the job. Next, I would make sure that you had about twelve kids and I'd bring 'em all up as Catholics and try to get a few nuns and priests out of 'em.'

'If you're going to talk to me like that, you can bloody well get lost and find another partner.'

'Adele, you're just a selfish, spoiled brat who should have been spanked across the backside years ago.'

'And you can piss off, Billy, and find yourself another partner. After tonight, I don't want to set eyes on you again. Now I'm off home, and please don't call on me again.'

'Thanks for a very sexy evening, Adele. I really learned something tonight. I hope the next man you try it with has a John Thomas that can see in the dark. I'll send you a coupla presents for Christmas – a torch and a sex manual.'

'Don't bother, lover boy. You're the one who needs a sex manual, not me. And if you go to that confession thing you lot have in your church, don't tell him you've had sex tonight, 'cos you haven't, and you never will till you learn a few basic facts of life. Good night and good bye.'

After that night, Billy's enthusiasm for ballroom dancing and teaching basic steps at Harrigan's went cold. He stopped going so often. He could not find the energy or the will to look for yet another partner with whom he could go through the same old routine all over again. On the odd occasion when he did visit the dance studio, the spectacle of the dancers looked hideous: the rictus smiles, the orange panstick and oil-slick hairdos, the bitchiness, and the stupid prancing about in time to the mechanical music; the whole scene had lost its appeal for him.

On the contrary, he had found a new interest, one that absorbed him and gave him greater satisfaction – philosophy! Reading Plato's *Republic* and attempting to follow the arguments of Socrates on the subject of justice and the ideal state became his chief preoccupation. Perhaps something at school had rubbed off on him after all, and perhaps his education had not been the waste of time that he had imagined.

Chapter Twenty-Eight

Jacob's Ladder

'I think we're in a corner of Hades,' said Billy as he copied out the umpteenth con-card.

'And Fiddler is chief Hell's Angel in this section, thinking up fresh tortures for us every day,' said Cliff Fernley.

'Nothing – but nothing – could be worse than that creeping-check torture he had us on for three weeks.'

'Don't you be so sure about that, Hoppy. He's got a vivid imagination.'

'Anyway, here's a stupendous piece of news for you. A really great piece of news. That con-card I've just filled in was the very last.'

'You really mean it? The very last?'

'The very, very last. The thirty thousandth. A bloke called Zechariah Zuckerman.'

'I can't believe it. We ought to celebrate it in some way. Any ideas?'

'Well, those whom God would destroy he first sends mad.'

'So?'

'See that large bottle of Waterman's ink we've been dipping into for the last three months?'

'The one with all the pellets of paper, dead flies, et cetera?'

'The very one.'

'Well?'

'I'll give you half a crown if you drink it,' said Billy, laying down a shiny new coin.

'Hoppy, you must think I'm mad!'

He paused and looked from bottle to coin like a spectator at a tennis match.

'Half a crown, you say?'

'He who hesitates is lost,' said Billy.

'Right on! Carpe diem!' he cried, then seized the bottle, took a long draught of the blue goo and ran out to the toilets.

He came back after a couple of minutes displaying a set of azure-coloured teeth and gums.

'Half a crown if you don't mind, Hoppy.'

'With pleasure,' said Billy. 'Worth every penny. But why so blue, Cliff? Why so down in the mouth?'

He had begun to croon 'Where the Blue of the Night' when Fiddler sidled up.

'I've told you two before. No singing on the job,' he growled. 'Get on with your copying.'

'Finished, Mr Fiddler,' said Billy brightly.

'What – all thirty thousand?'

'Yep – all thirty thousand.'

'In alphabetical order?'

'In strict alphabetical order!'

'Then your next job is to check that all the con-cards agree exactly in sequence and in details with all the files in the stock-room.'

'But that means sixty thousand items in total. That'll take ages and ages,' whined Cliff, grimacing and showing his pearly blues. 'That's a double creeping check!'

'More like a double-cross,' said Billy. 'No use wailing about it! Let's get on with it!'

'What a bloody rotten life it is, Cliff,' Billy said when Fiddler had gone. 'I live in a block of flats that I'm sure are worse than the Gorbals, I've got this bleeding lousy job under the Marquis de Sade, and I've blown it with my girlfriend.'

'Oh, things aren't so bad,' said Cliff. 'We can always get pissed on a Friday night. There's that to look forward to.'

'You mean a trip to Never-Never Land. Nah. What's the use? That doesn't solve anything. But Cliff, fancy having to do this job for the rest of our lives!'

'You're a miserable get, Hoppy.'

'You've room to talk. You're the one that's blue. Anyway, what I'm suffering from is divine discontent.'

'You mean you're depressed?'

'No, more than that. I just can't see the point of it all. Why we're here on this planet, I mean. A philosopher was once asked, "What's the best Fate that can befall a man?" and he answered, "First, not to have been born, and failing that, to die early." '

'I know why we're here,' said Cliff.

'Why?'

'We're here because we're here because we're here. There is no reason. We're just accidents of nature. The whole universe is an accident – a series of meaningless coincidences. God's sick joke.'

'At least you believe in a God.'

As they got down to the tedious task, on a sudden whim Billy raised his eyes to heaven as he'd seen Christ do in Pictures of the Garden of Gethsemane, fingered the rosary beads in his pocket and called out in an anguished voice:

'Is there anyone up there listening? Then hearken to me, oh God and all ye angels and saints. If you will send down a Jacob's ladder and haul me out of this bottomless pit, I'll believe in you for ever more. Let me do something better with my life.'

'And what about me?' complained Cliff.

'You pray to your own God and get your own bloody ladder!'

'Have a good day, son?' Mam asked when he got home that night.

'Don't ask!' he said. 'Good day? At the Inland Revenue? I should be so lucky! The only thing interesting that happened today was my friend drank a bottle of ink.'

'Well, wouldn't you think they'd give you coffee or tea – growing lads like you. You must have a very funny canteen, that's all I can say. Oh, there's a letter up there for you,' she said, pointing to the mantelpiece.

'Letter? For me? Who do I know that can write? It's probably a demand for money.'

He took it to read in the bedroom in case it was from Adele, threatening to come back to him or recommending a sex manual. He slit open the envelope and read:

Dear Hoppy,
How's it going in the world of commerce? Here at school, things continue much as they did in your day: Oscar still thinking up witticisms for our amusement; Baldy still as deaf as a post; Edie Dunn still on the verge of a nervous breakdown; Olly continues with his dictionary of obscene words and has now reached the letter 'P' and I leave it to your imagination to think of the words he's found; the smokers' club is still smoking itself

to death, mainly on Park Drive since our Yankee bonanza came to an end.

The point of this letter, Hoppy, is to tell you that we, the smokers, are all applying for places at a teacher training college in Chelsea, London. The college is opening up again after being closed since 1939 and has been used as a mortuary during the war. So if we get in, they'll simply be exchanging one set of corpses for another. Why not take a day off and come to see us? We still smoke in the alley at dinner times.

Your old shoe-shine pal,
Robin.

'Who was the letter from, son?' Mam asked as they settled down to their evening tea.

'That wasn't a letter, Mam. It was a ladder from my friend Jacob.'

'Sometimes I think that income-tax job has driven you barmy, our Billy.'

Billy took a day's leave to visit his old chums at school.

'Gosh, it's good to be back amongst you normal, sane people after some of the characters I've been rubbing shoulders with,' said Billy as they walked down Smokers' Alley.

'Us normal, sane people? Are you trying to insult us, Hoppy?' exclaimed Oscar.

'I mean it's great to be back in the old smokers' club alley. I notice there's been no let-up in the shagging down here, judging by the number of bags left lying about.'

'I suspect they're all left by one man,' said Titch. 'A latter-day Bluebeard who's trying to break some kind of record.'

'Yes,' said Robin, 'he probably goes into the chemist's and says, "Gimme a gross o' Durex – the usual week's supply." '

'Perhaps it's President Paul Kruger with our Edie Dunn,' ventured Nobby.

'No banana-flavoured bags yet?' asked Billy.

'We don't really know,' said Robin. 'No one's willing to stoop so low as to sample one. You're welcome to try, Hoppy, if you like.'

'No thanks,' replied Billy. 'Peaches were more my fruit. Remember Blackpool?'

'What about your sex life?' asked Olly. 'Still a virgin?'

'Yes and no,' replied Billy. 'It was all set up for me. I was invited, had an admission ticket, but when it came to getting through the doorway – well, it wasn't as easy as you think.'

The smokers' club was all ears for its street-wise, street-hardened member.

'These are all very penetrating observations,' said Oscar.

'Not easy, Hoppy?' asked Nobby. 'I've never had any problems. What went wrong?'

'The lady tending the door failed to show me the way in. I think that she thought that my old man could see in the dark.'

'Perhaps she thought it was a carrot,' said Olly.

'Or perhaps she thought it had a lighted bulb on the end,' said Oscar, 'rather like a miner's lamp.'

'What you needed,' said Robin, 'was foreplay.'

'Surely that's when you're teeing off on the golf course,' said Pottsy.

'Not quite,' said Oscar. 'Foreplay is when you're having it off on the golf course.'

'Did you know,' asked Olly, 'that according to the *Kama*

Sutra there are sixty-four ways of having it off?'

'I wouldn't mind trying any one of them,' said Pottsy. 'But I don't seem to be able to attract the girls to get them to do it.'

'Experiments have proved,' said Olly, 'that if you can get your tongue down a girl's ear, she's yours for the asking.'

'I've read,' said Robin, 'that there is a little spot on the base of a girl's spine that when stroked or touched sends her wild with desire.'

'Not what I heard,' said Titch. 'I've been told on good authority that if you can only get to fondle a girl's left breast, she'll do anything.'

'Just the left?' asked Billy. 'Not the right?'

'I'm only saying that's what I heard,' protested Titch.

'I would have thought that a girl's breasts were apolitical,' said Oscar. 'Are you claiming, Titch, that the breasts have political affiliations?'

'Why not?' said Titch. 'Maybe socialist girls respond to left-breast titillation and Tory girls to the right.'

'The next thing you'll be claiming,' said Oscar, 'is that a girl's left nipple is red and her right blue.'

'The nearest I've ever come to a girl's bosom,' said Pottsy, 'was when I saw my big sister's breasts as she came out of the bath. I nearly died of shock.'

'A case of "See nipples and die",' said Oscar.

'I've never actually been out with a girl,' said Pottsy, 'so how do I get to touch a girl's breast so that she can't resist me?'

'Try some of those blue-rinse ladies in your dad's Conservative club,' suggested Robin. 'Try their right breasts. I think they call them blue tits.'

'You lot are still as crazy as ever,' said Billy.

'We often envy you, though, Hoppy – leaving school

and getting yourself a job,' said Robin. 'How's that going, by the way?'

'Leaving school when I did was the biggest mistake of my life,' said Billy.

'But you were going to be a journalist on a newspaper,' said Oscar. 'What happened?'

'The first job, at the *Manchester Guardian*, was a calamity, but the second, the one I'm doing now at the Inland Revenue, is a disaster.'

'You're doing work and getting paid for it,' said Nobby, 'which is more than any of us is doing, surely?'

'I'm like one of those hamsters you see on a treadmill. Working like the clappers but going around in circles getting nowhere. If I don't get off the treadmill soon, I feel I shall go like one of those bags we've been talking about – bananas.'

'Sounds bad, Hoppy,' said Robin. 'Perhaps I wrote to you just in time – before you blew a fuse.'

'You certainly did, Robin. Now what about this college you're all applying for? What's the score?'

'We don't know too much about it, Hoppy,' said Robin. 'It made a sudden late decision to open its doors – which explains why it still has places.'

'The course is for two years initially,' said Oscar, 'but it's possible to go on to do London University degrees if you are bright enough and opt for a couple of extra years.'

'You lot will all have Higher School Cert – Subsid – by summer, whereas I've got only plain School Cert,' said Billy.

'But in nine subjects,' said Robin. 'And experience in commerce. I'm sure you'll get in, Hoppy. It'd be really great if the whole lot of us went together. Imagine it! The smokers' club in London – the bright lights, the theatres, the cinemas, the West End!'

'And we might even try to fit in some study too, if we can find the time,' said Titch.

'Surely all that's going to cost a packet. What about grants and things?'

'Tuition and boarding are covered by the Government – and Manchester may award a grant of twenty pounds a year provided you agree to teach for them when you've finished. And that's it!' said Olly.

'So we're looking at about two pounds a week for books, train fares, personal spends, et cetera,' said Billy.

'At least,' said Nobby. 'My dad worked it out at about two hundred pounds or so for the whole course over two years.'

'Then I'm just crying for the moon,' said Billy. 'My dad earns around five pounds a week. I don't see where we'll get two hundred pounds out of that.'

'But you won't need the whole amount all in one go,' said Robin. 'That's over a long period. About thirty shillings to two pounds a week should keep us going. And remember, we can always get jobs during the holidays.'

'If we can find jobs,' said Olly.

'It'll do no harm to apply, Hoppy,' said Robin. 'As for the money problem, why not cross that bridge when you come to it?'

'At this moment, Robin, I can't see any answer. Somehow I think I've had my chips. But it's my one and only hope – so I'll apply anyway, as a last desperate measure in case, as Mr Micawber put it, something turns up.'

Three weeks after submitting his application, Billy received an invitation to attend for interview at the Manchester Damian College office. The principal of the London college, Mr Michael Roberts, had agreed to make himself available for informal discussion and the answering of any questions that candidates might have.

'Please sit down,' Mr Roberts said. 'I'll just check your name first, if you don't mind, to make sure I'm talking to the right person. You are Mr William Hopkins?'

'Yes, sir. That's correct.'

'You have a name with poetic associations, did you know that?'

'Yes, sir. Gerard Manley.'

'Not related in any way, are you?'

'No, sir, I'm afraid not.'

'Have you read any of his stuff?'

'Yes, sir. I've read most of his poems, including his most famous – "Pied Beauty".'

'Good. Which one impressed you most?'

'I liked "Pied Beauty", of course, and also "Spring and Fall".'

'Yes. How does that last one go again?'

> *'Margaret, are you grieving,*
> *Over Goldengrove unleaving?'*

'You like reading, do you?'

'Very much, sir.'

'What are you reading at present?'

'I have two books going, sir. I'm reading Somerset Maugham's *Razor's Edge* and wrestling with Plato's *Republic*.'

'Excellent. And how are you finding our dear friend Plato and his teacher, Socrates?'

'Most interesting, sir. Though I think that Socrates often asks his students questions and then shoots their answers down in flames.'

Michael Roberts laughed.

'Quite true. He seems to enjoy letting them flounder a bit before he destroys their argument. Can you remember any of the arguments of his students?'

'A few, sir, though I'm only a little way into the work. There's Polemarchus, who argues that justice is rendering to every man what is due to him; there's Thrasymachus, who claims that "might is right" and that the just man always comes off worse than the unjust man.'

'Do you agree with that?'

'Oh, no, sir. The argument is like that of the Nazis we've fought the war against. It also reminded me of a little rhyme in the book of comic verse you've edited.'

'Oh, you've looked at my book, have you? Which rhyme did you have in mind?'

'The one by Lord Bowen, the one that goes:

> *'The rain, it raineth every day*
> *Upon the just and unjust fella*
> *But more upon the just, because*
> *The unjust hath the just's umbrella.'*

'Oh, very, very good,' he said, laughing and slapping the desk.

'Thank you, sir,' said Billy, laughing with him.

'Yes. Very good,' he continued. 'Now, on your form I see you've been working for the last year. What made you leave school before the sixth form?'

'I hoped to be a writer, sir, and wanted to get some experience on a newspaper.'

'Well, newspapers don't come any better than the *Manchester Guardian*. Why did you leave after only three months?'

'I wasn't getting anywhere, sir. I realised that I needed better qualifications.'

'Yes, I see. And now you feel you'd like to be a teacher?'

'Yes, sir.'

'Why is that? Why do you want to become a teacher?'

'I feel that I may have something to offer, sir. I have had some experience teaching and entertaining my young nephews, and I've always found great satisfaction when I see they've understood something I've taught them or enjoyed a story I've told them.'

'But there's more to education than mere entertainment, Mr Hopkins. What do you think we should be teaching in school?'

'The basic skills to start with, and then how to live fully and morally, and how to cope with life's problems.'

'Good answer. But what sort of people do you think our schools should be turning out?'

'If we are to believe Plato and Socrates, sir, good citizens.'

'Yes, but that begs the question: what do you mean by a good citizen?'

'One who respects the laws of God and the laws of the state.'

'That's all very well. But how are we to teach them all those things?'

Billy was stumped and felt he was getting out of his depth. Then he had a sudden flash of inspiration.

'Why, sir, that's precisely why I want to come to your college! To find out!'

'Oh, good answer!' exclaimed Mr Roberts, slapping the desk again. 'Good answer! Well, thank you, Mr Hopkins, for a most interesting discussion. We'll let you know the results in the next fortnight, when we've finished all our interviewing.'

'Thank you, sir,' said Billy as he left.

Outside the office, the smokers' club members were waiting.

'How did you get on in there, Hoppy?' asked Robin.

'Couldn't have gone better. I'm sure he'll offer me a place.'

'Fantastic!' said Robin. 'London, open up dem golden gates, 'cos here we come!'

The following Sunday, there occurred a family gathering. Steve and Pauline came round with their kids for tea and to receive a report of the interview. Sergeant Barry Healey was home on a weekend pass, and so seven adults and two children gathered round the table for high tea. Mam opened a tin of West's middle-cut salmon, there was the usual tossed salad, and the inevitable pineapple chunks.

'I've been saving these two tins since before the war,' Mam said.

'What are we celebrating, Mam?' asked Billy.

'The end o' the war with Germany, of course, and I allus said to meself that I'd open these two tins when the lights went on again.'

'This is just like the old days,' said Polly.

'Not quite,' said Flo. 'Our Jim is missing and the two lads are still in the forces.'

'But surely they'll be home soon – now that Hitler's killed himself,' said Mam.

'You've never said truer words than them, Kate,' said Dad. 'It won't be long before the whole lot's over and we've got that bastard Churchill out of the Gover'ment. He's all right when it comes to fighting wars, but he's not the man to lead us in peacetime. There was one thing, though, I was sorry to hear.'

'What was that, Mr Hopkins?' asked Steve.

'They're going to try that Lord Haw-Haw for treason –

probably hang him. They'd be better giving him a job on ITMA with Tommy Handley.'

'That's true, Mr Hopkins,' said Barry, chuckling. 'He gave us all a good laugh during the war. But the war's not over yet. We've still got Japan to beat.'

'You're right there, Barry,' Dad said. 'We've just got that Mickie Doo fella to finish off and then we can really start celebrating. But I tell you, I'm more worried about him than I was about Hitler. I hope they don't send our two lads to fight him, that's all. They could be out in them jungles forever.'

'You're right about that, Mr Hopkins,' said Barry. 'The Japs are ready to fight to the very last man. They even consider it a great honour to die for their country.'

'That's right,' said Steve. 'They believe that if they die for their country they will be given a very high place amongst their ancestors in heaven.'

'I only hope that when I get to heaven, we don't have to mix with a lot o' bloody foreigners,' said Dad.

'And who said you're going to heaven? More like the other place for you,' said Mam.

'He thinks there's a colour bar in heaven,' said Billy. 'All the blacks and coloured in one place, and all the yellow folk in another. And God is an Englishman.'

'No, He's not,' said Mam. 'He's an Englishwoman.'

'I read the other day,' said Dad, 'that some of them Jap snipers can stay up in the trees in the jungle for weeks, living off rats and anything else they can find. It'll take a bloody miracle to get them to surrender.'

'Let's stop talking about war,' said Mam. 'Let's change the subject, for God's sake.'

'How did the interview go, Billy?' asked Steve eagerly. 'Did you remember what I told you about not being too clever? About throwing the ball back into their court if the questions got too rough?'

'I did exactly as you advised, Steve, and the interview went like a dream. Almost as if someone else was answering the questions. I'm sure they'll offer me a place.'

'They can offer you a bloody place if they like,' said Dad. 'But you're not going and that's bloody final.'

'What's the problem?' asked Steve.

'Money!' said Dad. 'That's the bloody problem. He may have got away with it going to that Damian College, but this is different. This is bloody big money.'

'How big is big, Mr Hopkins?' asked Steve.

'About two quid a week for two years. That's nearly half my weekly wage,' Dad said. 'And that's not counting that we'll have lost his wage as well.'

'If you stopped drinking,' said Mam, 'we could afford it. You're too fond of the bevy, that's what you are.'

'I've not even been accepted yet,' said Billy. 'So we may be talking about something that's not going to happen.'

'It sounds to me as if you're in,' said Barry, 'from what you've told us.'

'Look,' said Steve, 'Pauline and I have talked it over and we're willing to contribute ten shillings a week towards his expenses. Will that make any difference?'

'And Barry and I have talked it over and all,' said Flo. 'And we're willing to give ten bob a week as well.'

'There you are, Ma,' said Steve. 'What do you say to that? Can you raise a pound a week to send your youngest to college in London?'

'Of course we bloody well can,' she said. 'His lordship here'll just have to sup a few pints less, that's all.'

'I used to be bloody master in this house before the war,' said Dad. 'I don't know what the world's coming to when women start telling a working fella what to do.'

'Then it's settled,' said Mam. 'He's going to college and there's an end to it.'

'I think you lot are the best family anyone could ever hope for,' said Billy. 'When I go to college I'll try to be a credit to you all, and I'll never, never forget the sacrifices you're making.'

'You can have the job of looking after us all when we're old and decrepit,' said Polly.

Chapter Twenty-Nine

Bombshells

On Tuesday 7 August 1945, the Allies vaporised the city of Hiroshima, a town of twelve square miles on the Japanese main island of Honshu, killing more than seventy thousand people. Mr Churchill said, 'By God's mercy, British and American science outpaced all German efforts. The possession of these powers by the Germans at any time might have altered the result of the war and profound anxiety was felt by those who were informed.'

In Sunlight House, young people from the various offices, not fully understanding the gravity and horror of the event, walked about pulling their eyes into oriental slits and saying, 'Please, Mr Truman, you no droppee bomb on Hiroshima, please. We have great honour to surrender, please.'

'Here,' Mam said when Billy got home that night, 'isn't this the day that memory man in Blackpool said the world would end? Well, it hasn't. So he owes me a bob.'

'Maybe it's ended for him,' said Billy. 'Anyroad, you'd have a bit of a job finding him now.'

'I suppose I would,' she said. 'Oh, and by the way, there's an official-looking letter up there behind the tea-caddy from that there college in London.'

'Why didn't you say so?'

Impatiently he tore open the envelope.

'I'll bet it's from the principal, Michael Roberts, offering me a place.'

'Come on then, read it out,' she said.

'Dear Mr Hopkins,' he read. 'We regret to inform you that, following your recent interview, we are unable to offer you a place at the college for the coming year. We are aware that this must be a disappointment for you but you will realise that we have received more applications than we have places. We have therefore had to restrict our selection this year to those candidates with HSC. You may wish to submit a fresh application for our intake in 1946. Yours sincerely, Michael Roberts.'

Billy's face fell. Bewildered, he continued staring at the letter in disbelief and dismay, and he could taste the bile rising in his throat.

'That's a bombshell, Mam,' he said thickly. 'I don't understand it – the interview went so well.'

'P'raps it wasn't meant to be,' she said. 'Anyroad, it's not the end of the world.'

'In my case,' he said in a broken voice, 'it is. That memory man was right after all.'

'Come on, cheer up, our kid. It's not as bad as that – you've still got your health and strength.'

'You don't understand, Mam. That application was my last hope. Now I have nothing ahead of me but that soul-destroying job in the Inland Revenue. I can see my future rising up in front of me like a solid brick wall.'

'You can allus climb over a brick wall, son,' she said,

'and see what's on the other side. One day you'll meet a nice girl and settle down. You'll see.'

'What a rotten hand fate has dealt me, Mam. Born in the slums of Collyhurst, bombed out of Honeypot Street back into the slums – to this dump which is even worse than the Dwellings. I tried to be a writer on a newspaper and ended up as a toe rag. Now what have I got to look forward to? I'm chained like a slave in a civil-service galley. I give up.'

He went into the bedroom and lay on his bed, staring at the ceiling. All his friends from school would be going off to college in September. He could hear Robin Gabrielson's voice in his head.

'The smokers' club in London – the bright lights, the theatres, the cinemas, the West End! London, open up dem golden gates, 'cos here we come!'

The sun began to set, the light to fade, and soon he was in the darkness. Still he continued to stare – his mind numbed at the thought of his prospects and the life before him.

His mam tapped gently on the door.

'Come on, our Billy. Don't just lie there moping. Come and have a bit o' tea.'

With heaviness of heart, he got up from the bed and went into the living room.

'I've been thinking,' she said, 'you used to be happy dancing. Why don't you go back to Harrigan's and find that lovely girl you was going out with? What was her name?'

'Adele. But I gave up Harrigan's after I broke up with her.'

'Well, you can't just lie there being miserable.'

'All right, Mam. You may be right. I've got to try and cheer myself up. I used to feel on top of the world when

I was out dancing with her. I'll walk over and see her. I'll try to make it up with her. Maybe she'll have me back.'

He washed, spruced himself up, put on a clean white shirt and a smart tie, and began to feel a little better. He walked the short distance to Adele's home and rang the doorbell.

It was a good five minutes before she came to the door. She was wearing a silk dressing gown but she looked as beautiful as ever.

'Hello, Adele. Thought I'd just call and see how things were with you.'

She stared past him.

'What do you want, Billy? I'm pretty busy at the moment.'

'I had a piece of rotten news today and I wondered if you felt like going out dancing.'

'You must be joking after the things you said to me last time. Get lost, Billy. Go and find yourself a nice Catholic girl to bear you a dozen kids.'

A voice from over Adele's shoulder called:

'Who is it, Adele? Tell whoever it is to bugger off. We're busy.'

Duggie Diggle appeared, fastening his shirt buttons.

'It's OK, Maximilian,' she said. 'It's only an old flame, but he's just going.'

'Oh, it's you, Billy,' he said. 'Too bad, old son. Adele's partnering me now. You blew your chance with her.'

'Hello, Duggie,' Billy said. 'Maximilian. That's a nice name. I didn't know you and Adele had got together.'

'That's one way of putting it, I suppose,' he leered.

'Sorry to have disturbed you, Adele,' Billy said. 'Parents at the Queen's Park Hipp, I suppose. I hope Maximilian there remembered to bring a torch.'

'Look, Billy, just piss off,' she hissed.

Billy walked back home, hands in pocket, shoulders slumped.

'Well, did you see her?' Mam asked. 'Did you fix up to go dancing with her?'

'Just leave me alone, Mam,' he said, and went back into the bedroom, where he lay, hands behind his head, staring at nothing.

The next day, he went into work as usual. Cliff Fernley took one look at his face.

'What in God's name has got into you? You look like a Scotsman who's lost a pound and found a tanner. In fact, come to think of it, you're getting to look more like Albert Fiddler every day.'

'Sorry, Cliff. I heard that I failed to get into college and I don't want to talk to anyone today. I need time to get over it. Best thing is to leave me alone.'

'OK, Hoppy. If that's what you want.'

There were to be no jokes, no pranks, no laughs that day. Simply the solid, hard grind of civil-service routine. A little later that morning, Albert Fiddler came up to Billy's desk.

'You look as if you got out of the wrong side of the bed this morning, Hopkins.'

'Yes, Mr Fiddler.'

'Anyway, I've got a change of job for you. You're supposed to be good at maths. Here's the invoice book of a taxpayer we suspect of cheating. The itemised details on each foolscap page have not yet been added up. That's a job for you, Hopkins.'

'I only learned to do quadratics and Euclidian geometry.'

'Look, just get on with it, and less of your lip.'

His spirits drooping, Billy added up page after page of

bills for over three hours that morning. By dinner-time, he had completed the task and went off alone for his midday meal at Joe's Chop House. On his way back, he stopped for a little while at Lower Mosley Street bus station and watched the great luxury coaches leaving for their long-distance destinations – London, Penzance, Glasgow, Edinburgh. Well, he could watch but he wouldn't be going anywhere this year further than Gardenia Court and Sunlight House.

Still dejected, he returned at one o'clock to find Fiddler waiting for him with a scowl that spelled trouble.

'You're supposed to be the whizz-kid at maths! Those invoices you added up this morning! Every bloody one of 'em is wrong.'

'Sorry, Mr Fiddler. I've got things on my mind.'

'You might well say sorry. What bloody fools we tax officers would have looked if we'd accepted your figures when we're supposed to be investigating a tax-dodger. It's about bloody time you started to get your mind on your job, or push off and find another.'

Billy's lips turned pale and stiff.

'Yes, Mr Fiddler. Sorry, Mr Fiddler,' he said in a dull voice.

That night he got home from work at the usual time, had his meal in silence, and went to lie on the bed to continue his contemplation of his old friend – the ceiling. He had been there for over an hour when he heard a stir and the sound of voices outside the bedroom door.

'Where is he?' he heard Steve Keenan say.

'He's in there, Steve,' Mam said. 'Just lying there. I'm worried about him.'

Steve tapped gently on the door.

'Billy, do you mind if I come in for a minute?' he said.

'OK. The door's not locked.'

'What's all this I hear about you getting a letter from the college and then going into the slough of despond?'

'I had all my hopes pinned on going to college, Steve, and now . . . well . . . I've just given up.'

'Given up! You must be crazy!' he said. 'Did you ever read that speech Churchill gave to the boys of Harrow School?'

'Can't say that I did, Steve.'

'I can still remember some of it,' he said. 'I was so impressed. "Never give in! Never give in! Never, never, never! In nothing – great or small, large or petty. Never give in except to convictions of honour and good sense. Never yield!" '

'How does that apply to my case, Steve?'

'I'll show you how it applies! Give me that letter from the college and we'll appeal. Never give in, Billy! Never give in!'

True to his word, Steve composed and typed a letter to the principal purporting to come from Billy's dad.

Dear Sir,

A few weeks ago, you were kind enough to grant my son, William Hopkins, an interview for a place at your college for the coming academic year, commencing September 1945. We were most disappointed in the family to learn that you were unable to offer him a place because of lack of an HSC qualification.

May we appeal to you, sir, to reconsider his case? In 1944 he passed the School Certificate in all nine subjects and was the only student in his college to do so. During the last year, as an alternative to staying on at school for a further year, he decided to gain experience in journalism and the civil service. He worked at the *Manchester Guardian* where he gained valuable understanding of the workings of a modern newspaper. Today he is employed in a busy office of the Inland Revenue.

We feel, sir, that his year in the world of commerce amply compensates for the year he missed in the sixth form, since it has given him a background knowledge which should prove of inestimable value to a prospective teacher.

We trust you will give this appeal your earnest consideration.

Yours sincerely,

Thomas Hopkins.

'Well, if that doesn't do the trick,' said Steve, 'nothing will. That's all I've got to say.'

It was a memorable, never-to-be-forgotten Saturday morning when Billy picked up the early-morning post and opened up the letter from the college.

'I'M IN! I'M IN!' he called at the top of his voice. 'Mam! Mam! I'm in! I'm in! The college has reconsidered my position. I'm in heaven!'

He pulled her away from the toast she was buttering and waltzed round the flat with her, singing 'I'm in Heaven'.

'Mam! Mam! I'm over the moon. I must rush round and tell Steve Keenan right away,' he called excitedly. 'And then I'm going over to Rusholme to tell my pal, Robin Gabrielson.'

Billy found Steve and Pauline just about to go shopping with their two children when he arrived with his good news.

'I felt in my bones,' said Steve, happily, 'that you would get into college. I just knew it all along. Never give in!'

'We'll make it a family motto,' said Billy. 'Steve–Pauline – I cannot put into words how happy I feel at this moment. It's all down to you, Steve, and your tenacity. I'll never be able to thank you enough.'

'Yes you can,' said Pauline, laughing. 'Just don't take up piano-playing again.'

'Come shopping with us,' said Steve. 'The kids would enjoy your company.'

'Can't,' he said. 'I've got to get over to see my pal to give him the good news. He'll be as pleased as Punch.'

'Right you are,' said Steve. 'No more depressions, Billy – OK? Happy days are here again! Now you get off and see your friend.'

It was Mrs Gabrielson, Robin's mother, who opened the door.

'You must be Hoppy,' she said, 'the one our Robin did the shoe-shining with. I can recognise you from his description.'

'Tall, dark and ugly, that's me, Mrs Gabrielson.'

'Not quite true,' she said, laughing. 'But do come in. Robin will be really glad to see you.'

'Hoppy!' Robin said when he saw Billy. 'What brings you to this part of the world?'

'Good news, Robin! I'm in. I've just heard from the college.'

'That is the best news I've heard all year. Absolutely out of this world!'

'I'd just about given up Robin, I tell you. It was my brother-in-law's letter that pulled it off.'

'This means that all the smokers' club – one hundred per cent of us – will be going together. You know we were all very miserable when you got that awful letter from the college telling you there was no place for you. It wouldn't have been the same with one of us missing.'

'Exactly how I felt, Robin. Now it's London, open up dem gates! Oh, Robin, Robin, I can't describe to you my utter relief at getting out of this job in taxes – it's been destroying me.'

'We all sensed that in the smokers' club, Hoppy. We could see it was getting to you. Now all our prayers have been answered.'

'It's like a dream come true.'

'Do you realise, Hoppy, it's just a fortnight before we're on that train together?'

'Don't I know it! There's an incredible amount to do between now and then. I've got to buy new suitcases, clothes, books, and so on and so on.'

'Most of us have already done our shopping, and even some of our packing, would you believe it. We're so ahead of ourselves that Titch and I have fixed up to go walking in the Peak District next week. Why not join us? It'll be a chance to talk about our big plans for the future.'

'Can't, Robin, I'm afraid. I have to work at the office almost to the bitter end, as I need every penny I can lay my hands on. Which reminds me, I must get back this morning as I promised to give my dad a hand before he wraps up in the market.'

'OK. I'll pass on your good news to the others and we'll see you in a fortnight at the railway station. What a day that'll be, eh! The bright lights! The theatres! The . . .'

'I know! I know! The cinemas! The West End!'

'Be seeing you then, Hoppy,' Robin called happily as Billy went down the street.

The week following his visit to Robin Gabrielson, Billy was run off his feet. There were a thousand and one things to attend to in preparation for college: the purchase of books, writing materials, clothes, sports kit, toiletries and name tapes, as well as packing to be done, along with visits to the barber, the dentist and the doctor. Most of his buying expeditions had to be done in the evening after the daily grind at the Inland Revenue office. It was after one of these purchasing sessions that he arrived home, happily exhausted, and collapsed in an easy chair. Mam was cooking the evening meal, and as usual, Dad was busy devouring the *Manchester Evening News*.

'Only a week left, Mam. I've just about completed all my shopping and I'm packed and ready to go. I'm looking forward to saying goodbye to that office. If I ever see another con-card or another file, I shall throw up.'

'Here, Billy,' said Dad, 'what's the name of that pal of yours – the one you're going to college with . . . Robin something or other?'

'Robin Gabrielson? What about him?'

'There's summat here in the paper about him. You'd better sit down afore you read it.'

Billy had a sudden premonition of disaster. His stomach turned over and a shiver went down his spine.

'Let me see that,' he cried.

MISSED HIS FOOTING WHEN CLIMBING DOWNFALL

Student's forty-foot death fall on Kinder. When climbing the Kinder downfall, Kinderscout, Derbyshire, with a friend, Robin Gabrielson, seventeen-and-a-half-year-old student of Rusholme, Manchester, missed his footing and fell to the rocks forty feet below. He was taken to Stockport Infirmary where he died last night.

His friend, Richard Smalley of Fallowfield, said

that Gabrielson was about twelve feet above him. Smalley shouted to Gabrielson: 'I can't climb any higher here, I will try to work my way round.'

A moment later he heard a scream and his friend's body fell past him on to the rocks. Smalley wrapped Gabrielson in his coat and left him in a sheltered spot while he went for help.

With a gamekeeper, whom he met on the moors, he summoned assistance but it was six hours before the ambulance could reach Gabrielson. On arrival at the infirmary, he was found suffering from injuries to the back of the head and internal injuries.

Gabrielson had recently won a place at a teachers' training college in Chelsea, London, and was due to begin in a week's time.

Billy's mind went numb and a freezing sensation enveloped his whole body. There was a tight pain in his throat and his heart pounded against his ribs. He stared, speechless, shaking his head at the newspaper, entreating it to say it wasn't true. He put his head down on the table but the tears would not come. He could not take in what he had read. It must be some other Gabrielson, some other Smalley – not his friends, surely. They were all going to college together in a few days' time. They had their train tickets and were all packed and ready to go. The room went cold, a violent trembling racked him, and he crossed his arms and wrapped them round his chest as if trying to ward off the cold.

His mother felt his pain. She put her arms around him to try to comfort him and stop the shivering.

'Don't take on so, our Billy,' she said. 'It's all right. It's going to be all right.'

'Another disaster, Mam. Will they never end? He was my best friend. We were going to college together on Sunday.'

'I know. I know,' she said. 'But it's God's will.'

'Don't talk to me about God, Mam. He's no friend of mine. He's my enemy. He's gone too far this time. He has done nothing but rain death and destruction down on my head. This is the last straw. Now I just want to be left alone.'

Once more he went to his bed, this time covering himself with a blanket in an attempt to get warm and stop the shaking. He gazed up at that grey ceiling he had come to know so well. In the semi-darkness, he could see Robin, and hear his voice. As he recalled images of his dear friend, his eyes grew wet and the tears flowed endlessly down his face.

He was awakened from his mournful meditation by a gentle knocking at the door.

'Billy, son, don't just lie there. Come out now. There's another little item about your pal y'ought to see.'

He got up and went into the living room.

'This is it, on page eight,' Mam said, handing him the paper.

GABRIELSON – On 10 September 1945, result of an accident, Robin James, aged seventeen (*requiescat in pace*), dearly loved son of Joseph Paul and Catherine. Deceased will be taken into St Joseph's, Longsight, on Thursday. Requiem Mass Friday, 10 a.m. Interment Southern Cemetery. No flowers by request.

'I'll go to the funeral on Friday, Mam, but right now I think I'll go for a walk. Maybe call on Pauline and Steve.'

'Will you be all right, son? Do you want me to come with you? You're not going to do nowt silly, are you?'

'No, Mam. Don't worry. I'd rather walk alone to think – that's all. I shan't be late.'

The evening was damp and wet. A raw fog had descended and it was nearly dark. The streets were deserted and quiet. Billy stumbled on, unconscious of the drizzle, head down, shoulders hunched. As he passed St Anne's Church, he suddenly became aware of the rosary beads round his neck. The beads his mother had given him for luck in the dancing competition, and the very same beads awarded to him by Sister Helen in another age when, as a stupid, innocent child, he had taken in all their stories and their lies about a merciful God. An involuntary shudder convulsed him, and with a great cry of despair, he wrenched the beads from his neck and hurled them into the rain.

'Take them, God, if there is a God,' he cried. 'I'm finished with you and all those tales of your goodness and mercy. Where were you when Teddy White was drowned in the Cut? When Henry Sykes was blown to bits by that German bomb? When Jim's lifeboat was lost? When Robin Gabrielson fell on the rocks? A saviour they call you, but you're nothing but a fraud. You do nothing but destroy those I love.'

He had reached Pauline's house. He rang the bell. It was Steve who opened the door. No words were needed. One look at Billy's strained, tearful face told all – that some dreadful misfortune had befallen him.

'Billy! For God's sake, come in.'

'Billy, you look awful,' said Pauline. 'Let me make you a cup of tea.'

'I've just heard of the death of my best friend,' he said. 'We were going to college together. Now I'm not sure any more that I want to go. Fact is – I'm not sure about anything any more.'

'But that's terrible, terrible,' said Steve. 'Tell us in God's name what happened.'

'I'll tell you what happened, Steve, but not in God's name. I no longer trust or believe in Him. It was He who allowed my closest pal to be killed falling from those rocks.'

'What a tragedy! We're so sorry to hear about it, Billy. And now you're wondering about your own future and whether you should go to college without your friend. And you've lost your faith in God as well. All hope's gone, eh?'

'That's right, Steve. Robin Gabrielson's gone, and with him all hope. As far as I can see, life's just one big lottery and without meaning. The universe is just a series of pointless accidents. "*A chequer-board of nights and days/ Where Destiny with men for pieces plays./One thing is certain, and the rest is lies/The flower that once hath blown forever dies.*" '

'You are in a bad way, Billy,' said Steve, 'if you think that there is no point or purpose to the universe. Only God knows why we and the universe exist. You seem to think that the death of your friend was pointless and meaningless.'

'Well, wasn't it?' said Billy.

'If I remember correctly, Billy,' said Pauline, 'it was through this pal, Robin, that you got the idea of going to college in the first place.'

'That's right, Pauline. It was because of a letter that he wrote to me. We had such big plans for the future, he and I.'

'You had your plans and the man upstairs had His. And they weren't quite the same,' said Steve. 'Have you thought that that letter from Robin may have been part of God's plan for you? What you are suffering now, at this moment, may be God's way of showing you the way you must go.'

'I've thought about all the sufferings, all the deaths in my life and I no longer believe that there is a God.'

'Life is not simply the pursuit of pleasure,' Steve said. 'Remember that bit of the prayer – "To Thee do we cry, poor banished children of Eve, mourning and weeping in this vale of tears." That's what the world is, Billy, a vale of tears. You may not believe in God, but He believes in you. You may not be looking for Him, but He is looking for you all right.'

'I've thought about God and all that and cannot accept the arguments for His existence.'

'Well done! You've worked it all out by logic, eh?' Steve said. 'Listen, Billy. Faith in God has nothing to do with logical arguments. God is a supreme being who is beyond all reason and all knowing. You simply accept Him and there's no way we can unravel his divine plan or the way he treats us. Faith, you will remember from your catechism, is a gift and not something you arrive at by intellectual arguments.'

'Have you never doubted, Steve?'

'Of course I have. We all have. There is a prayer we used to say, "Oh God, I believe in you. Please help me overcome my unbelief." '

'Right at this minute, Steve, I feel that He has deserted me, and I am alone.'

'Don't you remember that story?' he said. 'How a man thought God had deserted him when he noticed only one set of prints on the sand at the very time when he was at his lowest. You will recall that there was only one set because at the most difficult time of his life, the Lord had carried him. And God will help you through this rough patch, Billy. Trust Him.'

'How do we know that? It doesn't seem that way at the moment.'

'Look, I don't want to go all heavy on you, but let me remind you of that passage in St Matthew. *"Come unto me, all ye that labour and are heavy laden, and I will give you rest. Take my yoke upon you, and learn of me; for I am meek and lowly in heart; and ye shall find rest unto your souls. For my yoke is easy and my burden is light."* '

Billy walked home heavily that night in sombre, pensive mood. Steve had given him much to think about.

St Joseph's Church was packed that Friday morning for Robin's Requiem. Everyone who'd ever known Robin seemed to be there. Billy looked round the church slowly: Robin's grieving parents, his relatives, his teachers, his fellow-students, his neighbours filled all the benches to the very back. In the main aisle, at the front of the church, stood the oak coffin with the polished handles. From the choir loft a small group of Damian brothers sang the plain-chant Mass. Solemn-faced, the members of the smokers' club sat together towards the front of the nave.

Billy could not take his eyes off the coffin. Inside that box lay his closest friend, fast asleep in a dream from which he would never awaken. His eyes closed never to open again. His lips sealed never to speak or smile again. Past all help or need of it.

'Eternal rest grant unto him, O Lord,' intoned the priest.

'And let perpetual light shine upon him,' answered the congregation.

'May he rest in peace. Amen,' said the priest.

After the Introit, Robin's father began the first of the readings in a quiet, melancholy manner, and it seemed to Billy, as he listened, that the words were being directed specifically at him.

'*Death is nothing at all . . . I have only slipped away into the next room . . .*'

Mr Gabrielson's voice faltered; he paused and swallowed hard. For a moment it looked as if he might break down. He took a deep breath and in a low, grief-stricken tone continued:

'*What is death but a negligible accident? Why should I be out of mind because I am out of sight? I am but waiting for you, for an interval, somewhere very near, just around the corner . . . All is well.*'

For a minute or two there was a solemn stillness – not a sound in the church except for subdued sobbing, and the blowing of noses, amongst that anguished congregation. Then the brothers began to chant the Sequence of the Dies Irae and the Mass continued.

After the communion rite, a distraught-looking Titch went forward to give the final reading:

> '*Lead, kindly light amid th'encircling gloom,*
> *Lead thou me on, the night is dark*
> *and I am far from home, lead thou me on.*
> *Keep thou my feet; I do not ask to see*
> *The distant scene; one step enough for me.*'

There was a catch in his voice, and Titch broke down – unable to continue. Sorrowfully, he looked appealingly towards Billy, who nodded his understanding, walked forward and took over the reading of Newman's verses.

> '*I was not ever thus, nor prayed that thou*

shouldst lead me on; I loved to choose
And see my path; but now lead thou me on.
I loved the garish day and, spite of fears,
pride ruled my will; remember not past years.

So long thy power hath blest me, sure it still
Will lead me on o'er moor and fen,
O'er crag and torrent, till the night is gone,
And with the morn those angel faces smile
Which I have loved long since, and lost awhile.'

At the end of the Mass, the coffin was borne out by the pall-bearers, followed by a grieving procession of mourners. The smoking-club boys, who had known Robin best, stood together in a forlorn, melancholy group. Mrs Gabrielson, her eyes red with weeping, came up to them.

'Thank you, boys, for coming, and for those beautiful readings,' she said softly. 'Robin so loved you all. And now he won't be going to college with you after all. I can't tell you how hard it is to take it all in and to accept that he is dead. Everywhere in the house are hundreds of little reminders of him – his clothes, his shoes, even his collar studs and cuff-links. And his half-packed suitcase is still in his bedroom, exactly where he left it. I haven't had the heart to move it.'

She was about to break down, but recovered her composure.

'Go to college,' she said, 'and, for the sake of his memory, do well and succeed. That's what he would have liked. He will be with you down there in Chelsea in spirit.'

They watched the cortège proceed slowly down Plymouth Grove until it was out of sight. There was a song which went round and round in Billy's head:

> *All the birds of the air*
> *Fell a-sighing and a-sobbing*
> *When they heard of the death*
> *Of poor Cock Robin.*

'When something like this happens,' he said, offering his cigarettes round, 'everything in one's life falls into perspective.'

'Too true,' said Oscar. 'You begin to get your priorities right. What's important and what isn't.'

'We spend all our time,' added Titch, 'worrying about exams, about money, about sex, about career, about tomorrow.'

'All the time taking it for granted that we're going to have a tomorrow,' said Olly.

'Poor Robin has no tomorrow,' said Nobby.

'We've got to take each day as it comes,' said Billy. 'Act as if each day was our last.'

'And one day,' said Oscar, 'we'll be right.'

'Robin's mother seemed keen that we should stick to our plans, go to college without Robin and succeed for his sake,' said Titch.

'I'm not so sure,' said Pottsy. 'Academic study, as you all know, was never my strong point. I'd like to go to college with you all, but my father wants me to go into his business to learn the ins and outs of the retail trade. I'll sure miss you lot.'

'That goes for me too,' said Billy. 'I'm not sure about anything any more.'

'Oh, surely not, Hoppy,' said Oscar. 'Don't say you're changing your mind about college.'

'It's enough the gang's going without Robin, without you pulling out as well,' said Nobby.

'I'm having second thoughts,' said Billy. 'College

doesn't have the same attractions now that Robin's dead. He was the one who encouraged me the whole time.'

'All the more reason you should go, surely?' said Titch.

'Well, the way I see it, I did an awful lot of moaning and complaining about my job – how boring it was and all that. That doesn't seem to matter any more. Life isn't all that bad. I've got my ballroom dancing, and if I worked hard in the civil service, I could end up as a fully fledged tax officer.'

'What about your ambitions to write and all that?' asked Olly.

'A pipe-dream, Olly, a pipe-dream. That's all it was. If I went to college, I'd have to consider the tremendous expense I'd be putting my folks to. That's apart from the fact that they would lose my weekly wage too.'

'We hope you change your mind, Hoppy,' said Oscar.

'I've not decided yet,' said Billy. 'Robin's death has got my brain in a whirl and I don't know whether I'm coming or going. I thought I might get away this weekend, say back to Blackpool for a couple of days, walk the beach at Cleveleys where we used to play together, and think things through.'

'But we're supposed to leave on Sunday,' said Titch.

'I know! I know!' sighed Billy. 'I'm just confused, that's all. Do I really want to go to college? Do I really want to be a teacher? I can't see the point in anything any more.'

'Well, just in case, Hoppy, here's my hand,' said Nobby. 'Goodbye, and we'll see each other when we see each other.'

'Same goes for me,' said Pottsy, shaking hands.

'Cheers!' said Olly, taking Billy's hand. 'But I hope to see you in a couple of days.'

'I'm not shaking hands,' said Oscar, 'because I just know you'll be going with us to London.'

'Neither am I,' said Titch. 'Please, Hoppy, be sensible and make the right decision.'

Sadly they parted company at the corner of Plymouth Grove and went their different ways.

Sunday afternoon. A taxi pulled in at the Central Station approach. Billy got out with his luggage, paid the driver and struggled his way across the station concourse. He consulted the large railway timetable board.

'Platform six,' he said aloud.

He handed his ticket to the collector at the barrier.

'Better hurry, mate,' said the man. 'That train's due out in a few seconds.'

He hurried as best as he could with his suitcase along the platform, looking for a particular compartment.

And there they were! Heads sticking out of the windows as if it were a cattle truck – the Damian College Smokers' Club.

'Trust you to be late, Hoppy!' called Oscar.

'Come on, Hoppy!' shouted Titch. 'Get a move on or you're going to miss the train!'